Blood

by Roland Ladley

The sixth of the Sam Green novels

i

First edition prepared for publication with CreateSpace June 2020

ISBN: 9798653479786

For my brother, Kevin, my number one fan ...
who we loved and lost to covid-19 this year.

Rest in peace.

Communism is not love. Communism is a hammer which we use to crush our enemies.

Mao Zedong

Prologue

37 Ngõ 91, Hà Nội, Vietnam

Three weeks previously

Her back was stiff. Towards the bottom of her spine. It was a new pain. It joined her smashed nose, a loose tooth, the burn marks around her wrists, throbbing in her legs and the constant buzz in her torso – which lingered for hours after the taser assaults. She had to admit out of all of the abuse, the wet blouse and taser routine was easily the most effective. The first time had been explosive. She remembered catching her inner thigh on a 12-volt fence which was keeping cows from running amok on the edge of her mum and dad's village. It had sent a spike of electricity to her heart and left an unpleasant burn on her flesh. The taser treatment felt like it was fifty, maybe a hundred times worse. She was convinced on the third or fourth time (it was a blur – she couldn't remember) her heart had stopped beating. As her body had collapsed, its fall stopped abruptly by the rope wound round her hands and tied to the ceiling, she felt a gap where her heart should have been.

And then, *thump*, her ticker had rebooted itself.

1

Not that she was particularly bothered at that point. Within days of her incarceration she had an overwhelming sense of resignation. That this was it. She would end her time in this baking cellar. In a room about the size of a double garage. No windows. Two doors, only one of them used. She had no idea where the second one went. The first, she was pretty sure, was where she had been delivered through. Her legs and hands tied, her head covered in a dirty hessian sack. It was also the door her abusers used. She had been taught not to call them interrogators. That gave them a badge – a side, like in a netball match. *Your side; my side*. Abusers was a more helpful description. They hurt her and, at some separate point, asked her questions.

Abuse. Questions.

Disassociate the two.

Label them as criminals, along with murderers and rapists. Hate them for what they do to you. Channel your energy against them.

And ignore the questions.

She *had* to ignore the questions for as long as she could.

It wasn't like the films. It wasn't name, rank and number, thank you very much. There was no Geneva Convention here. Not in the bowels of South East Asia. She was at the mercy of people who were governed by their own rules. Who worked outside of international norms. They had a job to do. And they would use whatever means necessary to get it done.

That meant punches to her face. Hanging her for hours by her wrists with only her toes touching the grey, damp floor. Living among her own faeces. Wearing clothes stained with urine and sweat. Eating weak rice and drinking wretched water, which passed straight through her and, when she was alone and couldn't be released from her ceiling tie and be manhandled to the bucket in the corner, dribbled down her legs. No showers. Her teeth hadn't been cleaned for … how long was it? Three weeks, maybe.

There was no natural light. She gauged the days by the number of meals: morning and evening. But she had lost count of how many breakfast and dinners she had been given. Even when she wasn't trussed, her hands and ankles were tied, the latter chained to a spike cemented to the floor. Her bed, if you could call the thin, filthy straw mattress a bed, was in the centre of the room. She had tried to etch the number of days with her fingernails on the floor, but they weren't strong enough. Instead she had found a hole in the mattress and pulled out a handful of straw. She had separated the strands and placed one stalk at the right-hand side of the mattress for every meal. It had worked for about a week …

… and then her abuser had found the straw and made the connection.

She'd been hanging at that point, maybe for over an hour.

He'd picked up the fifteen or so strands and walked to her.

Her face was set higher than his. She was naturally taller and, on tiptoes, her eye level was at least six inches above his. He was looking up. She was staring into space, above his head, a glaze of hurt etched on her face. She'd been trussed up after 'meal one' of the day and had spent the time alternating between the agony of hanging from her wrists and the knotting throb of cramp and muscle ache when she pushed off the floor with her toes.

'Don't ... do ... this.' All of them spoke English to varying degrees.

He had the numbering stalks in one hand and was using the index finger of his spare hand to tap her on her nose – which had been re-broken the previous evening. Even though she twisted and turned, the man holding the straw had made contact. And each time the pain was as bad as if her nose had been smacked by a bat.

Single injury. Play on it. Perfect interrogation technique.

Stop it. Abusive *technique*.

She'd then given up counting time. Not that it mattered. The days would go on. The beating, the hanging, the tasing, the fatigue and stomach cramps. They would all go on. At some point she might crack. At some point she might tell them what she thought they wanted to know.

4

At some point she might begin to feel something for her abusers. If they relaxed the pressure, maybe offered her a shower and a decent meal, she might warm to them in some way. If one of them displayed kindness, some sympathy, she might not be able to stop herself from rejoicing in a newfound friendship.

At some point she might become subject to Stockholm syndrome and develop a psychological alliance with her abusers. It happened.

At some point.

Until then she would deal with the abuse as best she could.

And not answer the questions.

There was a clunking from the door. It opened.

Another day.

Would it be trussing and tasing first, or would she be placed on the wooden chair and take another smack to the nose? Or would they ask her the same questions – again?

'Hello, Miss Ruby.'

It was her abuser. He had the metal, figure-of-eight hook in one hand.

She was about to be hung by her wrists again.

Jane Baker squeezed her eyes shut and waited to be lifted from the floor.

38°19'48.7"N, 128°06'16.2"E, North of Ihyeon-Ri, DMZ, Korea

Jae-joon pushed the mine cart the final couple of metres until it reached the makeshift rock buffer. It was heavy and he was tired. The narrow gauge railway ran for just under a mile, almost the full length of the original tunnel. Between him and his brother they had pushed the trolley all the way. The railway started – or stopped, depending whose side you were on – at the bottom of a long, slanting shaft that once emerged north of the Korean peninsula's Demilitarized Zone (DMZ). That entrance had been blocked off with tonnes of concrete over thirty years ago.

The track ran out of rails about 15 metres from where the tunnelling finished – where they were now – digging halted abruptly, Jae-joon reckoned, when his country had discovered the 'Third Tunnel of Aggression' in 1978, or certainly after the United Nations had accused the Democratic People's Republic of Korea (DPRK) of threatening the 1953 Korean Armistice Agreement a few months later.

If it hadn't been for the really bad rains of 2015, the tunnel he was in now might well have remained a secret; along with, so myth would have it, another ten to fifteen others the Korean People's Army had been digging to enable a mass invasion of the South. Four were documented and in the public domain. One of those, and the most famous – the Third Tunnel of Aggression – was just 50 kilometres from Seoul, the

South Korean capital. It was now a major tourist attraction.

His – yes, he could call it his – was one from the book of myths.

Except, as he touched the wall to cool his hands, it certainly wasn't a myth.

Jae-joon wasn't a civil engineer but he knew a good tunnel when he saw one. Like the one close to Seoul, his had been blown out of bedrock. It was vaguely circular, just big enough for a single man to walk upright; maybe two or three abreast in places. Although, as he recalled from his conscription days, possibly not carrying a weapon and other equipment. The sides were ragged, but solid, and scored with drill holes where dynamite had been placed. There was damp everywhere, and whilst the tunnel did fill with water after an extended period of poor weather, it never became unusable.

Poor weather! How lucky had they been?

The summer rains of 2015 had been among the worst on record. Korea wasn't a wet country. Average rainfall was low. The climate was best described as 'humid continental', with cold, dry winters and warm, damp summers. The short summer rainy season, the *jangma*, was normally unexceptional. And the odd typhoon, if it missed Japan, could bring heavy showers. But 2015 provided the perfect storm – literally. A *jangma* unusually brimming with heavy rain and two wild typhoons, one following the other.

His village, in a valley in the Baekdudaegan mountains, had been badly hit by flooding. Slabs of the mountainside had slipped away, blocking roads and destroying hamlets. Everyone had helped each other. Families, driven out of their homes by thick, muddy sludge, had been put up by others who hadn't been so badly affected. The local monastery had opened its doors and the monks had set up a soup and rice kitchen for people who couldn't heat their own food.

The deluge had lasted for a week. The clear up had taken two months.

And for that what they needed was stone and brick. And plenty of it.

Jae-joon worked for the government. He was a quantity surveyor and travelled daily down the valley to the local town. After the flood he'd been released for a month, along with a number of the men from the village, to help with the clear up. They had worked collectively – and tirelessly. Everyone had chipped in, young and old.

Even in the 21st century there was something about the Korean work ethic which constantly surprised him. His grandfather was in his eighties. His normal routine, like many of the elders in the country, included exercise: walking; Taekwondo and Hapkido; gentle push ups and sit ups on the village's outdoor weights area. After the flood his grandfather was among the first to volunteer to move rubble and carry stores. He worked until rest was the only thing he was capable of. And he did all of that without complaint.

And he was not alone. There was never a shortage of men to help with the rebuild. And there was never a shortage of *jupchae, hoeddeok* and sweet tea from the wives, sisters and daughters. Within three weeks all displaced families had returned to their homes. A few weeks later village life was close to how it had been before the rains.

It was a Saturday, about two weeks into the clear up, when they'd found the tunnel. Or, more accurately, a sinkhole that led to the tunnel.

Jae-joon was working in the far corner of a temporary quarry he'd established to provide rock and aggregate for the rebuild. His cousin was driving an 8-tonne excavator, pulling away at a new seam of rock. The digger was working hard, its bucket struggling with a large boulder, when the ground had given way.

Thankfully the hole wasn't wide, although it was, at first glance, very deep. His cousin slewed the digger's tracks and reversed out of harm's way. Jae-joon, who had been standing to one side waiting to check the quality of the seam of rock that might be exposed, tentatively shuffled forward.

The grey and white of the far end of the quarry had now been joined by a black chasm, about a metre wide – and dropping straight down.

'What is it?' His cousin was now at his side, his hard hat worn at a slight angle.

'I've no idea,' Jae-joon had replied.

He was at a loss. They weren't digging in limestone; there should be no water-drilled gullies and underground rivers. And there were no local caves other than a disused, village-dug coal mine. And it was over a kilometre away.

'Have you got a torch?' he asked his cousin.

'I think so. In the cab. Let me get it.'

He and his cousin had spent half an hour inspecting the hole, but were none the wiser. Jae-joon was concerned the quarry might be riddled with caves and he could lose the digger. Or, worse still, one of his family or a colleague lost to an accident caused by an unseen danger.

So they'd taped the area off and, for the next four weeks, avoided that end of the quarry and dug elsewhere. The earth never opened up for them again.

But the hole was an itch on his scalp which needed scratching.

Jae-joon wasn't an experienced potholer, but had joined the university caving club for a semester. During the term they had spent a weekend exploring the Gossi cave, in the centre of the country. On that trip he'd learnt the dos and don'ts of moving underground. And he'd also bought some of the gear – ropes, hard hats and head-torches – a decision he'd often regretted as he'd left the club soon afterwards. By his second semester, evenings with his girlfriend in Gangnam were a much more exciting prospect than messing around underground.

He still had the gear. And now he had a hole – maybe a cave?

Six weeks later, when the air in the valley was so cold his breath froze as it left his lips, he had made the decision to venture underground. If nothing else it would be warmer down there.

He'd taken his brother with him. His brother was older. But stronger. And, whilst he'd never caved before, he was as brave as a dragon. With Jae-joon's limited expertise and his brother's heart, they should be able to tackle the toughest of tasks.

Jae-joon had used his car as an anchor for the descent rope, and had tied the safety to a nearby tree. He had led, with his brother acting as belay. After a short struggle to get through the opening, the shaft widened and he quickly found a ledge. Below him was a black abyss and the only next step was to abseil into the darkness. He reckoned he had 30 metres of safety rope before he'd run out. At that point his brother would have to pull him in; and that would be that.

He lost count of the drop. As the rope fed through the figure-of-eight, his head torch illuminating earth and rocks off to his side, he tried to fathom how far he had dropped.

20 metres?

Maybe 25.

...

Clunk.

His foot struck something. Something *very* un-rock like.

He pulled his feed rope up and toward him. His descent stopped. Holding the up and the down rope in one hand he reached to unclip the torch from his hard hat with his free hand ... which slipped through his fingers and fell.

No!

Clank!

The beam rolled and then, *thud*, it stopped.

Jae-joon peered down. It took him a few seconds to work out what he was looking at.

My God.

As his fallen torch lit up the inners of an open metal box about the size of a shopping trolley, he knew he had discovered ... a fifth tunnel of aggression.

And now, three years later, he and his brother were making use of the tunnel. Not as it was intended. Not as a conduit for the military, or a passage for spies.

But for a much more humanitarian purpose.

He and his brother, with the help of a limited number of village elders, had opened a channel to the North. They'd started using it formally just four months ago – over three years after he'd first clanged his foot on a mine cart, the one he had just finished hauling along the track.

Yes, it had taken them nearly three years to prepare the tunnel so it could be used safely by those who needed it most: the young and the elderly; pregnant women and the infirm. A safe passage between the DPRK and his own country, South Korea.

Three years. But the wait had been worth it.

And Jae-joon knew it couldn't last. That this project was destined for failure. There would be a leak. Someone, either side of the border, would tell someone else. The authorities would come crashing down on them. And rather a hero of the people, an honour that would probably have been bestowed on him if he had told the police or the army of his find three years previously, he would be considered a criminal. Maybe even a traitor.

But that didn't matter to him. As soon as they had broken out of the far end of the tunnel and confirmed what they knew – that they were in the North – he only wanted one thing: to reunite his extended family. A family shattered by war at the end of 1953. A family split in two on the 27th of July that year when the Korean Armistice Agreement was signed – a treaty which formalised a border between north and south. A border that tore families apart; families separated by a line drawn by a human hand. A line that had been randomly etched on maps in countries other than his own.

In New York.

In Washington and Beijing.

Scribed on maps by foreigners, but drawn from the blood of his people.

From a war to which there was no end.

No peace treaty.

A war which had kept his grandparents apart. His grandfather stoic and resolute. His grandmother – well, who knew? She had been kept safe in the neighbouring village to the north whilst visiting her sister. But the battles and then the ceasefire had stopped all movement. And then the DMZ, the most fortified strip of real estate in the world, had ensured that they remain apart.

But not now. Not since the tunnel had become operational.

Once they had broken turf in the North it had taken him and his brother three weeks to ensure the route to his great-aunt's village had been clear. That there were no troops, or police.

Initially their trips had been short; reconnaissance. But, even so, they had been overcome by the destitution they had found. All of their visits had been at night but it very quickly became clear that what they had heard about the North Koreans' economy was an understatement. The fields were sown with struggling crops. There were no tractors. No cars. There were some bicycles. And there were chickens. But no other livestock.

They found their great-aunt's house easily, having casually quizzed their grandfather about his past – something, after a couple of glasses of *soju*, he was more than happy to share. Jae-joon had no idea what she looked like, as he had never met her, but his grandfather had given him a photo. It was black and white ... and grainy ... and old. But it had been enough.

On their fourth visit, late one evening just before the sun had disappeared behind the trees on a westerly hill, his brother had spotted her. She had left a ramshackle house carrying a towel toward an outbuilding – Jae-joon had assumed it was where the family did their ablutions.

They had waited.

The door of the shack opened and the woman emerged, the light of a candle in the window of the main house catching her face.

It was her!

Jae-joon was about to leap to his feet, when his brother had stopped him.

'Not now! You'll frighten her to death. Let's come back. Maybe next weekend. And stay until it gets light? And then we can make an approach, maybe pretending to be people from another village. Or tourists?'

'Tourists? Are you mad?' Jae-joon had been following his brother's logic until that point.

'We'll think of something. We need a photo of Grandad. And possibly some memorabilia. Something to persuade her?'

That had been the plan.

And it had worked.

They'd come the following weekend. They'd brought one of Grandad's pipes the old man had said he'd had since before the war.

They had waited until after dawn and had made contact. It had taken most of the morning and more tears than Jae-joon thought were possible to shed, but his grandmother had been persuaded.

That had been the start ...

... which was now history.

Now, as Jae-joon lifted a young girl from the mine cart, a girl who weighed nothing and whose clothes were as ragged as a tramp's, they were on their fourteenth trip. And so far, with the help of the elders in both villages, they had delivered maybe a tonne's worth of supplies into the North whilst, in return, smuggling forty-seven of the most needy from the North – including Grandma Eun Ae.

And what a reunion that had been!

Horror

Chapter 1

Plaža Kupari, Kupari, Croatia

Present Day

There were some benefits to doing his job. Sure, Kupari Beach was hardly one of the gems of the Adriatic but, with the mid-fall sun nicely warming the day and with a single white yacht interrupting the clear waters of the bay, Jackson White Jr felt great. He was sitting on the beach wall, his feet dangling a good three feet from the sand below. The view to his front was perfect. A block of dolphin-green sea, lightened by a white sand bed that seemed to last to the horizon. Above it a clear, soft blue sky, darkening to the heavens, broken only by a solitary gull which was circling rocks off to his left.

Behind him things were a little different. Abandoned hotels peppered with bullet holes formed an imperfect semicircle, the gap between them and the beach decorated with broken blacktop and angled paving slabs. It was a mess. A mess that had started life as a Croatian military resort only to be ransacked by Serbian forces in the Bosnian war. Twenty-five years later it was still disused with the original damage exacerbated by partying youths and vandals. The Grand Hotel, a two-storey *maison* placed centrally to the beach, was a shell. The modern, five-storey Hotel Goricina looked more multi-storey car park with its open sides and concrete plinths, than officer-quality accommodation. Other broken buildings littered the vista, trees and shrubs taking over where, Jackson assumed, manicured grass used to flourish.

There were no paying guests at the resort. He'd reconned the site four months ago, along with seven other possible meet locations on the coast either side of Dubrovnik. This was possibly the best – if you were looking for something close to total exclusion. The site was open, but uncrowded. There were five locals relaxing on the beach. And a scruffy, lime-green Opel Corsa was parked up on the small quay to his right, its occupant a fisherman sitting on the end of the rock and concrete pier next to an empty net and bucket.

There was no one else. Jackson knew that to be so. He'd arrived an hour ago; shorts, a polo shirt, and flip-flops, a small camera bag and a rolled towel under his arm, dressed and equipped like any American tourist. It had taken him thirty minutes to sweep the area. A half-decent road brought you into the resort, along a mile and a half spur off the D8. And there were two other coast-side approaches. A track from the east, competent enough to allow vehicular access with a 4x4. And a cliff footpath from the northwest. He'd hidden infra-red sensors with wide-angled cameras on all three routes. Each sensor was wirelessly linked to his phone. If anyone broke the lines, he'd know about it. With a glance at his phone he'd have a good idea whether the latest visitors were a threat.

Yes, the place was a mess; hardly a beacon for visitors.

And that's what made it perfect for a meet.

He checked his watch: 10.34 am. His agent would be in position in six minutes; the fourth floor of the Goricina, southwest corner.

Jackson had taken responsibility for Bae Ki-tae as soon as the Korean had arrived in Croatia; a DPRK defector high up in the regime's civil service. Bae, not his original name which had been changed to protect his identity, was the CIA's most current agent. But his currency wouldn't last long. Jackson's boss reckoned they had about six months of useful intel from the North Korean after which, such was the churn in the upper echelons of the DPRK, the man would be out of date. Other than having an encyclopaedic knowledge of the regime's doctrine and mantras – for which they had five or six Harvard professors who were experts in the field – his utility would dwindle.

Jackson's job today was to extend that time. And for that he had a present for Bae: a cell phone, with a difference. The phone could reach any number in North Korea from Croatia, whilst seemingly calling from a number inside the North Korean capital, Pyongyang. It was clever stuff. Too clever for Jackson. He was happy with the front end of computers. He could carry out low-level hacking and some coding, and he was completely comfortable with the Agency's IT applications. But microelectronics wasn't his thing.

He had other skills.

One of those was persuasion. He was a very good HUMINT (human intelligence) operator. He had that type of face: kind and considered. He had natural empathy. And he was *very* good at agent research, both prior to a meet using the complete gambit of Agency tools and that from other mission centres and embassies, and he had a highly effective *cascon* (casual conversation) manner. With a decent *cascon* he reckoned he could establish date and town of birth, marriage status, workplace, and the type of car a prospective agent drove within the first five minutes of an engagement.

And that was just the beginning.

Meets were never programmed to last longer than an hour, unless they were conducted in a safe house. An hour was an age to him.

The key was offering your own soul – your own indiscretions.

Jackson had four aliases in Croatia and he knew them as if he were looking in the mirror. Today he was Harry Pence, a US Embassy officer from Zagreb (which wasn't far from the truth). Harry was married with three children. He loathed his job, he hated his wife (but doted on his kids) and he drank – not heavily, but enough for it to linger on his breath. Bae already knew Harry was struggling at work, but not so much the Korean felt

21

unsafe. He knew Harry had his eyes on a pretty blonde in the secretariat, and that his eldest kid was smoking dope he bought from a market stall down by the River Sava.

And much more.

Because of that Jackson knew a great deal about Bae Ki-tae. And no topic, either personal or professional, was off limits. Today, therefore, he hoped his relationship with the North Korean was such that he could persuade him to use the cell to make contact with friends in Pyongyang. To start the gradual process of establishing agents from a distance. To extend Bae's utility to something more than a walking encyclopaedia of North Korea. To foster a growing network of agents within the DPRK.

Bae would push back. Of course he would. He had escaped the murderous regime, breaking from his minders on a visit to Singapore as he prepared to have an operation on his liver; treatment which was unavailable in Pyongyang, but accessible for senior government officials – loyal party members. His trip and medical expenses were funded by taxes raped from destitute farmers working the fields around Hamhung and Tanchŏn.

Instead of heading for surgery he had made it to the US Embassy and sought asylum. He was out of the country two days later, without any ceremony. Neither Jackson's government nor the DPRK's regime had made the asylum public. It was the best kept secret in the

22

history of defections. The current President of the United States was making overtures of peace on the Korean peninsula. There was no way they were going to refuse asylum to any defecting North Korean. But neither were they prepared to make hay when there was a bigger fish to fry: denuclearisation. And the last thing Pyongyang wanted was to be humilliated by the defection of a high ranking official.

Bae had defected and no one was the wiser.

After a successful liver op at the Walter Reed National Military Medical Center followed by a seven-week debrief, Bae Ki-tae was asked to choose a country – within reason. Bae had told Jackson there had been a map of the world on the wall at Langley. He'd asked one of the CIA interviewers where they would prefer to live if they had been given a choice. The man had pointed to Croatia, 'where his parents had emigrated from'.

And that had been that.

Jackson had taken responsibility for him from there. A new identity had been issued, accommodation provided and now, four months later, the two of them were meeting for the eighth time. Originally the meet was planned for next week, but his contact had called it forward. No reason given; changing dates by a couple of days was not unusual.

So, for today, Jackson had a set of questions concerning a forthcoming summit between the President and the Supreme Leader. He'd received them yesterday from the State Department. Apparently they already knew the answers but were interested in any nuance Bae Ki-tae might add.

That would take them maybe half an hour. And then, under instructions from the Head of Mission Center in Zagreb, he was to push Bae on opening up contacts in the DPRK. Hence the very advanced cell phone.

Jackson would make it happen. Bae and he were best of pals. They'd already shared some pretty deep secrets. He'd built up trust ...

... now it was payback time.

He stood, opened his camera case and took out a Nikon 3500 DSLR – on the face of it, a standard $400 camera. What any reasonably affluent tourist might have in their bag.

Jackson turned it on and raised it to eye level.

There were still five locals on the beach. And the fisherman. There had been no notifications on his phone that his infrared beams had been tripped. That must mean Bae was already within the perimeter ... or was late? The latter was unlikely. Part of Bae's extended tour at Langley was a briefing on the protocols he and his in-country case-officer would use.

One of the practical demonstrations was how to take part in a meet. Get to the RV early; maybe thirty minutes before. Position yourself where you can see the location. Somewhere between 100 to 300 feet, depending upon the terrain – urban, close; rural, distant. Stake it out. Look for possible tails. Approach the meet three minutes beforehand, and only if you think the route is clear. Linger for no more than five minutes. Leave if your case-officer doesn't turn up.

Jackson knew he'd have practised it at least three times. More if necessary.

Bae had been spot on for all of their previous meets. It would be the same today.

He looked at the camera's 3-inch LCD, twisting the focus. The normal Nikon's screen would repeat the view that entered the lens, matching colour for colour. Not so Jackson's model. His Nikon had been specially adapted by R&D in Washington. His screen was just shades of two colours. Reds and greens. Infrared. Hot and cold.

He turned the camera toward the Hotel *Goricina*; fourth floor. On the southwest side.

A cool, mid-green concrete hulk, framed by colder, dark-green sky.

Nothing.

He moved position so he was better able to see the corner of the hotel.

Jackson looked again at the screen.

The fourth floor.

No. Wrong floor?

It was difficult to be exact. The hotel was in two parts. One half was further up a small incline. The southwest corner was closer. Its ground floor lower than the main part of the hotel.

The fifth floor?

He moved the camera. Played with the lens. Held it steady.

There!

A man-sized blob of fuzzy dark-orange, obscured by a plastic sheet which covered a window.

A short, man-sized blob.

A Bae-sized blob.

Good.

Jackson lowered the camera and reached to open the bag.

But he stopped; he wasn't sure why.

He raised his camera again. It took him a second to find the previous spot.

What?

The short, dark-orange sized blob had changed. It was no longer Bae-sized. It was ... *two people?* The combined mass of warm flesh was moving about.

Struggling?

Jackson stared at the screen for a few seconds trying to rationalise what he was watching.

Shit!

In his effort to respond quickly Jackson missed the camera bag and the expensive Nikon crashed to the floor.

Shit!

Seconds later, with the pieces of the camera now shoved into the bag, Jackson was sprinting towards the gap between two concrete posts from which the entrance doors to the Goricina Hotel once hung.

26

HQ Secret Intelligence Service (SIS), Vauxhall, London

Frank was more stressed than usual. He was struggling with a series of images he'd had through from the BND (*Bundesnachrichtendienst, the German Federal Intelligence Agency*) concerning a right-wing grouping that was now working cross-international borders. Calling itself Universelle Freiheit, or Universal Freedom (*UF*), the network was thought to have members in all northern European countries, including Scandinavia. The intelligence community view was UF's gestation started in Leipzig University where a hard-right, anti-immigrant drinking crowd had factioned. From that split a German politics student, Jakob Christofel, had set up a quasi-political party taking a few pals with him. That was over a year ago and whilst Christofel had managed to stay above the law, his fledgling group had expanded via chat rooms on the dark web and was now considered to be a major pan-European terror cell.

German law made eavesdropping on its citizens next to impossible. As a result much of what UF was orchestrating could only be stopped by arresting the perpetrators when they had done, or were in the process of doing something illegal. And that had only been marginally successful. There were three trials against German citizens in train: six men, all white and

27

all from more impoverished backgrounds from cities in the east of the country. The alleged crimes were criminal damage, riotous behaviour and the latest, attempted murder.

A mosque in Dresden had been firebombed three months ago. Bizarrely the BND had been granted over-watch on the mosque because there was clear evidence of an Islamic plot to attack the upcoming Christmas market, probably by way of a 'drive through' where a random truck would be stolen and driven by a martyr through the crowd.

Instead they'd stumbled across a fascist attack. A lone UF attacker had been picked up by the driver of a BND cell which was operating a high-powered listening device from the back of an unmarked van. The driver had spotted a motorcyclist pull up to the mosque, take out a Molotov cocktail from a satchel he had slung around his waist and set it alight. The driver had alerted the team in the back of the van and they had broken cover. Whilst they hadn't prevented the first petrol bomb from smashing through one of the mosque's Moorish windows, the bomber hadn't had a chance to light the second. In all he had four homemade devices in his bag. Two months of investigation found links to UF which the BND were now investigating further. The man was due to attend his first court session next week.

What Frank was attempting to do, between multiple cups of fruit tea, was match known British UF members with images taken by his continental

28

counterparts – make the pan-European connection. He had a series of mugshots on his central screen, all of whom had form … and all of whom had travelled to Europe in the past four months. The key was matching one of his faces with one – among hundreds – the BND had shared with him. He had the dates of when his set of imageo had travelled to continental Europe, and the BND had worked within those parameters. They had CCTV and some hand-held photos of seven UF gatherings during the period.

The German images were on his left screen.

His job was to make the link. In light of the UK's recent position on the European Union, it made him smile that doubtless his thugs would have voted to leave the EU whilst, when it suited them, they were more than happy to collaborate with their 'friends' in Germany.

And Holland.

One of the sets of BND images was of an anti-immigrant march in Arnhem, just over the border from Germany. The AIVD (Algemene Inlichtingen- en Veiligheidsdienst – the Dutch Security Service) had held a joint surveillance op there with the BND five weeks ago. Frank had forty-seven photos of that event.

He had his group in a line across the top of the central 32-inch screen. They looked two-dimensional, but Cynthia (SIS's mainframe) was clever. If he touched a face and wiggled his finger the headshot twisted from side to side. Such was the technology, he could rotate the image through 360 degrees with Cynthia's image-enhancing software filling any gaps.

Frank stared at them.

Twelve men.

All connected via chat rooms and dark web messaging. All but two with police history. All with far-right political affiliations. And all had money. He had access to their bank accounts and credit cards. He knew where they lived, what they did for a living and which pubs they drank in. GCHQ had their phones tapped and their internet browsers monitored. And MI5, the Security Service, was close to recruiting at least one of them.

Twelve men. Lined up in a row on top of his screen.

One, two, buckle my shoe; three, four, knock at the door ...

... eleven, twelve, dig and delve.

OK, then.

With a flick of a finger he launched one of the BND images from his left-hand monitor. It crossed the gap between screens and settled under his line of fascists. He compared the images, picking a face in the crowd from the outside, in.

No.

No.

Wait.

He enlarged the central image. It was a side shot taken at the Arnhem march. There must have been sixty people in the photo. Most of them had their heads covered with a hood, or a scarf. Getting any facial match was going to be difficult. But there were always more clues than just the shape of their face, the colour and set of the eyes. British people dressed differently from their European neighbours. The brands of clothes they wore were different. Even though many shops were pan-European, the stocks were subtly different. Frank was an expert on the Next catalogue. And Primark. And Nike.

And others.

Simple markers were football shirts and emblems. More complex were watches. More subtle still: brands of e-cigarettes.

Last week his list was only eleven strong. On Monday he'd found the twelfth. He was working on a BND photo of a meeting in a *Gasthaus* in Cottbus, just west of the Polish border. The image was pixelated and oblique. But one of the men in the photo was wearing a brand of glasses that could only be found in the British Specsavers range. He'd spoken to a pal of his at Counterterrorism and they'd shared a set of images they had been working on of a cell in Eastbourne. Hey presto – same glasses, this time a frontal shot. With Cynthia's help he'd attributed 78% likelihood they were the same man. That was good enough for government work.

And eleven had become twelve.

He moved the enlarged image of the march around, looking for clues.

No.

31

'Frank.'

?

He abruptly sat back in his chair. It was Claire, Jane's PA. She had crept up on him whilst he was intent on his work, his face far too close to the screen for good eye health.

Although she wasn't Jane's PA – not for the moment. Jane was away on sabbatical. Somewhere east. His last contact with her had been an e-postcard from Langkawi, a delightfully tropical island off the coast of Malaysia. Or was it Angkor Wat, the Cambodian temples?

It's OK for some.

He spun his chair so he faced her.

'Sorry. Yes, Claire.' He smiled.

'The boss wants to see you. Now.' She forced a smile back.

'What, Marcus? He could have pinged me?'

Marcus was Jane's stand-in. But he wasn't Jane. That was the only good thing he could say about his temporary boss.

'No. Clive.' Claire raised her eyebrows, opening her face in an attempt to display as much surprise as Frank was now feeling.

'Clive ... as in C? The big boss.' Frank pointed to the ceiling.

Claire nodded.

Frank had never been into C's office on day-to-day business. He'd met him on a number of occasions, but that was always as part of a team ... either a debrief, or some congratulatory affair, such as post Switzerland last year after Sam had prevented the Dalai Lama from taking a bullet.

'On my own?'

'I think so, yes.' Claire was nodding again.

'Does his nibs know?' Frank pointed in the direction of Marcus's office. He really didn't like Marcus. 'His nibs' was the best he could do.

'I don't think so, no. The call came from Janet, PA to PA.'

That's odd.

Frank stared back at the screen. Twelve mugshots. All of them dangerous. And a photo of something close to a riot. One of the twelve would be in that crowd. He knew that. And he had to find him.

'You should go now.' Claire sounded impatient.

Frank's concentration was broken for the second time.

'Sure ... OK.' He stood. He was the same height as Claire. He was younger. But she looked in much better shape than he did.

It was his turn to nod.

He picked up his notebook, circumnavigated Jane's PA and headed for the stairs.

Chapter 2

There was a note on the kitchen table. It read: *Gone for a run.* Frank picked it up, smiled to himself and placed it in the recycling. He unloaded the single bag of groceries he had bought from Anbu's convenience store and put the kettle on. He reckoned Sam would be back anytime in the next hour. He'd prepare a cup for her, but not make it.

What a day.

His meeting with C had been disturbing. On one hand he'd been delighted the boss had singled him out to share the intelligence. On the other, the picture the intelligence painted was not good. Not good at all.

He took a standard tea bag from the cupboard and placed it in his Dire Straits mug. Next to the builders' tea was a pack of Whittard of Chelsea, 'Very Berry Crush' bags. Sam would have one of those. No sugar.

He smiled to himself again as he dropped the new bag in her bone china mug. It was decorated with, 'I'd Rather Be In My Camper'.

It was at times like this, when he was in the comfort of his own home, that he felt wholly conflicted. Work was massive. It always was and always would be.

Leading on UF, and all far-right groupings in the UK with overseas connections, was a huge job. Some of the work, including the contacts in foreign embassies and associated travel, was much bigger than would normally fall to an analyst. Whilst he didn't run agents, what he was doing was closer to the load of a case-officer than it was matched against his original analyst's job description.

And he loved it.

His meeting with C this afternoon had pushed that boundary further still.

What C was asking of him would require more hours ... and possibly more travel. Which didn't fill him with glee. As an introvert, he was naturally a home bird. His two forays abroad – Munich, and Italy, leading to Switzerland – had taken him out of his comfort zone and parachuted him into a whole new world of anxiety. Munich had almost got him killed; he had made it out of a burning house minutes before it would have engulfed him. Italy, and then Switzerland, hadn't brought him quite so close to his own death, but it had laid out death before him in grizzly detail. And he hadn't signed up for that. If it hadn't been for the subsequent intensity of being Sam's carer, he was pretty sure he'd have been having his own breakdown by now.

Maybe that was to come?

And that's where the conflict arose.

Work. And Sam.

She was so much better than she had been just under a year ago. She was up and about. Clearly running. And talking too. It was never deep stuff. But it was better than nothing at all. She prepared the weekday evening meals – simple but wholesome food, with carefully selected ingredients free from sulphates and additives, and other nasties. She did her own laundry and was ever so good around the house. On weekends they walked, read the papers and even went to the cinema – just like an older married couple. He cooked then, more flamboyantly than her, and they sat on the sofa together watching the box. Physically close, so much so he could feel the warmth radiating from her thighs and shoulders. But never so close that they touched.

He understood that. He knew the boundaries. There was no need for words. He could read the messages in her eyes. He knew her that well. And he knew the last thing she needed was him making her already fractured life more complex.

If she wanted to be his, she would let him know. In time.

And he had all the time in the world … for her.

He loved her.

There was no one else. There would be no one else.

He'd never had a girlfriend and he was emotionally mature enough to know he never would. And that didn't bother him. He liked his own company. He had a small circle of gaming friends. They played together on the net and, every second weekend, met at one of the houses and fought the board game equivalent. Once Sam was up for it his pals had descended on his house one Saturday night. Sam had stayed in the background, sat with her feet under her bum on a large cushion in the corner of the sitting room. His friends were aware of some of her mental health issues and knew not to press. In return she had been delightful. At that point she was still not talking, but that hadn't stopped her pointing to empty bottles of beer and cans of coke, and nodding to ask if they'd like a refill. And she had helped Frank clear up at the end of the evening.

If it had been possible he would have loved her even more just then.

Other than one or two old Army pals, Frank didn't think Sam had any close friends. Once she'd started to talk, he'd asked if there was anyone she'd like to visit. The answer had been, 'no, thanks'. He pressed later on relatives; again the answer had been, 'no'.

She seemed content.

But wistful.

More so recently.

He couldn't put his finger on it. There were lots of smiles and some laughing, but every so often he caught her looking out of the window, beyond the row of houses opposite as if to some imaginary horizon. When they walked in the park, she didn't seem focused on the here and now: the squirrel which darted across their path, or the butterfly dancing with a nearby bush. If he

37

spotted something for her – there was a small murmuration of starlings a couple of weeks back that swirled and twisted low across the trees – and pointed to it, she would immediately come to, as though he'd woken her from a trance. In that case she'd stared at them, smiling at their antics and following their every turn ... until he sensed they'd lost her interest and something else had taken its place. He had no idea what.

And he wasn't going to press.

Questions like, 'Are you OK, Sam?' weren't on the prescribed list of helpful asks. He just knew that. It was much better to let her be and only ask specific questions rather than generalities.

'Have you taken your meds?' was OK. Although he had given up on that after a couple of months. As with everything she did, she was utterly reliable with process and timings.

At some point she might open up. In the meantime he loved having her in his house. And he loved looking after her. She was more delight than trouble. And when she smiled ...

The kettle had boiled.

He poured the boiling water into his cup.

'Make that two.' Sam's small voice from behind him. She was as stealthy as a stalking cat.

'Sure.' He didn't turn around, but filled Sam's cup. 'How was your run?' He was stirring his tea bag, fishing it out with a spoon and putting it into the composter.

She didn't reply.

He turned and handed her her cup. She was dressed in black male running shorts, an un-logoed yellow singlet, a red showerproof, long-sleeve top and a microfibre, blue and black beanie. Her face was plastered with sweat and hair was hanging from the hat like the roots of a recently weeded dandelion. You would never say of Sam that she had 'all the gear, and no idea'. The opposite was more apt. He knew nothing of running, and hoped he never would, but a month ago Sam had joined the local Saturday Park Run. The 9 am start time was too early for him and she had made her own way to the event by public transport. He was still in his pyjamas when she got back.

He'd asked her the same question then.

'How was the run?'

'Mmm? Oh, OK ... thanks. I must shower,' had been the response.

Frank had checked the Park Run website later that day. Sam's five-kilometre time had been 19 minutes, 25 seconds. She was the third female in the race and first in her age group by a margin. Just as significantly, she had beaten all but twelve of the men.

'OK' was clearly a relative term. She was in the, 'no gear, every idea' category when it came to running. Actually she was in that category for almost everything she put her hand to.

Other than, of course, interacting with her fellow humans. That wasn't her forte.

Sam had the mug to her mouth. She pointed upstairs.

'Sure, Sam. I'll put supper on whilst you shower. It's *University Challenge* tonight.'

'Good,' was the short response as she headed down the hall. Followed by, 'I'll beat you again,' as she turned to take the stairs.

She would. She always did. There was so much stuff in her head. All of it, even after what might be described as an adult lifetime of trauma, immediately accessible. And all of it available well before he'd had a chance to reach into his own memory. She was still sharper than flint, although on first meet you would never have thought so. She was quiet and unforthcoming in company. Brusque when questioned. Unresponsive to trivia.

Her forensic ability had proven to be an enormous asset when it came to deciphering the many complex threads of a myriad of intelligence operations. Her patience and diligence key to spotting things others wouldn't. Her fearlessness sown from a complete disregard for her own wellbeing.

Today, however, after his meeting with C he was unsure having Sam around was such a good thing.

It was that conflict again. This time, in a way he could never have imagined.

C had briefed him on an operation which was on the closest of holds. A series of events which were both incendiary – and personal. A pink folder: Top Secret. UK

40

Eyes only. The title, in red capitals, was Op MANDOLIN. There was a distribution list pinned to the front. The paper detailed four names. C was one. The second was the Cabinet Secretary. The third was the Chief's PA.

He was the fourth.

A pink folder. Top Secret. Four names.

Op Mandolin.

Frank.

'Cynthia's mainframe has an equivalent file,' C had said. 'Janet will sign you in and furnish you with a password. I want you to look over it in the reading room and come and see me first thing tomorrow. Then we'll talk about what to do next.'

C had briefed the outline of the case to him verbally. What he had told him had shocked Frank to his core. At one point he had to put his hand on a chair to steady himself. What caught him wasn't necessarily the possible global impact of the report, although that was potentially both dangerous for regional stability and highly damaging to SIS's reputation across the world.

It was its personal nature which had caught his breath.

Jane Baker was in trouble. Big trouble. Indeed it was possible that she was already dead – although C thought that unlikely.

The report, which he'd read three times in the isolation of the reading room, was an extraordinary tale. From where he sat it was, almost certainly, one of the most intricate operations SIS had ever undertaken in peacetime.

And it was currently failing; the ramifications of which could be huge.

Just as pertinent, Jane was in peril. That is why, apparently, C had chosen him. Other than Sam, Frank was as close a colleague to Jane as anyone else in the building. He knew her really well. And C was hoping that knowledge would unearth something useful.

His conflict today, standing in his kitchen with a steaming mug of tea in his hand, wasn't about work versus Sam. It wasn't that he wanted to attend to her so much, but only had enough energy to manage what he was currently doing. The conflict now was between him having access to the details of an operation that had endangered Jane's life, versus ... well, the fact the best person to unstitch this and sew it back together was obviously Sam.

And she was no longer codeword cleared. Even if she were, Frank would struggle sharing the information with Sam for fear of the impact it might have on her.

He would probably get through losing Jane.

He would never cope if he lost Sam.

CIA Mission Center, Undisclosed Location, Zagreb, Croatia

There were more people in Conference Room 2 than Jackson had ever seen. Every chair was taken. Three men and two women were standing shoulder to shoulder, squashed at the back. And there were some faces he didn't recognise, which surprised him. The murder of Bae Ki-tae was clearly the biggest event to have hit Zagreb for some time. In his two years at the Center he'd never come across anything like this.

He'd just finished his briefing. It was the fourth time he'd recounted what had happened. First had been over the phone to the chief about ten minutes after he'd found Bae Ki-tae lying in a pool of his own blood on the fifth floor of the Goricina. Jackson had called in once he'd made best endeavours to find his killer ... or, not, as was the case. The instructions he'd been given had been clear: 'Get out of there – now!' That was the Agency's IA (*immediate action*) in the case of a dead agent. The CIA spent a good deal of time and money recruiting informants, but a dead one was worthless. And, however well placed, all agents were expendable. They all had watertight backgrounds, either real or fabricated, and history had proven the best way to deal with a loss was to let the local, and in some cases, national authorities deal with the body. In Bae Ki-tae's case Jackson reckoned the local *policija* would probably come up against a brick wall and pass the case to the Ministry of Interior. If that became uncomfortable for the US, the Mission Center had a couple of well-placed contacts to help brush it under the carpet.

His second debrief had been a replica, this time face to face with his chief.

His third had been last night – via video link to Langley. The man he'd spoken to was the Deputy National Intelligence Chief (Europe). Jackson knew his wiring diagrams, and DNIC (Eu) was the big man. Bae Ki-tae's death obviously involved some shit and some fans. By the end of the hour-long debrief Jackson didn't yet know whether he was being held responsible for the agent's death. He clearly wasn't getting any medals.

And he'd just finished his fourth briefing. This time to the biggest crowd of staff he'd seen gathered in the same place, other than last year's Thanksgiving party. But that had included wives and children.

The director had told him to break his briefing into three parts: Bae Ki-tae's background; the recent history of meets and dead-letter boxes in country; how yesterday had played out. And he was to make absolutely no deductions.

He'd done all that rather well, he thought.

The chief summarised.

'OK, people. The second highest defector in the history of the DPRK chooses our country to retire to. He's living in Dubrovnik, working as an independent tour guide for Koreans visiting southern Croatia. We know where he lives, we have his bank details etc, etc. He's met with Jackson eight times before; this would have been his ninth. All previous times had been routine and as per schedule for an agent of this standing. The

44

ninth was planned for next week and had been brought forward by Bae Ki-tae. No reason given and no flag to the contact to say the need to amend the date was urgent. That's right, Jackson?'

'That's right, sir. As I said, we were due to meet next week, but Bae called it forward.'

'SMS?' His chief interjected.

'That's correct.' Jackson pressed and swiped at his tablet. He was prepared for this. He had screenshot his SMS exchange with Bae. He sent it to the screen. It read:

Coffee as usual? Tuesday would be good. The green bar?

'As you'd expect, Bae's used a SIM that was one of ours,' Jackson continued. 'Untraceable. Routed randomly around the world. The "coffee" code is for a non-scheduled meet. Tuesday means Monday. The green bar in the pre-agreed location and time, the Goricina. Note if there had been a crisis, the final sentence would have finished with a smiley. If his life were in danger, he'd have used a Croatian flag emoji. In short, I just assumed he had something else planned which messed with our prearranged schedule, and needed a change.'

'Or he had something key to add to the forthcoming summit?' The supplementary came from one of the men Jackson didn't recognise. He was sitting at the far end of the conference table.

'Could be, although the timings of that meeting aren't yet in the public domain.' The chief answered the question for Jackson.

'No, sir. I don't agree,' Jackson interjected. 'There's an emoji for that. Smiley face for minor crisis; national flag for imminent danger to life; coffee cup for postpone, I'm unwell; and a heart for important information. All four emojis are found on different swipes of the Android OS. We had rehearsed them – and he was clear. If he had something for the summit, he would have posted a heart.'

There was a suppressed chuckle from a few of the team in the room.

'Enough!' Jackson reckoned the chief looked under pressure. 'Moving on. Jackson follows procedure and secures the meet site. He spots his agent at the agreed location. He then sees his agent struggling with another person. By the time Jackson gets to the meet, the agent is dead – stabbed – and the assailant gone.' He took a breath. 'Bae has been stripped of anything of monetary value, there's no wallet, no phone, no watch.' The chief paused again. Jackson thought the man had lost some of his tan since yesterday.

'Questions? Deductions?'

They came thick and fast.

Jackson was convinced this was not a mugging. He'd spoken to the embassy late yesterday and they had trawled the *policija* database. Kupari Beach was not a crime spot. Yes, there had been a number of arrests in the area but it was mostly drugs and the odd alcohol-fuelled fight. Mugging was a popular pastime in tourist hotspots, such as Dubrovnik. But even there the records show none in the past five years were linked to murder. That, of course, didn't mean it wasn't a possible explanation, but it was very unlikely.

Second, was the nature of the stabbing. Last night he'd had a quick chat with the embassy's pathologist showing him one of the stills from his camera. There was a single wound. In the chest, left side; likely, straight through the heart. Whoever had killed his agent was either a professional, or incredibly lucky.

Jackson poured water on that particular wildfire.

'No, sorry, folks. I think we're dealing with a professional hit. Removing consumables is just a way to make it look like robbery. Although it does us one favour: we might assume that's what the *policija* will conclude, but I'm completely unconvinced. Next question?' He lifted an open hand by way of invitation.

'Was anything else left at the scene?' It was Kim, a case-officer buddy of his who worked on the same floor.

'Not that I could see. I took sixty-five photos at the scene in about two minutes. I've not yet had a chance to look through them in detail – you've seen just a couple today. You have to remember the hotel is a garbage tip. There's broken doors, windows, porcelain from smashed toilets and sinks, and thirty years of party debris, including beer bottles, cans, cigarette butts and plenty of drug-related paraphernalia. It's the perfect place to lose evidence. Sorry.'

There was silence. The questions had dried up.

'OK, team.' It was the chief again. 'I got you here because this is the biggest thing to hit this mission since the war. Other than natural causes, we've only lost one agent in the past decade, and that was suicide. I may be the first Zagreb Mission chief to have lost an agent in living memory, but I refuse to be the first to have lost one and not, as a result, uncover the biggest conspiracy since Ukrainegate. So, whilst it's natural for Jackson to lead on this, I want everyone to do their own digging. And if Jackson needs your help, you drop everything. Clear?'

'Yessir's and other acknowledgements percolated around the room.

'Anything else, Jackson?' the chief asked.

'No, sir. I think that's it.'

'No stone unturned, then. Let's go, people.'

Triệu Quang Phục, Lào Cai, Vietnam

An unnamed guard brought in Jane's supper. It was chicken and rice, her staple food for the past two weeks. On the tray was some sweet tea and a Chinese candy bar – she could tell by the characters on the wrapping. She wasn't an expert in either Vietnamese or Mandarin, but she recognised the purity of the Mandarin lettering on the packaging.

That didn't mean she was now in China, although it was a possibility. The absolutely awful trip from Hanoi to where she was now had been long enough to take her north and over the border. Although, quite frankly she could be Laos or even Thailand. But the packaging spoke of China. Or somewhere close.

She didn't want to be reminded of that trip. The six hours or so in the boot of the car. The unworkable heat, which had brought on heatstroke ... a headache like she'd never experienced before; sweating without any sweat and, towards the end, dizziness and blackouts. The banging and lurching, a process that played on her smashed face, her weak limbs and her swollen wrists. The exhaust fumes.

The misery.

Thankfully, once she'd been manhandled out of the car and into her new prison, some bright spark had recognised her heatstroke for what it was and had thrown her into a cool bath. She was *compos mentis* a couple of hours later.

However the sickness, diarrhoea and lethargy that followed had lasted three days. If she could have lost any more weight, she would have, her walking skeleton impression unable to give anything else.

But, fair play to her captives, the move had brought with it some compensation. They were obviously at altitude. There was no air conditioning in her room but it was a good ten degrees cooler than the black hole of Hanoi. She was no longer in a cellar and her new place was presidential in comparison to her previous jail. It was big enough and had the worn decorations, including ornate plaster friezes, to be the dining room of an old colonial house. It was a corner room with two tall windows on the long wall, and a single window on the short; two doors, opposite the windows. The windows were sealed shut, and outside of them were substantial metal bars that looked impenetrable. The floor was parquet, but much of the wood had lifted or had been lost. The walls had once been wallpapered, but only a tiny fraction was left. The pattern was difficult to pick out, but she thought it might be repetitive *fleur-de-lis*, which reinforced the notion of an old French estate – which would shout Vietnam or Laos over China. What remained was plaster, and that had started to fall off the wall. There was a central ceiling light, its wire meeting a decorative rose – which needed a good wash. Jane reckoned in a previous life the single bulb might have been replaced by a chandelier.

And it wasn't just the decoration which had changed. She was being fed. Half-decent food. Three times a day. She had a bed … on a bedstead. And a chair and table. There was a bucket to wash with, and a toothbrush. The first time she used it her gums ached straight afterwards as if she'd brushed them with a file. There was a second bucket for her business – and soft paper. Luxury of luxuries, she also had a chance to visit a shower and a proper loo, although the latter was a French squat variety.

In her waking moments she was neither tied, nor hung from the ceiling. Her nose was still two sizes too big and, when she had a chance to stare in the mirror in the shower room, her eyes were still framed with yellows and browns. But they hadn't touched her face, or any part of her anatomy since she'd been brought from Hanoi.

In fact, other than one conversation with an older man dressed in a communist-style, baggy, grey casual suit, with big lapels and loose fitting trousers – all held together with a brown leather belt – she'd not been questioned.

It was all very puzzling.

And disconcerting.

What do they want from me?

In the cellar in Hanoi she'd held out for about four weeks, although time hadn't been something she recognised as a construct in that previous hell hole; so it might have been a good deal longer – or shorter. She had given the scantiest of details of who she was, where she worked – *government; security* – and what she had been doing in Asia. She knew that her story would hold. SIS were experts at developing bombproof covers and laying a web of background that was irrefutable. Her 'sabbatical' story would survive investigation, however interrogated. She'd been with government for eighteen years. The last three had been particularly taxing. Her mental health had been dodgy. She had been given six months paid leave. She was due back to work in January.

Why not pack a rucksack and push off to South East Asia?

Wouldn't anyone?

When questioned on what she meant by 'security', she fell back on a Security Service (MI5) alias. She knew enough about how 'Box' (one of the colloquial names of MI5) worked to easily pass off as an intelligence officer of theirs. The beauty of the cover was that foreign intelligence agencies felt less threatened by MI5 because their work was internal to the UK and rarely made it into the international arena. Her passport, bank cards and driving licence had her as Gemma Ruby. You didn't need to look hard on social media, or interrogate Google, to find her. She was as described: a middle-ranking officer in the Security Service.

However.

Two weeks ago she had been broken.

The constant pain, the heat, the enervating hanging from the ceiling, accompanied by the bucket of water and taser assault, the weakness, the smell of her own insides ... the vomiting, it all became too much. Her abuser (she still didn't know his name) hadn't needed to lift a finger. One morning he had untied her from her bed and sat her on the chair with her arms forced behind her. Jane assumed a smack to the nose, possibly with a spanner, would come next. Followed by some questions.

That morning he didn't draw a weapon. Instead, he brought his face to hers and studied her nose, as if inspecting for damage. She noticed his blinking as he rocked his head gently from side to side. He was so close she smelt his breath above the stench that filled the room; it wasn't an unpleasant smell, there was a whiff of coffee, maybe some spearmint? When she looked into his eyes, she thought she spotted some humanity, but it was fleeting.

And then he pulled back – Jane remembered flinching at that point – but he just stood upright, doing nothing. He blinked again, his hands held together in front of him.

Blink. Blink.

It must have been a minute before the tears came. She couldn't stop herself. It was a trickle at first, then a torrent. Her shoulders heaved and her body rocked. She couldn't face him anymore. She looked to her side – one way then the other. And then her head dropped, her chin bouncing off her chest as she sobbed some more.

'I work for MI6.'

The man walked around the room as she spoke – more like ranted. Jane told him her real name. She told him her job title. And she explained what operations she'd been involved in over the past year, focusing on Rome and the bringing down of the 'Ndrangheta Mafia – although she had enough of her wits about her not to mention the American involvement. She then rattled off a whole load of inconsequential information about herself. Her parents. Where she had gone to school. Where she lived and what she drove.

It was as expected. It was as she'd been trained to do.

There was no blueprint for surviving interrogation. No right way. Just conjecture – a feel of what had worked before. Supposition by people who had back-briefed officers who had broken, survived and not sold the crown jewels.

She was in what was known as: stage two.

Give them something. Something real and tangible. Something immutable. Then talk about yourself. Once you've broken, you're broken. Fill the void with useless facts ... but make sure they're facts. Don't lie again. If you lie, they will find out and that will be it. They will never trust you. You will be of no use to them.

And you will be dead.

She had been broken, that was for sure. And she couldn't have stopped herself. But in that moment of abject despair, when her life had become worthless and the thought of more torture had been overcome by inconsolable self-pity which had instantaneously led to self-preservation, she had still managed to stick to a script.

Of sorts.

Tell them something. Something real.

But not something they want to know.

The sessions had become less painful. And shorter. She had given them plenty of information that could have been lifted from SIS's website. She was indiscreet here and there about previous operations in the Middle East and Europe; closed ones with all the agents safe and their case-officers protected.

Her interrogator had pressed her on South East Asia, as he had done before. What had her itinerary been ... as opposed to what she had told them previously? She amended that a little to be in line with much of the truth, but stuck to the original story that she was on sabbatical. A sort of lie. She included her visits to SIS missions in Singapore, Thailand and Cambodia. And added that she was due to visit the mission in Hanoi, but they – her captors – had picked her up before she'd had a chance to make that meet. By way of explanation she told them that these had been courtesy calls from a senior SIS officer to colleagues in missions she'd never been to before. She was hoping to be given the Far East desk at Vauxhall (a little white lie which had made her nervous) when she returned.

Then, abruptly, she had been bagged in the middle of the night, stuck in the boot of a car and bounced all the way to ... wherever she was now. Somewhere near the Chinese border, possibly.

And that begged the question. Having now spent five days in captive rehabilitation, in the likely dining room of a French colonial villa, what was the plan for her? Who were these people and what were they going to do to her next?

That would be stage three. And nobody had taught her about that. And there was a good reason. Because the intelligence services didn't know of anyone who had come out of it alive.

As she took a mouthful of chicken and rice, an involuntary shiver spasmed through her body. More rice fell to the floor than made it to her mouth.

Jane knew something was coming.

She just didn't know what.

Roseberry Gardens, Orpington, London, UK

Sam took another spoonful of granola. She knew it was good for her, but she also knew it was like eating wood chippings which had recently been rained on. Every so often she got a taste of something which wasn't bark – a fruit, or a nut that scratched at her gums. It wasn't an unpleasant breakfast experience, but neither was it her childhood favourite: Frosties and warm milk. One day she would be old enough not to have to care.

She knew she chewed like a mouse. *Maybe a hamster?* Small, repetitive cheekfuls. She didn't eat with her mouth open – she hated that in others – but her lips were slightly puckered. Overall, she guessed, her chewing demeanour was petite and possibly feminine.

Like a hamster.

Which made some sense. Her hair was a multi-mix auburn, another wood analogy sprung to mind. Its hamster-esque colour was distracted by the odd and wildly disconcerting grey strand which, on its own – plucked from her head – seemed innocuous. But somehow, in amongst the mid-brown mass of curling swirls, stuck out like a crack on a smartphone's screen

Hamster cheeks and hamster hair.

And, now the wrong end of thirty: hamster hips.

She was fit, though. Back close to her very best. With Frank's as a base, and no commitments other than not unnecessarily pissing him off, she had put all her energies into her physical strength. Running was her top priority; other core strength exercises a close second. She'd remembered enough yoga – having accompanying Jane Baker to her classes all those years ago in Vauxhall – to be able put together a weekly programme that stretched her mind as well as her limbs. Frank's sitting room was hardly gym-sized, but it worked after she'd moved the furniture. He was particular about where everything was placed and once she'd finished abusing the room, she had to put things back *exactly* as she'd found them. He was never fussy with her – to her face. But she noticed him nudging a chair, or sliding a coaster when she wasn't meant to be looking.

So she was fit. But despite some decent muscle building, waist downwards she was more bulky than she cared for.

Hamster-like.

It didn't help that, whilst she had no tummy, she was hardly more than a couple of handfuls in the chest department. Narrow shoulders continued the beer bottle image.

Oh well. No one was looking. And she was hardly advertising.

What had surprised her was that mentally she felt pretty well. Sure, the first couple of months post-Davos had been a struggle. The flashbacks, the continual anxiety, the need for complete calm – to the point that she only wanted to look at one vista, and that was nearly always the view out of Frank's front window.

The inability to form words and then articulate them.

Her new meds, a name and a brand she couldn't be bothered to recall, were working their magic. She hadn't told the doc, but she was now down to a quarter dose and, so far, there had been no ill effects. Frank assumed she was still bottled up. Still not quite with it. And she hadn't dissuaded him of that notion. She was building up her physical and mental strength, whilst appearing semi-mute and flaccid. And he left her alone – whilst meticulously looking after her. It was a neat trick and one she was thankful for. But, and it was a big but, she wasn't ready for a normal relationship, even if it were only to be platonic; not that Frank was pressing.

Bless him.

She liked the quiet, and the calm. She always had. An outspoken introvert, she enjoyed her own company – relished non-pestering space ... and freedom.

Freedom.

That's what was missing now. Now she was on the up. Now she was fit and almost stable.

Now that ...

She had taken another mouthful of cereal, stood and had made her way to the kettle. Frank was making noises upstairs and would be down in a minute. She was always up before him (he was hardly a morning person) and she always made his tea. Today would be no different.

Now that ...?

As the water in the kettle made noises close to boiling she tried to finish the sentence. But couldn't. She knew it was about dreams. About nightmares. Things that went bump in her night. People who stalked her; nasty people – people with intent of malice. But none came into focus. Sure, she could remember what had happened. She could put names to faces ... to places. Afghanistan; Germany; Italy; Venezuela; Switzerland. But that was a functional process. It wasn't emotional. She knew there was a huge psychological chunk of stuff that was there somewhere. She hadn't been able to utter a word for three months, after all. And something had caused that. But she had managed to tuck it away. Lock it in a vault.

She hoped it stayed where it was. Forever.

Freedom.

That's what was missing.

She was ready for it. She just needed to break it to Frank that that's what the problem was. That she was leaving. Heading for ... *freedom.*

If there were such a place.

He was on his way down. And today probably wasn't the day.

She finished making his tea, stuck it on a mat so it was closest to the door between the kitchen and the hall, and sat back down. She had bits of damp tree to finish.

'Hi, Frank.' He looked like he'd just got out of bed and thrown on the first thing he'd come across. Greying black jeans, a green t-shirt with the black 'egg-timer-inside-a-circle' logo of *Extinction Rebellion,* bold as brass, on its front. No belt and tatty blue plimsolls. He was the perfect model of a middle-class liberal facing down the terrors of today's world. A woke in an arena full of sleeps.

He grunted in return, picked up his tea and then, recognising he should already be a human being, smiled at her.

'What have you got planned for today?' he asked as he sat on a stool opposite her, reaching for a bowl.

'Oh, just stuff. You know,' Sam replied. 'Just stuff' was actually looking at a second-hand VW camper in Camden. But Frank didn't need to know that. Not yet.

She finished her granola and placed her spoon dead centre in the bowl, perpendicular to the edge of the table. It wasn't quite right the first time. She nudged it so it was.

Talk about Frank and his particularness!

'You?' she continued.

'Ahh ... well.' He stopped mid-sentence, a grimace on his face.

Something's not right.

He'd been quiet last night, but she'd thought nothing of it. He had been late back from work and she knew only too well a vegetative state often followed. Normally by morning, however, he was more communicative.

'What's wrong, Frank?'

He managed to fill his bowl with cornflakes and was reaching for the soya milk. He stopped mid-movement as though he was going to add something.

'Nothing, it's nothing,' he said, before continuing to pour.

Sam studied him. It wasn't nothing. In fact, it was definitely something. She'd never seen him like this before.

'What's wrong, Frank?' A tougher tone this time.

He put his chin in his hand and turned his head so that he was staring out of the kitchen window.

'I can't tell you.' It was a whispered response.

Sam was immediately frustrated.

'What? Why?'

He turned to look at her.

Silence ... then.

'Because you're not codeword cleared.' A resigned quiet.

There's dampness in his eyes.

Sam sat back in her chair with a thud. It was her turn to raise her hand to her mouth. She gnawed at a knuckle.

A pause.

'What is it, Frank? What is it that you can't tell me?'

He'd picked up his spoon and was now pushing his cereal around the bowl. He stopped and looked directly at her.

'Jane's in trouble.' And then he immediately added in a rush, 'That's all I can tell you. I've already said too much.'

Shit.

Sam gathered her thoughts. Frank would tell her everything ... if she pressed him. He was utterly reliable at work and his integrity was unbreakable. But he *would* tell her everything. She knew. But she didn't want him to break that trust. She didn't want him to have to make such a decision.

But she still needed to know what sort of trouble Jane was in.

'Is she in Asia?'

'Yes.'

'Is she hurt? Had an accident?' she rushed.

He thought for a second.

'I don't know.'

She blew a soft raspberry.

'Is she working?'

Frank's expression changed. His neck stiffened and looked at her as though she were an alien.

A raw nerve.

'OK. Don't answer *that* question,' she added.

Sam had never bought that Jane had taken a sabbatical. Not working wasn't what Jane did. She was tipped to be the next-but-one Chief. Taking six months out when the world was beset with chaos and its leaders prone to idiocy, wouldn't be her way. Sam had assumed her old boss was on assignment, maybe travelling the world carrying out a review of overseas missions – or similar.

'Are you on the periphery of what's happening? Did you pick this up in the margins?'

Frank shook his head. He still hadn't eaten any of his cereal.

'Is the circle a wide one?' Sam continued.

Without lifting his hand he raised four fingers.

Wow. The smallest possible cabal. The Chief, a senior politician, the Chief's PA and an intelligence operative. The closest of holds.

This was big. And potentially *very* damaging.

And Jane was in trouble.

Just then it came to her. Like stepping out between two cars and being hit by a bus.

'Eat some breakfast, Frank. You're going to need all of the energy you can stuff down your throat.' The flash of inspiration coalesced. The veil had dropped and an opportunity had revealed itself. It all made perfect sense.

She stood, taking her bowl in her hand.

'What are you doing?' Frank asked, a touch indignantly.

She stopped by the sink and turned to him.

'The last time you and I heard from Jane was a WhatsApp message from Siem Reap, a selfie taken outside one of the Angkor Wat temples. That was six weeks ago. The previous photo was from KL, overlooking the Petronas Towers, a month previously? She was travelling north. Unless you tell me I'm heading for the wrong part of the globe, I'm getting on a plane to Ho Chi Minh City. Which, if I remember rightly, was her next stop ... on her sabbatical.' Sam made a quotation mark sign with her hands.

'But ...'

Sam walked over to Frank and clumsily put a hand on his shoulder. He looked up at her, all dewy eyed.

'Jane's in trouble. It seems to me that you're C's point man in Vauxhall. I know there are plenty of SIS staff in the South East Asian capitals who will be brilliant at helping you sort out Jane's problem. But ...' now *she* was beginning to feel a little tearful, '... I need to do something, Frank. I can't stay here much longer, sitting on my hands. I'm feeling better than I've been making

out. An overseas break, the heat, some foreign food ...'
she'd taken her hand off Frank's shoulder and was
pointing randomly at the window, '... it will do me a
world of good. And, just maybe, if you need someone to
follow a lead because you can't share what you have
with others, then I'll be on the ground. And I know Jane
better than almost anyone."

'But ...'

Sam leant forward and pecked him on his cheek.
It was all the affection she could conjure.

'I'm going to pack some stuff and then pop
downtown to get what else I need. I'll book a last minute
flight on the way to the airport.'

Frank didn't say anything. He turned his head
away from her and stared at his cereal, his shoulders
hunched. Sam sensed at that point he was deeply
unhappy. That, what with whatever was happening to
Jane, she had joined the short queue of mayhem makers
and taken a hammer to his personal life. And it hurt. A
lot. But not so much it was going to stop her. Not now.
She had been preparing to go somewhere indeterminate.
Freedom – wherever that was. All of a sudden, she had a
real destination.

And a purpose. And that was more like it.

'She's not called Jane Baker.' It was another
whisper from Frank.

'Sorry?'

'She's travelling under an alias. Gemma Ruby.' He took a resigned mouthful of cornflakes. 'I now deserve the sack.'

'Thanks, Frank.' She tapped his shoulder and headed for the hall. 'I'll keep in touch, every step of the way.'

Chapter 3

E71, South of Modruš, Croatia

Jackson knew he was taking a risk. The Dubrovnik *policija* had submitted an initial report. Bae Ki-tae had been named as the body found in the abandoned hotel on Kupari beach. The details issued were as the mission centre had hoped for: recent South Korean immigrant; working as a tour guide in the city; no previous record. The man had been murdered, likely as a result of mugging. Investigations were ongoing.

However, the not so good news was that they were looking for a man linked to the death. The man was around five-ten tall and had been wearing shorts and a polo shirt, and carrying a small black bag. He had been spotted at the same time as the murder, running in the direction of the hotel. A man of similar description had been caught on CCTV after the murder getting into a silver Golf which had been parked in the main village. Unfortunately, or fortunately in Jackson's case, the number plate had been obscured.

Jackson was now a wanted man, something the mission Centre could expunge with a single telephone call. But as things were, nobody in Zagreb wanted to draw attention to a murdered Mr Bae Ki-tae. Not yet, anyway.

His choice to head off down to Dubrovnik to meet up with a *policijski inspektor* agent of theirs who worked out of Split, was a tough call. The *policijski inspektor* had been on their books for four years, was a safe pair of hands and didn't work in the Dubrovnik office. As such he was far enough away from the case to prevent cross-contamination. But of high enough rank to get access to Bae Ki-tae's apartment without sending any hares scurrying. Jackson's worry was, although the Dubrovnik *policija* had already searched Bae's flat – and, apparently, found nothing untoward – the last thing he wanted was to bump into someone who might put two and two together and make an answer which looked like Jackson White Jr.

But that wasn't the problem that was chomping at Jackson's heels as he drove south.

A much bigger issue hung over him.

Bae Ki-tae had been murdered.

No, that isn't enough.

Bae Ki-tae had been exposed, either by chance or design, and had been tracked down – and followed. He had then been murdered. Jackson thought the place and time of death was significant. His murderers could have ambushed him in his home. Beaten him up in a dark alley. Put a pipe bomb under his car.

But they hadn't done any of that.

They had waited until Bae was due to meet his CIA case-officer and murdered him in plain sight. That was no coincidence. Whoever had done this was sending a message. They knew more than just Bae's previous identity. They knew that he was an informant. And they weren't having any of that.

Last night he and his now expanded team had brainstormed the possible antagonists. Clearly North Korea was an option, but the considered view was they were a blunt weapon and lacked the resources and finesse to murder a defector at a distance, let alone whilst sticking their middle finger up at the US. But his team hadn't discounted them.

Second was any of three major players: Russia, China and Iran.

Russia was unlikely. They had the reach and they always had the intent – in this case just to mess with the US's intelligence network. But they had little in common with the North Koreans and, in many ways, supported the US's drive to denuclearise the Korean peninsula.

The Iranians were an option. There was a long held, but unproven theory, that the DPRK and the Islamic Revolutionary Guard Corps were working together to deliver a nuclear weapon capable of being fired from both North Korean and Iranian strategic missiles. According to UN inspectors the (now defunct) Iranian nuclear deal had prevented Iran from pursuing their ambition of building a nuclear device. The DPRK, however, already had such a capability – albeit crude, unwieldy and non-transferable to other missile systems. The doomsday scenario was that if you glued together the DPRK's nuclear arsenal and the Iranian's Meshkat, medium-range cruise missile – which could fire out to 2,500 kilometres – much of the Western world would be in danger. Should the Iranians believe that Bae Ki-tae was in a position to jeopardise such a programme, if it in fact existed, then they certainly had the ability to track him down and kill him, pretty much at will.

The third, and most likely player, was China. They were the DPRK's greatest ally. And, whilst the Chinese rarely used the MSS (*Ministry of State Security*) to interfere in other countries' affairs, in the last ten years – with China's 'Belt and Road' initiative pushing their influence worldwide – the MSS had begun to travel. It was certainly a possibility.

The four credible options were: the DPRK, Russia, Iran and China.

But there was a fifth. And Jackson didn't want to think about that.

An internal hit.

The US security infrastructure was a wide and prickly beast. The US political scene was just as wide, just as prickly and now more partisan than ever. Mix in the power of defence companies and their lobbyists, and even some of the other major conglomerates, and you have plenty of people who might want a North Korean defector dead. There were those who wished nothing more than a unified Korea. Big business was in favour – the opportunities endless and profitable. Major defence companies were less sanguine about reconciliation. The US military strength in South Korea was 25,000. If peace broke out, that number wouldn't survive the cuts that followed. The defence budget would take a hit and programmes would be lost. Many admirals, generals and air marshals would be put out to grass.

Closer to home the CIA and the NSA would also both be lanced by a peace deal.

As his team discussed the 'fifth option', Jackson had looked around the room and taken in his team. Bae Ki-tae, as a repositioned informant, would have been on limited distribution; maybe less than a handful: the director, the deputy, Jackson and maybe one or two others. He'd need to check that list. It should be impossible for someone in the office not on that list to access the file.

Unless you had higher and wider clearance.

Like, maybe, the Deputy National Intelligence Chief (Europe), or a myriad of other top brass at Langley?

He'd need to check the file for electronic fingerprints when he got back.

In the meantime he had someone speaking to the mission centres in Beijing and Seoul. Another working Tehran and Moscow. Someone was pushing Langley and the NSA hard to see if they had anything. And he had the two sharpest analysts in the building poring over the sixty-five photos he had taken of the scene of the murder.

And he was going to slip into the victim's apartment, illicitly. His *policijski inspektor* contact had texted him this morning to say that the Dubrovnik force had searched the place yesterday and found nothing untoward. Jackson had no idea what he was looking for. But he had to look for himself.

He was due in Dubrovnik in three hours. He checked the GPS. He was going to make it with half an hour to spare.

HQ SIS, Vauxhall, London

'Clive will see you now.'

The Chief of SIS's PA, Janet, broke into Frank's oblivion. Sitting on a soft chair, nestled sensitively next to an antique coffee table littered with glossy magazines, he was away with the pixies. His mind was trying to work out how he was going to cope with Sam's bombshell whilst, concurrently, meeting with one of the most powerful men in the country. Tears lurked, like a persistent stalker. He'd cried leaving the house, Sam upstairs in her room, packing. He'd cried on the tube. And, just now, he'd shed a tear in the loos on the way to his one-to-one with 'Clive'.

The mirror in the lavatory told the story. No amount of splashing of water, or rubbing with a towel, had made a difference. He looked a mess. And C would spot it straight away. He was a spy, after all.

In a lucid moment, on the walk between the tube station and Babylon, he reflected on what he knew: that

Sam wouldn't stay with him forever. That she was a wanderer, incapable of an in-depth relationship. She'd never made any secret of it. In Davos last year, at the height of the 'Ndrangheta affair, he'd blurted out that he loved her. And her response had been clear. She was incapable of love. It wasn't a gift she could bestow.

Since the horrors in the forest a few miles from the Hilton Garden Inn, he'd looked after her as though she were a recuperating partner. An abused woman who needed as much space as possible to recover from the horrors of being pursued and then almost killed by a deranged man. In that time she had accepted his warmth, but never crossed the boundary between friend and lover; and he had never asked her to, even though it pressed on him like an overcast day.

Deep down he hoped his devotion might be reciprocated at some point. But he knew if he looked beneath the layers, it could never be.

She was everything to him.

He was a brother to her.

She'd been in love once before. With an army officer, seven years ago in Afghanistan. He had been killed in a mortar attack in which she had been badly injured. That horror, that stain, had remained with her. And that was part of why he loved her so much. Her integrity was bigger than a power station. She had made a commitment to another man. And she had no intention of breaking it.

He knew that, deep down.

And now she was gone.

...

'Frank.'

It was Sir Clive Morton, standing in the frame of his door.

Shit. I bet I look as dishevelled as I feel.

'Oh. Sorry, sir.' Frank was on his feet, moving to the door. C stood aside and showed him to a chair that had been pulled out from under a small conference table. As Frank sat, the boss took the chair beside him.

'You've read the file?' C looked at him, his head on one side. Then, quickly, 'Are you OK, Frank?'

Bugger.

'Yes. Sorry. A bit of bad news at home. Nothing to worry about.' Frank moved about in his seat. 'I'm on this.' He grimaced a smile.

'Sure?' C's tone was paternal.

'Yes, of course. Sorry ... again.'

'Good.' C didn't look convinced. 'What do you think?'

Frank assumed he meant Op Mandolin, and not the fact Sam was about to get on a plane to Vietnam ... and he might never see her again. As for Mandolin, he thought if Jane wasn't dead, she could well be in a matter of days. *Which clearly isn't helping.* She'd started something she hadn't got anywhere close to finishing. And, as a result, she would likely pay for it with her life.

'I'm really worried for her,' Frank replied quietly.

'Sure, Frank, me too.' C paused. And then, 'How do we find her and, maybe more importantly, how do we finish what she started?'

'Let me recap,' Frank suggested.

C nodded.

Frank took an audible breath.

'I think after she took over responsibility for running Dusit Rattanatari from Singapore Station, he opened opportunities in South East Asia. That included two new agents, both business partners of Rattanatari. One in KL and one in Cambodia. As her reports say, she held prelims with both men, Fai Zhao and Atith Jafarov, the latter in Phnom Penh as recently as eight weeks ago. Rattanatari was good for Singaporean business intentions, but nothing spectacular on the intelligence front. Zhao, similar in Thailand; with Chinese descent he had connections with senior officials in Beijing. That could lead somewhere. Jafarov, whilst living in Cambodia, was native Vietnamese. His business crossed the border between Cambodia and Vietnam and would also be a useful agent if he could be recruited. Both men were keen to engage with us, or should I say, Jane, because they feared for the future of the region.' Frank stopped and sniffed. 'I've got it so far, sir, yes?'

'Yes, Frank, spot on.'

He continued. 'That's where Jane gets a little hazy. Her reports paint Zhao and Jafarov as anti-communist and pro-free market. Which isn't a surprise. Zhao's father was killed at Tiananmen. Jafarov's

75

background is southern Vietnamese and so innately anti-regime. And his grandmother was French, so he may well be a Europhile. In the first instance, I suspect what Jane was working on was business-based.' He paused and shuffled in his chair. He looked at C and was met with impassiveness.

He didn't take that as a criticism and continued. 'Whatever, what the two men were rubbing against was probably as much to do with their empires, both of which – according to Jane – reach into the hundreds of millions, as it has to do with ideology. Although, as we know, a bucketful of money is its own God. Significantly, though, her final report hints to a Level One intelligence disclosure, possibly to be offered at her next meeting with Jafarov. That was planned for the Cambodian border town of Kampot and would have happened about a week after we lost contact.'

Frank blew out a long breath. One of his legs was bouncing on its toes. He put a hand on his knee to stop it.

C didn't say anything. Instead he stood and walked across to an espresso machine.

'Coffee, Frank?'

'No, thanks, sir.'

The whirr of the espresso's pressure system squeezing boiling water through ground coffee was the only noise in the soundproof room. It was followed by a momentary splash as brown fluid graced a delicate, white-china *demi-tasse*.

'Sir.'

76

'Yes, Frank?'

'Why did Jane go to South East Asia in the first place? Surely Singapore, KL, or Bangkok could have run with this?'

C was standing by his chair, tiny cup in one hand, saucer in another.

'That's a good question.' He took a sip 'Beijing Station told us something was going down. Something big. But nobody has any idea what it was. Langley's out on a limb – they are as lost as us. And then we get a call from Singapore. They've been handed something from a low-level agent. A Chinese immigrant, working on the docks. He's a foreman, or similar. Apparently he's overseeing the unload of a Cuban registered container ship, *La Teja*. A spot check by customs uncovers a crate of sophisticated weapons and ancillaries, including rocket launchers, night sights, timers and similar; hardly a huge arms shipment, but a significant find. Unsurprisingly the crate is not on the manifest. The local feds are called, and the cargo is impounded – usual procedure.' C finished his coffee and placed his delicate cup and saucer on the table. 'Except, it isn't impounded.'

'What do you mean?' As time was progressing thoughts of Sam were being pushed to the back of Frank's mind. It was helping being busy.

'A crate *is* craned off the ship and taken to the police compound ...'

'But it's a fake. A replica?' Frank was ahead of him.

77

'Exactly.' C raised a single finger to his nose in a 'game of charades' signal to let Frank know he was spot on. 'It's done well, but not well enough. The foreman spots the switch. He's confused, but it's more than his job's worth to point out the anomaly. So he keeps quiet ... until he meets his case-officer.'

'Do we know where the shipment was destined?'

'The paperwork is not clear. But the ship is due to empty all of its cargo by the time it gets to Tianjin, that's Beijing's main port of entry. There it will be reloaded with humanitarian equipment and shipped to Nampo ...'

'Pyongyang's port of entry.' Frank completed C's sentence, an action he immediately regretted.

'Correct.' C's reply was shadowed with a bemused look.

Oops.

Frank sat back in his chair and stretched his back. And then quickly sat up straight when he realised he was making himself far too comfortable in the big man's office.

'But this is hardly earth-shattering? A quick phone call to the UK Ambassador to the UN and it's sorted. The ship's breaking a UN embargo. Their problem?' Frank asked.

'Correct again. That, or something similar, would be our SOP (*standard operating procedure*). But it's more complicated.' C picked up another pink file from his desk, walked across to Frank and placed it on the table.

'This is Operation Abraham. It's on a slightly wider distribution than Mandolin. It's a worldwide op looking at the flow of arms between four countries: China, North Korea, Vietnam ...'

And Cuba.

Frank was ahead again. This time he didn't complete C's sentence for him, he'd learnt his lesson.

'... and Cuba. Jane was point man on this ...' C was tapping the file with an index finger, '... at Vauxhall. You know that Harry Belton, D(GC), (*Deputy, Global Coordination*), is leaving at the end of the year?' Frank nodded quickly. C continued. 'Well, it may not be a secret, but Jane was being lined up to take over Harry's role. Op Abraham is a D(GC) operation and I thought it best for Jane to get her teeth into it.'

'So she flew to Singapore – it was a good a place to start as any?' Frank asked.

'Yes. Cuban ship, illicit defence equipment and a route which finished in the DPRK. Singapore was the hub.'

'She might have travelled to Vietnam? Or China? I've not looked at the details, but I guess all of the four countries are helping each other? There's a *quid pro quo* here?'

'Yes. You'll see the details in the file. The equipment is mil-spec US. As documented it's as good as it gets. Any country without a first-world army would be delighted to have access to the gear. And you're right. It might be any of the three.'

Frank opened the pink folder, had a quick glance at the summary, and then closed it again.

'Abraham is less than eight months old. Mandolin, about four months. And Jane shacks up with two anti-communist businessmen … who, on the face of it, seem unlikely to be pro-Chinese and Vietnamese regimes getting their hands on state-of-the-art military equipment. But, looking at it another way, as businessmen with wide portfolios, they might just have a finger in a pie that looks something like this? They could be involved?' Frank was now pointing at the pink file. 'Or the two operations could be completely unrelated? Businessmen one side; a ship full of weapons the other?'

'Exactly,' C continued. 'Jane was non-specific. She was just starting out – following a lead she thought might be linked to Abraham. Was Fai Zhao and/or Atith Jafarov pushing Jane to something which would help expose Operation Abraham? Or, might they be part of it? Or … there was no link? Her hope might have been to recruit one of them to get inside the cycle.'

C had sat down next to Frank.

'The issue for me, Frank – and this is why Mandolin is on the closest of hold – Jane tagged her next meeting as a lead to a possible Level One intelligence source. Level One is, as you know, a very particular categorisation.'

International level grouping; global destabilisation. Frank rehearsed the definition in his head.

'It's above my pay grade, sir, but do you really think Abraham, a ship full of armaments, is an operation which is likely to cause global destabilisation?'

'No, Frank, I don't. Not as it stands. The supply of arms, up to but not including nuclear warheads, is a Level Two categorisation. Jane wouldn't have attributed a Level One tag to her next meeting unless she were absolutely convinced. And that lack of clarity concerns me.'

So why pick me, a lowly analyst?

'So why not break this open to a large team? CIA liaison, multi-station teaming, etc?' To Frank it seemed like the most obvious approach. Big problem, big hammer.

'That may come. But we're not there yet. I want to keep this low key. Maybe for the next thirty days or so. If the enquiries come from you – someone at your level – it's unlikely to raise any alarms. Not in the first instance. And, as you, me and the Cabinet Secretary are the only players who know Jane is missing, we might be able to keep this close for a good while. Which might increase our chances of finding her.'

You, me, the Cabinet Secretary ... and Sam Green.

Frank thought it best not to mention that.

'So. If I understand you correctly, I'm not a big enough fish capable of making waves which might

81

breach the defences. That means I can thrash about, maybe push harder and wider than a more senior team – without getting noticed.'

'Yes. Absolutely. And, might I add, you are the best analyst in the building. You have good contacts in GCHQ and friends, as I understand it, across the Thames. And you know Jane.'

C stood and walked behind his desk. The meeting was over.

'I'll get Janet to issue you with an Op Code. And Marcus has been told to delegate your current work for the next month. I think that should give you enough time to work out whether or not you have enough time. For now, I'd like an email one-pager, close-of-play, every day. Anything more immediate, just come on up. Any questions?' C asked.

About a thousand.
'No, sir, thanks.

47 Apartment Tomy, Gornji, Dubrovnik, Croatia

Jackson let the *policijski inspektor*, Stjepan, ahead of him so he could open the door to Bae Ki-tae's apartment.

The key turned in the lock but when the policeman tried the door it only moved a few inches. Stjepan frowned in his direction. He pushed harder. The door gave some more, which allowed Jackson to spot the problem. The floor was covered in household debris; as if the mail hadn't been lifted from the floor for an age.

Except it wasn't the mail. It was a piece of furniture. And some books, maybe a magazine or two. If this were the entrance hall he wasn't looking forward to the mess in the rest of the apartment.

The policeman stepped over the wreckage. Jackson followed.

'This wasn't in the local police report? That he'd been burgled?' Jackson's Serbo-Croat wasn't bad.

'No. The house was very tidy, according to the report,' Stjepan replied. He'd stopped in the doorframe between the hall and the lounge. 'I'm not sure we should carry on with this. I should call the local station.'

Jackson was right beside him, having navigated a bookshelf, its contents and, what looked like, a couple of days of laundry.

No. Not yet.

'Not yet, Stjepan. Give me twenty minutes.'

Jackson brushed past the policeman and made it into the longue.

The apartment was small, maybe 60 feet square. A single living/kitchen/dining room. A bedroom, and a bathroom. But, on the plus side, a fabulous balcony overlooking the old town with the Adriatic beyond. Not a bad pad for a single man with a decent US government salary supplemented by some Croatian pin money.

But not at the moment. Whoever had been in the flat between the local police and their arrival had done a good job. Everything, *everything*, had been ransacked. Nothing was in its original condition. The sofa had been split apart, the kitchen drawers emptied and pulled from their casings. Pictures were off the walls, the mattress in the bedroom torn, its contents spewed on the carpet. There was a computer monitor on the floor, its screen cracked. It took him five minutes to find the mouse – It had been smashed.

But the tower was gone.

It took him longer than twenty minutes to see if there was anything left that might help him. If Bae had kept any personal possessions which could link him to unknown contacts, maybe on the Korean peninsula, they were gone. There was no diary. No spare phone. Nothing with his handwriting on it. Anything that might present itself as a lead either didn't exist, or had been taken. The flat had experienced an expert trawl, carried out by people who knew what they were looking for. Textbook stuff. All that was left was the debris of a single man's life, smashed to pieces and strewn all over the apartment's floor.

Save one thing.

Which might be nothing.

It was a coincidence really.

Part of the Agency's professional development was a six-monthly newsletter that summarised new procedures, some delivered from post-op reviews, others, more casually, borne from experience gained by case and intelligence officers from across the CIA's mission centres worldwide. Staff were encouraged to submit articles to '*Breaking New Ground*', for which there was a $250 royalty. The latest copy had arrived last week and, in a moment of quiet, Jackson had scanned the magazine for interesting snippets.

A few things had caught his eye, one of which might just be useful now.

Apparently, and this was especially so in the Far East, criminals were saving data in places you wouldn't really expect. Dark-web, cloud-based storage was still the favourite, and that worked for organisations who had people with the skillsets to put it together. The advent of 512-bit crypto keys, which were unbreakable – even with the most powerful of supercomputers – made dark-web encrypted storage the gold standard choice for criminal organisations. With the right equipment and access to the right software they could guarantee access to their data anywhere in the world. And that data was completely safe – out of harm's way.

But it cost. A lot.

And, whilst it was super-secure, some people still didn't trust the cloud. Your stuff was elsewhere. Surely if it wasn't in your safe, someone could access it without you knowing?

Neither did it have the same old-fashioned feel as having your files and spreadsheets with you. In your hand – so you could touch them. And he got that. It was like holding a DVD. You owned the film. It was yours ... and provided you looked after it, it would always be yours. Streaming the same film from somewhere in – who knew where: *Ireland? Denmark?* – was great when you were travelling. But you couldn't caress it.

Physical storage had always presented a problem. Solid state drives could be broken. And stolen. Pen drives. Laptops. Computer towers.

Things that you could touch.

And steal.

Well ... according to *Breaking New Ground,* people had started to get ingenious.

Hoods were now hiding data in plain sight. It was obvious if you thought about it. Anything that could hold an e-drive – something about the size of half a sugar cube – could be disguised as, or in, a common object; one not normally given a second glance by a thief.

The magazine had six examples. The first five were just clever hides: the handle of a kitchen pan; an owl ornament; the cuff of a heavy coat; glasses case; a tin of sweets. The marker to look for was a micro-USB port. Small enough to miss, but big enough not to lose. Behind the port wasn't a battery – the usual accoutrement – but a solid state drive. All you needed was a cable with a mini-USB connector and you have access to the drive.

The sixth one was so obvious, it was easy to ignore.

An electric toothbrush.

A case-officer in Manilla had found a solid state drive inside an electric toothbrush. The toothbrush worked and was charged via the mini-USB port. But, when dismantled, he found the charging point also doubled as a port to a tiny solid state drive. It was genius. Who would look there?

And Jackson had found an electric toothbrush, on the floor in the bathroom. It was intact.

There's no way?

He smacked the bottom of the brush on the side of the sink. The white plastic casing cracked. He took out his keys and prised the gap apart.

And there it was. Exactly as displayed in *Breaking New Ground*.

Unbelievable.

'Have you found something?' Stjepan was at his side.

'No. Unfortunately not.' Jackson kept the toothbrush in his hand, which he surreptitiously placed behind his back. 'We should go?'

'Yes, please. I'll phone my opposite number when we get outside.'

'Good. And thanks a lot. Sorry for wasting your time.'

Jackson led the way, the toothbrush now in front of him.

Triệu Quang Phục, Lào Cai, Vietnam

87

Two days. And more chicken and rice than she could manage.

But no interaction. No visits, apart from her unnamed guard.

She'd tried to move on. Attempted some exercise. Yoga.

It had been tough yesterday. Her face was sore. Her body wretched, emaciated after an age of poor food, something which might have been dysentery and no sunlight. The new eating regime was helping and her stomach had settled and she was sure she was putting on a little weight. Walking to the shower was no longer a meandering totter, with the walls acting as props.

The trajectory was upwards. But slow.

So yoga it was.

There was a large rug on the floor. She had doubled it up so it acted more like a mat. She'd used a sequence she'd put together as a fallback for when she had been struggling for time at work. It was a fifteen-minute session: heel to hand stretch; semi-supine; a yogic three; cat/cow to big toes; sinking eventually into downward dog. Nothing too complicated. Nothing too strenuous. Just a balance of stretching, muscle tone and relaxation.

And it had hurt like hell.

Her muscles had screamed at her. Her joints as stiff as a strong breeze. She didn't know if it had been the leftover effects of the tasing or that her body, which had experienced nothing but pain, was jacking it all in. Whatever, fifteen minutes had felt like fifteen hours.

Three days later and she was up to half an hour. It still hurt and her body still complained, but she was making progress.

Less so the relaxation. The longer her captors kept her in the dark, the longer her mind had a chance to play through all the scenarios available. None of them ended happily.

They had broken her. She had told them who she was. They had moved her immediately and stopped the torture. And now she waited.

Phase three. Whatever that looked like.

Jane was mid-'cat/cow' when she was interrupted by the door opening. She quickly broke the pose, clambered to her feet and went and sat on the bed. It felt safer there.

It was a new man. With the same flat Asian features. Mid-height, stocky, round Chinese face, black shiny hair. He was wearing a suit, a white shirt and a red tie. The suit was charcoal grey with a thin, light-blue pinstripe. Short, white cuffs emerged from the sleeves by about a centimetre. He looked like a Shanghai banker. Not from the trading floor, but higher up. Possibly an accounts manager or senior broker: wealthy and connected. He was accompanied by her unnamed guard. By the time she had sat on the bed, they were a metre into the room, standing still. The stockbroker was forward centre. The guard, who had a folding table in

89

one hand and two collapsible chairs in the other, slightly further back. There was a power play here. And the man in the suit had clearly won.

The stockbroker barked an order to the guard. *Mandarin.* Jane had learnt some key phrases. She could say hello, goodbye, thank you and order a coffee. She had hoped to pick up more. If she hadn't been interrupted.

The guard set out the table and chairs. He was efficient and particular. Then, with his back to the door, he bowed to the stockbroker – hands together in the prayer position – and scuttled out of the room. Jane heard the locks being turned.

'Hello, Miss Baker.' The stockbroker's English was spoken through tight cheeks and a narrow mouth. 'Please join me at the table.'

Jane felt very cautious. Even more so, once she'd spotted a folder in the man's hand.

Where's this going?

The man was offering a seat by pointing at it.

'Who are you?' A small act of defiance.

The man laughed; short but derisory.

'Please sit, Miss Baker.' He nodded graciously. 'Please.'

Jane thought for a second … but no longer.

She tentatively stood, the yoga having drained what little energy she had. She took the three steps to the plastic and metal chair … and sat.

The stockbroker did the same. He carefully placed the folder on the table in front of Jane. It was unmarked. Blue faux leather, with plastic folios. Whatever was in there was being protected.

There was a moment's pause. The stockbroker was sitting impassively, but his eyes told a different story. They were intense and lively.

The man opened the folder. Blue on the inside of the cover. The first folio had a single line title: Miss Jane Baker. Secret Intelligence Service. He spun the folder through 180 degrees.

She stared at it. And then at the man. Their gazes met.

And then he turned the first folio over.

...

Jane's heart rate was probably running at close to 80 beats per minute before the man turned the page. It had still not settled from the yoga.

Within a few seconds, the shock of what she saw on the page sent that rate through the ceiling. She reeled. Her neck weakened and her head wobbled. She was going to faint.

And it had only just started.

The man turned the pages. One by one. Slowly, but with purpose. He was telling a tale. Painting a picture – of horror ... without saying a word.

Eight pages. Fourteen photographs.

One message.

Tell us everything we need to know, otherwise: these images of the ones you love, your mum, your brother and his family ... we know where they are.

The photos were new. Each taken with a camera that had an associated date, superimposed in orange on the bottom right of the image. The one of her mum was shot yesterday, in the local pub. The photo could have been an old one, and the date etched on later, but Jane knew that wasn't the case. Her mum was wearing the M&S jumper they had bought together the day before Jane had flown to Singapore.

It was a lovely photo. Her mum with her pal Cynthia, sat in a corner seat which Jane remembered. Mum had a G&T. The pair of them were smiling at the camera as though someone, bold as brass, had asked them to pose.

The last photo was of her sister-in-law's dog. A cockapoo. Misty. It was sitting in the kitchen window looking, Jane guessed, for squirrels. The guy with the camera must have been in her sister-in-law's back garden.

Jane's strength had left her, but it didn't stop her from lifting some of the plastic inserts and folding them back until she found the one of her mum in the pub.

She touched her face with her own finger.

It all made sense now.

They had left her alone because, having been given her name, they wanted to find her family. To take photos to show her that they knew where they all lived. That they were reachable.

Touchable.

Jane was no longer the target.

They were.

She took her finger from the folder and lifted a knuckle to her mouth.

She stared at the man in the stockbroker's suit.

'What do you people want?' she stuttered.

Chapter 4

Jackson was sitting next to one of the Mission Center's data-cryptanalysts. His name was Ron and he was a big guy, more rotund than hefty. And he was very good at what he did.

'Look, Jackson.' Ron was pointing at a line of code on his screen. It was the outcome of half an hour of Ron's work on the toothbrush solid state drive. It had all been a mystery to Jackson, and what Ron was pointing at now was equally hieroglyphical.

'What's that, Ron?'

'It's the key, Jackson. We're there. You, see what I've done is ...'

Jackson put a hand on the big man's shoulder. Ron stopped mid-sentence.

'We've been through this, Ron. I really don't need to know the detail. Just get the damn thing unlocked. Have you?'

Ron's shoulders were facing his screen, his round face with accompanying extra chin facing Jackson. His finger had left the screen and was now pointing in the air, as if to signal victory.

'Almost. This line of code, here ...'

'Just do it, Ron.'

Ron got the message and smiled. He returned to his work, his fingers gracing the keyboard like a world-class pianist.

Jackson leant back in his chair and placed his hands behind the back of his head. He looked to the window closest to Ron's desk. It was opaque. And bombproof. All the windows were. After the 1998 Nairobi bombing of the US Embassy all of the CIA mission centres had been reinforced to withstand a drive-in bomb. The Kenyan attack was 2,000 pounds of TNT. The result: 224 people dead, twelve of whom were Americans. The programme of rebuild and the worldwide refurbishment had taken over a decade. They were safer in this over-engineered building in Zagreb than they would be in a nuclear bunker.

That felt good. But it also felt wrong. Jackson wasn't sure that a bunker mentality was the best way to reach the people of the country in which you served. It was like wearing sunglasses on a meet – he never did that. He always took his Wayfarers off as he approached an RV. He wanted those with whom he was meeting to see his eyes – for his demeanour to be open. If he expected them to be candid, if nothing else, he needed to look like he was prepared to be the same.

His last liaison, of course, hadn't made it to that point.

So far all the meet had given him was a dead body and debris. Photographs of flesh, clothes and trash.

And a blurry, infrared clip of a man being murdered on the fifth floor of the Goricina.

But he now had a small, solid state drive. Which Ron was currently hacking.

He stood, stretched and made his way to a side office.

The initial read out from the photos he'd taken was not encouraging. He'd put a team together: a CSI – who was an FBI woman on secondment; a photo analyst; and the embassy's pathologist. After six hours the story was of a short, but intense struggle. The murderer had stabbed Bae Ki-tae in the front of his chest, between the third and fourth rib – left side. It seemed likely Bae was being held from behind with one arm, and the assailant had forced a medium-sized blade (around 5 inches) into his chest with his spare hand. The pathologist's view was in order to do that, the attacker would probably need to be a man, and that man would probably need to be bigger and stronger than Bae.

Death had occurred whilst Bae had been in the assailant's arms. This conclusion had been reached because the ground where he had been attacked had been disturbed, but not as much if he had been thrashing about on the floor. And the blood had pooled very locally. Again, pointing to an initial struggle, but not a long one.

There was nothing about Bae's body which indicated anything other than he was preparing for his meet with Jackson. His clothes were clean and unremarkable. His shoes were new, or nearly new. And the CSI thought Bae had recently washed his hair.

And, although they were still working on it, there seemed to be nothing of note to be found from the debris; just smashed concrete and tile, broken glass and litter. The team had all of the sixty-five photos blown up and pinned to a large cork board in the office he'd just entered. Whilst he was waiting for Ron he'd had a quick glance at them all. Most were clean, but the analyst had sharpied a few with red ovals.

Four seemed to be of interest. Jackson was about to interrogate the analyst when Ron put his head round the door and whistled.

'I'll come back to talk about those.' Jackson was waving a finger vaguely at the image-strewn cork board.

'Don't rush. It's a whole load of nothing,' the analyst replied.

Great.

Hopefully the solid state drive would have all the answers.

Jackson followed Ron to his desk.

'I'm in.' It was a whisper from Ron.

Jackson leant forward and looked at the screen.

The lines of code had been replaced by a small box, like any notification box on any computer monitor, anywhere in the world. The box showed three yellow files. They were numbered: ox_1; ox_2 and ox_3.

'What are you waiting for?' Jackson barked.

'Just … well. I wanted to be sure you were ready.'

'Of course I am. Open one of the damn folders.'

Ron double-tapped on the folder marked ox_1. A new box materialised. In it was a vertical list of files alongside four columns: name, size, type and date modified.

Jackson put up his hand to stop Ron from messing with the screen.

He studied the list.

'Scroll down.'

Ron did as he was asked.

The list of files was longer than a few scrolls, but Jackson reckoned there were no more than thirty files in the folder. Most were Word files and pdfs; the titles, unsurprisingly, were written in Eastern characters. There were a couple of jpeg files and one mp4.

'Open the jpegs.'

Ron obliged.

Three images, all of Bae's family. Jackson recognised them instantly.

'The mp4 file.' Jackson leant slightly further forward.

Ron got it running.

It was a short pornographic clip. Nothing nasty, just a Western man and a woman getting it on.

Shit.

'Open the other two folders.'

The set of files in the other two folders was a similar balance to the ones in the first: common stuff – Word, pdf, jpeg and mp4. Jackson knew he wouldn't have a chance with those written in Korean script. Not without a translator. He ignored them for the moment.

There were two mp4s in the second folder. They were both stupid, madly humorous clips. One was a man falling off a chair, and the second was a bride crashing into the table which held her wedding cake. At least there was no more porn.

The jpegs were more interesting.

There were five in ox_2. They were photos of Bae and a group of other men. They were wearing fishing garb and carrying rods and tackle. There was a group photo of six men standing on a quay by a boat. It was hardly conspiratorial stuff and was dated over a year ago, but he'd need to get the new faces checked out.

There were four photos and no video in ox_3; the images were curious. For a start they were not staged. It was though they had been taken surreptitiously. The images were shot in a quarry, or something similar. There were a group of people milling about, of various ages and both genders. And they appeared to be centred round something Jackson couldn't make out. An object of some description on the ground.

'What's that, Ron?' Jackson asked, pointing at the black smudge in the middle of the quarry photos which had a piece of metal rising from it.

'I've no idea. What do you think it is?'

Jackson tilted his head on one side. And then the other.

'It seems a really odd thing to say, but it looks like a well. You know, a hole in the ground with water in it.' Jackson had no idea why he'd needed to add the description. 'But it's unlike any well I've ever come across.'

The problem was they didn't have a clear shot of the image's centre of attention. People had either their back turned on the splodge – one or two of them were carrying boxes and plastic bags – or they were heading for it, or looking over it; more like into it.

Jackson used his hand to expand the photo. The image correction software sharpened up the pixelated edges, but it didn't help. He reduced it again.

'Might it be a crash point? You know, where maybe a drone has hit the ground. That silver thing there ...' Ron was pointing at a curled piece of metal which appeared to rise from the splodge, '... could be the remnants of a drone – or, I don't know, a missile?'

Jackson sat back in his chair.

'What's the date on the images?' he asked.

Ron did his magic. The date displayed on the screen.

Jackson blew out hard.

'That's five days ago, two days before his murder.' Jackson's mind raced. 'Any of the Word or pdf files in ox_3 dated similar?'

Ron prodded and swiped.

'There's one Word file, dated within a minute of the three photos. Your man must have picked them up all at the same time. Maybe attached to a single email.'

'Open it.'

Ron swiped and prodded.

Eleven lines of Eastern characters; about a couple of hundred marks altogether. Jackson had no idea whether a single character was the same as a single letter in the Roman alphabet, or the same as a whole word. Even so, it was hardly an essay.

But ...

Bae was talking to someone?

Five days ago. Just before he was murdered.

What was he playing at?

Jackson needed to get all of the documents translated.

'Do you know of anyone in the building who can translate Korean?' Jackson asked.

Ron looked at him, his big, open face attached to a shaking head.

'Lucy!' Jackson shouted over his shoulder. One of the intelligence officers half-stood, her face rising above the computer screen from a couple of desks away.

'Yes?' she replied.

'Over here. I need you to get hold of Langley. We have some files which need translating ASAP.'

Frank tapped the 'send' button and his last email shot off into the ether. He checked the time on his screen. It was 5.56 pm. Singapore would be asleep. As would KL, Bangkok, Hanoi and Seoul. Langley was up; the Americans were about to head off for a late morning coffee, or an early lunch. Cheltenham – the headquarters of GCHQ – would be heading home soon, if they hadn't already; they were the first people he'd spoken to this morning. He'd also sent asks to the SIS stations in all of the major European cities. And, he'd put a red tasker across the UK's counter-intelligence and terrorist police networks. The Security Service, Counter-Terrorism Police, SO15, National Crime Agency, Border Force, The Border Agency, Defence Intelligence and the UK's Special Forces were now all seeing if they had anything on Dusit Rattanatari, Fai Zhao and Atith Jafarov. Europol and Interpol were also in the loop.

He tapped his fingers on his desk. And then pushed his chair back, thought for a second, and then pulled it forward again.

Six in the evening was a good time to be going home. He'd been in the office for eight and a half hours. Normally, about now, he'd have taken his Super Furry Animals mug to the sink, given it a good rinse and headed home. Sam would have been waiting for him; or maybe out exercising. But she would have been 'at home'.

On any normal evening.

Tonight she probably would have prepared pasta with vegetables – maybe with some fried chorizo thrown in. A cuppa first, supper, TV, the latest disasters on the news and then bed. Sleep, breakfast, work. Repeat.

Repeat.

Or not.

He should have spotted the signs. She had become restless. She was always on her phone, trawling the internet. Her long sits in the bay window looking above the roof line of the houses opposite told the story. Her constant exercising, burning off all of the excess energy.

Her diet. The menus she was producing had become more flamboyant. During the week they were no longer following a regime of straightforward, set menus. Her ingredients were now more exotic.

He could see all that now.

I am a fool.

He was a fool. He hadn't allowed for it.

He should have sent her away. Bought her a surprise plane ticket to somewhere and packed her toothbrush.

He hadn't seen it coming.

And now it was too late? He felt himself welling up.

Possibly.

Whatever, it left a huge hole in his life. A Sam-sized hole.

And that hurt.

Where is she now?

He'd popped up to her room just before he'd left for work. She had her rucksack on her bed, around which was scattered – neatly – various items of clothing. Her passport was on her bedside table. Next to it was her phone and a small power pack.

She'd stopped what she was doing and looked at him, a beige pair of shorts in her hand, her sunglasses resting attractively on her head.

'Hi,' he'd said.

'Hi.' The reply accompanied by a defensive smile.

'You OK?'

She'd nodded in response.

On the verge of packing, but waiting politely for this conversation to be over, was his best guess.

'There's nothing I can say to make you stay. Just for a day or two? Until you're completely clear that this is what you want?' he'd asked.

Sam had stolen a quick glance at her rucksack, the destination for her shorts.

She shook her head.

No words.

'Will you keep in touch?'

At that point she'd raised herself to her full height and taken a deep breath through her nose, letting it out slowly in a whistle.

'Sure, Frank. Of course.'

It was his turn to nod a reply.

...

He had turned to leave. She caught him by surprise.

'Let me know if you need my help, Frank. I'll be on the ground. You can trust me.'

He looked over his half-turned shoulders.

Can I trust you?

It was a huge question. To which the answer wasn't straightforward. He could *definitely* trust her to do the right thing. Given the slimmest of chances, she would find Jane and save her. And she would put her life in jeopardy doing so. But, and it was a big but, if she were faced with a decision between Jane and some other course which might have equally disastrous or advantageous consequences, he didn't know he could trust her to take the path he was directing her to take. Sam did what Sam did. She would look at the facts and make her own decision, even if SIS policy was contrary to her choice. Her history showed she always favoured saving lives above all else. But, in her head, she would – without fear of the consequences – do what she thought was right. And sod everything and everyone else.

It was a moral courage thing. She had it; almost blinded by it. And he couldn't help but respect that.

But ... could he trust her?

He didn't know how to answer her question, so he didn't.

It was his turn to nod, albeit in a noncommittal way.

He'd put up a hand and waved shallowly.

She smiled and did the same.

And that was the last time they had been in touch.

He had no idea where she was. She had told him she was heading for Saigon, or Ho-Chi-Minh City – its more formal title.

Saigon. The American Embassy – 1975 – with the Hueys on the roof, extracting the last of the tens of thousands of US and South Vietnamese personnel who faced incarceration or even death if they had stayed. Evacuated at the very end of the war. The largest helicopter operation ever undertaken. And the US's most ignominious defeat.

And no longer the capital of Vietnam. That was Hanoi, in the north of the country.

He'd never been to either and, if Sam had got her ducks in a row quick enough, she might be mid-flight, somewhere over Iran or Pakistan – heading east. Frank had checked the visa requirements this morning. UK citizens could enter the country without one, provided they stayed for less than two weeks. Knowing Sam she'd have gone for that option: check visa requirements, book the first flight to Saigon, and then search for a hostel to stay in. All before she'd got to the airport.

She's definitely in the air.

But he didn't know. Because he hadn't heard from her.

On the way to work he'd drafted six different WhatsApp messages, and deleted them all. In the end he'd sent her an SMS. It had read:

Good luck. Let me know if you need anything. Γ xx

There'd been no reply. And, as SMSs don't offer e-acknowledgements, he had no idea if Sam had got the message. That's why he'd used a text. He didn't want to learn she'd ignored him.

Maybe she'd be in touch when she landed?

Maybe.

So, what now?

He could still go home. He had to go home. He couldn't stay here all night and he certainly had nowhere else to go.

But. He didn't want to go home. Not when it had a Sam-sized hole in it.

Not yet, anyway.

His fingers hovered above the keyboard.

He pushed his mouth to one side and then typed, 'Dusit Rattanatari' into Google.

The first headline was from *The Straits Times*'s website:

Singaporean businessman, Rattanatari, murdered.

The date/time sticker was ... twenty minutes ago.

Frank was immediately frantic.

He opened two new tabs and typed in 'Fai Zhao' and 'Atith Jafarov'.

This time the news wasn't quite so shocking, or immediate. Neither had been reported murdered in the last half an hour. And what there was, was low-level business-related stuff. Atith Jafarov's search showed a link to a *Facebook* site – which was private – but that was hardly unusual. GCHQ would, almost certainly, be onto that by now.

It was a relief, though, that both men, the key men in Jane's itinerary – with the latter due to meet her at Kampot with a hint of Level 1 intelligence – had not recently hit the news for being dead.

And that was a good thing – in one way. Two out of the three of his leads were alive. *I hope.* However, it didn't begin to answer whose side the two men were on.

Were they trying to help Jane unpick Operation Mandolin or Abraham?

Or, were they in the thick of it and had hooked Jane with the view to using her and then ... Frank metaphorically gulped ... getting rid of her?

He pushed back in his chair again. A fleeting image of Sam, curled up on a Cathay Pacific flight with a blanket tucked around her legs watching the latest *Deadpool* movie materialised, and was then banished.

He stood. Took his mug and made his way to the kitchen. He found his small package of Rooibos teabags in the cupboard and plopped one in his mug. He then filled it with boiling water from the scalding tap that scared the hell out of him.

He waited for the tea to brew, the water spinning quickly in the mug, the bag struggling to keep up with the liquid's momentum.

Sugar.

Just one. A lump of exorbitantly expensive, unrefined sugar. Sam had weaned him off sweeteners. They were, according to her, 'a present from the devil, given gladly to those of us who want to hasten bowel cancer'.

He waited for the bag to slow and then fished it out with a spoon.

Back to work.

In the few minutes he'd been standing in the kitchen he had formulated a plan.

First, he would dig out everything Google had on the three businessmen – he'd cut and paste them into a new document and read it later. That would take him maybe ninety minutes. Then he would drop C an email telling him what he had done, what he had found out ... and, what he was planning to do. C had told him to start his briefing from tomorrow. But Frank had something *now* – the death of Dusit Rattanatari.

And he needed to run a plan past the boss.

It was a plan that didn't suit him. In fact he disliked it on so many levels. But, if he pushed aside his own misgivings and preconceptions, it was the logical thing to do.

Complete C's email briefing.

Tell him what his plan was.

Go home.

And come in tomorrow and see what C's response was.

Chez Minosa, 71 Co Giang, District 1, Hồ Chí Minh,
Vietnam

This is weird.

Sam looked at the palm of her hand, inspecting her fingertips. They were tingling. *That is strange.*

Her eyes were taking in too much light, as if her pupils were dilated beyond optimum. Her hearing was too finely tuned. The noise wasn't deafening, it was just too … full. It was as though she could hear everything. Even people's thoughts.

There was too much colour. Too much light, considering it was well past midnight. And the noise was too percussion-like. The cars, the people. The motorbikes. Tap, tap tapping away. There were scooters everywhere. Two wheels were clearly preferred over four. Hundreds and hundreds of them filled the gap between her seat outside her 'boutique hotel' and the buildings on the opposite side of the road. And they were coming from every direction. She thought the Vietnamese drove on the right-hand side of the road, but you wouldn't know. Scooters clearly had their own rules.

Or made their own rules.

And the preferred mode of transport was obviously multi-purpose. Yes, there were single people on smart scooters as you might see in any capital city – Hondas appeared to be the chosen marque. Some managed two people. Others, three. And it didn't stop there. Two adults and two children, the larger of the child standing on the plate with their hands on the handlebar. The smaller sat on the lap of the pillion. Three adults and a dog. Two adults and more boxes than you could fit in the boot of your car. A single adult and a felled rainforest. Or a lathe and assorted bits of metal. Jeans, hundreds of pairs – hung from a couple of rails under a canopy; a mobile, two-wheeled shop. Vegetables laid out in baskets. Bananas. Pineapples. Skinned joints, chased by a swarm of flies which sparkled in the neon of the night.

Sam, who was still fidgety, glanced left and right. The pavement, which was broken and missing in places, was more often than not blocked with street traders. Between makeshift, plastic awnings, covering more goods than she had words for, what pavement that remained was still puddled with rain from a sharp, late-afternoon shower.

It was crazy.

The heat. The rain. The scooters. The noise and the lights – sharp and penetrating. The tingling, as though she was plugged into a socket. Or had one of those nine-volt rectangular batteries permanently placed on her tongue.

Drugs?

She didn't take any – not the recreational kind. Sure, she was still popping a smaller than prescribed pill for her anxiety (or whatever it was), and she'd swallowed a lifetime's measure of Valium in the past year. But she'd not had one of those for a couple of months. In any case, that particular drug made her sleepy and accepting. Her current mood was as if she'd overdosed on speed and just staggered out of a rave.

Perhaps it was the jetlag? That she hadn't slept for thirty-six hours? Or, maybe it was just her shredded emotions, dissected and unravelled like a worn rope, its ends exposed to the madness of Saigon's streets. Deserting Frank. Losing Jane. And the dash for freedom.

Just a peck on Frank's cheek. That's all it had been. And then – gone; a thief on a moped.

Did she feel bad about that?

Do I?

She didn't know. She was a mess up top. Like her hair, all curls and strands and damp and shaggy.

She couldn't have asked any more of Frank. She couldn't. But it hadn't been enough. For the past couple of months she'd been looking over her shoulder.

112

Searching. She had to get out. He was lovely. She wasn't. He deserved better. She didn't.

It wasn't an itch. She wasn't being pulled away by some mysterious world force. There was no calling.

It was the cage. Walls and fences. Bars and glass.

The normalness. Suburbia.

Parks. And TV.

Supper and sofas.

It wasn't her. It could never be. She was a ... Sam was struggling with the simile. Which animal best described who she was? Frankly, anything in a zoo. A dog on a leash.

She was feral. That was it. Pick an animal, provided it was wild.

She didn't do cages. She recognised that now.

So, she was in a new country – and a new, strange city. And she was at home.

Free.

And it felt good, even if there was every chance her mind would explode before the sun rose.

Sam put a finger in each ear and pressed hard.

She didn't know if that was going to help, and she knew she looked ridiculous. But if she kept her fingers there she might stop her sanity from escaping.

Idiot.

CIA Mission Center, Undisclosed Location, Zagreb, Croatia

Jackson was back, standing by the display of images his team had put together. The wall with four photos marked with red sharpie swirls. However there were now four more images added to the sixty-five: the ones of the 'drone crash' from Bae's pen drive, the strange dark splodge in the ground with the bent metal spike sticking out of it.

The analyst, CSI and pathologist were with him.

'Tell us about the original sharpie photos,' Jackson asked of no one in particular.

The analyst took the lead. He pointed to one, then immediately at a second. Jackson could see the red circles were different shots of the same thing, a small dark – maybe black – multi-angled shape.

'These are the same object,' the analyst stated. 'Taken from different angles.'

'OK. I can see that. What is it?'

'We don't know. Plastic, probably. Smashed, broken, possibly from an electrical item, maybe a broken cell,' the analyst replied.

'Or a bit of plastic off a larger piece of equipment. Say a simple bathroom pipe,' the CSI chipped in.

'Why have you highlighted it?' Jackson asked.

There was quiet for a second.

'Because ... because there's nothing else like it in any of the other photos?' CSI again.

Move on.

'OK. And this one.'

The third image had a red oval identifying an almost indistinguishable mark on Bae's shirt. Jackson wouldn't have spotted it if they hadn't zoomed in and marked it. He also couldn't tell which section of Bae's shirt he was looking at as the blow-up had removed all helpful references.

'This?' He pointed at the photo of light blue material.

The pathologist had a pencil in her hand. She pointed at a strand, possibly thread, of light grey.

'Again, we can't be sure, but this is alien to the blue material of the shirt. The victim might have picked it up anywhere, but the photo is of his right shoulder. We've told you we think the assailant attacked him from behind ...' The woman grabbed the analyst – by surprise. One arm held him tight around the top of his chest, the other mimicked stabbing motions. '... like this. If I'm wearing something grey it's possible I could have left that evidence on the body.'

She let go of the analyst, who looked happier than he had moments previously.

Jackson nodded.

'And this one?' He was pointing at the fourth image. In the centre of the final sharpie circle was a used match. 'It's a match?'

'Correct,' the CSI replied. 'A recently used match.'

'How do you know?' Jackson's mind was already ahead of his own question. *Did Bae smoke?* He was convinced he didn't.

The CSI continued. 'We checked the meteorology for the previous twelve hours. There had been heavy rain the night before. You can see that from looking at the damp patches in the photos. The balcony where the body was found was prone to leak, by the look of it. The match, which we're pretty sure is dry, has fallen onto such a patch.' The CSI was using a finger to draw round the edge of a darker pile of broken masonry and other debris. The match was lying to the edge of the damper area.

Jackson leant forward and touched the image.

'But the victim didn't smoke.' Almost to himself.

'Are you sure?' the pathologist asked.

'Pretty certain. In any case, anyone could have dropped this before Bae turned up.' Again, Jackson's brain was working quicker than his mouth. *If the murderer was there prior to Bae ...*

'It stopped raining three hours before the murder. What's the chance a smoker was in the same place prior to your agreed meet? In a derelict hotel?'

Jackson didn't say anything. If the assailant had beaten Bae to the meet location, then they knew everything about the liaison, rather than tagging him to the meet. And that added a whole new level of complexity to what was already a tricky situation.

He shook his head.

'Let's move on. Away from the crime scene. You've all had a chance to look at, what we're calling "the drone strike". Has anyone had any thoughts on what this is?'

The pathologist raised a hand.

'Do you want me to stay? There are no dead bodies here.'

'Yeah. Four brains are better than three,' Jackson replied. He had already moved along to the new images. 'Any ideas?'

The CSI started.

'First, the photos are taken undercover. So, either the object – this black affair here,' she was pointing at the dark shadow, 'is an illicit thing of interest. Or, one of the faces is POI (*person of interest*), and the photographer is nailing the mugshot to the place.'

Jackson had that, although his intuition told him this was about the splodge of dark, more than the people moving around it.

'That's fair. But if we ignore the heads, what is it they are looking at ... heading into ... coming away from?'

The analyst chipped in.

'If you remove the images' perspectives, you have an area of ground as long as it is wide. It looks like a crater of unknown depth, probably six feet wide. The rubble around the edge looks new – that is, it's been moved from its original location. Which might indicate a violent event, such as a bomb or explosives, but none of the rocks are charred. Look here ...' The analyst was pointing at a medium-sized rock on the edge of the dark mass. Jackson moved closer to the image.

'... this section of small rock appears to have come from the bigger rock it's next to. This face and this face look like they match. It's as if it has fallen, or broken off. The break looks new-ish. You can see from the shade difference between the old rock here and the area of the break. Key, though, is that there are no char marks. The boulder has been broken, but possibly not by an explosive event. Indeed, if you look at all of the earth surrounding the crater, including this metal, curvy spike affair, I can see no signs of burning.'

'So no explosion?' Jackson asked.

The man was shaking his head.

'Anyone else?' Jackson asked.

Nothing.

'What about the metal pole?'

'A rod of some sort, like an implement to poke around in the bottom of the pit,' the pathologist added.

'Or the end of something that's fallen into the crater?' the CSI said.

Jackson scratched his chin. He had no idea, so he didn't offer anything. Instead he summed up.

'So it's a hole. Either one that has naturally opened up. Or, it's manmade? But no explosion.'

There was silence for a second.

'I think that's a fair summary,' the CSI added.

'What has this got to do with the killing of Bae Ki-tae?' Jackson added, not expecting a response.

He stood back from the board. The other three followed his lead. He had one final glance up and down the images.

Nothing.

He screwed up his face.

A match, a minute piece of thread, and a hole in the ground. Or maybe a face in a crowd, next to a hole in the ground.

'OK. Let's do facial recognition on all of the mugs in the shots. I know it's incredibly unlikely, but let's see if we can get a fix on any of them. Got it?'

They nodded, and the analyst whose responsibility it would be to undertake the work was nodding more vigorously than the others.

Let's hope the translator comes up with something.

Chapter 5

'OK, that makes sense to me. When can you get moving?'

Frank was standing in front of C's desk. He'd been called up to the office as soon as he'd got into work. The boss, so far, was happy with his plan. Which was, travel to Singapore and then try and match Jane's itinerary. If he took a work laptop and other electronic paraphernalia with him, he'd be able to keep up with all the 'paperwork' – reports from Europol and Interpol, the UK's counterterrorist organisations, other SIS stations, etc. He'd have much the same level of security access as he had here and, if he needed more, he could find a friendly embassy and get patched through. In Singapore he'd also be able to lead the initial investigation into the death of Dusit Rattanatari, which they might appreciate.

Then head north.

It was a huge decision – for him.

He was an analyst, not a case-officer. He didn't step outside a protective environment unless it was to pop to the shops and get a sandwich. Although, to be accurate, he had worked with/for Sam in Munich a couple of years ago. And twelve months ago he had been her wingman in Switzerland. But at no time in either of those excursions had he felt comfortable.

He was an introvert. Being an introvert didn't make him furtive. It didn't make him a natural spy.

It made him scared.

He was no good in the shadows – not comfortable with taking risks. His idea of a risk was a 'yes' to the barista in Costa when they asked him if he wanted to sample the new blend of coffee from Colombia.

However, and he knew this part of his reasoning was plain wrong ...

... South East Asia was calling him.

Shouting at him.

It was an electromagnet and he was an iron filing.

And it was madness. He hated travel. The idea of stepping off the plane into an unknown world sent shivers down his spine.

Professionally, the moment he left his desk he'd be all at sea. He didn't have the confidence to waltz into Singapore Station and lead an investigation. He needed to be instructed. Told what to do. He wasn't a leader. He was an investigator. He studied stuff and spotted things. He then asked for more stuff and spotted new things. He didn't lead.

How could he? He didn't know which way to go.

But the magnet was strong.

And, as C had just concurred, him travelling to Singapore wasn't a stupid idea. From an operational viewpoint it made sense.

Emotionally, however, it was crazy – but he couldn't stop himself.

Stepping back and squinting at the plan, all he could see was calamity. He would mess up. Something would go wrong. He didn't have the capacity to manage what C had agreed to.

Not without help.

He took a breath. His eyelids closed involuntarily; he quickly forced them open.

'There's one more thing, C.'

Sir Clive looked as if he was about to get out of his chair. He probably had another meeting to go to. Or he was going to politely usher Frank out of the office so he could get on with being very important and saving the world.

C stopped, mid-rise. He sat down again.

'Yes, Frank?' There wasn't a hint of frustration in his voice.

Here goes.

'I've been looking after Sam Green for the last ... almost a year.'

Frank waited. He didn't know why.

'Go on.'

Another breath.

'I told her about Jane. Nothing to do with Op Mandolin or Abraham ...' Frank was at a canter now, '... She pressed me yesterday morning. I was too obviously carrying the weight of Jane's disappearance. I must have been looking hangdog. And I ... told her. That Jane was in

122

trouble. We'd been getting electronic postcards from her as she moved north through Thailand and Cambodia, on her sabbatical. They stopped about a month ago. I wanted Sam to know that I'd had an update.'

Frank was rocking from foot to foot. And he was gently sweating, even though the temperature in C's office was cool. C had raised a hand to his chin. His stare was impassive, but penetrating.

Frank was about to lose his job.

'She understands that what you have told her is Top Secret?'

Frank nodded. He'd brought his hands together. He managed to stop himself from wringing them.

C snorted. And then pushed back in his chair.

'What will she do when you travel to Singapore? Who will look after her then?'

Frank looked at the floor; then to his left. There was a photo of the Queen on the wall. It was on its own. About A3 size and tastefully framed in gold. The wall was painted dark blue. It was all very regal.

All of a sudden he felt completely out of his depth.

'Frank?'

He looked back at the boss. In a fidget he raised his hands to waist height and then dropped them to his side. He wasn't getting very far.

C broke the impasse.

'She's on the way to Asia already, isn't she?'

Frank nodded.

'Saigon, I think. It was the last contact we had from Jane. Sam … well, she needed some air. I was probably stifling her and she was looking for any excuse to escape – normality? And, inadvertently, I gave her that opportunity.'

Frank shrugged. It was out now. And it could well be over.

'Sorry,' he added.

C stood. As he did he reached for a folder on his desk. He picked it up and walked round to Frank's side. He rested his hand on his shoulder. Frank turned to look at him. He was greeted with something close to serenity. He didn't know what to expect next.

'Go to Singapore, Frank. Go and find Jane. Do what you do. But …' he had let go of Frank's shoulder and moved towards the door, '… Mandolin and Abraham are for your eyes only. The names are codeworded. The events inside them are codeworded. In the same way I know you won't have divulged any unnecessary details to the agencies you tasked last night, those rules continue to apply. Wherever you are. And whatever you do.'

He had opened the office door and was offering Frank an escape route.

Frank took the chance, but he didn't get past C's outstretched hand.

They were close again now. Frank looked at the Chief. Any hint of softness he had displayed earlier had gone.

'You have a month. If, during that time, you were to recruit an agent who could help you find Jane – or untangle any of the conspiracies in Mandolin or Abraham – then that would be good practice. And, as any case-officer would do, you can use whatever discretion you wish to get the best from that agent.' He paused. And then added, 'Provided the security of the operation is not undermined. Am I clear?'

Frank was completely clear.

'Thanks, sir. I won't let you down.'

And with that C dropped his arm and Frank slipped away down the corridor.

Highlands Coffee, 39 Mạc Đĩnh Chi, Đa Kao, Quận 1, Hồ Chí Minh, Vietnam

Sam had her 8-inch tablet unfolded. The Facebook app was open. She was studying Gemma Ruby's timeline. It was, unsurprisingly, public. Jane would have wanted anyone who might be interested in her alter ego to match a picture she painted on her fabricated social media. As Sam had only been told of Jane's alias as she left the UK, this was her first check to see if there were any clues.

And there were none – almost. At first glance Gemma Ruby's timeline told the same, albeit much fuller, story as the WhatsApp messages Jane had been sharing with Frank and her. The timeline was of an early middle-aged woman (government employee, according to her profile) on sabbatical, journeying around South East Asia. It followed her journey from Singapore, via Kuala Lumpur, Langkawi – an island off the north western Malaysian coast – to Bangkok, a trip along the Death Railway (to the Bridge over the River Kwai), and then on to Cambodia. She had travelled by coach and train. There were countless photos of glorious beaches and modern skyscrapers. There were endearing images of local children, and spectacular shots of temples and palaces. She'd shared plenty of pictures of the inside of overnight trains, and of 'sleeper' buses, with the occupants in bed-like seats, one on top of the other.

Sam reckoned there were over 100 images.

And they all stopped six weeks ago at Angkor Wat, the massive, 12th-century temple complex outside Siem Reap in Cambodia. Sam counted ten photos of the huge religious site. Eight were landscape shots of the temples, all looking fabulous, and two were selfies, with the temples as the vista. One of the two selfies had a tuk-tuk in the background. Sitting in the front seat of the small taxi was a local man. Sam used a finger and thumb to expand the image. She clocked the driver's face and the details of the tuk-tuk: it was mustard yellow – badged with a firm's logo: *EZGo* – and she could make out a partial telephone number.

She googled *EZGo* and was immediately directed to a Facebook page. She explored further. They were

Phnom Penh based. And she now had the full phone number.

But it was six weeks ago. And, at that point, the pictures had stopped telling the story.

Sam looked at Instagram. There was no account name that matched Gemma Ruby.

Snapchat: *nope*. Twitter: negative.

So, Jane's alias had one public outlet – and that was Facebook. And it wasn't helping.

What about 'actual' Jane?

Other than her WhatsApp messages, did she have a social media presence? SIS didn't ban their staff from having Facebook accounts, or using Instagram, although few ventured onto social media.

Sam hadn't. She struggled enough with living amongst real people. The idea of making her private life public was anathema to her. So she wouldn't have known if Jane Baker was out there – she would never have looked.

She googled her.

Unsurprisingly there were lots of Jane Bakers, and lots of Facebook, Instagram and Twitter references. She scrolled through the first couple of pages and didn't recognise anyone. *This is going to take some time.* If she still had access to Cynthia, SIS's mainframe, life would have been a whole lot easier.

Undeterred, Sam pursued this line of thought.

How did Jane keep in touch with her family? As far as Sam knew, Jane's mum was alive, and there was a married brother living in Surrey. *Godalming*? And they had a daughter, Sophie. Sam remembered Jane talking about knitting her a winter cardigan.

Had Jane been in touch with them after her last WhatsApp to her and Frank?

What was the latest communication from Jane? They had to find it.

She looked up from her screen.

Very little had changed in the two hours she'd been sitting in the café.

Highlands Coffee was the Vietnamese *Starbucks*. It was decked out in different drops of flowered wallpaper, the room scattered with tasteful round tables and soft, red leather and wood chairs. The menu was clearly franchise, but it was different – and better – than its Western equivalents. If she stayed much longer she was definitely going to try the shredded chicken *Bánh mì*.

And the place was clearly popular.

But that was no surprise. Vietnam was an overly busy country – its geography tree-like, with the southern Mekong Delta the bulbous roots, the trunk a 800-kilometre thinnish strip of land with Cambodia and Laos in the west and the South China Sea its eastern border, before the landmass widens and rises to the tree's canopy, the Annamite mountain range, which Vietnam shares with China and Laos.

With a population of close to 100 million, Sam reckoned most of them had transited the café in the past two hours. It was very busy. But manageable. Especially as the air conditioning was working overtime and her third iced-lemon was super-cold. Unfortunately the first had made it to her bladder and she now needed a pee.

Which she would take in a minute or so.

She put her hands behind her head and focused on the picture window in the mid distance. Her view was frequently interrupted by a miasma of bustling, but seemingly happy locals, most of them patched into their smartphones.

One young woman caught her eye. She was sitting on her own on one of the few red sofas. She was absolutely stunning, with porcelain skin, small, tight lips adorned with cherry red lipstick, a super slim, but well-proportioned body ... and a delicate hat with a rim the size of a helicopter landing pad. Her dress was diagonal, black and white stripes. Her shoes white stilettos. And the hat was gloss white straw, with a black silk band.

She was something out of the pages of *Asian Vogue*, if there were such a publication. In one hand she held a clear plastic *Highland Coffee* mug which was carrying dark liquid, topped with cream. In the other was a selfie stick, at the end of which was a larger than average phone.

Sam couldn't hear the *click* of the phone as it took picture after picture, but she could tell when the girl had taken a shot – her pose altered, ever so slightly. Her lips pursing; her head tilting. She was in her own world. A fashion icon of rare beauty – on the *Highland Coffee* catwalk. Just her. With Sam as the audience.

Sam knew that she'd only been in Vietnam for a day. It was her first visit to anywhere further east than Afghanistan. But she was already coming to a conclusion.

Vietnam was a so-called communist country; a one-party, socialist republic. It's government arguably in tight control, with its people towing the party line.

You could have fooled me.

The gorgeous, black and white clad woman, with selfie stick and oversized hat, told the story. The communists might think they were in charge, but the young population were having none of it. They were chic and cute; the girls were fashionable … the boys aspiring sportsmen. And they were plagued with gadgets, and loving it.

But some of the recent history of civil conflict, north versus south – of winning an ideological war against the greatest superpower on earth – had left its mark: of trouble; and of toil. Anguish and effort was still etched on the faces of the elderly. And the work ethic seemed present in the bustling young. Yes, they were taking a break. But they didn't pause for long (apart from the selfie-taker). They had things to do. And, likely, a living to make.

And Sam loved them already.

Her phone pinged. She picked it up from the table. It was a WhatsApp message from Frank.

She held the phone at arm's length. And hesitated. She closed her eyes.

What time is it in the UK?

Her brain answered the question before it had formed in her mind. Four-thirty in the morning; six hours behind.

What was he doing up at this hour?

She hadn't replied to his text from a day ago. She hadn't found the energy. There was too much happening. Too many events invading her senses; scratching at her time. She was going to reply. *I am going to*. Soon.

She opened her eyes.

Frank was pestering her now.

And she didn't want that. She had come over here to find space. To escape from the walls which had been closing in. Frank, *bless him*, had been part of the problem. She hated herself for feeling like she did after how he had looked after her. But that's the way it was. Whilst her mind often played many tricks on her, delusion wasn't hiding up her sleeve.

I need to pee.

Her eyes hadn't lifted from the phone.

She was going for a pee. But she didn't want to lose her seat, and that was likely in the melee ... but pee she must.

Wait.

She blew out through her nose.

Let's do this.

She opened Frank's message. It read:

Hi Sam. I really need you to read this. I'm heading out to SGP. I have been tasked to look for J. I have access to new info. It doesn't look good. And it's part of a bigger picture. I need help. Ack. F

Sam didn't need to pee anymore. That would have to wait.

En route to Heathrow Airport, London, United Kingdom

Frank laid his phone on his lap and stared out of the window. He was tired. It had been a bit of a day. Yesterday there had been a swathe of emails and numerous telephone calls after the previous evening's taskers. He'd scanned most of it – and much of it was interesting, but not game-changing. GCHQ had tracked down numerous electronic and phone accounts of the three South East Asian businessmen, including the now deceased Dusit Rattanatari. Via the lawyers on the third floor he'd been able to grant the Doughnut (the colloquial name for GCHQ) authority to explore the men's accounts, including – when GCHQ found the capacity – to monitor calls. The problem they had was lack of resources. ELINT (*Electronic Intelligence*) now overmatched HUMINT (running agents) by a factor of hundreds. And that made sense. The exponential growth

132

of the internet and the constant use of smartphones – plus the ever expanding proficiency of e-cryptology on all electronic platforms – was how criminals and terrorists did their business.

It was also where governments did theirs.

Much of GCHQ's work now was letting our senior politicians know whether other parties were eavesdropping on us, or tracking down those messing with our e-systems. It was an ever-expanding world which included a new subset of GCHQ, the NCSC (*National Cyber Security Centre*). The NCSC was the government's new counter-ELINT arm. It had been set up because there were plenty of foreign national and individual players who wanted to know what we were up to. And electronic eavesdropping was the best way to unearth our secrets. NCSC's job was to prevent that.

There was so much to do. And the list of asks from people like Frank to the hub at the Doughnut was huge, too big for the number of staff to manage effectively.

Except, he was working directly for SIS's Chief. And the Op Code he'd been given finished with an '*x*'. And that meant Operation Mandolin was at the top of the pile of SIS taskers.

But it wasn't as straightforward as that. SIS weren't the only people who could put a request into the Doughnut. MI5, Counter-Terrorism Police Network, any of the major police forces, even the tops of the pile – the Cabinet Office, the NSC (*National Security Committee*) and the JIC (*Joint Intelligence Committee*) – all had good reasons to press GCHQ for ELINT, or support from NSCS to counter electronic threats. There just weren't enough desks, nor were there enough analysts to fill those desks.

And the complexity didn't stop there.

It wasn't anywhere near as simple as to offer the Doughnut a name, say that of Dusit Rattanatari, and wait for the intelligence to pile up in his in box.

Dusit Rattanatari was Singaporean. But he was ethnic Indian – Tamil, in fact. His father had emigrated to the island in the 60s. Rattanatari had been brought up in Singapore and had taken over his father's import and export business five years ago. Whilst English was widely spoken and was the business language of choice, Singapore was predominantly ethic Chinese, with some Indian and indigenous Malay communities making up the numbers. Frank had spoken to a desk officer in SIS's Singapore Station yesterday lunchtime. They had a file on Rattanatari, which they'd now shared with Frank – it was brief and not helpful. However it did tell Frank that the Singaporean-Tamil spoke English fluently ... and Mandarin, the latter because most of his staff were ethnic Chinese.

So, when Frank put a tasking email to GCHQ to get them to start to unpick Rattanatari's electronic profile, they had to do so in multiple languages. And, and this was a big and, Frank had to provide 'keywords', or triggers, to the Doughnut. Much of their work was based on huge computers using complex algorithms to scan hundreds of millions of lines of data and tens of thousands of phone lines. Those computers needed to scan for something.

Keywords were it.

That was Frank's job, and he'd done that as soon as he'd been given the Mandolin file. GCHQ liked to keep the keyword list for a single entity down to twenty, otherwise the machines in their basement overheated; their in-house joke. But Frank wasn't allowed twenty as his sift for Rattanatari would need to search in three languages: English, Mandarin and Tamil. As a result his list was restricted to ten – which then had to be translated. He'd chosen:

Dusit Rattanatari; Gemma Ruby; Jane Baker; La Teja*; arms shipment; Vietnam; Cuba; Tianjin; DPRK; Fai Zhao; Atith Jafarov.*

He had no idea whether or not the ten would reap any reward, and he might have to amend them as time went on. But that was all part of the job. And he'd provided similar lists for Fai Zhao and Atith Jafarov. The supercomputers in GCHQ's basement would now be heating away quite nicely.

He stared out of the taxi's window. Pre-dawn London was flashing past; currently the Chiswick High Road heading for the M4. Next stop Heathrow and a Qatar Airways flight to Singapore. It was the earliest he could find: 9.25 am. And then thirteen hours in the air. If the traffic remained as it was he'd be three hours early for check-in. Time to grab some breakfast, log into the SIS secure net and continue the sift of the reams of intelligence that would have come through since he'd taken responsibility for the operation.

He closed his eyes ...

... just as his phone buzzed in his hand.

He checked it. It was a return WhatsApp from Sam.

His heart made a little flutter.

He swiped and prodded. The reply in the first speech bubble read:

> *I'm in Saigon. Have you checked to see if J has any personal social media that's more recent than our WhatsApp? What about her parents and brother? Anyone checked with them?*

There was an immediate second bubble:

> *I have a tuk-tuk company to investigate in PP. Might go there tomorrow. Sleeping coach seems the most effective way.*

He waited to see if there was any more.

...

Nothing.

He stared back out of the window. There were streaks of rain now, meandering diagonally down the pane.

Is this what I want?

Where was this going? They had no future, surely? He knew that. So ... was this as good as it was going to get? He and Sam working together? And was that enough for him?

Do I have any choice?

His phone buzzed. Another message from Sam.

Going for a pee.

Another buzz; another WhatsApp speech bubble:

⁇

Frank smiled. That was it. He was hooked. Sam had found his button and pressed it. He knew that. And he knew there was little he could do about it.

CIA Mission Center, Undisclosed Location, Zagreb, Croatia

Jackson was looking over a secret update from Langley on the planned Korean summit, for which there was no exact date and the detail was scant. Even within the CIA some things remained 'need to know'. He'd moved on from scanning all 273 pages of the, now translated, documents that were on Bae Ki-tae's toothbrush drive. As soon as they had arrived he'd immediately scrambled for the Word file Ron reckoned had been sent to Bae at the same time as the photos of the dark splodge, surrounded by the crowd. It was of no help whatsoever. It was just under a page long and, now in English, it was alphabet soup.

Which meant it was coded.

Or the original file in Korean characters was a cipher. In which case the translation was worthless.

He'd gone straight back to Langley and asked them to put their best people on it. The response had been immediate and unhelpful: do it yourself.

Which, when he thought about it, was understandable. Langley had enough on their plate. And, on reflection, maybe it wasn't such a bad thing? Zagreb was equipped with high-powered software and the team had employed a couple of very decent data-cryptanalysts, one of whom was Ron. They also had on the staff a lady named Jolene. Apparently she was an old-fashioned code-breaker on her last tour before heading home to a small dairy ranch in Wisconsin. Her main job was as a voice analyst but, as an old-school intelligence officer, early on in her career she had majored in decoding ciphers. And, although her skill was less and less utilised because the machines had taken over, she was, apparently, very good at it.

With before and after translation copies of the printed document in his hand, he popped along to Jolene's desk.

'Hi, Jolene.' He was standing at her shoulder.

'How may I assist you, Jackson?'

He felt as if he were shopping for perfume and the store assistant knew he had no idea what he was looking for.

He didn't reply. Instead he held the documents in front of her, the Roman plain text on full display. She wiggled her shoulders in a 'this is exciting' way and snatched the papers out of his hand.

She had a quick glance at both folios and then, looking over a pair of steel-rimmed, half-moon glasses, asked, 'This is it?'

'Well. I don't know which is code. The original is Korean; that's a foreign language to me. The English is the translation. You choose. One or the other. Anyhow, why do you ask? Should there be more?'

'It depends. If it's a standard cypher, like a Caesar's shift ...'

'Caesar's shift?' Jackson didn't know if he were interested.

Jolene raised her eyes to the ceiling as if Jackson had forgotten how to tie his shoelace. She opened a notebook and scribbled down *a, b, c, d* and *e*, and directly underneath each of those letters wrote *b, c, d, e* and *f*.

'Every letter is displaced by one; '*a*' is a '*b*', etc. The simplest of Caesar's shift. You can displace by five

139

backwards, or seven forwards. Whatever you wish. It's the least complex of codes, but one of the most difficult to break. Get it?'

Jackson nodded his head.

Jolene was just starting.

'It might be a pattern-based, which is a straight random, but consistent cipher. Say an 'a' is always a 't', and a 'b' is always a 'g'. It helps to know the sort of message you're looking at so there's some context to work with. But, if there's enough code – and there may be here – we can normally sort something out. It could be polyalphabetic, or a displaced-qwerty, where you use the letters on your keyboard to lead you to another ...'

Jackson put up his hand.

'I believe you, Jolene.' He forced a smile. 'There are 273 pages of other documents which have been translated. They mostly make sense in English: letters to a bank manager and other mundane stuff. In amongst those are a couple of spreadsheets and ...'

It was Jolene's turn to interrupt.

'Do the spreadsheets seem cogent?'

Jackson accessed the bit of his brain where he held that information. It seemed to help that he played with his ear at the same time. He remembered thinking one of the sheets didn't look like anything he recognised.

'One doesn't seem to make any sense.'

'Good,' she said with finality. 'That might be the details of a rectangular cipher. Two characters, one along the top and one down the side. They connect to a new letter in the spreadsheet.' Jolene used the index fingers on both hands to sketch how it worked. She held one hand high, and moved it horizontally; the second dropped gracefully, top to bottom. She then brought both fingers together in front of her face, indicating a brand new character from the middle of the sheet.

'I have an eye for these things. But we also have some decent software that might be able to help.'

'What about the fact the coding might be the original pages, using Korean characters?'

'That will make it more difficult. But, I've cracked Russian codes in a previous life – and I didn't speak the language before I started.' She smiled and tilted her head.

'How long do you need?'

'How far to Mercury and back?'

Jackson had never heard that idiom before, but got the gist. He frowned.

'Depends on the speed of your spacecraft,' Jolene added.

He hadn't lost his frown. With it still plastered to his face, he had turned and started walking back to his desk.

'I'll share the docs with you now, Jolene.' Over his shoulder.

'I'll go and put my spacesuit on,' was her response.

Half an hour later the truth was Jackson wasn't much further forward with the 273 pages. This sort of work bored him; he was much better with people. And, other than the recent, potential coded sheets he'd handed to Jolene, everything else seemed innocuous and unhelpful. Unless Jolene could pull a rabbit out of a hat, the documents and the strange photos of the hole in the ground might well remain a mystery.

He was convinced they were key. That they were what had prompted Bae to call the early meeting. And, as a result, they now had some images and a coded message. Which told a story. A story Bae had wanted to share with him.

And he was still waiting for the office's face recognition software to see if there were any matches to those from the four photos. He thought it extremely unlikely ... and that the story here was of the hole, and not the people in the pictures. But, it was worth a shot. The mission centres in Seoul and Beijing had yet to report back. And, of course, he had a bit of plastic, a grey piece of cotton and a dry match.

It wasn't much. But these were early days.

The problem was, if Bae's meet was meant to provide some intel concerning the upcoming summit, early days wasn't in the lexicon. He had to crack this. Very soon.

He scanned the final page of the short Langley update.

What is going on?

What did Bae know? Was it to do with the summit? If so, was it key?

He couldn't get his head straight with it. And his stomach was messaging him.

He was hungry and it was almost lunchtime. He'd not managed to make himself something before he'd left his apartment this morning. That was, of course, one of the downsides of being divorced.

Yeah, but not being cheated on was an upside.

He'd go out to the local Konzum and get himself a sandwich.

He stood, stretched and then lifted his jacket from the back of his chair.

He walked towards the door, touching Ron on the shoulder as he passed. Ron didn't lift his head from his screen, but raised a hand in recognition.

Two minutes and one flight of stairs later, he was out through the metal detector and onto the street. The warmth of the late morning sun soaked him like a shower. It was mid-fall, so the heat was a perfect temperature. He'd play some basketball after work and then throw a burger on the barbeque and break open a can. His balcony was ideal when the weather was like this.

With his jacket over his shoulder and a spring to his step, Jackson strode out along the sidewalk in the direction of the supermarket.

Three steps later he was on the ground, feet from where he had been milliseconds earlier. A wall of

143

superheated air had lifted him and spat him to the floor. His flight ungracious – his limbs floundering as his torso spun.

Fuck!

What?

His face and exposed arms singed.

His ears rung like church bells ...

... and the pain in his shoulder was instantaneous. And immense.

Heat, blast, noise and then agony – in that order.

The dance steps of an explosive device.

Jackson knew.

He'd been there before: Iraq, 2011.

Then he'd been in the wrong place at the wrong time. A suicide bomber had detonated themselves at the entrance to a police station in Karbala. Jackson had been inside the station, having just arrived for a meeting. A minute earlier and he'd had been blown to pieces. A minute later and his calf would have remained intact – and he'd have seen out his tour.

The heat of that explosion had been hotter than any Iraqi summer's day. The blast which immediately followed had sent him flying. And the noise of the explosion messed with his head for a long time afterwards. A piece of shrapnel, later found to be a ball bearing that had been impregnated in the bomber's waistcoat, had ripped through his calf muscle like a high velocity bullet.

But he had survived. Just the one hole.

Seventeen others hadn't been so fortunate.

Now, eight years later, he knew he'd just been through the same ordeal. Shrapnel from the centre of the blast was still falling from the sky, crashing and tinkling beside him on the pavement. The sour smell of burnt ... he didn't know what ... was already filling his nostrils.

And some part of his body, maybe his shoulder or chest, had been joined by an alien object.

Wait. Was there more pain? Or might that be bruising from the fall ...

His brain wasn't working fast enough. He was losing consciousness. Day was becoming night.

Zagreb was morphing into Ramallah.

The pain was strengthening ...

... and then blackness.

Chapter 6

Krong Bavet Border Crossing – Vietnam into Cambodian

Sam was waiting in the customs queue. There were around twenty people in front of her, and all but two of whom were locals. Behind was the same story: mostly locals. The white couple ahead were older-age, hippy-esque with bright backpacks, long hair, more beads than Woodstock and badly fitting but comfortable clothes. Behind her, a way back, were two younger white women, possibly gap-year students; again backpackers. They were more contemporarily dressed: shorts and t-shirts.

Sam was piggy in the middle. She was wearing an un-ironed, pale-green loose top and a dull-yellow sarong decorated in an indescribable pattern of reds and whites. Flip-flops were the order of the day. As was a narrow-rimmed, floppy hat. She wouldn't be mating any time soon.

Her 40-litre backpack was aging, but sturdy. In it was a change and a half of clothes, an all-in-one frumpy swimsuit, three pairs of knickers, running shoes, shorts and a singlet, two weeks of out of date malaria tablets, and not enough toiletries. Her wallet, passport, phone and battery back-up were in a money belt around her waist. She was travelling light.

And it felt good.

Their coach driver had dropped them off and driven ahead. The resulting foot crossing between Vietnam and Cambodia was ordered but ramshackle. Her present country seemed second-world; tarmac more prevalent than potholes. As she glanced ahead it looked like her future country might be more at home in sub-Saharan Africa. There was a distinct degradation of infrastructure. Reasonably smart custom officials looked set to be replaced by poorly attired soldiers where money probably spoke louder than up-to-date documents.

Oh well.

They all shuffled forward. Sam forced her mind to empty, although that was always problematic. As a result it didn't last long. Instead she played with a loose thread on her sarong, immediately recalling her dad's response to the photo of David Beckham wearing a black, wrap-around skirt to the '98 World Cup final.

'I'm off to shops, luv,' he'd said to her mum. 'I'm going t'get one of them sharons, like Beckham's got. What colour should I go for?'

Her mum, always the adult in the room, had replied, 'Don't be daft, dear. You'll get very breezy knees and who knows what will fly in to join them.' They'd all laughed at that.

Mum and Dad.

God, how she missed them.

She'd managed to unravel the thread so that it now twisted around her index finger three times. She'd need to nip it off before the whole skirt fell apart.

That, however, would be a job for later. She'd reached the front of the queue, dutifully waiting behind a yellow line that had been badly painted on the concrete. Ahead of her was a simple wood, glass and tile booth. In it was a man wearing a peaked cap. He looked earnest.

He gave her a 'you can come to the booth now' nod.

Sam moved to the window.

He nodded again, this time at her passport.

Sam handed it over. It was clean. After Switzerland she'd got a new one. She knew she'd travel again, and multiple stamps from a strange array of countries wasn't always helpful if you needed to take a break without drawing too much attention to yourself. It was habit.

The man with the peak cap was Vietnamese. He was 'stamping' her out of the country.

And it didn't take long. And, surprisingly, it hadn't cost her anything. Along with some larger notes she had ten five-dollar bills in her waist-belt. That level of denomination was usually enough to grease the palm of a sticky official.

Now temporarily nationless she walked out of the building into the shade of the huge concrete edifice that proclaimed, from the other direction, that you were entering the 'Socialist Republic of Vietnam'. Big red letters on a huge white, fake-marble arch that was topped with a precipitous red-tiled roof.

The Cambodian entry point was 25 metres ahead. Immediately the tarmacked road disintegrated. There were potholes of all sizes, mud and dust and, looking either side of the road-cum track, a build-up of plastic waste. The office ahead was more Nissen hut than customs checkpoint. And whilst half of her coach in front were either in, or were leaving the hut, such was the lack of order Sam was pretty sure she could have walked straight past the checkpoint.

Their coach was ahead of them, along with more taxis, mopeds and tuk-tuks than she could count. People were milling about and a discord of buildings in various states of repair littered the entrance to the 'Kingdom of Cambodia'. There was no triumphant arch proclaiming that fact.

Sam decided to stick with convention. She entered the checkpoint.

Ten minutes of un-air-conditioned heat later, she was at the booth.

There were three men in various states of uniform; two at a desk (one eating a packet of crisps), one serving. They didn't look anywhere near as officious as their Vietnamese counterpart, but she spotted a handgun on the belt of the man chewing on a mouthful of crisps. On one corner of the desk was a scruffy pile of US dollars.

Never argue with a man with a gun.

Especially one who's probably not paid a great deal.

'Passport.' The serving man, who had too many shirt buttons undone to be considered uniformed, extended a hand.

Sam handed over her passport.

He looked at it for a minute and then passed it to one of his pals – the non-hungry one.

The new man flipped through all the pages without paying much attention and unceremoniously gave it to the official who was pouring the last few crisps from the packet into his open mouth.

He's going to get grease all over my new passport. Grrr.

Sam waited. More angry than anxious.

...

She broke into the charade that was the checking of her passport.

'I have the two photos,' she said, holding them together between finger and thumb. Sam had read that in order to get into Cambodia you needed two passport-sized photos. She tried to do as she were told.

'Paper,' was his response.

What?

'Sorry. What "paper" do you want?' She tried not to sound indignant.

The man, clearly used to tourists reading the instructions on the official website but not understanding that those details were at odds with what the border officials actually needed, pointed lazily to a pile of forms off to her right.

Sam paused.

She really didn't want to let the passport out of her sight.

Sual it.

She took two paces to her right, glanced quickly at the form, picked up a pen from a nearby shelf and, without too much thought, filled it in.

In less than a minute she was back in front of the serving man. Her passport was still being fingered by the bloke who had just finished his mid-morning snack.

The serving man nodded towards the form. Sam handed it to him, along with the two photos ... which he immediately pushed back to Sam, shaking his head as he did.

More poor advice from the website.

'Sixty dollars.'

What?

The government website had visas into Cambodia at $30.

'I thought the visa cost was thirty dollars?' Sam replied calmly, trying her best to hide the grit between her teeth. She knew where this was going.

'Administration.' The serving man shot a glance over his shoulder at his two colleagues.

Sam sighed inwardly. She had been here before. Which meant she had two alternatives. One of which was pricey and painless. The second – well, it could end up anywhere, including jail. And be messy.

She took out a fifty- and a ten-dollar bill from her wallet.

She reluctantly handed them over.

Serving man checked the money, turned and handed the wodge to the non-eating man. The crisp packet man passed Sam's passport to serving man, who gave it back to her without ceremony.

Thirty seconds later – and sixty dollars poorer – she was out of the customs house and into a new country, her second in three days.

A little grumpy and without particular interest in her surroundings, she made her way to her coach – which had the air-conditioning running – found her seat, and settled in for another two hours of wacky races.

So far, so ...

At least the coach, which she'd booked after she'd finished her WhatsApp conversation with Frank, was comfy. She'd searched for the most recommended operator from the net – Giant Ibis – who, for this route, had laid on a conventional 'sitting up' bus. The journey, up until now, had matched the website's described itinerary. They'd left on time and arrived at the border crossing four hours later. Once they were through customs it would be another two hours to the Cambodian capital.

As soon as she got to Phnom Penh she had two jobs, the order dependent upon Frank. She was determined to check out the tuk-tuk company – the one in Jane's last series of photos from Angkor Wat. And, once Frank had OK'd it, she had to get to the British Embassy.

That was going to be complicated. Her WhatsApp conversation with him had been necessarily vague. They never spelt out Jane's name, instead used the abbreviation 'J'. Everything else was noun-less. *No names, no pack drill.* What she had managed to elicit from their exchange was that Frank was looking at three contacts, one of whom was 'no longer operating' – which, Sam assumed, was a euphemism for something a lot deadlier. Frank's, 'we're looking internationally, wider than South East Asia', was helpful. However his, 'could lead to concerns at the very highest level', wasn't new. Frank had told her a couple of mornings ago he was one of only four in the circle of intelligence. Whatever he was investigating was top-level.

Not helpful either was, 'I won't be able to share much'. Sam assumed that meant Frank had been given the authority to recruit her as an agent, which attracted a whole range of restrictions ...

... most of which she was pretty sure she could circumvent. If she felt inclined to press.

Whatever, Frank had asked her to stand by to go to the Cambodian Embassy: 'Main building only'. She wouldn't be allowed into the SIS station. On the plus side the embassy would provide secure comms. And he'd be able to update her from there.

Their conversation hadn't been all one-sided. Sam had pushed Frank to look at what social media was live in Jane's real name; and to check with her parents and brother to see when their last contact had been. And she'd pressed on SIS's last recorded position for Jane. Frank had replied:

South East of our final message from J. Still in the same country.

Sam had thought about that. She'd pushed:

Timing?

Frank response had been short:

Two days after ours.

And that had been it.

In short, there wasn't much to mull over as the driver propelled the coach onwards to Cambodia's capital, overtaking cars, oxen, mopeds and strange, hand-walked tractor-looking devices with hollow metal wheels which looked as if they should be driven from the inside by over-sized gerbils. She eventually worked out they were for cultivating the paddy fields.

Had Jane made it this far?

Sam was heading in the opposite direction to Jane's likely movements; the coach was motoring west

154

towards Phnom Penh; Jane would have been travelling southeast by unknown transport from Angkor Wat.

How far did she get?

Were their paths about to cross?

Sam looked absently out at the splurge of lush green grass that was sprouting from a mirror of blue and cloud decorated paddy field. In the distance were low hills, equally as vibrant. Cambodia, like Vietnam, was clearly a very fertile place.

The bus swerved past the shell of an old Renault 4 which looked as if it had been in a helluva accident and then pecked clean by locusts of straw hat wearing locals.

Could that be ...?

She shook her head violently.

Idiot.

One car crash doesn't make a conspiracy.

Jane had made it to Cambodia from Singapore. Frank was heading for the latter. Sam, on the other hand, was currently close to the end of Jane's known route. Between her and Frank they were making a 1,000-mile pincer movement.

On her journey Jane had recruited, or started the process of recruiting, three agents, one of whom was already dead – *that didn't augur well.*

And Frank was a lone wolf, which meant the Chief thought discretion was key. That might mean he was worried about intelligence contamination – and/or the prize was big, but not pressing.

Jane, the Chief, Frank ... and me.

155

Why am I now in the loop?

That was a good question.

It might be Frank's way of staying close, or at least in touch. And she got that, although it would really piss her off if it were his main driver.

Or, he genuinely felt she was the best help he could find. That didn't make complete sense either. He'd have the support of all of the staff in the local stations. Singapore was at least twenty strong, and she thought the case-load there wouldn't be onerous?

Although ... *would Frank be up to leading a close-hold operation such as this?*

Could he be discreet *and* effective?

Sam couldn't see it.

Is he out of his depth?

She wasn't sure.

He was a fabulous analyst. And hard-working. But, he had the breaking strain of a warm Mars Bar. Should things get overwhelming – and with the climate of these countries any pressure would be amplified – she didn't see him holding it together for too long.

Am I right?

If so, did he need her – professionally? Was he asking her to be his prop?

It was a possibility. There'd be an instantaneous connection. No 'getting to know you' and, just as important, 'looking forward to trusting you', required. She and he would easily pick up where they left off in Switzerland.

And that isn't so bad?

Possibly. Although, should Frank hold back vital intelligence because she lacked the necessary clearances, she could see this going north very quickly.

And did C know she would be in the loop?

Another unknown. It would be one of the first questions she'd ask Frank. If the Chief did, then she might be able to work some levers.

It was all very complicated, to be sure. When what they needed more than anything else was clarity.

Hopefully, once she got into the embassy some of this might become clearer.

British High Commission, 100 Tanglin Rd, Singapore 247919

Frank stared at the screen. He blinked. And blinked again. He closed his eyes and let the air-conditioning waft over him. If he stayed like this for long he might well nod off. And he couldn't afford to do that.

He needed to reply to the SO15 email.

Another minute …

The journey from the airport had been simple but, as was ever the case with him, stressful. His secure work phone had taken an age to fix to the Singaporean server. As he waited for his luggage it had connected. The news was he had 157 unread emails. As the carousel snaked the luggage around the hall he scanned the messages titles. Straight away he knew he could delete around forty of them. Another forty would have been automatically forwarded to the analyst Marcus had chosen to take on his responsibilities. He could ignore those. The remainder were all linked to Op Mandolin or Abraham.

There were over fifty emails related to the ops; some new, some replies to his previous asks. Before he'd had a chance to look through any of the detail his bag had arrived. Ten minutes later he was on the city's MRT. The metro was clean, driverless and uber-efficient and, having alighted at Orchard, he decided to walk the remaining 500 metres to the British High Commission.

Which had been a mistake. The temperature was 35 degrees. Combined with the humidity, the conditions were sapping. He was hot, sweaty and a little irritated by the time he'd arrived at the main gate. The guard, looking very imperial in a white, short-sleeve military suit and plenty of badges, was, thankfully, all smiles. However, the High Commission building was a good five minutes' walk through sumptuous gardens from the gate – which hadn't helped his humour.

He was met by Tanya, one of the SIS Station's admin assistants which was, as was often the case, at the rear of the embassy, shoe-horned into a prefab extension. It was 10.30 am by the time he had been offered a cup of tea, although his body clock was telling him it was due at least another three hours kip before it was prepared to join him.

This is going to be tough.

The small number of staff – there were desks for over twenty, but Frank had counted eight, including Tanya – politely ignored him. Tanya busied herself with setting him up on a free desk a short distance from one of the air-conditioning vents, next to a semi-opaque window.

It had taken him a couple of minutes to boot up the machine by which time Tanya, *bless her*, had delivered the tea.

'Thanks, Tanya. Where's the Enigma portal?' Frank wanted to know where he could access the Top Secret Mandolin and Abraham files. It would be the same terminal he'd need to report back to C.

She'd given him directions to a small office down the corridor, the key to which was held in a safe that only SG1 and SG2 (*head and deputy of Singapore Station*) knew the code to. He'd have to get onto that before the end of the day.

In the meantime all of the work he'd generated – all fifty-odd emails – were classified Secret. He'd made sure that was the case. A standard Cynthia machine would manage those.

Frank thanked Tanya again and got to work.

He was five emails in when he came across a report from SO15 (*Special Operations 15*), the Met's counter-terrorist branch – formally Special Branch. In his original email he'd asked them to carry out a straightforward systems' search on Dusit **Rattanatari,**

Fai Zhao and Atith Jafarov, not expecting any flags. However, after Sam had pressed him from Saigon, he'd tasked them, The Service and GCHQ, to do a search on Jane's mum and brother. He needed to know what was Jane's last communication to the UK.

He knew he was pushing his luck with SO15, as they were predominantly London-based. His request should have gone to Surrey Police Force, the county where both Jane's mum and brother lived. But on the way to the airport with sleep in his eyes and without the appropriate email address for the Surrey force, SO15 had been it. He'd made an appropriate apology in his message.

SO15's reply, which was open on his screen now, was a cut-and-paste police report from the Surrey force.

And it made his stomach churn.

The report was signed off by a police constable. It was dated two days ago. And it was ... horrible.

Jane's sister-in-law had come downstairs that morning to make the tea and had noticed the family dog was not at her feet, begging to be fed. After calling his name, and searching the house, she'd gone into the garden.

Where she'd found 'Misty'.

She was hanging by her rear legs from a tree, her head no longer attached to her body.

After throwing up, plenty of tears and then, with her husband, forming a plan that meant their daughter

Sophie didn't get to see the headless pet, she'd called the police.

The initial report was inconclusive: there had been no other similar crimes called in across the county; the family knew of no reason why anyone would want to mutilate their dog; investigations were at an early stage … blah.

Frank's cursor hovered over the attached jpeg. He closed his eyes. And double-tapped, opening it and involuntarily pulling his head away from the screen as he did.

He knew what was coming … but the montage of four photos showing a headless dog hanging from a tree was too awful to look at. He fought back rising bile and closed his eyes again.

I need to sleep.

But he couldn't.

Not now. Not yet.

Think.

This wasn't an act of a serial dog murderer. This wasn't a local, incidental crime.

It wasn't Jane's brother and sister-in-law who were the targets.

Headless Misty was a message for Jane: if we can do this to a pet dog – we can do the same to any member of your family.

Which was harrowing news – for Jane.

But good news for them.

Jane was alive.

Or she had been when the dog was murdered, otherwise what was the point?

Jane was alive … two days ago.

And they had a crime scene.

It wasn't as straightforward as that. They were dealing with international-level criminals; the area would almost certainly be clean. But, if the dog-killer had left even the smallest trace of evidence, maybe they could track them down?

Provided the local plod hadn't stamped it all into the grass.

Frank was with it now.

He clicked 'reply' to the original email. He added his pal in The Service to the list of addressees. This was now a UK terrorism case – he was sure of it. Between them they needed to see it that way.

After he'd sent the tasker he picked up his phone and opened WhatsApp. He found Sam's contact details and pressed the white-on-green telephone button and waited for it to ring.

Two buzzes later and then …

'Yup.'

Hello to you too.

'Where are you?'

'I'm with the tuk-tuk company. I've got as far as Siem Reap. Just arrived. You?'

'I'm here. Settling in. How soon can you get to the embassy?'

There was a pause.

'How quickly do you want me to be there?'

'I've just got here. I need a couple of hours to process a number of emails and get my head together. I also need to get the admin staff here to book you in. Say three hours?'

There was a further pause.

'Four. I've just come from the capital. I've been travelling all day, although stock car racing is a more apposite description – let's say it hasn't been the most fun I've ever had. It'll take me another harrowing three hours to get back.'

'Sam?'

'Yup.'

'I think J may be OK ... that is, she is still with us. But we might not have long.'

...

The pause was louder than any words. Frank sensed that Sam was gathering things together; getting ready to move having stepped up a gear.

'OK. Three hours.'

The phone went dead. Frank looked at the small screen. There was a message from WhatsApp asking him to rate the call. He dutifully pressed '5-stars' and closed the App.

With his phone back on the desk his eyes were drawn to what was left of Misty. And that jolted him. He quickly reduced the report and pushed back in his chair.

He needed help. He had no idea what other bombshells were in the forty or so emails. And he knew he had to process them quickly. Getting Sam in now was the right call. And three hours might be enough time to read his messages in detail, scribble some notes, elicit support from a few of the team here and, once Sam was in the picture, start to piece together a plan.

Except.

He was about to stand and go and find Tanya. He stopped himself.

Sam was not on SIS's books. She was, at best, an agent.

He looked above his screen to the window. Frank reckoned a sandwich of glass and polycarbonate, probably one and a half centimetres thick, with a grey, thin film coating. Bomb proof – and too hazed to pick a target through.

It was a perfect metaphor for where he found himself. Well protected but without vision.

Sod it.

Jane was missing; in trouble, but possibly alive.

And he had been tasked to chase down a Level One intelligence source: *international level grouping; global destabilisation*.

Sam Green was the best help he could hope for.

Triệu Quang Phục, Lào Cai, Vietnam

Jane was sitting at the table again. The Chinese-looking man in the stockbroker suit was back. She hadn't seen him for three days. Not since the gruelling four-hour session. With no tasers. No hanging by her wrists. No smacks to the nose. Just four intense hours of questions … and answers. After which had been the usual routine. Chicken and rice three times a day. Some candy. Coffee.

A shower; a toothbrush.

And yoga.

The yoga hadn't helped. Yes, she was feeling stronger. More human, although the mirror in the bathroom told a different story.

But it hadn't settled her. Hadn't stopped her mind from reeling from her disclosures. The detail of some of her work in London. The reasons for her trip to South East Asia. And her liaison with the Singaporean, Dusit Rattanatari. She'd kept a lot back. She'd not mentioned Fai Zhao or Atith Jafarov. Nor had she spoken of the Cuban registered container ship, *La Teja*. And its illicit, military cargo destined, she thought, for the DPRK. She'd kept that to herself.

She spoiled some secrets. But protected others.

She only hoped that whatever damage she had done – and she had no idea what that looked like – had sent SIS teams scurrying around to pull agents and protect sources.

I hope.

The man sitting opposite looked as if he were about to fill in some of those gaps.

165

But not yet.

She stared at him. Him back at her.

He had a round face topped with archetypically short, shiny black hair. His eyes were small against the breadth of his face, giving them an intensity that hurt. And his small top lip turned up and over his even smaller bottom one. There was no smile. No graciousness.

He still didn't utter a word.

Worryingly – so much so Jane felt her stomach tighten – he'd brought the folder back in with him. The family album.

What's in there this time?

His hands were clasped together on top of the file.

There was a further minute of silence. Jane's heart was beating so hard she was surprised the stockbroker couldn't hear it.

'Well, Miss Baker.' An introduction, not a question. And then a pause.

Jane didn't respond.

'We found Mr Rattanatari.'

Shit.

Her shoulders dropped and her intestines felt as though they had slackened. She wasn't going to survive this.

'We had a conversation with him.' The stockbroker's face held the same expression: business-like. A poker face. No trace of emotion.

She looked down at the table and closed her eyes.

I have likely killed a man.

'Is he alive?' she whispered.

The stockbroker didn't reply to begin with. Instead he let out a short snort.

'Do you think we're animals, Miss Baker?'

Jane lifted her head.

'Is he alive?' she asked again. Still a whisper.

The stockbroker twisted his mouth.

'He told us he had passed two names to you, Miss Baker. Two names you didn't give to us?'

Jane looked closely at his features, trying to establish if the stockbroker were lying.

Two men. Not one. Or three. Two. Fai Zhao and Atith Jafarov. The stockbroker knew. That meant they had tortured – *or bribed?* – Dusit Rattanatari. And he had told them about Fai Zhao and Atith Jafarov. That they were similarly-minded businessmen: anti-regime; pro-capitalist. And they were willing to talk to the UK's intelligence agencies. Because something wasn't right in East Asia. And they were powerless to do anything about it.

'Rattanatari didn't give me any names. He was my only asset,' Jane lied, her voice sounding a lot weaker than she had hoped.

'Mmm. So, Miss Baker. You continue to lie to me. Which is unfortunate. Unfortunate for me. And unfortunate for you.'

The stockbroker lifted his hands from the folder and spun it through 180 degrees so it was directly in front of Jane. He motioned for her to open it.

Unfortunate for you.

She didn't know what to do. She didn't know where to place her hands. She certainly didn't want to touch the folder. She knew inside would be an immeasurable horror.

Tears formed in her eyes. One escaped a bottom lid and fell on the plastic covered file. It splashed, forming three very small, discrete puddles. Another was about to follow it when …

'Open it, Miss Baker. And then we can talk about Mr Atith Jafarov and Mr Fai Zhao. And everything else you have been keeping from us.'

She couldn't. It wasn't possible.

With a sigh, the stockbroker turned the opening leaf. It fell to the table, leaving the inside blue of the cover and a plastic folio containing two images.

Jane couldn't stop herself.

She retched.

The stockbroker leapt from his chair, not before a spit of Jane's puke had splashed onto his shirt, tie and very smart suit. His chair spun, and toppled, clanging on the floor.

Jane hadn't budged from her seat. Her body was heaving and her head shaking. Tears were cascading, mixing with half-digested rice and coffee and strands of chicken … and bile. The smell was putrid and, as a background to her terror, she was softly wailing an extended, 'Nooooo.'

As she rocked she held her chest tight, but even as her head moved to the beat of her pain, her eyes remained focused on the portion of the image she could make out from between the sick and tear cocktail.

It was Misty. Her brother's dog. Before. And she couldn't finish the sentence.

They had murdered something precious to her family.

They had gate-crashed what was so interminably dear to her and, as a ruthless example, murdered the easiest of targets.

What would her family be thinking?

And then the absolute reality hit her.

They had murdered a pet. But not a person.

She was in no doubt that they could – and they would. In the same way she knew Rattanatari was dead. These people were merciless. Beyond reckless. Gangsters with motives but no morals.

And what happened next was up to her.

She was damned.

It was her fledgling agents. A huge divulgence of SIS secrets.

Or her family.

She let the tears, now accompanied by snot which was dripping from her nose, cascade away.

Still staring at the table, she blinked; bits of half-tear spread wider than the mess in front of her.

'I need to go to the loo. Then I'll talk.' A soft, weak noise.

She had made up her mind.

The stockbroker had already called in her guard and was barking orders at him whilst he frantically brushed lumps of sick from his suit.

She lifted her head.

'I need to go now.' Louder. She was emphatic.

More indecipherable instructions to the guard ... who took Jane by the forearm and pulled her quickly out of the room.

Twenty steps later and they were by the toilet door.

The guard let go of Jane's arm and pushed the door open.

'No lock!' He barked his usual order.

Jane didn't acknowledge, nor wait for any further directions. She dived into the loo and immediately locked the door.

The next sixty seconds was a blur. As soon as the latch was across, the guard started banging on the door. With the sound of heavy percussion reverberating around the windowless, small room, Jane stared at the circular vanity mirror which hung loosely from a nail on the wall above the sink.

Bang, bang – loud, foreign shouting – bang, bang ...

She closed her eyes. And counted.
One, two, three, four, five.

170

She opened them, blinked, spraying more tears, and then took the mirror off the wall ...

... and, in one motion, hurled it to the floor.

As it broke into hundreds of pieces, the frantic banging on the door continued.

She needed to find one shard; one that was woman enough for the job.

There.

She picked up a sliver, the size of her middle finger, turned and sat on the pan.

Six, seven, eight, nine, ten.

With the shard of mirror in her right hand, and her left forearm exposed ...

... she cut.

Shit, that hurts!

And cut.

And cut.

Fuck, no!

She wasn't very good at this, but in seconds she couldn't tell flesh from red.

She gritted her teeth, let out a low-pitched scream ... and cut again.

The door broke open just as Jane joined the draining blood on the floor.

She thought she heard shouting. Maybe she felt someone grab her by the arm?

Which arm?

She really didn't know.

Because the blackness came.

British Embassy, Sangkat Srah Chak, Khan Daun Penh,
Phnom Penh, Cambodia

Sam was alone in the Deputy Head of Mission's office, logged on to the FCO's (*Foreign and Commonwealth Office*) secure portal. She hadn't been allowed in Phnom Penh Station, but Frank had enough clout to get her a secure machine in a soundproof room. It was the best she could hope for.

The young lad who had shown her in and set up the machine had just dropped off a glass of water, and did she want anything else? *Yes, please. Four more of these.* The journey back to the capital had been as much of a fairground ride as the original to Siem Reap, just in reverse.

'No, thanks,' was the actual answer. And, as she waited for Frank to make the connection, she looked over the deputy's office.

It was an old-fashioned room with a sash window, but replete with modern furniture and classy touches. There was the obligatory photo of Her Majesty next to which the second-in-command had hung some very tasteful, if abstract local art. The desk was big and tidy and there was a single silver photo frame of a good looking, middle-aged woman and a child. It could be wife and daughter. Or, maybe, single mum and her kid? Sam didn't know.

She took a sip of her water.

And then, there was Frank. Thirty-two inches of LED with his face as large as life.

He smiled at her, and half-raised a hand, making a small waving movement.

And that froze her.

She didn't know what to do. Somewhere, far off from the left field, a bolt of guilt hit her like a swinging punch bag and took the wind from her lungs. She immediately felt her face redden and her mouth dry.

Here, now on the same continent and in high definition, was the man who had professed his love for her. Over the past year he had waited on her hand and foot, never once asking for anything in return. He had looked after her, first as an invalid and more lately as a favourite sister. Other than a final peck on the cheek, he'd never touched her. Not even a hand on her forearm.

And what had Sam done in return?

She had run out on him. At the first possible opportunity. Without discussion and without a shred of empathy. At best she had been careless. At worst, completely heartless.

But he was still there – here. Still the same Frank. Still undemanding and – very likely – still giving. She wanted, no *needed* this, whatever 'this' was. This job ... this operation. This chase. She hoped it was her desire to find Jane which was driving her. Trying to find the woman who had been alongside since Sierra Leone. Who had covered her back, even when there had been differences. Who was now lost ... maybe worse.

Yes, this is about Jane.

But it was also about the job. The exhilaration.

The distraction.

Sam was an automaton. A machine that needed input.

And Frank was about to feed her.

Still giving.

Still taking.

And she hated herself for it.

She smiled at the monitor.

'Sorry.' The quietest of apologies.

'Don't be, Sam.' There was no delay between the two countries, even with the security protocols doing their thing.

Frank smiled again.

'Are you OK?' he asked.

She nodded sheepishly.

'I am sorry, though. For ... walking out like that.' Frank was shaking his head, but Sam wanted to finish. She added, 'Thank you for looking after me. Means a lot.' Her smile had gone; her face genuinely sad.

She couldn't be sure, but it seemed it was Frank's turn to be embarrassed.

'Are you on your own?' he asked, shifting in his chair.

'Yes. And the team here assure me the room is soundproof.'

174

'Good. Thanks. I can't let you take notes,' he added.

Sam nodded. She had never taken notes. It wasn't necessary. She heard things – she remembered them. It was the way she was wired.

'OK. There's quite a bit,' Frank continued. 'And, from a strictly agent/intelligence office relationship I am going to give you much more than I'm authorised to. And by doing so, I am putting you in danger.'

Sam nodded again. It was a curt nod, one that might be construed as impatient.

Come on, Frank. Let's get to this.

Her embarrassment had gone. She had said her piece, however uncomfortable that had been. Now she wanted everything.

'OK.' Frank took a breath. 'There are two operations running concurrently. One may be a subset of the other. Jane was running both ...'

Frank outlined Operation Abraham, the intelligence effort to expose arms running from Cuba, via Singapore, to Vietnam, China and on to North Korea. He told her about the Cuban vessel, *La Teja*, and the switching of the crateful of US-spec military equipment in Singapore which might be bound for Pyongyang.

'Are you with me?' Frank asked.

'Yes. Carry on.' Without taking her eyes off the screen Sam took another drink.

'The station here were the ones to get the *La Teja* intelligence. And they also put Jane onto a Singaporean national, Dusit Rattanatari ...'

'Spell,' Sam interrupted.

Frank did as he was asked. He then briefed her on Operation Mandolin, on Fai Zhao and Atith Jafarov, giving both of their names phonetically. He explained a little about the men's backgrounds, and how he was unclear whether or not they were in this for ideological reasons, or that their businesses were suffering and SIS intervention would go some way to levelling a playing field.

'Did Jane meet both of them?' she asked.

'She had a half-hour meeting with Zhao. I have her report; it was a prelim. It doesn't add much of substance. She was due to meet Jafarov at Kampot, that's in Cambodia close to the Vietnamese border ...'

'I know where it is,' Sam added unnecessarily.

'Quite.' If she had pissed Frank off, it didn't show. 'The thing is, her next meet, the one with Jafarov was, apparently, going to discuss a Level 1 source – or so her final report indicated.'

Wow.

International level grouping; global destabilisation.

Like the mafia from last year. Reach and effect at the highest level.

'And that's when she went missing.' It was a statement from Sam, not a question. 'You said when you called earlier you think she's still with us?'

'Correct. And I hope I'm right. Rattanatari was found dead in a warehouse on the Singapore docks. He could only be recognised by his expensive shoes ... and eventually by what was left of his dentures.'

Sam wanted to say something, but Frank stuck up a hand.

'That was four days ago,' he added. 'Which could mean Jane has been broken and she has given them something.'

'Or ...'

'Let me finish.' Frank was being surprisingly sharp. Sam was impressed.

'Two days ago someone butchered Jane's brother's dog. Cut off its head and strung up the body like a pheasant.' Frank stopped as if, this time, he was waiting for Sam to finish his thought process.

Bastards.

It was clear to her and she took his lead.

'She's definitely broken. She's given them Rattanatari and disclosed her own name. They've made a statement with the dog. A member of her family is next unless she tells them everything. It's textbook stuff. No need for waterboarding when you have the interrogee's relatives on the wrong side of a sniper rifle.'

'That's my view as well, Sam.'

Sam's eyes were dry. The air-conditioning was pumping out cold air but, as always, it was leaching moisture where it could. She blinked, holding her eyes closed for a second.

'You OK?' Frank came straight back.

'Yes, sorry. Dry eyes.' She needlessly pointed at her head.

'I have more,' he added.

'Go on.'

'I've tasked all of the local stations, including where you are now. I've also gone wide to all of the intelligence cells here in the UK, and to Europol and Interpol. GCHQ are working the electronic presence of all three men. And they've covered *La Teja*, as have the MCA (*Maritime and Coastal Agency*). I've had a couple of preliminary reports.'

Sam couldn't see, but off screen Frank appeared to be moving paper around his desk.

'None of the men have a record; police or intelligence. So far a blank there. *La Teja* is a Cuban workhorse. It sails worldwide, but over the past three years it appears to have stuck to a single itinerary: Cuba, Cape Town, Singapore, Vietnam, China and the DPRK, and then back home via Panama. I have a huge spreadsheet of ships logs and cargo. I will get onto that later.'

Frank lifted a pile of paper and waved it in front of the screen.

'What else have you got?' she asked.

178

'Beijing Station has sketchy intelligence of an upcoming major operation somewhere in East Asia. They have an agent in the Politburo. The information is coming slowly and is loose. But there's certainty there.'

Sam had never served in Beijing but had been to a presentation once on the workings of the Chinese Communist Party. The leadership was typically pyramidal. The Politburo was twenty-five strong. It sat below the Standing Committee, a smaller grouping of seven, which was one down from the General Secretary. Beijing Station's source was well placed.

Frank hadn't finished.

'Beijing also have their fingers in a "bot" farm. I'm not allowed to know the location. It's one level up in terms of capability from the "click" farm that was uncovered a couple of years ago in Kotaku. Do you remember it?'

'Sure. Ten thousand SIMs, a thousand phones and a small army of users promoting whatever the highest bidder paid for. They focused on WeChat – the Chinese equivalent of WhatsApp and Instagram combined. But the farm was capable of boosting any Instagram profile – for a price.' She remembered it well. She remembered everything well.

Frank shuffled in his chair.

'Beijing reckon the Chinese government, or maybe just a senior member of the government, is running a very capable bot farm just outside the capital. Over the past three months its focus has been Hong

Kong. Thousands of fake profiles with millions of followers peddling fake news ...'

'Supporting the government; anti pro-democracy riots?' Sam knew the answer to the question.

'Correct. They've focussed on WeChat on the mainland, but have a sophisticated operation into Facebook and Twitter. Fake websites and social media accounts peddling the government's line. It's effective, but not bombproof.'

'The protestors are still protesting,' Sam concluded.

'Yes. And in any case, the news from Beijing Station is within the next couple of days the farm is going to switch focus.'

'To what? The major operation? The Level One intelligence, whatever that it is? What?' Sam's tone was sharp; pressing.

Frank wasn't fazed. 'They don't know. But when they do they'll put out a charlie-charlie. And I'm now on that distribution.'

There was quiet for a moment. Frank sat impassively, his briefing finished. Sam's mouth twitched and she played with an ear.

'Is that what we have?' Sam broke the impasse.

'At the moment, yes.'

'And we have no idea where Fai Zhao or Atith Jafarov are?'

'No. Unless Phnom Penh or Hanoi come up with something. Or we get a breakthrough from GCHQ on their electronic or signals presence.'

Sam's mouth twitched again.

There were so many questions.

What was this about? What had Jane unearthed that was important enough for her to disappear? Why was Rattanatari murdered? Where were the two businessmen? If Frank had put a request in two days ago and there was nothing back from any of the multiple sources SIS had at their disposal, then the pair had either gone the same way as the Singaporean and nobody could match their dental records – or they were hiding for their lives.

And where is Jane?

'What did you get from the tuk-tuk company?' Frank broke into Sam's thought process.

'Nothing. Well, almost nothing. I found Jane's driver and I have her hotel details – where he picked her up from that morning. He dropped her off in town late afternoon, after she'd done the temples. At a restaurant. So I need to go to both locations.'

'Sure,' Frank replied.

There was another long silence, and this time Sam's thoughts were interrupted by the hum of the DHM's air-conditioning unit in the background. It was cold enough in the room. So much so her body involuntarily shivered.

They should turn the bloody thing off.

'What do we do now?' Frank asked.

The question surprised her. She was his agent, not the other way round. He should be giving her instructions.

Sam scratched her nose.

When you have nothing, make something happen.

It was the mantra of an instructor of hers at Fort Monkton.

Make something happen.

'You do the ship's logs. Find out where it is now. Keep pressing the intelligence community. Get a copy of the police report from the Rattanatari murder ...'

'Hang on!' Frank was writing Sam's instructions down, and he was struggling to keep up.

'We need to find Fai Zhao or Atith Jafarov. Put your best men on that. And, if nothing else, find out where *La Teja* is. If it docks somewhere, someplace soon, at least we've got one physical thing we can interrogate.'

Frank finished his jotting.

'And what will you do?'

'I've got a restaurant and a hotel to visit.'

Her hands were hovering above the keyboard. She was about to sign off. But something was bugging her.

If this is big as it sounds ...

'Frank?'

'What, Sam?'

'Why aren't we all over this like cheap emulsion?'

182

'We are, Sam. You and me. I suppose I could recruit one of the station here. In fact, I will do that.'

I don't mean ...

'I don't mean that. No offence to you, but why is this being headed up by a senior analyst at Vauxhall, and not a cross-agency team?'

Frank paused.

'I did question the boss. He said it was too sensitive and probably had too long a gestation for him to authorise that.'

Sam wasn't convinced. Not at all. Something wasn't right. And it was too early to pinpoint why.

'OK. Keep in touch.'

She pressed the escape key and Frank vanished into a charcoal screen.

Chapter 7

Matthew Stringer pushed his head back and let out a soundless yawn. It was coming towards the end of his shift and he was beginning to lose concentration. His buddy, Travis, would be along in an hour and, after a short handover, he'd be on his way home.

There wasn't much to tell him.

The subject, The Right Honourable Anne Bertram MP, hadn't left The Reform Club during his watch. And the traffic into and out of the club was all 'knowns'. Matthew had dutifully photographed and logged them. As for noise, the single mic in Miss Bertram's suite was transmitting a good deal of nothing but Classic FM. The woman had showered, if you believed the mic's output. And she had been working on her laptop, if he'd interpreted the tapping noises correctly.

She had also used her phone three times. Thanks to GCHQ his laptop had a direct link to the mainframe in Cheltenham which was tapping her phone. Two 'out calls' had been to her builder, who was renovating her house in the Chilterns – hence this three-month sojourn to her club – and the third was an 'in call', from her

184

sister. He had listened to every word, checked the compression waves against the known phonetics of the builder and Anne Bertram's sister, and typed 'Normal' against the file. The team would not need to refer to them again.

In fact, if things stayed as they were, in two days the operation would fold – an operation he'd been on it since its inception. It was a 'cabal' op: MI5, GCHQ and SRR (*Special Reconnaissance Regiment*). Two months over-watch of the house, the tapping of the Member of Parliament's phone, a mic in her constituency office in Tunbridge Wells, and a tail, which was a combination of a mobile officer on foot and navigational tracking of her car.

They reckoned they had her covered for 75% of the time, which was a good score. It would have been better if the Home Secretary had signed the wider submission, which included internal video and a GSM 'handbag' transmitter – for when she was travelling by train – but in the end they were restricted to two internal mics in the house, the phone and over-watch. And since she'd moved to the club, a mic in her suite and a front aspect obs. Things had been better in the house because SRR had very competent laser microphones and, with two perimeter teams, they had been able to get most of the voice, most of the time.

But in the end they still had nothing.

If The Right Honourable Anne Bertram was a conduit between her brother's firm and UK government policy, they'd not been able to establish it.

Which was a shame, because the intelligence pointed to a connection.

The Bertrams were old money. They'd not traced it all the way, but there was a line of succession between the brother's current firm, Tilsdent Holdings, and the East India Company. Tilsdent was nowhere near as prolific as its imperial original, but it was not without weight. Or ambition.

Tilsdent was a London-based holding company for a raft of industries and financial services that stretched from central Europe to Tokyo. On interrogation, most of the firms were legit. A couple, one of which was an arms broker, ran very close to the edge of legal – and certainly on the wrong side of moral. A few of them, however, were so opaque that, even after a year's worth of investigation, The Service still had no idea what they did.

Except one: Parker Global Bank (*PGB*).

PGB was Geneva-based and came to their attention three years ago. It wasn't a bank. Not in the conventional sense. It was a grouping of five individuals who spent their time shorting and going long on global currencies. The practice, of betting the future value of, say, Sterling, was not against the law.

Unless you had insider knowledge as to which way the currency was going to move.

And PGB seemed to have the right people in the right places. So far the cabal had put together a matrix which included an insider in the European Parliament, two individuals in Far Eastern governments and three key players in the always volatile countries in South America, where the currencies might as well be underwritten by a trampoline company.

Ordinarily an up-to-no-good Geneva-based bank with British credentials would be of interest to SIS, not The Service. But just as they were about to hand the file over to their sister organisation, Anne Bertram had been promoted to Financial Secretary to the Treasury. And that had raised a UK mainland flag. Before a cabal operation had a chance to be pulled together to investigate the newly promoted Anne Bertram, the pound had taken a 4% fall after the Trade Secretary failed to secure a previously 'guaranteed' US trade deal.

One of the biggest winners of that failure had been PGB. They had shorted the currency two days previously – and had made £560 million in the deal.

Anne Bertram's move and her family connection with Tilsdent was seen as too much of a coincidence to be a coincidence.

The cabal was on her case within a week.

But now, four months in, the operation was drawing down. And, other than establishing that Anne Bertram was very good at her job, they had uncovered nothing of note.

Matthew knew the feeling. He'd been here countless times before. Whilst the Home Secretary's signature gave them a six-month operational window, resources were so tight they could ill afford to stay on task. Indeed, he'd been called to a meeting tomorrow which had nothing to do with his current work. He reckoned he'd pulled by the evening, about the same time Anne Bertram would be free to walk the streets without company.

He yawned again, but stopped halfway through.

Hello?

He looked over the top of his tripod-steadied Leica to the entrance of the club.

A taxi had drawn up.

Visitor.

He steadied his hand on the shutter button.

According to the log, the average number of daily entries and exits to the club was 105. 'The Reform', as it is colloquial known, had around 2,700 members of which 400 or so were women. Anne Bertram was one of the 400. She also had secured one of the thirty-two residential suites.

This visitor would be entry number 43 for today, which on current track was unlikely to break any records.

Click. Click.

He spun the zoom.

Click.

He lifted his head and looked above the camera.

What?

The visitor had taken the three steps and had made it to the door.

Click. Click.

Now the visitor was inside.

That can't be?

Matthew paused ... and then he turned to his laptop to download the photographs.

It took him a couple of seconds to get the images onto the touch-sensitive screen. He dragged them round, three above two, and then enlarged the clearest one with a finger and thumb.

No doubt about it.

He reduced it.

And then looked at the last photo he had taken.

He enlarged that.

It was a difficult image to interpret as the glass in The Reform's front door was reflecting the façade of the building next to his.

But that is her?

Yes?

Anne Bertram had met the visitor just inside the main door. Which was very unusual.

Nobody does that; that's the doorman's role.

Unless ...

The visitor was special.

Was she going to take him to her suite? Surely not?

Could I be so lucky?

He reached for his headphones and put them on.

Nothing. A slight background hiss. Some very low level knocking.

Probably the floor above.

He waited.

And waited.

…

He took off the headphones and stood up, his eyes always fixed on the door.

He sat down again.

He poured himself some tea from his flask.

There was nothing from the speaker. Nothing from the phonetics app.

…

He fidgeted.

…

Twenty minutes later and still nothing.

Then there was movement. And he was on it.

Click. Click. Click.

The visitor was leaving. This time Anne Bertram's face was in the frame. She was there, by the door.

Click. Click.

And the taxi was gone. The meet was over. The front door was closed.

He breathed out. And then, just as last time, he quickly transferred the images, got them up on the screen and started playing with them; picking out the best for the main report – the rest would go straight to file.

Ping – ping.

An SMS from the MP's phone. It popped up in a dialogue box on his screen. It was to a +41 number – *Switzerland*, via Cheltenham. He opened it.

It read:

Meeting successful. There is benefit on both sides. We should talk.

Matthew stared at his screen for a couple of seconds. This was crazy. *Just crazy*. The Financial Secretary to the Treasury had just met with Sir Clive Morton, the Chief of the Secret Intelligence Service, at a discreet private club in central London. The outcome of the meeting was a text to a Swiss number that could well belong to PGB, an organisation known to undermine national currencies. And the message was, 'there was benefit to both sides'.

What the hell am I going to do with this?

Axis Hospital, Petrovaradinska 1, Zagreb, Croatia

Jackson was feeling groggy. His head was full of wood chippings and his shoulder was thudding away to the beat of some far-distant drum.

At least I'm here.

'Here' was both here in hospital – and not a bad one by the look of it – and also of this world. He'd only been with it for an hour or so and most of that time had been occupied with a deep reflection of how lucky he had been – twice.

The explosion was with him. Front and centre. He remembered every little detail, as he had from Iraq. He was walking down the sidewalk, which was broad, maybe nine feet wide. He was still parallel with the Mission Center, its high-walled perimeter and barbed wire top on his left, and row of vehicles on his right. Sedans, not pickups. Two silvers and a red? *Maybe*.

The bomb had detonated in front of him, possibly two cars further down. He remembered seeing the sun-bright light of the explosion forward-right. It was a split second of whites and red and yellows – and a black shape, probably a car, which was rising and contorting. And then he was over, in the air and finally on his back with a thud.

He reckoned he was maybe thirty feet from the seat of the bomb.

That close.

He'd been further away in Karbala.

And yet, here he was. Sitting up in bed with nothing more than a hole in his shoulder and some splintered bones to moan about.

Elation. That's what it was.

He'd felt it before. The acute sense of surviving something he shouldn't've.

And, if it was like before, the darkness would come. Maybe in a month. Maybe longer. That overwhelming sense of sorrow and lethargy. That nothing mattered anymore.

That's what he'd got last time. That he'd survived when others hadn't.

Maybe this time ...?

Maybe it wouldn't be so bad.

Maybe.

He'd only seen a nurse so far. She'd been at his bedside when he woke, redressing his shoulder. She was short, young and slim; dark haired, angular ... pretty. What a vision to be greeted with when he'd woken from the dead.

He'd asked if she spoke English.

'No.' Thick and gravelly.

Sexy.

He needed to get a grip. The last thing the young girl needed was a forty-something American making her feel uncomfortable.

She had smiled, more forced than natural. And he had let her finish her job.

'Anyone else injured?' he'd asked speculatively.

She'd stopped dressing him at that point.

Another forced smile and a shake of her head. He hadn't known if she hadn't understood the question, or he was only one injured,

She had finished his bandage with some tape and left him in a bright, single room. It had one outside

193

window. The place was decorated with the usual medicinal paraphernalia: drips; machines with wires; a noticeboard with papers hanging from clips. There was an over-bed table which sported a jug of water and some fruit, and a further window with half-closed blinds which looked out onto a corridor. To his right was a TV. It wasn't on. His clothes were hanging from a hat stand in the corner and, as he took this all in, he reached for the drawer to his right (*shit, that hurts*) and found his phone – which was out of juice – and his wallet. He had no reason not to trust the staff, but he checked for ID, his bank cards and his cash. They were all there.

He forced his backside against the pillows, lifting his torso a touch. His shoulder stung whilst his mind churned.

Was he the only survivor? He remembered seeing at least one other person on the sidewalk, and the gate guard was just a few feet behind him.

Why? Why did this happen?

Was the Mission Center the target?

His mind was empty then. There were no immediate answers.

Think.

He pressed on.

Was this to do with Bae Ki-tae?

No.

No. That didn't make any sense.

What did make sense?

194

Zagreb's threat level was 'Guarded': *general risk of terrorist attacks.* 'Guarded' was one up from 'Low', and one down from 'Elevated'. Mission centres didn't operate at 'Low'. They were always at least 'Guarded'. As such Zagreb was as likely to be attacked as he would play for the Giants.

But it had been

Was there a connection?

His shoulder wrestled with further thought.

'Jackson!'

It was the boss. At the door.

'Hi, Chief.' Jackson acknowledged him, raising the hand that wasn't attached to a shoulder which was doing a deal with the devil.

The man was at his bedside in a couple of strides. His facial expression was mixed. Concern, relief and tiredness played with the lines on his face.

'How you doing?'

Jackson nodded and forced a smile. 'Fine, thanks. I've not yet spoken to a doctor. But, the shoulder's sore, and my face hurts when I smile 'cos of the burns. But I sense it will all heal.'

'Good. Good.' It was hardly a chorus of sympathy. The Chief was distracted. Lost for words almost.

Jackson felt obliged to fill the void.

'What happened, Chief?'

The boss looked for a chair. He found one, pulled it up and sat down with a finality that might mean he might never leave. A bomb in your own backyard must be one of the most difficult things to deal with.

'An IED. In a Ford. Not big enough to bring down a building, but big enough to turn the car over ...'

'Was anyone else hurt?' Jackson interrupted.

'There was a young girl on the opposite side of the street. She took shrapnel to her face. Looks set to lose an eye. Our guard, Jimmy, was blown over, but no real damage. And there was an old man, behind you, walking away, he was knocked over. Had a heart attack. It's touch and go.'

There was a natural pause. There were others, then. Of course there would be. But they were minor players, weren't they? The bomb was meant for him? Jackson stared ahead, his eyes focusing on nothing in particular. As his brain emerged from the fog, he could only find one plausible answer.

'It was my bomb. They wanted me.' Jackson's comment was quiet, but strong.

The Chief was rubbing his forehead.

'That's my call, too. But why?' the Chief asked.

'The North Korean? It's all too close. Too much, too quickly not to be linked. We know there's nothing from the murder scene, apart from a match and some thread. And they're probably irrelevant. But the solid state drive, the cipher and the photos. Maybe they'd put in train a series of questions to which the answer was, "take out Jackson White Jr"?'

He stared at his boss. Who was looking bewildered.

'Cipher? You told me about the photos – I've seen them. But I don't know anything about a code?'

Of course.

He doesn't know.

The images from the solid state drive of the hole in the ground had been in his last report. They were on the board with the sixty-five from the murder scene. But the code ... that was as green as grass. He'd just got the translation back from Langley and, other than him, the only two people in Zagreb who knew about it were Ron and Jolene. He'd just handed the documents over to Jolene when he'd stepped out of the building. And then, *boom ...*

It took him less than a minute to update the Chief on the cipher.

'Is that why Jolene is sitting outside, waiting for you to come around? I told her to stay where she was until I'd seen you.'

'Is she?' Jackson's tone was caught between excitement and resignation. All of a sudden his shoulder was yelling at him louder than the drugs could mute. And he was hungry – and he needed a piss. She had something? Already? God, she must be good. And yet he was struggling to summon the energy to be bothered.

'Sure. Do you want to see her? There's been no movement on the Bae Ki-tae case since the bomb. We've had our hands full. But if the two are connected?' The

Chief was at a canter. Jackson guessed he was clutching at straws. Any straws would do.

Jackson must have been grimacing because the next thing the Chief said was, 'Do you want me to put someone else on this?'

Yes, please.

'No' He was shaking his head, sending all the wrong signals. How long after Ramallah had he broken down? Three weeks? A month? It had come without warning, hit him like a truck and hung about for six months. And then left just as quickly. If the same scenario played out, he didn't have long before he'd be as useless as saddle without stirrups. 'Let's get her in, can you, please?'

'Sure. Right away,'

The Chief was out the door two strides later.

Residence 101, Sala Kamreuk Road, Siem Reap, Cambodia

'Thanks.' Sam's smile was as big as the welcome she'd received at the boutique hotel. The price was ridiculously inexpensive, the rooms magnificent and the staff genuinely friendly. She could afford to move in and never leave. It was a thought.

The local woman pulled open the sliding balcony door and Sam followed her outside. They were two out of three floors up. The view, overlooking a compact courtyard pool and, at eye level, across the rooftops of the neighbouring houses to a perfectly round, setting sun, iced the cake. She had no idea how long she was going to stay here, but a good night's sleep and a decent breakfast would go some way to expunge a combination of jetlag, a round trip and a half from Phnom Penh to Siem Reap, and the emotional exhaustion that was pulling at her arms and squashing her spine as if she had been lugging around a couple of jerry cans.

I need to rest.

She needed rest. Everything was catching up with her. Leaving the UK; the long flight; the damp heat; Frank; the constant travelling; the batshit driving; and the fact neither the restaurant nor the hotel could add anything to the Gemma Ruby story.

No one at the restaurant recognised Jane's photo on Sam's phone. That didn't surprise her. It was packed full when Sam had got there. There must have had over sixty covers and with a one and a half hour turnover, she reckoned on close to 250 guests a night. And Jane had been there six weeks ago. Sam's face recognition was the best there was … but there was no way she'd have remembered Jane unless there had been a particular reason to.

The hotel scored at least one point. The woman who had just left Sam's room remembered Jane. 'Lovely lady. Very generous.' Sam didn't know if that had been a hint. *Probably not* – Jane was always generous. But the woman couldn't offer anything else. As far as she was concerned Jane had not met anyone in the hotel. And,

199

only after Sam suggested Jane was lost and possibly in danger, had she given Sam Jane's stay-dates – which were not a surprise.

'She left very early in the morning. She had booked in for three nights, but only stayed for two. She left quickly.' The woman had added, 'She had paid for all three nights,'

So, Sam was caught between a real desire to do something – to make something happen – and the need for rest. There was nothing she could actually do that might be helpful other than, maybe, head down to Kampot which Frank had said was Jane's likely destination post Siem Reap. The small riverside town was about 300 kilometres due south from where she was now – probably six or seven hours in a car. Although they did fly from Siem Reap to Phnom Penh, which was an option.

But why? What would she do when she got there? She needed something more specific. Do nothing, unusually for her, looked like a sensible choice.

For now.

She needed a shower, and probably handwash some smalls – and eat the remaining nuts and fruit she'd picked up from the market. That was unless the sleeping bear didn't bite her backside first.

And she had to call Frank. They'd not spoken since this morning's video link at the embassy. It had taken her three hours to get to Siem Reap, courtesy of a swerving taxi driven by a toothless Cambodian rally driver. No gap was too small; no corner too sharp. At least she'd got here in one piece. Just. She'd kept her knees together and her eyes half-closed most of the way. In a previous existence she might have hollered at the driver, but in her exhausted and fractious state of mind, if that had been her final journey she could hardly say she hadn't lived.

Shower.

Then eat. Then sleep.

A phone rang. It wasn't hers.

What?

Of course. It was the on-loan embassy satphone: old, larger than any of her pockets, and with an antenna that could take your eye out. But it was encrypted; which was a 'tick'. She'd had to sign three forms before they'd handed it over. It was hardly Q at Vauxhall, who gave away gadgets like his stores were on fire.

She dug it out of her bag and pressed the green phone icon.

'Sam?'

It was Frank.

'Yes.'

'We've got Atith Jafarov. That is, we have his phone.'

Sam's head cleared. Instantly.

'Where is he?'

'Are you in Phnom Penh?' His words were sharp – staccato.

'No. Siem Reap. Restaurant and hotel. It's been a yo-yo day. Where is he?'

Get on with it, Frank.

'Good. He's in a small village, due west of you: Krakor. The phone is in a house. You're on the wrong side ...'

'Wrong side of what?' *Come on, Frank. Make sense.*

'I've got an overhead open on my monitor. There's a body of water between Siem Reap and Krakor. Quite a big one. Think ...' Frank was clearly the one thinking, 'Windermere.'

Sam could picture it.

'Give me the LOCSTAT.' Sam reverted to military shorthand for 'location state'.

Frank dithered, as if he were about to handover the password to his bank account.

Then, 'You ready for a "what3words" location?'

'Send.' Sam again resorted to the military vernacular.

'Visibility-dot-gruff-dot-elevator.'

What3words had overtaken lat and long as the guaranteed method of location tagging. It mapped the whole globe, was accurate to 3 metres and bombproof. As far as Sam knew, every Western intelligence service now used it. The UK security infrastructure had gone one step further and provide a daily-changing code which switched each of the fixed words with a series of numbers. She didn't have the decode protocol – and Frank hadn't used it.

visibility.gruff.elevator.

It took her two seconds to get the what3words app up on her phone.

Frank continued. 'Jafarov's phone's pinging as we speak. I have it on the monitor here. Where you are is as closer than a team from Phnom Penh Station, if I could get one together. And I don't know how quickly they would act. And, frankly, I'm not sure we should barge right in. Maybe recce the place first?'

Sam didn't reply straight away. She already had the what3words map open with the location highlighted. The village of Krakor was 120-odd kilometres from her, a long detour around the bottom of Tonlé Sap, a large lake in the centre of the country. Forty klicks as the crow flew.

Why is nothing ever easy?

'I'm on my way.'

She threw her phone on her bed and started repacking her backpack.

Axis Hospital, Petrovaradinska 1, Zagreb, Croatia

Jackson placed the three-page report on the bedcovers. Jolene, who had now left, had done a fabulous job in a ridiculously short space of time. The problem was, what she had decoded didn't make any sense. Sure, it was written in English, but he couldn't understand what the output was telling him.

> *We have found 5toa. It's operational. Could be used by both sides.*

He'd pressed Jolene on the '5toa'. It was the only word that didn't make sense.

'Yes, I'm sure,' she had replied. 'That's what it says. That's the decode.'

Jolene had explained the coding was unique – one she had never come across before – but not so difficult to break. It was, apparently, a four-stage process.

'You start in Korean, and that's translated into English: stage one. Stage two ...' she had been using her fingers by way of demonstration, '... is turning the English into Morse code. I've ain't ever seen it done before; kinda clever. It's not difficult, but you've gotta know what you're at. Easy to miss.' She was now pointing to the translated sheet and her pencil marks. 'Vowels are "dots", and consonants are "dashes". Morse code. See here: consonant-vowel pair. That's a dash-dot. Translated from Morse, an "N" in real life. You see, it repeats twice, here and here. That's clever. I really like it.'

Jolene certainly was clever. And, just then, Jackson really liked her.

'But it's not as straightforward as that. Stage three is sorting all of the permutations. In code the number five, you see, is five dots – five vowels. But in Morse five dots, as well as the number five, could be two "Es" and an "S", or an "H" and an "E", or twenty-three other combinations. That's stage three. Sorting that all out. And stage four, well that's taking the mess and making the message.'

Jackson had kept up – sort of – although his shoulder was telling him not to care.

'So, Jolene, 5-t-o-a could be any number of other mixture of letters and numbers?'

'Correct. I have listed all of those on the third page. But there's a rhythm here. And I found it. So I think you just need to establish what 5toa means. That's the key.'

He couldn't. No matter how key.

Jolene had left him an hour ago, the Chief thirty minutes before that. And he was no further forward. He was tired and sore. And the drugs were turning his mind to mush. Ten minutes ago he'd asked the very attractive nurse if he could use the men's room. She'd helped him out of bed and, with tears of pain forming in his eyes, he had waddled his drip carrier out of his room with the nurse keeping an eye a few feet from him. As he hit the corridor he was initially surprised, and then comforted, to see an armed Croat policeman sitting on a chair. When he got there, using the john introduced a new

205

level of pain. By the time he got back to bed he was shattered.

Sleep was not far away.

But what is 5toa?

He was convinced it had something to do with the hole in the ground. *Definitely*. The cipher had arrived at the same time as the photos. They were inextricably linked.

He glanced at sheet three of Jolene's report. There were seventy-one different versions of the code which she'd interpreted as 5toa.

He had a hole, so he looked for the letter 'H'. It was in six of Jolene's possible decodes. The one that caught his eye was 'HASK'.

Hole above … something … and Korea? Or South Korea?

Could be?

Possibly not.

He tried again. But he couldn't see any connection.

He closed his eyes. Scrunched them together, fighting tiredness.

Jolene had the rhythm. She did.

So 5toa would remain his best bet.

The number five. And then: tango; oscar; alpha.

He opened his eyes, picked up his phone which had been charging and googled, '5toa'.

It surprised him to find there were some sensible entries.

The first told him that TOA was an abbreviation for a Swedish industrial company. He'd ask one of his team to press Stockholm Mission Center to see if that lead took them anywhere.

Next, and more promising, 5toa was a biological protein. He didn't begin to understand the papers that Google offered but, away from context of the photographs, the message now made sense.

We have found 5toa. It's operational. Could be used by both sides.

We have found a biological protein.

It was operational and could be used for both sides.

Was it a biological weapon?

Could proteins kill?

But what about the images? The hole? The bit of metal, sticking out of the ground?

He wasn't sure.

And what about the IED – the bomb with his name on it? And the timing of all of this. Bae's death. The toothbrush solid state drive. The images and the Korean translation, just as the bomb with his name on it had exploded.

And the upcoming summit.

It was all so quick. So *precise.*

Someone was in the loop.

Who?

And …

… who do I trust?

The Chief, probably. Jolene – clearly. Ron? The three members of staff running down the images?

Anyone at Langley?

Come on. What sort of question was that?

He closed Google, opened the telephone app and phoned Ron, who picked up immediately.

'Yeah, hi, Jackson. I was going to come and see you later. How are you doing?'

'Fine, Ron. Well, not so great, but I'll live.' Jackson had his phone in one hand and Jolene's report in the other. 'Have you got some free time?'

'Sure. The Chief is getting us together every six hours for IED updates, but I'm not on anything ... not really.'

'OK. Good. Get on with this. First I need a secure link and a laptop. By tonight. Second, get hold of Jolene's cipher report, the one she's just done for me. Read it and then, as quietly as you can, try and get to the bottom of the word, "number five, letters tango-oscar-alpha". It will mean nothing to you now, but it will do once you see the report. Happy so far?'

There was a pause. Jackson assumed Ron was finishing writing something down.

'Sure, Jackson. Next?'

'I want a report on what sensible permutations there might be for 5toa by lunchtime tomorrow. Got it?'

If Ron was concerned by the deadline Jackson didn't feel it.

'And let me know as soon as the center gets anything on the IED.'

'You think there's a Korean connection?' Ron came straight back at him.

'I think the bomb was meant for me.'

There was a pause. Ron was processing.

'But that doesn't add up?'

'Why?'

'How can someone pull an IED off that quickly? It must have been planned for months?' Ron's incredulity poured out of Jackson's handset.

'Maybe, Ron. Or maybe they're just very, very good at this?'

'What, you mean ...?'

'Exactly. So be careful. *Very* careful. And see you later with the laptop. Bring some cookies.'

Krakor, Pursat Province, Cambodia

Sam asked the taxi driver to pull over. They'd reached the centre of Krakor, a small but bustling town on one of the country's national routes. The road was single carriageway and paved, and they'd stopped just short of a junction. Here a minor track crossed the main road, and headed off into the dark of the countryside. And it was just that: tracks. According to the information Frank had sent her, the location of Jafarov's phone was off to her right some 60 metres away. She'd asked the taxi driver to stop short as she wanted to approach on foot.

She paid the driver and stepped out of the poorly air-conditioned car. She was met by a wall of heat. It might be gone ten in the evening, but nobody had turned down the thermostat. She reckoned it was still well past 30 degrees.

Krakor was alive. A roadside market was still open – a multiple of stalls appeared to be selling anything you ever needed. They were haphazardly covered with dark canopies under which naked flames in pots and glasses displayed their wares. And it was still attracting customers. Opposite the market, a shadowy, two-storey colonial arcade whispered of a more prosperous past. Breaking the mould and set back from the road, one or two of the houses were ostentatiously smart, with outlandishly decorative entrances of pillars and, now mostly grey in the dark, pastel-painted balustrades. The display of limited wealth stopped there. It seemed that, apart from the few, everyone else wasn't quite so fortunate. Shabby block and rust coloured, corrugated iron-roofed buildings made up much of what Sam could see. In the distance, lit by the lights of a passing car, she spotted makeshift dwellings constructed with wood frames and plastic sheeting.

And, as she headed north along the track that ran perpendicular to the main road, the poorer dwellings won.

Barely a house.

210

A shack.

Then, on her left, a more palatial building: three-storey – the bottom incomplete, with room for a paddy field tractor – with a tiled roof.

Wasteland both sides.

Another wood, canvas and plastic-sheeted dwelling.

Two more.

She reckoned she was 15 metres short now. The what3word, 3 metres square, was ahead of her and slightly right.

It was properly dark now. Much of the ambient light from the town was behind her. Even though her eyes were now attuned to the lack of light, anything below the horizon was a black cat in a coal scuttle.

She moved off the track to her left, giving the what3word location as much room as she could.

She came across a car: *mid-80s, blue Toyota Corolla.* She walked around it. And a second: *silver Lexus RS 250.* Both facing back the way she had come. She clocked their number plates. Across from her: a tuk-tuk. She captured the image. Further down was a yellow – could be green in the lack of light – Hyundai, H100 minibus. It was facing down the track which led to the lake. She walked until she could make out the plates.

Gotcha.

And then. To her right, set back – and exactly where the app on her phone told her it would be – a hut. It might be a house, or a large garage; wholly corrugated iron with a wooden door and window on the front aspect.

Planks and rust.

With a light on inside.

It was a dim light, but it was better than darkness.

Sam jogged forward to the minibus and crouched behind it, the sweat on the backs of her legs sticking flesh to flesh. She dug out the embassy satphone from her rucksack. And dialled Frank.

'Sam?'

'Yeah. I'm here. The location is a large hut. There's a light inside, three vehicles on the road opposite. I'm going to read out the registration numbers. Ready?'

Sam waited.

'Go,' was Frank's response.

She read out the details.

'I'm going for a look see.'

'Sam, wait ...'

She hung up, slung her pack and then, checking the coast was clear, jogged across the road onto the far verge. A second later she was at the front left corner of the shack. Now enveloped in the night and shadows, she knelt down.

And listened.

...

Insects. A distant car.

Nothing.

The route around the outside of the building needn't be a journey into the inky unknown. She could use the light on her phone. Or ...

... with her hands straight out in front of her she shuffled forward.

Bush, next to the wall. She pushed past that, some branches scratching at her face. Bush finished. A clearing? Rubbish underfoot. *Careful*. As dark as pitch.

But a glimmer ahead.

She stopped. And listened.

...

A muffled cry. Could be. Might be an animal?

A thud. Definitely from inside the building.

She strained her ears.

...

She moved onto the corner, to where the siren-like light was singing.

She knelt. And listened.

...

Nothing.

...

She poked her head around the corner. A small, scruffy garden lit by the dull glow from the panes of a half-glazed door. It wasn't much but it was better than nothing.

Crouching, below window level, she shuffled to the door.

Pring, pring!
Shit!

It was her satphone. Which was in her bag.

Idiot!

The ringing pierced the darkness like a wolf's cry, she scrambled for her bag.

And then it was off, the sound muted.

She waited, poised – ready to turn and run.

She listened some more. But all she heard was the blood punching her eardrums.

...

A new sound. The engine of a car turning over. Petrol. Big. Throaty. Six cylinders.

It was one of the cars from the front?

The Lexus.

Yes.

Two choices – she didn't have time to rehearse them.

She turned and, as quick as no visibility allowed, she made her way back to the front of the building, her face scratching against the bush, her balance almost lost by a poorly positioned piece of rubble. She skidded to a halt short of the front of the hut.

And looked.

The Lexus was gone. The tuk-tuk, Toyota and minibus were still there.

The satphone, which was still in her hand, buzzed. She checked. It was Frank.

There's an issue.

He wouldn't have kept phoning her. He knew better than that.

She connected.

'Yes?' As quiet as a light breeze.

'Jafarov's phone's on the move. Heading back towards the main road.' Frank was also whispering.

Fuck.

'One of the vehicles from out front has just left. The Lexus. I'm on foot. No transport. There may still be people in the house.' She stopped for a second and listened. Nothing but the buzz of the phone. 'Track the phone. I'll see what's in the building. We can catch up later.' Sam didn't wait for a reply. She disconnected and made her way back round the house.

A few seconds later and with more scratches to her face, she was kneeling at the back door again.

She lifted her head up and peered in. Her eyes adjusted.

And then she immediately dropped down.

Fuck.

This doesn't look good.

She raised her torso again, the top of her head looking over the wood of the door like a Chad.

Shit.

A mid-sized room with a door on the far wall leading into a darkened second room. A lit, low-wattage light dangled from the ceiling.

What it illuminated was a grotesque mess.

The room was completely empty apart from a chair and a man. They were as one, lying on their side in the centre of the room, their backs to Sam. The man was

215

trussed to the chair, his hands tied behind the wooden uprights – his feet to the front legs.

Neither man nor chair were moving.

Nor was the pool of blood in which he was lying.

She watched for any sign that the body might be alive.

No. Nothing.

No ripples from the shallow pond of blood.

She listened.

Nothing.

...

Either the body was that of Jafarov and his assailant(s) had taken his phone. Or he had been involved in the murder, and had just left the scene phone in hand.

There was only one way to find out.

Still half-crouching, Sam tried the door. It clicked and opened. She pushed it ajar. And listened.

Nothing.

She stood. Waited. And was just about to enter when she looked to her left. She spotted a fist-sized rock on the floor. She picked it up.

Then she tentatively walked in.

The badly drawn oval of blood was a couple of metres wide and there was no way she could check for a pulse without getting her sandals wet. And she didn't want that.

Instead, she walked round one side of the body and stood in the frame of the door of the second room, looking into the blackness.

And listened.

Nothing.

She turned and, now facing the corpse, walked to the edge of the blood. She crouched.

The man's face was a mess. His shirt had been ripped open and there were cuts and gouges across his chest.

And ... *holy shit* ... his fingers were sticking out at all sorts of angles.

She stood and made some calculations. She walked around the body and checked her numbers from a different angle.

She placed her weapon on the floor, took out her own phone and snapped some photos, the flash exposing the torture and death horror show.

Then, using the satphone, she phoned Frank.

'Sam?'

'Do we know what Jafarov looked like?' she asked.

'We have one image. Not a great one. We're working on it.'

'OK, I'm going to send you some photos of a dead man. He's been tortured. His face is a mess, but you might be able to get something. As far as I can tell he's got nothing on him to assist, and I'm not prepared to sully the evidence by stepping in five pints of blood. The photos won't tell you his height. But I reckon he's 182, maybe 185. Which is tall for a local …'

'Wait one,' Frank interrupted.

There was a pause. Sam wasn't sure Frank had fully registered she was hanging about where someone had recently been brutally murdered.

'I'm not in the queue to have my nails done, Frank.'

'Sorry. 182 is the height we have for Jafarov. Could be a match.'

Clunk.

Scrape.

Sam froze. And disconnected the phone. She slowly and gently reached down and picked up the rock.

There was a shuffle from next door.

Choices?

There was only one.

In a single step she moved silently to the side of the doorframe.

Shuffle. Shuffle.

A pause. Then …

… the belly of a short man announced itself through the doorway at the same time as a hand holding a pistol. In that instant, Sam switched off the light.

'*Que?*'

Self-defence training at Monkton was just that: self-defence. She was good at it, but it didn't teach her how to disarm a short, fat man carrying a handgun – with only a rock.

Sod it.

In one motion Sam pulled her arm back and swung it, short-fat-man head height and with all of the strength she could muster.

Bearing in mind she was now working in a darkness she had orchestrated, the sound of rock smashing against flesh and bone was a satisfying one. Even more to her liking, she heard the handgun *twang* against a nearby wall ... and then the *thud* of a short, fat man, now pistol-less, collapsing to the floor.

Lights on.

The man was out of it – semi-conscious. The fingers on both hands were doing a bad job of stopping the blood from his face spoiling more of the floor. The good news was that they were dulling the sound of a low-pitched scream.

It took her twenty seconds to collect the gun, grab the man's wallet and phone from his trouser pockets and make it to the front door.

Wait.

She sprinted back to the short, fat man and checked his pockets again.

Nothing. *Shit.*

Hang on.

His short-sleeve shirt had a breast pocket.

Keys. Good.

No fob. *Bad.*

Toyota or Hyundai?

She knew she had limited time. She'd try the Toyota first.

Sam was out of the shack in seconds and sprinted across the road to the Toyota. She stuck the main key in the driver's-side lock.

Nope.

Move

As she ran to the Hyundai she glanced across at the tuk-tuk.

Knowing my luck ...

She pushed the key into the minibus's driver's door. It worked.

Thank fuck for that.

She jumped in and turned the van over. It started first time.

In seconds she expertly spun the yellow – could be green – Hyundai H100 through 180 degrees and, now with a hand and shoulder that were reminding her they had been involved in a fight, she sped away from the dead man and the not so dead short, fat man.

Chapter 8

Anchor Bankside Pub, 1615 Thameside, London

Matthew was sitting on one of four red, faux-leather dining room chairs that served a highly-varnished table. The table was one of fifteen or so that were hemmed in by wood panelling, in a pub which always tried its best to belong to a previous existence. The purple, red and cream paisley carpet, which finished short of the bar to show off wood tiling, was displaying signs of wear – which added to the olde-worlde effect. Sepia pictures of old barges, quays and riverside warehouses reminded of a once industrial past. Between which, chalkboards told a different story. One where food and drink prices had easily kept pace with London future.

Matthew's pal and senior colleague, Howard, was at the bar collecting a couple of pints. Mathew had asked to meet his friend off-site because, well, he had no idea what to do next.

Which was as mad as a fish; off any chart he'd could think of.

It wasn't that what he had seen from the over-watch across from The Reform Club was out of the ordinary – which it was. It was that something, somewhere, told him not to stick the photos or names in the log. There was little he could do about the SMS from

221

Anne Bertram's phone to, what he now knew was, the number of a Swiss national. That's because the text would be on GCHQ's file which he couldn't amend. His report had, therefore, noted the details of the SMS (*Meeting successful. There is benefit on both sides. We should talk*), but made no further comment.

But he hadn't transferred the images, or made any remarks about Anne Bertram's visitor. And, so far, the operation's manager hadn't quizzed him on the SMS entry into the log. Matthew struggled with that, which all added to where he found himself now: confused, and a bit lost.

Howard arrived with the pints. Matthew pushed a couple of beer mats around the table; his friend placed a glass on each. And then sat down.

'So, mate. What's the problem? Career? Ex-wife? Sex?'

Matthew laughed, took a sip of his beer, licked the froth from his lips and replied, 'Yeah, mostly all of those.'

His pal smiled and nodded.

'Thought so.'

They both took another sip.

In the pause Matthew looked up at an old brown and white photo on the wall next to the table. It was a shot taken from the pub looking across the Thames. He guessed the photographer wanted to show the river at work. There were ships and barges of all shapes and sizes. Most of the boats were open topped, and piles of coal and aggregate climbed from the hulls like miniature mountains. On the far bank was a continuous line of brick wharfs and warehouses, reaching five storeys, but no higher. Significantly, although paler, above the horizontal slabs of quays and toiling river was the lone silhouette of St Paul's Cathedral. Perspective meant that the image had only captured the mighty dome although, if he squinted, he could make out the two, square bell towers. They popped up further to the left, seemingly disassociated from the cupola.

For a reason he couldn't grasp, he suddenly felt even more uneasy about what he had done, and what he was going to do next. He wasn't a religious man, but there was something resolutely honourable about the cathedral. It had survived the Blitz. It spoke of generations of Brits who'd done the right thing, even when the world had thought it sensible to head off in a different direction.

And that's where Matthew thought he was now: heading off in a different direction.

In the past few years his country had become polarised. It wasn't necessary the left and the right, nor the religious and the atheists, although there was some of that. It was more nationalist versus globalist: England against the world. And that was being mirrored elsewhere, particularly in the US.

Bizarrely, and this was why he'd asked to meet Howard, it had permeated through his workspace. There were plenty of the staff who didn't wear their views on their sleeves. And there were a number who feigned 'no opinion'; they just wanted to live out their busy albeit comfortable lives. But it was a badly kept secret – in one of the three national institutions where secrets were paramount – that there was conflict amongst the senior echelons of The Box (*colloquialism for MI5*) as to the UK's place in the world. Matthew argued the smart money was to continue to share resources globally. But many were now advocating holding their expertise close. Sharing intelligence and assets with a very select group. A month ago he'd picked up this was no longer an issue of making a choice between nations; those countries we can trust, and those we should not. But the talk was of decisions being made on the basis of personality. Which individuals could we work with in the NSA, the BND and DGSE? Which names could we trust at Interpol?

More worryingly, who could we trust at Vauxhall and SO15?

In Thames House?

Who was on *our* side?

And was he on the right side?

In amongst this ideological conflict he was unsure about the manager of the Anne Bertram operation. He was a vocal nationalist and, at times, Matthew sensed a deep-seated xenophobia – which was a particularly unattractive trait for a member of The Box. He was also young and ambitious. And he had the ear of a couple of the deputies.

In short, Matthew didn't like him – and didn't trust him – although he was clearly good at what he did.

But why keep the Clive Morton/Anne Bertram meet from him? What possible reason did Matthew have to hold close a highly irregular and possibly suspect liaison between the Chief of Secret Intelligence Service and the sister of a man who ran a global business, where a good chunk of it was at best below the radar; at worst illegal?

He didn't know. But something nagged at him. Something strong enough to make him doctor a report. An action that, if discovered, might mean he would be out of a job.

'What's the issue, Matt?' Howard asked.

They were both a third of a pint down their glasses and they'd hardly said a word to each other.

Matthew scrunched up his face and breathed out through his nose. He looked to the bar, and then back to his pal.

Here goes.

It took him a hushed five minutes to describe the events of late-afternoon yesterday and his report's omissions. After which he downed the rest of the pint and then asked his friend, 'One more?'

Howard nodded, a touch solemnly.

'Please.'

A couple of minutes later they both had fresh beers and his pal was staring right at him, eye to eye.

'And you tell me this because you don't trust the operation's manager?' Howard asked. Matthew had purposely not mentioned the man's name.

Matthew nodded. 'What with everything ... you know, the supposed conflict at the top, I dunno? Either Vauxhall's chief is working an angle – on our patch – which directly infects an operation we're running. That sort of shit happens, although it shouldn't. Or, it's something much bigger. More nefarious.' He paused for a second, concern etched on his forehead. 'The reason I bring it to you is, first, I trust you.' He paused a beat, hoping that would score some points. 'And second, I don't have the contacts at Vauxhall, not ones high enough placed to let us know if Sir Clive Morton is running his own operation in which Anne Bertram is an agent. Or, something more unspeakable. You do. You can ask around.' He raised both hands and sported an 'I'm lost' look.

Neither man said anything for a while. Both took sips of their drinks.

'OK. I don't need to know anything more. This whole thing is highly irregular and, if you don't mind me saying, slightly paranoid. But I'll chase it down for you.' Howard paused as he finished off his pint. 'On one proviso.'

'What's that?'

'If I get nothing from this. Or something which relieves you of your paranoia, you'll take everything you have and stick it back on record.'

That caught Matthew. He took a gulp of the quarter of a pint that was still resting on the table.

All of a sudden the reality of what he was doing hit him hard.

He would need to think of something very plausible to fill the gap he'd created. He just didn't know what. His career might be over, regardless.

'Deal,' he replied.

Axis Hospital, Petrovaradinska 1, Zagreb, Croatia

'I'm thinking that perhaps the best person to answer this is a Korean, preferably someone from the north.' Ron was helping himself to a couple of the grapes he'd brought along for Jackson.

'I think that's a great idea. The problem is, other than Bae Ki-tae, I don't know any North Koreans,' Jackson answered. He was sitting up in bed having slept fitfully for a couple of hours overnight. He felt more human having washed and shaved with the help of the second shift nurse who, with more facial hair than the apparition he'd initially woken to, had made collaboration easier, but nowhere near as much fun.

'We could try Langley. They'll have the database of known defectors and could get a couple of opinions soon enough.'

'No.' Jackson's response was immediate and firm.

His sleep had been fitful because it was laced with a recurring dream – more like nightmare. His waking recollection of the explosion was still surprisingly vivid. And that scene had been amplified in his sleep. In the depths of the night the bomb was bigger, the casualties greater. He was simultaneously injured and uninjured. As only dreams can do, bits of his body had become detached at the same time as he was orchestrating the event. He'd used one of those comic ACME detonators – the red box with the plunger handle. Every time the incident was reconstructed by his subconscious, it was he who forced down the plunger.

And each time he was receiving his instructions from a man in the shadows; dark-suited and sunglass-wearing.

He'd woken in a sweat, his shoulder jabbing at his nerves. But the image from his dreams stayed with him. The subliminal message was clear: he was being manipulated.

By a man in the shadows. In a dark suit and shades.

'No.' His repetition was softer. 'I can't see how the IED could have been pulled together without insider knowledge.' He paused and looked at Ron, searching for any tell-tale signs he might be against, rather than with him. 'At the moment, no one at Langley.'

'What about the mission centre in Seoul?' Ron suggested.

Ron's work had been excellent. Overnight he had written a thorough brief on the interpretation of '5toa'. He'd spoken with a US scientist at the UK's military nuclear, biological and chemical research centre at Porton Down, Salisbury. Since the 80s both nations had shared this facility, the Pentagon's arm being the DTRA (*Defence Threat Reduction Agency*). Ron's report had made it clear: proteins don't kill unless you ingest tons of them over many weeks. There were at least five known deaths of bodybuilders in the US, but they'd got super fit first. And, according to the scientist, 5toa was considered benign – both useless and harmless to humans.

Ron had looked at every conceivable explanation. He'd even written a computer programme to run all of the other possible Morse-code permutations through Google. None of them added anything to the sum of all knowledge.

Jackson had already thought about asking Seoul if they could check out 5toa. But the same red flag had been raised: what if a simple enquiry alerted whichever team had killed Bae and then targeted him?

He wasn't prepared to go there – yet.

He had one other avenue.

'Which Limeys do we know?' It was a question to both of them.

Jackson had worked alongside a member of Secret Intelligence Service a couple of years ago in Ramallah. He was pretty sure the woman was on her last tour and would probably have left the service by now. Other than that?

'I got to know a guy last year. We did a week's course together. Residential. I think the course was called, 'Distance Surveillance', or something. I was on it for the techy bits. He was more high-browed than me. If I remember right he was an intelligence officer working for MI5. Decent guy. We shared a beer a couple of times.'

'Do you remember his name?' Jackson asked.

'Mmm. Not sure. I can dig it out. I think we exchanged emails afterwards. Soccer stuff.'

'OK. That's good. Let's try that. My only contact is a woman from Iraq. I'm pretty sure she left soon afterwards. So give yours a go.'

'Sure,' Ron replied. 'And if nothing comes from that, do you want me to contact Seoul?' Ron asked. He was already collecting his things.

'Maybe,' Jackson acknowledged. 'And, before you go ... and thanks for this ...' Jackson was patting Ron's report which was on the bed table. '... any news on the IED?'

Ron was on his feet. He reached for a couple more grapes.

In between chews he replied, 'Not much. The boss is running around like he's got the wind up his ass. We've got permanent press on our doorstep and someone from Langley arrived today pushing for answers. So far there's nothing. Not from any of our sources. It just doesn't make any sense?'

It does to me, Ron.

Jackson was tired now. He'd have to let Ron do his donkey work. The boss seemed happy with that. Everyone else in the team was off the Bae case and now chasing their shadows. Hopefully that meant he and Ron could operate in the margins. The last thing he needed to do was to make a splash. Somehow he didn't think his friendly hospital policeman was man enough to prevent the tidal wave that might wash over them if he pressed this too hard.

11°37'38.5"N 104°45'53.5"E, Unknown Street, northern Phnom Penh, Cambodia

Tap, tap, tap … tap, tap, tap.

Sam woke instantly, her eyes darting to the sound of the tapping. As her head turned, her right arm snapped across her body, her hand dropping into the footwell of the rear seats of the L100. She immediately found the MP-443. The safety was off and her finger on the trigger, just after her eyes had focused on a smiling local whose face filled half of the rear, kerbside window. The other half was a bowl of rice with bits in. With his spare hand he was pointing at the food.

Rice, chopped-root crop and meat. It wasn't something she could get used to for breakfast.

'*Non, merci.*' She waved her free hand, releasing her grip on the handle of the pistol. French was at best tolerated in Cambodia. English worked in tourist areas. Khmer was the universal language, which might as well have been Klingon to her.

The man wasn't taking no for an answer. The bowl of rice now almost upturned showing off his wares.

Sticky rice, stuff and meat.

Still no.

The man's grin was unwavering.

Bugger.

'Wait. *Attendez.*' Louder this time.

She sat up, her joints nudging her: find a bed, not the backseat of a minivan next time.

She should give the man some money. And then get on with her day.

The rear windows of the van were of the sliding type. She'd made sure they were closed and locked before her eyes shut of their own accord about four hours ago.

She undid the one closest to the man with the rice and stuff. As soon as the window slid back, the bowl was shoved through the gap. She was having it for breakfast.

Sam breathed in.

If I must.

As she took the bowl, which was quickly followed by a pair of chopsticks, she asked, '*Combien?*'

The man with the rice and stuff didn't say anything. He just continued smiling, his head tilting to one side.

As she dithered, the man found words of encouragement.

'*Mangez! Bon! Bon!*'

'OK. OK.' She tried her best not to sound irritated.

Sam thought chopsticks were the cutlery of the devil, forcibly introduced in the Middle Ages by a wealthy Eastern class to keep the hordes from becoming gluttons. Many years ago, when she was still in the army, she'd played the game where you have to eat single grains of rice with chopsticks. It had been her first sergeant's mess formal dinner, which was to be combined with the inevitable mess initiation.

She knew something was coming – and she knew it would involve a lot of drinking. She just wasn't sure what.

That night had been a curry night, the on-loan Gurkha chef's speciality.

After a couple of drinks before dinner, the two newly-promoted sergeants – her and a male physical training instructor the size of a small tractor – were sitting across from each other, the huge expanse of mess table between them, the regimental silver laid out on a central velvet runner. The rest of the mess had taken sides: small tractor versus slip of a woman. The result of which hadn't been a surprise.

Sam knew the drill. This was a drinking game, more than one of dexterity. In front of both the competitors was a bowl which, apparently, held exactly

233

100 grains of cooked rice. Next to the bowl was a line of pint glasses that, if needed, would be endless. On the word, 'Go', each player had to select a single grain of rice with their chopsticks, elevate it and then eat it. The forfeit was for every grain dropped, and typically that would happen more times than not, two fingers of beer would be drunk.

The winner? The person who ate all of their rice without throwing up.

It was hardly *Mastermind*.

There were eighty-two warrant officers and sergeants in the battalion, and Sam reckoned seventy were in the mess that night. And nearly all of those were standing behind small tractor man. Five were with her – all of them women (twelve other girls were betting against her, which was slightly irritating). And, yes, money was changing hands.

Sam had never used chopsticks before, so this was going to be a first. And she wasn't a great drinker. After a couple of pints she was normally all over the internet, typically ordering fifteen bras from Victoria Secrets, all of them at least two cup sizes too big.

But she was a *very* quick learner. As the members of the mess were about to find out.

She didn't need practice – at anything. Not really. All she had to do was watch. Once, maybe twice. And then she got it.

'Go!'

234

The dining room was in uproar. Small tractor man, who had clearly used chopsticks before, dropped his second grain, swigged his beer, and then managed to down the third speck of rice. He was motoring. Sam, on the other hand, was being screamed at by her very small group of high-pitched fans, and pointed and laughed at by the others ...

... because she didn't immediately pick up the chopsticks. Instead, she stared intently at small tractor man's technique.

That's one way of doing it. I wonder if ..?

Sam started slowly at first. Not necessarily because she was worried about dropping grains and having to drink too much alcohol, which would inevitably lead to a headache and a large parcel full of very pretty, but oversized bras. But because she didn't want to give her game away. She wanted to beat small tractor man. She knew she'd have to drink some beer – but she also knew that this wouldn't be the last event of its kind and she needed to keep her powder dry.

She took her time, but still beat her opposition having drunk only a pint of beer. Key though – she didn't embarrass him. She dropped the 96th and 97th grains on purpose. Then the house came down. Her team were delighted with her performance and definitely a few quid richer.

And she was right. This wasn't the only test. After a quick pee she was back at the table. Sitting opposite her was, apparently, the mess champion – a mid-50s, wily stores sergeant. He'd been in the battalion since the Boer War and was an old hand at beating young pups at this game.

'Go!'

It wasn't tiresome. It was a game, and everyone was having fun, even if it was at her expense. The aim, of course, was for all new mess members to get plastered. And that was fine. She would do that. It wouldn't be the first time.

But, they – all of them – missed a key point.

Above everything, certainly at that time in her life, Sam was a competitor.

So she matched the ancient, wily stores sergeant grain for grain. On purpose. She had the speed to get ahead of him. But she was starting to enjoy herself. And when she inevitably dropped a grain of rice which, before the last twenty grains the opposition had done three times, she had expertly caught up.

And then it was back to ... grain for grain.

It did cross her mind to lose. Would she get a hard time for beating the man who, in living memory, had never been beaten? Would there be a bad taste left in everyone's mouth if more money had been lost than earned? The big man, the regimental sergeant major, was leading the chanting for the old, wily stores sergeant. Did she really want to get on the wrong side of him? Or would he be secretly impressed?

In all honesty that thought process was over before it started.

She was going to win.

Under pressure the stores sergeant dropped three of the last ten grains. Sam slowed down to allow him to drink his swigs, before getting ahead of him again.

Then it was over. The unbeaten had been vanquished. She was the new mess champion. There was close to a riot – but it was a happy riot. She should have known. No one cared. And everyone was impressed. They loved it, even if one or two of them were a tenner down. Best of all, she didn't have to buy a drink all night.

And she got so drunk she woke up the next morning with that headache and who knew what else in the post.

That victory was good news just now – in the suburbs of Phnom Penh – as she really didn't want to eat the rice and stuff. She would have much preferred to have made her way to the embassy, stop for a decent coffee, use the loo at one of the cafés in the centre of the city, clean her teeth, and then be prepared for the start of another day.

Whatever that looked like.

Frank had called her last night when she had been roadside, about twenty klicks south of Krakor. She had come off the main road next to a garage – if you could call it that, it was more a collection of battered vehicles and a shack. She wanted to change the number plate on the van and pulled over where, if someone were looking, the L100 would be lost amongst a cluster of similar vehicles.

She'd put down her penknife and found the satphone.

'Sam, are you alright?'

'Sure. I've got some stuff for you. I was going to phone – but just now I'm changing plates.'

'What?'

She'd explained to Frank about the short, fat man with the pistol, his phone, wallet ... and minibus ... and smashed face. She gave Frank what details she could from the man's bank cards. The phone, however, was locked; there was currently nothing she could do with that.

'You should get to the embassy,' Frank suggested.

It wasn't bad advice but Sam had already made up her mind. She needed to sleep, before it ambushed her. The embassy would be shut until working hours and any duty officer would need to be called in.

'No. I'm making my way to the capital. I'll get as far as I can and then I'll get my head down. The embassy will wait until the morning.'

She assumed Frank would argue the point, but he didn't.

'OK. For update, we've still got Jafarov's phone. It's on its way to the Vietnamese border. Nothing other than that.'

'Get some sleep, Frank. We need to use what we have to find Jane. And we both need clear heads to do that. Get up tomorrow and put your best people on it.'

And that had been that.

Now, a bowl of rice for the better and five dollars poorer (the rice and stuff man couldn't conceal his delight), she was ready to re-join Frank on their search. Jane's main contact, Jafarov, might have been brutally murdered, but they had a pinging phone in a Toyota – and they had its registration. They had bank cards and a mobile from a short fat man. And they still had a ship carrying mil-spec arms and equipment steaming north, probably to the DPRK.

She reckoned they were further on than Jane had been before she disappeared.

The thing was, though, was that enough?

The rice and stuff man now gone, Sam pulled the side window closed, discreetly picked up the MP-443 and clambered into the driver's seat.

The L100 started first time.

Another day, another dollar.

British Embassy, Sangkat Srah Chak, Khan Daun Penh, Phnom Penh, Cambodia

Sam was back in the Deputy Head of Mission's office, staring at a blank screen wearing a pair of headphones. She'd asked to see an SIS analyst from the station. She assumed that the station had the wherewithal to conduct a thorough search for any details of the short fat man, and hopefully break open the phone. Its contact list would be really helpful, as would any SMSs it stored. If they didn't have the technology the phone might have to be couriered to a larger station such as Beijing. Or, worse case, all the way back to GCHQ. The analyst had promised Sam their best efforts.

Without something from the short fat man, or maybe a static ping from Jafarov's phone indicating it had arrived somewhere (and how long would the battery last?), she admitted it seemed unlikely there was much she and Frank could do for now. It was possible that one of the stations, or GCHQ, had something from Frank's previous taskers. If not she might have to be a tourist for a while; look around Phnom Peng, which wouldn't be a bad thing. Apparently the Tuol Seng genocide museum, which was the centre of the Khmer Rouge regime's torture and murder apparatus was a must-see, if that form of tourism ticked your box.

She wasn't convinced it did hers.

After all, she had seen her fair share of death. And had been very close to it herself a couple of times. Torture was also not an unknown experience although, as she understood it, what she had been subjected to wasn't on the scale of those who suffered at the hands of Pol Pot's regime.

Whilst she waited for Frank to connect she surprised herself by reflecting, albeit briefly, on her

240

recent past. Berlin, Munich, Caracas, Freetown. Miami, Rome, Zermatt. And, of course, most recent, Davos.

And she almost forgot Camp Bastion.

Camp Bastion.

How could she forget?

The mortar rounds. Her insides sticking out of a gaping hole in her combat jacket. Chris her love. Killed at the same time. A picture of him flashed into her consciousness, but it was fleeting.

Then ... Davos. The mad man, Freddie Derwent, her most recent nemesis. Her own death so close – his life taken from him just before he was going to finish her.

Bang.

She really thought the bullet had been for her.

She remembered longing for it.

And Ralph Bell – evil personified. Dead in a concrete cell in the jungles of Venezuela.

Freddie and Ralph. It could have been a comedy double-act.

And tonight, for one night only, iiitttt's ... Freddie and Ralph.

They used to scare her witless. Stalk her, day and night. In her dreams; in the corners of her waking moments. There were many times she'd rather have been dead than know they were alive. She didn't fear death. Not even now. At times she had screamed out for it, even as early as Kenema in Sierra Leone. Bell was there. With his smashed face and can of diet Pepsi. He'd

241

hurt her more than she could bear. And when they'd drugged her and left her to die in the fire, she had been thankful.

Jane had saved her then. Jane and a bunch of Sierra Leonean soldiers. They had braved the fire and pulled her and her UN pal, Henry, out the burning hostel.

Jane.

The big sister she'd never had. The women she loved ... and fought, like in any relationship. They'd often had different views of the world. First time in Rome, Sam had pressed ahead when Jane had ordered her to stay. In a twist you couldn't write, two years later Jane had ordered Sam back to the city, whilst she and Frank had pushed on through Switzerland. Common causes; different methods.

Between them, Jane and her, they had sorted out some stuff; put some bad guys down – that was for sure. But it wasn't always a harmonious relationship.

But she did love her.

I do.

And now there were new adversaries. New foes, currently unseen. And Jane was, very likely, in their clutches. That made it Sam's turn to find Jane and pull her from the fire.

That was what she was going to do.

'Sam? Can you connect the video?'

Frank's voice shattered her unstructured thoughts.

But not before she had come to a realisation.

242

There are no dreams now?

There hadn't been for many months. There was no Ralph Bell, and no Freddie Derwent. And, even having brushed with death last night and captured the image of a short fat man so she now had someone new to fret about, she had slept soundly.

No dreams.

No nightmares.

No massive anxiety in daylight – no flashes of a would-be killer in her peripheral vision.

She just had clarity. And focus.

Which, when she thought about it, surprised her.

Maybe it won't last?

That was a sobering thought.

She found the appropriate key, pressed it, and Frank's mug appeared on the screen.

'Good work,' he said. A small smile followed.

'If I'd have been there five minutes earlier I might have saved Jafarov, if that's who it was. Do you know?'

'We've done a match between the shots you took last night and the only image we have of him. And we're getting 73%,' Frank replied.

73% wouldn't stand up in court, but it was good enough for government work. It was Jafarov.

'Shall we assume the same fate has come to Fai Zhao?' Sam asked.

'We don't know. We've got Hanoi, KL, Bangkok and Phnom Penh on the case. He may well still be in hiding. In any case, reading between the lines in Jane's last report, I think Jafarov was our lead man, I'm sorry to say.'

'Do you have anything else? What should we do now?' Two questions from Sam. She was impatient. Jane was waiting for her. Somewhere.

'In no order. *La Teja* is coming alongside at Cai Mep, which serves Saigon. According to the MCA it is due to sail to Tianjin in thirty-six hours' time …'

Sam interrupted Frank.

'Tianjin, that's Beijing's container port?' She had no idea why she posed the question; she knew the answer.

'Correct. So, anyway, that's one possibility.'

'And?' she pressed.

'I'm waiting on Bunroeun Phy, that's the guy whose face you smashed last night. I've got an all stations out on him, but nothing yet.' He paused for breath. 'Jafarov's phone has gone dead. It made it as far as Krong Svay Rieng, that's about forty klicks short of the Vietnamese border. It's difficult to make assumptions, although the likelihood is they were on their way to Saigon.'

There was a natural pause, but Sam broke it.

'Have you got any good news?'

Frank let out a small sigh.

'Yes, possibly. Jane's last message to the UK. It was a WhatsApp exchange with her brother. A day later than her final report to us.'

'Did she say where she was?'

'Outside a bar in Kampot. There was a photo. It's called the "Lemongrass Bistro".'

'What did she say?' Sam pressed.

'She gave her brother some indication of where she was staying, but no names. She called it a "glamping spot, north of the town". She was thrilled about it. Said it was great to be close to nature, that sort of stuff.'

'Anything else?'

'What, from Jane's WhatsApp?' Sam could see by the expression on Frank's face he was struggling to keep up with her questions.

'No. General intel.' She asked.

'No. Nothing from Beijing ref the bot factory. Just the ship, the now dead phone and Jane's WhatsApp.' He still looked perplexed.

'Send me the WhatsApp exchange.'

'Sure. I'm not sure there's much more you can get from it?' He sounded tired.

'We'll see.' She took off her headphones and stood up. Frank now had a screenful of midriff.

'Where are you going?' A small bleat from the headphone speakers.

'I can be in Kampot in, maybe, three hours. It's due south of here. My understanding is it's a small colonial town, full of ageing expats, many living an inexpensive high life. There can't be many glamping spots north of the town. Send me the clip and I'll find it.

245

If you get anything before I get there, I have wheels. I can divert.'

She'd finished packing her stuff in her rucksack. She paused and took in Frank's two-dimensional, expressionless face. She stopped what she was doing and let out a small, feminine sigh.

I have to do something.

'I have to do something, Frank. And if I get nothing from Kampot I can be at Cai Mep before *La Teja* sails. It's almost en route.'

Frank didn't say anything. Nor did Sam.

'Look, Frank. It's either a minivan ride to Kampot, or a trip to the genocide museum.'

He was nodding now.

'OK. But, be careful. Kampot could well be where we lost Jane. We wouldn't want to lose you as well, Sam.'

Indeed not, Frank.

Hell

Chapter 9

167a, Town Road, Tottenham, London

Matthew was sitting on his bed, tying the laces on his trainers. He was close to being late for his gym session at the Edmonton Eagles Boxing Club, which was a short jog away. The nights were closing in, it was getting cold and, given the choice, he probably would have stayed in and watched something on Netflix. That was the beauty of having a gym partner. You did your best not to let them down – and he knew he would feel great afterwards. It's just today had been a sod and his mind needed time to declutter. There was nothing better for that than a couple of hours in a vegetative state in front of the telly.

But not tonight. He wasn't going to let his mate down.

He stood, opened his wardrobe and pulled out a tracksuit top.

Done.

Where were his keys?

Yep. Got those.

Next stop …

The jog to the boxing club would take him ten minutes. There'd be a one-hour gym session – a combination of circuits and punch bag workouts – and then he and his mate would finish off with a twenty-

248

minute warm-down jog around the park. He was normally done for after that.

He locked his front door, stuck his keys in a zip pocket of his tracksuit top and took off.

The cold air caught the back of his throat, and his right tendon, which was always on the edge of misbehaving, twinged. He'd need to keep it steady until he warmed up.

Overall, though, he didn't think he was in bad shape for someone technically in middle age. At 181 centimetres and smack in the middle on the BMI chart, he was probably best described as 'chunky'. He kept himself fit, he ate well enough but, since the divorce, he would be better off if he drank a little less red wine. His last MOT had him close to the wrong line when it came to cholesterol. And his blood pressure was a little high.

'How are the stress levels?' had been the doctor's final question. Which was the wrong thing to ask an intelligence officer in MI5. He'd been noncommittal.

If he'd been asked today the answer to that question would definitely have been: *bloody awful*.

It had been a combination of things.

First, he'd got this strange email from a CIA analyst based in Zagreb. Apparently he'd met the man on a course last year. It took a couple of seconds, but then Matthew recalled the event and eventually remembered the American. His name was Ron and he was a huge Newcastle United supporter – which was very odd considering he came from the Midwest. They'd had a couple of drinks one evening and spent the whole time reminiscing over Kevin Keegan. They hadn't communicated since and he would hardly have called him a friend.

So that was a surprise.

The email was at best arcane. The words were in English, but the intent behind them was very unclear. Did he, Matthew, have any reliable contacts in, say, the Korean peninsula? And, if so, could he ask if anyone could decipher the alpha-numeric '5toa'? Was it an abbreviation anyone recognised? Or did it ring any other bells?

There was no explanation as to why the question had been asked, although Matthew suspected the CIA in Zagreb would be working round the clock and following every available lead to unearth who had planted the recent IED. Ron's ask was from lefter than left field. It was like Matthew emailing the CIA's Moscow Mission Centre and asking someone if they had a decent recipe for Yorkshire pudding.

Unless there was a Korean link to the bomb?

Which would be very strange.

In any case, he didn't know of any SIS staff in Seoul of whom he could easily ask the question.

An option was pass the buck to a pal of his at Babylon, who would probably have a couple of avenues to explore. It was a thought.

Anyway, before he put any horsepower behind the question from Ron he needed to know his intent. So he had pinged a short response:

> *Hi Ron. This is interesting. Are you able to give me a bit more background before I put something round the houses? Time is money at the moment, and my pals will want some flesh on the bones, so to speak.*
>
> *As an aside, the Magpies could do with some help. Any spare cash kicking around in the States? Matt.*

He'd pressed 'Send' and then gathered his things to head off to a meeting on the new operation he'd been assigned to. It was, strangely, a target over-watch on three well known, left-wing politicians. The operational lead was the same person as the Anne Bertram op, which was due to close tonight. Matthew could imagine the man rubbing his hands together with delight having been assigned this new job. Anything to undermine the 'snowflakes' in this country.

He'd been about to leave his workstation when his monitor had pinged. It was an immediate response from Ron. It read:

> *I can't give you much, I'm afraid. Everything here is a bit sensitive, so please don't share too widely. 5toa was in a cipher we've found. It's from the*

Korean peninsula. And, for security reasons, we can't press too hard here. Time is money here too, so anything you can do. BTW, I've sent $50 to Steve Bruce. I hope he uses it wisely. Ron.

A bit sensitive? We can't press too hard here?

Why wasn't this ask being channelled at chief or deputy level? Ron's address block told Matthew that his Zagreb pal hadn't been promoted since they'd met last year. As such it was a very odd exchange, almost as though Ron was a singleton, working his own theories which he daren't share with his bosses.

That sounds familiar.

He'd replied to Ron before he left for the meeting:

On it. I'll hopefully have something by the end of the day.

And then he'd emailed the pal of his in MI6, giving as much information as he had. He'd made the point to avoid US contacts and 'could he have something by 4 pm this afternoon'. With that he was now late for his meeting.

The operation on the three left-wing politicians was standard over-watch stuff. But the rationale behind it seemed purposely opaque. Matthew liked to work with 'intent'. That way, if something cropped up that needed an immediate decision which had not been covered in any briefing, he could make an informed decision based on what he thought the operational commander's intent was. This morning, that had not been clear – which had frustrated the hell out of him. It was as though they were unpicking the lives of two men and one woman for the sake of it. And he wasn't happy with that.

After lunch his friend Howard had phoned. And that hadn't lightened his mood.

Howard had spoken to a well-placed SIS director and, as carefully as he could, he had asked the question as to whether their Chief was running a female agent in the government. Apparently the response had been raucous laughter. Not in a disparaging way, more in a 'you've got to be joking ... the Chief?' way.

So, that had come to nothing – which was hugely frustrating. And it had left him in a very difficult position. He had promised Howard he would come clean about not including the Chief/Bertram liaison in his final report. And at the end of their call, Howard had reminded him of that.

Matthew had taken no action since, but he had dwelt on it for most of the afternoon.

To cap it all, just before he left the office to come home he'd got a response from his pal at SIS. And it had been a call, rather than email, which spoke volumes. What he had told him was extraordinary, both in terms of what 5toa stood for, and how that potentially mixed into current events in East Asia. More extraordinary was the tone in which the intelligence was passed to him.

'I think you, or should I say wherever your ask originated, has unpicked something which has set some hares running here. And there was nothing I could do to stop them running. I sense this is going strategic sometime soon. Sorry about that.'

That had presented Matthew with another problem.

What should he say to Ron?

In the end he went for brevity, and signed off a simple email to the American which gave one version of the abbreviation '5toa'. He then pressed 'Send', packed up his things and headed straight out of the office.

He'd slowed his run to cross the main road. A gap appeared between two cars and he dashed across. The club was now about 800 metres away; it took him five minutes to get there, by which time he was both warm and tired.

The single-storey, poorly lit brick building, was set back from the road – a gravel carpark to its front. The club was placed on the edge of a small recreation ground although, with the sun now set, the trees and grass looked like they disappeared beyond the horizon.

He slowed to a walk, hands on hips, breathing a little too hard. As he crossed the carpark he slowed further to let a silver-grey Ford Focus pull across the front of him, right to left.

It stopped.

Which was annoying.

He turned to walk around the back of the car, but it reversed. Just a couple of feet, but enough for him to know the car was deliberately blocking him.

What the ...

The passenger's window dropped. Inside was a shadowy figure, made more obscure because the man it was definitely a man – was wearing a hood.

'Oi, Matt.' An East End, almost gangster accent.

What?

Matthew had started to move to his right, to circumnavigate the boot of the Focus. But he stopped. His nerves spiked as he turned back to the passenger's window.

'What? Who are you?'

'Never mind.' There was now a forearm resting on the door at the end of which was a black leather glove. The man's face was still in shadow. 'Trust me. Leave the Croatian thing well alone. It's not worth your while. Are you listening?'

Of course I'm bloody well listening.

'Yes, of course.'

'Mark my words, Matt.' There was an arrogant chuckle. 'We know where you live.'

And then the most extraordinary thing happened. The man's other arm appeared, his hand holding a bundle of fur. It took Matthew a second to make out that it was ... a rabbit.

255

A second black glove holding an unmoving rabbit – by its ears.

The glove released the furry ears and the rabbit fell lifeless to the floor.

The window glided to a close and the car accelerated, turning sharply, and sped off, its front wheels spraying dirt and pebbles in its wake.

Matthew, who had not had the time to get nervous, even less to get angry, turned to catch the plates of the car.

There were none.

Bewildered, he looked back to the rabbit. There wasn't a great deal of ambient light and the grey-brown fur was much the same colour as the dark gravel of the carpark. The corpse was lying on its side, as if it were sleeping. It appeared cuddly …

… like a rabbit.

Except.

He crouched. And looked more closely. There was something different about the rabbit.

God.

There were no eyes in its sockets.

Just then any residual heat from his run deserted him. And he felt very cold indeed.

Retro Kampot Guesthouse, Kampot, Cambodia

Sam pulled the L100 into the gravel drive of Jane's glamping spot. She was pretty sure this was it. There were other 'camping under reed roofs' north of Kampot, but Retro Kampot was the best known and, as Jane had described on her WhatsApp message home, what Sam could now see were four *beautiful* straw-topped huts next to a river.

She had narrowed down the list of likely camping guesthouses from the internet and had presented the options to one of the staff at the Lemongrass Bistro half an hour ago. That was after she'd been told that nobody recognised the photo of Jane that Sam had shared from her phone; it was the same story as the restaurant in Siem Reap. The bistro was busy, the footfall large and they couldn't possibly remember everyone. What they were able to say was Jane would probably have taken a hut at Retro Kampot. The staff at the bistro's description matched the message sent by Jane: small, upmarket and riverside.

This was it; she was sure. A clearing in secondary jungle next to a small river. There was a large central, open atap with a wooden bar and room for numerous comfy sofas and low tables. And there were four accommodation huts; bluey-grey painted wood with straw roofs – covered patios sporting hammocks with mossie nets. It was all very tasteful.

She parked the minivan beside the central atap and got out.

It was hot. Sticky. The L100 had air-conditioning, but it clearly had not been serviced and at best recycled warm air. She was pretty sodden, her light-green singlet more dark green than its original colour. Her underwear was wet and there was sweat between her toes. She needed a shower. There was only so much deodorant she could wear before it mixed with the smell of stale sweat, and the recycling of her clothes was running out of momentum.

Against that background Retro Kampot was particularly beautiful.

So was the 20-something Frenchman who met Sam as she climbed the three wooden steps up into the open hut.

'Hello. How may I help you?' The French accent was syrupy and the smile disarming. He was wearing cut-off jeans just above the knee, a plain yellow t-shirt and Havaianas. With his cropped, dark hair, olive-brown skin and a physique that suited a member of the French Foreign Legion, Sam felt her ovaries twitch.

Stop it.

'Hi. Do you speak English?' Of course he did. He was one of those fabulously talented Frenchmen who spoke every language, had a first-class degree in biochemistry and played outside centre for Toulouse.

I wish.

'Sure.'

They were within feet of each other. He smelt nice. Sam didn't do perfume and certainly had not been sufficiently close to enough men to distinguish Brut from Boss. She, on the other hand, probably smelt like an eight-month-long backpacker.

He smiled again with a closed mouth. No teeth. She reckoned they would be perfect.

'I'm looking for a friend. I'm pretty sure she stayed here a couple of weeks ago. Maybe for a night or two. Have you been here for a while?'

The Frenchman left Sam, taking his scent with him, and moved to behind the bar. He opened the lid on a laptop at the same time as he extended a hand to a bar stool and offered her a seat. She took it.

'I'm on duty here five days out of seven. I have the weekends off. But even then, I stay around. I have a room upstairs.' He pointed at the stairs in the corner of the building. Sam hadn't realised the roof was tall enough for a second floor.

'What was your friend's name?' he asked.

'Gemma Ruby.'

The Frenchman stopped tapping away on the keyboard and looked across the bar at Sam. His face had lost most of its charm. It now looked sad – even a bit nervous.

'What?' she asked.

'You don't know?' the Frenchman replied.

'Know what?'

'There was an incident here, with your friend. We called the police. I assumed that it would be all over the news?'

Sam could see where this was going, but needed the whole story.

'Tell me ... please.'

The Frenchman looked at the laptop, as though he was unsure as to what to do next. Then he nodded.

'Sure. Would you like some coffee, or tea, first?' It was a nervous, meek offering. And with that, any idling thoughts of having found the perfect man evaporated. She was very choosy. And he had lost it under pressure.

'No. Tell me what happened.' *That was too sharp.* 'Please.'

It took the Frenchman ten minutes to tell the story. Jane had phoned and booked a bed the day before she arrived. She was delivered by taxi and pitched up mid-afternoon. She'd enquired about food – they had a simple menu – because she was meeting someone at the guesthouse that evening and they would need feeding. After that she had settled in before taking one of the canoes onto the river for an hour.

The Frenchman had not seen her again until she turned up for dinner at about 7 pm.

'I can tell you what she was wearing, if you like?'

'Go on,' Sam prompted.

'It was a cotton trouser suit. Cream with red flowers. Long sleeved. I remember commenting on it. She looked very attractive, for a more elderly woman.'

If the Frenchman realised he was being patronising, it didn't show. Or maybe he liked his woman more mature? Jane was in her mid-forties. She was hardly 'more elderly'.

'And then it all happened.' The Frenchman had reached below the bar and retrieved two cans of coke. He put one in front of Sam and opened his own.

'What happened?'

'Her guest turned up. He came by taxi. Probably 7.15 pm ...'

Sam stopped him. She took her phone out of her pocket, prodded and swiped and then showed him the photo she had of Atith Jafarov which Frank had shared with her.

'Is this him?' she asked.

The Frenchman took the phone and stared at it for a couple of seconds and then looked back at Sam, his face painting a picture of suspicion.

'What is this woman to you?'

She got it. This was looking much more like police work than an enquiring friend. She'd been a fool and had gone too far, too fast.

Idiot.

Think.

'I work for the British government. We're looking for Miss Ruby. She was one of ours and she's been missing for a number of weeks. She is also a very good friend of mine. And I need to find her.' Sam placed a smile at the end of her explanation.

The Frenchman handed her phone back and took a swig of his coke.

'Yes, that's him.' He paused.

'Please, go on,' Sam pushed – gently.

He took a deep breath and continued the story. From what he'd seen Jane and the man did not know each other and were meeting for the first time. There were pleasantries and, whilst he didn't hear what they were discussing – much of it was in hushed tones – he'd got the impression it took them a little time to get down to business.

And then it all went crazy.

A car had pulled into the drive and stopped short of the main building, blocking the exit. Two men got out. Jane didn't react, but the man from the taxi was off before the two new men got within metres of the main hut.

'He ran, over there, towards the river.' The Frenchman was pointing. 'The two new men were confused. One followed him and the second held your friend by the shoulders. She struggled, but he was too strong.'

'What did you do?' Sam failed to hide her exasperation and the question caught the Frenchman off guard.

'*Rien*. Nothing.' His voice was defensive and had raised a pitch. 'It all happened too quickly. The man your friend had met was already in the river. I heard a splash. And *l'homme* who had followed him shouted something I didn't understand. A different language. But I'm sure it was an expletive ... swearing because the other man had got away. And seconds later they were gone. They took your friend with them. She shouted and struggled, but it didn't matter. They put her in the boot of their car. And then they backed out of the drive. And disappeared.'

The Frenchman was clearly uncomfortable; his hands were shaking. He took a final swig of his coke, the can steadying as he pressed it against his lips. And then he stared back at her, wetness in his eyes.

'Did you see the car?' Sam demanded. 'The marque?'

'I think so. It was silver ...'

'A Toyota?' Sam completed his description.

'Yes, for sure. Mid-sized.'

'And can you describe the two men?'

'They weren't Cambodian. But neither were they Western,' he quickly added.

'Tell me as much as you remember.' Her voice was more relaxed now. She needed him to think calmly.

Slowly.

He started. It was good stuff, like remembering Jane's clothes. He'd make an excellent witness and probably a good analyst. But he wasn't Foreign Legion material – for sure. In the end what she got was hardly a Photofit, but it was better than nothing.

Bring! Bring!

It was the satphone. Sam had left it in the minivan.

'Excuse me.' Sam stood up and jogged to the Hyundai.

263

It was Frank. She stayed where she was and lowered her voice.

'Hi, Sam. How's it going?'

'Some progress.' She glanced across at the Frenchman. He still looked uneasy. The sight of a satellite phone with its fat antenna probably didn't help. He had been living the life of a French Riley – until a couple of weeks ago. And now, all he probably wanted to do was head home.

She told Frank what the Frenchman had explained to her.

'So, it was Jafarov?' Frank asked.

'I'd say yes, definitely. And I have an inconclusive description of both of the thugs who took Jane. My contact here is convinced they're not Cambodian, maybe not even Vietnamese. For me that leaves Laos, China and Korea.'

'Neither match your man from last night, the one with the smashed face?' Frank added.

'No.'

Frank continued. 'That's something, though. Well done. Good idea to go to Kampot.'

Sam didn't need complimenting, she needed new intelligence.

She needed to find Jane.

'Do we have anything on the Toyota? Or my minivan?' she asked.

'The minivan belongs to the bloke you smacked last night. He's a local hood, with a record – works for the highest bidder. We're still digging there.' Frank paused for a second. 'The Toyota is a loss. It was stolen from a garage in Phnom Penh four weeks ago. But we do have access to the Vietnamese border crossing logs, although not in real time. So if the vehicle has crossed towards Saigon, we will get a confirmation, but likely twenty-four hours behind the curve.'

That didn't help. They weren't getting anywhere quick enough for Sam.

Frank continued.

'We do have more on Jafarov's business dealings. Rather than bore you, I'll send a file through for you to look at in slow time. In big chunks of stuff, it seems he has fingers in every pie along the Pacific Rim. All of it above board. Key, though, are opportunities on the Korean peninsula. Shipping. Steel. Coal.'

'North, or South?' Sam asked.

'Both. North is latent, but there is a real possibility for very quick expansion if, say, sanctions were lifted.'

Sam closed her eyes. Her mind raced, catching up with all of the input she'd had from scanning the news over the past week.

The Korean summit?

The editorials were talking up a rapprochement when the leaders next met, although no date had yet been given.

Whatever.

'Anything else?' she asked.

'No. Sorry.'

Sam looked back across at the main hut. The Frenchman was no longer at the bar, he was tidying up one of the large coffee tables.

I wonder where Jane's stuff is? She walked towards the wooden steps.

'What are you going to do now, Sam?'

'Ehh ... sorry.' She was back in the main atap now. 'Missed that.'

'What are you going to do?' Frank asked again.

'If my French totty allows, I'm going to have a shower.' *On my own.* 'Then I'm going to find Jane's stuff, if it's still here.' She stopped short of the Frenchman who had a polishing cloth in his hand. He stood up. They nodded at each other. 'And then I'm heading for the ship. Unless you tell me otherwise.'

Axis Hospital, Petrovaradinska 1, Zagreb, Croatia

Ron pressed the '4' button on the elevator control pad; it started to move. As it rose he stared straight ahead, fixating on the vertical rubber seal between the two silver doors. The elevator hummed. Like his brain.

He was out of his depth. And uncomfortable. Now that it had sunk in, he wasn't at all happy that a bomb had gone off just outside his window. Everyone in the office was on edge. During the Balkan War in the 90s, Zagreb had been a key mission centre. One or two old

266

hands talked of scores of clandestine missions into northern Bosnia, running informants on all three sides. Stories of joint CIA/Delta Force teams laser-marking Serbian targets for F16s to destroy were stuff of local legend.

Back then.

Now it was comically known as 'Zzz...agreb'. Sleepy city, where the sun was blue, the skirts short and the beer cold. So much so they were due to lose another five staff next week due to the Agency's European reconciliation. He'd seen a paper that proposed relocating all staff in Zagreb, Bratislava, Budapest and Ljubljana to Vienna. Zagreb was the furthest from Vienna, at just over 200 miles. And it did naturally look south to Sarajevo, and southeast to Belgrade. You never know, they might be left out of that move.

In many ways Ron hoped they weren't. He'd only been at the centre for a year and was originally hoping to do two more. He had a Croatian girlfriend and was settling in nicely. But the bomb had put an end to that. Zagreb was no longer a backwater; and that made him uncomfortable. He was a hacker, not a hero. He didn't mind hard work. But he wasn't keen on being on the front line.

Which is where he was right now.

The terse email from his Limey pal reference 5toa had given him the jitters. On the face of it the words said nothing. But against the background of what Jackson was investigating, they added up to something

267

mighty raw. Ron didn't have the experience or knowledge to contextualise what the email meant. But he knew that it didn't sound good.

That added to his sensation of unease. The bomb – meant for Jackson, who was convinced it was orchestrated from within. The change of focus for the mission centre. Away from Bae Ki-tae, to chasing shadows; looking for leads when Jackson was clear that they should be investigating themselves. And now, potentially, a bombshell bit of news from his Limey pal. Bae Ki-tae was onto something. Something big.

Out on a limb, Jackson would know what to do. The problem was, Ron wasn't sure he could stand the pressure of working that way.

He'd have it out with him. Once he'd told him what the Brits had said.

The elevator jerked to a stop. The doors slid open. Ron turned right into the corridor; his boss's room was at the end, on the left.

The ward was quiet. He waved at a nurse, who recognised him and nodded back. A man pushing an empty gurney passed him coming from the opposite direction. A door to a two-person room was open. Ron caught sight of a couple of visitors standing around a bed, one holding a bunch of flowers.

Jackson's door.

It was closed, as usual.

But something was different. He couldn't place it.

He opened the door and entered.

Jackson was as he'd left him yesterday. Almost horizontal. A heavily bandaged shoulder, one of those short electronic sleeves on his finger to feed the machines with statistics, and a couple of drips. His laptop was on the bed table, open.

He was asleep.

Ron stopped halfway across the room.

For some reason he listened. Intently.

The room was almost noiseless.

Is that odd?

He glanced at the monitoring machines.

...

There were no readings. No lights. No *pings*. They were turned off?

He looked at Jackson. He was ... pale.

Oh my God.

Two steps and he was at his side.

Everyone in the CIA carried out annual first aid training; it was the law. And what was it?

Breathing, bleeding, brakes and burns.

He'd never used the four Bs before. Not with a proper, live body.

Live?

He grabbed Jackson's wrist. Fumbled for a pulse.

Then it hit him.

I'm in a fucking hospital!

'Nurse! Nurse!' he turned as he screamed. He'd seen a nurse earlier. She would know what to do.

He was out the door in a second and saw the nurse rushing towards him.

'I think he's dead! I think my friend is dead!'

The nurse, who didn't reply, was already on him. Ron moved his bulk to the side and let her through.

And then he noticed what he'd missed earlier.

An empty chair, by Jackson's door.

The Croatian policeman wasn't on guard. His seat was there, but he wasn't.

Conspiracy flooded into Ron's mind, so much so there was little room for rational thought.

They've finished the job.

He had to sit down. Now. He fell into the policeman's chair.

This isn't happening.

Tears of hopelessness formed in his eyes.

I'm going home.

He was due some vacation. He'd take it now. The Chief would understand. Anything to get away from this madhouse.

Chapter 10

Matthew had cleared his desk, both metaphorically and physically. He had finished a series of calls and emails regarding the three MPs. His role was checking their financial propriety – looking for tax and bank irregularities, mortgages and similar. The operations manager had secured the necessary court orders and that allowed the team to use their own in-house search resources, as well as conversations with HMRC (*Her Majesty's Revenue and Customs*), the Treasury and, if necessary, the fraud offices of the banks and business with which the three had accounts. The GCHQ rep was onto the three's electronic footprint. And a joint team of MI5 and SRR were now on the ground setting up over-watch on houses and places of work. Unless and until the intelligence showed real intent by the MPs to do something nefarious, the court wouldn't sanction mobile cover.

Matthew still thought this was a witch hunt. He'd pressed the manager on the operation's intent and got a poor response.

'The three travelled to Russia six months ago. Their itinerary was jam-packed. We know two of them are ardent supporters of the left-wing think tank, "Impetus". The DG is keen to see if there is any connection between the trip and their own left-wing ideologies.'

Matthew had made the point the trip to Russia was a cross-party affair, and they weren't investigating the two Tory and one Lib Dem MPs who also travelled.

'I think you've answered your own question,' had been the curt response.

Anyway, he'd done what he could for now. The question set was in train, there was little more he could achieve until some replies came in.

Which was good news. Because he had to get his head round an eyeless rabbit.

He had an empty sheet of A4 on the centre of his desk.

He stared at it.

And then, along the top of the paper, he drew a timeline. It was short; just three days. Underneath that he scribed, left to right, a series of events:

> *Chief SIS/Anne Bertram – the Swiss SMS – chat with Howard at the pub – response: no agent operation – email from CIA Zagreb/5toa – email to SIS ref 5toa – response/hares running – dead rabbit/no eyes*

Last night, when he had been hitting the punch bag with everything he had, he'd come to the conclusion the whole 5toa/dead rabbit saga was an unbroken circle. CIA to MI5. MI5 to MI6. And back again. Zagreb had uncovered something. Something which, bearing in mind the ask had come from just an analyst, was much bigger than they thought it was. Not meaning to mix species, it had certainly scared the horses across the Thames.

And it had certainly unnerved him, eyeless rabbit 'n' all.

Any normal person would have gone straight to the police. But ... he wasn't any normal person. He worked for the Security Service. Whilst it wasn't every day someone tried to threaten him with a dead animal, he and his colleagues often found themselves in harm's way. It was in the job description.

He took a breath and tapped his pen on his forehead.

So, 5toa was the central big issue.

That had played on his mind when he and his pal were cooling down round the park at the end of their session. As he jogged, a mid-distant memory nagged him. It was something he'd read over the past week. Something to do with the stretch of Anne Bertram's brother's company, Tilsdent Holdings. But no matter how hard he tried, the memory didn't completely form.

He'd got up early and made it into work for 7.30 am, about forty minutes earlier than usual. He'd used that time to read back into the Anne Bertram op. Most of it was dull, repetitive stuff, but after fifteen minutes he found his mid-distant memory. Tilsdent was a major investor in SE Telecom, a burgeoning start-up in Seoul. They also owned a dormant energy company working in Kaesong, the collaborative industrial zone in the DPRK, close to the South Korean border. The zone was currently closed, but the infrastructure was still in place. And, Matthew assumed, would boot up should relations thaw.

Was it too much of a stretch to go from the Chief of Secret Intelligence Service, through Anne Bertram to her brother's company – which had business links to the Korean peninsula – and then step over to a rogue piece of Korean-based intelligence from Croatia, of all places? A piece of intelligence that as soon as he shared with an SIS desk officer, it had squared a circle?

Matthew's pen was now poised above the sheet of A4, its nib next to *dead rabbit/no eyes.* From there he drew a circular, connecting line back to *Chief SIS.*

He sat back in his chair; his pen went back to tapping his forehead.

The man with the hood and the gloved hand and the dead rabbit had made it clear last night: *leave the Croatian thing well alone ... we know where you live.*

That had come about because he had spoken to pal in SIS about 5toa and that had sent, according to his mate, 'some hares running'. And 'he couldn't stop them running'.

Hares.

Dead rabbit.

No, come on. That's ridiculous. *That's, like, they're listening to my telephone calls.*

Surely not. The stats didn't make sense. Sure, tap his phone ... now. After he's made the connection. But the notion that they were already listening to him, or his mate at SIS, could only be nonsense.

The rabbit was just a rabbit. *Not a hare.*

His pen stopped tapping.

The circle *was* still a circle. One thing led to another which, in the end, led back to the beginning.

What should he do now?

There was no way he was going to quit, to leave the Croatian thing alone. He wasn't paid to do that.

Who should he speak to?

SIS was out. That's how this had started.

His current boss was a fool, and a nationalistic one at that. Matthew wasn't going there.

So it was back to Howard. He was the only person he could trust.

Or ... he could go it alone.

He had the resources. The current op was hardly taxing. In fact, against protocol, he could use the current op code to put out some feelers. If he were careful he could disguise, what should he call it ... *Op Blackberry*, that's it, the clever buck rabbit in *Watership Down* ... in amongst his current intelligence gathering in a way no one would notice. He had that freedom.

And if nothing came of it in the next couple of days he would then take some advice.

Yes. That's what he would do.

British High Commission, 100 Tanglin Rd, Singapore 247919

Frank was worried about Sam. She'd already had a close run in with a local and a pistol. She had stolen a minibus, stolen a second set of plates and had just made a big noise in Kampot where Jane had been kidnapped. She was now on the way to the Vietnamese border, if she wasn't there already. He'd spoken with Hanoi Station and alerted them that 'one of theirs' was inbound and did they have any agents in customs or the Vietnamese equivalent of Border Force who could ensure she made it through without a scratch.

They didn't, although they had a man well placed in the military who might be able to reach someone in the Vietnamese Border Defence Force and pull some strings.

'No.' Frank had stopped the conversation in its tracks. Whilst Frank wasn't a qualified case-officer he knew the rules – and so would they. The only safe hands were your agents, and they were never to be fully trusted. It was hardly a comparison, but it reminded him of his mum's dating advice: *if she sleeps with you, she'll sleep with anyone*. He was pretty sure she was commenting on the liberal attitudes of the girl he might be seeing, rather than his ability to date effectively.

276

Although, as his girlfriend list was short on names, maybe she was making a point about his ability to attract women *per se*.

Whatever, SIS recruited agents and informants because those people had issues which could be extorted. Indebtedness was at the top of that list, although there were many other indiscretions in the pile. It made sense that if SIS could find and exploit a weakness, others would too. Agents turned. All the time. And asking them to speak to someone they knew concerning a sensitive issue, such as Sam crossing an international border, was not proscribed. The links too long, too tenuous and highly unreliable.

You dealt with your agent. You didn't ask them to deal with others when your own people were at risk.

So. Sam was on her own.

And she wasn't answering her phone. Which worried him.

He reckoned it would take her three hours to get from Kampot to Saigon Port. If he were her he'd drop the van short of the border, walk through and then pick up a taxi on the Vietnamese side of the crossing. The journey looked about 400 kilometres. If you added in the crossing – and he hoped she was aware it closed at night – he reckoned she'd be there by lunchtime.

Frank had no idea what she'd do when she got there. According to the latest from MCA, *La Teja* was still dockside and not due to leave for another eighteen hours. Doubtless the port would be fenced off and guarded. When he'd spoken to Hanoi earlier about the border, they also confirmed they had no tags to anyone at Saigon Port; there was no help there.

And what would Sam do if she got into the dock? If she got onto the boat?

What was she up to?

Indeed, what were *they* up to?

Clearly they needed to find Jane. Bottom up that meant finding the silver Toyota and the man/men driving it. So far he'd got nowhere with that. Top down he had more information from various sources, but little useful intelligence.

They had found the second of Jane's businessmen, Fai Zhao. That is, they had found his body. A car crash, apparently, just south of Bangkok – a week ago. The wreckage had made identification almost impossible, so that's why it had taken them so long to find him. Jane's businessmen leads were – literally – dead. That hadn't stopped GCHQ from trampling all over their electronic footprints. There was a lot of stuff; too much for him to sift through effectively. He'd asked the station chief if he could borrow some manpower; the boss had given him an analyst, Riley, to help out. It had taken Frank a couple of hours to bring Riley up to speed, always mindful of the security caveats of both Op Mandolin and Abraham. Riley, who had seemed excited to be taken away from some other more mundane task, had worked late into the night, and was up and in before him this morning.

He'd checked on her just now; she was still beavering away. She was, apparently, making progress, but needed a little more time.

With Riley on the businessmen, he'd had a long and unfruitful conversation with Beijing. Their Politburo agent, who had informed them of an upcoming 'major operation', had gone to ground. They had no idea why and it worried them. And, as a result, that source had dried up. Insofar as the re-tasking of the bot farm – from targeting Hong Kong to another focus – again the news was interesting but inconclusive. The output from the farm had fallen dramatically, as though someone had sent the staff on holiday. The tech team in Beijing Station suggested that maybe the farm was undergoing a major upgrade and was out of action as a result? The bottom line was: they didn't know.

And that also worried them.

Their best placed agent had gone schtum and the bot farm they had an inside track into had closed for business. And both of these things had happened prior to a major event Beijing Station had been trying to get a handle on for over a month.

They were an unhappy and nervous bunch. Frank could see why.

He'd also got nothing from the Chief. As directed he had sent daily 'for his eyes only' reports and, whilst he'd always got a response, they were perfunctory – and lacked further direction.

So. What now?

Should he stay in Singapore?

Should he try and stop Sam from gaining access to the port?

His questions proved unnecessary. As he stood to go and make himself a cup of tea three things happened at once. As a result, the decision was made for him.

First, an email pinged in from MCA. It was short:

La Teja is no longer quayside. Next port recorded as Tianjin. Sailing time est under 10 days.

What?

Then Riley appeared at his shoulder.

'Frank?'

He was still taking in the news from the Maritime and Coastal Agency. He needed to divert Sam before she jumped the fence in a communist country that didn't take too kindly to Western interference …

… just as his phone rang.

It was Sam.

Thank God.

He sat back down and motioned for Riley to do the same at a chair next to his desk. He connected his phone.

'Hi, Sam.'

'Hi, Frank. I'm looking at a three-metre fence with spikes on top and more cameras than a Hollywood film premier. Before I stake out the whole perimeter and end up in the Hanoi Hilton, do you have anything for me?'

'Yes. Glad you phoned. *La Teja* is at sea. It's on its way to Beijing. I've literally just found out.'

'Fuck it.' It was a resigned statement of frustration from Sam, rather than one of anger. Frank thought she probably wasn't relishing getting into the port. Now she didn't have to. On the other hand, she might now feel lost for direction. He had some sympathy with that.

He continued. 'And I don't have any direction for you, I'm afraid. Unless ...' He turned to Riley, who was looking very pleased with herself.

In his briefing to her he'd told Riley half the story. Her job was to look for anomalies within ELINT and SIGINT from GCHQ. She knew about Jane, but not what Jane was onto. And she knew about Sam. During their conversation he had stepped close to but, hopefully, not yet over any line.

'Hang on, Sam. I've got someone here with me who might have something. I'm putting you on speaker.' He nodded at Riley.

'Hi, Sam. It's Riley.'

'Hi.' An unsurprising curt response, which didn't put Riley off.

'I've got a whole load of stuff from the Doughnut on Jafarov and Zhao. I'm about ten hours into a mountain of phone logs and emails ...'

'Cut the intro, Riley. I'm tired and hungry and need to sleep. Give me what you know. And strip that to the bones.' Frank could hear the weariness in Sam's voice. It was all right for them here in the air-conditioned comfort of an office.

Riley blushed a little and coughed. Frank gently touched her forearm and then gave her a thumbs up. She'd get over it.

'OK. Zhao is clean ...'

'Hang on, Riley ... *was* clean,' Frank interrupted. 'Just to let you both know I found out earlier Zhao was killed in a car crash last week. It almost certainly wasn't an accident.' He paused. Neither the phone nor Riley said anything. Frank motioned for her to continue.

She coughed again.

'Zhao's businesses are ... sorry were ... all above board. His contacts match his businesses and business links. There's nothing I've found financially, politically or ideologically which throws up a flag.' She paused, snatching a quick look at Frank, who smiled and nodded encouragement.

'Atith Jafarov, however, was a different kettle of fish. His business dealings are more opaque. His call log includes numbers associated with both the Chinese and Vietnamese governments. His emails are less telling, more business orientated ... except one.'

'Go on.' A croak from the phone's speaker.

'There's a five-week long email string between Jafarov and a man called, "Wang". Wang's address is a

282

Hotmail. GCHQ has four locations where it has pinged: two in Beijing, one in Hanoi and a fourth between three towers on the Chinese/Vietnamese border. I have triangulations to within 500 metres of all four locations. What's interesting is the way the email chain degenerates over time.' Riley took a breath. She was staring at the handset. It remained quiet. 'The first email in the string included a selfie of two men. One we know for sure is Jafarov. The second is Wang; I'll tell you why in a minute. They are standing next to each other. Big smiles ...'

'Where's the photo taken?' Sam interrupted.

'I don't know. The background is a non-typical, large house. Behind which are mountains. Tall ones. They're snow-capped. The caption is, after my poor translation, "We got a lot done. Thanks for inviting me.".' She paused, possibly expecting questions.

There were none.

'Over the five weeks, and the chain is twenty-seven emails long, the tone of the conversation deteriorates. It's business orientated. Opportunities in China and North Korea. There are no names. It's all non-specific. But the final three exchanges become vitriolic. Wang's responses include, "You must remember who you are dealing with – we are not inclined to work with you anymore." His final email reads ...' Riley flicked over a page in her notebook, '... "I would stay well out of Vietnam and China, if I were you, Mr Jafarov. You are not welcome here. Under any circumstances."'

283

Again, Riley let her briefing hang.

'That might explain why Jafarov reached out to Jane?' Frank suggested.

'I've not finished,' Riley interrupted.

'Go on,' Frank encouraged.

'I think I've found Mr Wang. It is an incredibly common name, like Smith or Jones, but I got lucky. At first I looked for all CEOs, COOs and CFOs of the major Chinese conglomerates. Nothing. I then looked at the Chinese political hierarchy. Bingo. I found a "Wang" on none other than the Politburo's Standing Committee ...'

'That's one level down from the General Secretary and one level up from the main Politburo. There are only seven members,' Sam interjected.

'Correct.' Riley sounded surprised at Sam's knowledge of the Chinese Communist Party's wiring diagram. But it didn't stop her. She continued. 'Mr Wang Huwinh is "Secretary for the Central Commission for Discipline Inspection". In short, he's the Communist Party enforcer.'

'How do you know it's the same Wang?' Frank asked.

'Because I have two photos to compare. The one from the email and one from the internet of the Standing Committee. Cynthia gives an 87% corroboration.'

All three of them were silent.

And then Sam chirped up.

'OK. This is making some sense. I found Jane's stuff in Kampot; they'd kept it in a room behind the kitchen. Anything valuable seems to have been taken and there was nothing left in her bag but clothes and a dog-eared notebook. In it are notes from her meetings and telephone calls with Rattanatari, Jafarov and Zhao. The Rattanatari and Zhao stuff seems undescriptive and unhelpful. As, on the face of it, does her only exchange with Jafarov before her abduction. It was a long telephone call the night before their meet at Kampot. Her notes on that are two pages long. It's mostly generalities, but, and I recite word for word, there is this entry towards the end. Jane's notes read: *it all went downhill from Lào Cai.* Jane's side note is: *throwaway line from AJ.* AJ is Atith Jafarov, just in case you're not keeping up.'

Frank glanced at Riley. She shrugged her shoulders.

'Spell Lào Cai, Sam,' Frank asked.

Sam spelt Lào Cai phonetically, including the *grave* accent. And then continued.

'I've checked. Lào Cai is a Chinese/Vietnamese border town; Vietnamese side. That could well tie in with the GCHQ triangulation and maybe your photo, Riley. Good work, by the way.'

Riley smiled.

There was a further pause.

Frank thought about saying something, but nothing of use came to mind.

'I'm off,' Sam announced. 'Send me everything you have. And try and find the location in the photo. Start with the triangulation. Cynthia's 3-D mapping might do the trick.'

'Hang on, Sam. Where are you going? And how do you intend to get there?' Frank asked.

'I'm going to the Chinese/Vietnamese border,' Sam replied, as if it were that simple.

'It must be 1,000 kilometres to the north.' Frank couldn't hide his exasperation. 'Book into a hotel and get some sleep.'

There was another pause. Frank looked at Riley, who shrugged her shoulders again.

'Jane's still missing, Frank.' Sam's tone was soft, almost desperate. 'This is the only lead we have, unless you have anything else? I'll catch a flight out of Ho Chi Minh to Hanoi as soon as I can. I'll then head north from Hanoi. Send me any stuff you have ASAP.'

The phone clicked off.

God, she was annoying ...

Frank looked at Riley. She shrugged her shoulders ... again.

'Is she always like this?'

Frank's grimace turned to half a smile.

'Yes, 'fraid so.'

'I better get onto Cynthia and find this location.'

'Good idea,' Frank replied.

286

Headquarters, The Security Service, Thames House,
London, SE1 9EL

That's interesting.

Matthew was looking over the results he'd had back from GCHQ concerning further investigations into PGB, the Geneva-based bank working under the umbrella of Jonathan Bertram's Tilsdent Holdings. He'd pressed the Doughnut for more on Tilsdent and the Korean peninsula. Having drawn a sweeping line between the rabbit with no eyes back to Sir Clive Morton, he needed to establish something more than just a nascent energy company working, or currently not working, in Kaesong.

He hoped GCHQ's mass of financial spreadsheets might confirm what he thought might be the case ...

... that it all came back to PGB.

The sheets were confusing – the analyst at the Doughnut providing the information, not the intelligence. That was Matthew's job. There were seventy-four pages of accounts showing financial interactions between one of the five PGB brokers and the CFO at Tilsdent, Jonathan Bertram's parent company. It was page after page of numbers with the only helpful indicators the column and row headings. And there were plenty of 'hidden' comments.

287

He'd searched the sheets using the Ctrl-F function for a number of keywords looking for any Korean peninsula link.

He'd tried: Korea, DPRK, Pyongyang, Tilsdent and Bertram. Nothing. He put in ten DPRK cities, and then ten from the south. Nothing. Then all of the major South Korean industrial groupings: Samsung, Hyundai, Hynix, etc.

Nothing.

He'd googled North Korean industries, which was a very small list. But none of them came up from the search on the spreadsheets. He was then about to give up when he decided to search for North Korean banks. There appeared to be three sets: the Central Bank, local banks and overseas banks. He started with the Central Bank. He found its SWIFTBIC (*international bank sorting code*) and searched for that amongst the spreadsheets.

Nothing.

He did the same for the overseas banks. Nothing … except. He scrolled down the Google listing and found a later entry.

Hang on.

One of the banks had recently amended its title. Donchan Bank had changed its name to the Wang-Chang Credit Bank. He googled that, found its SWIFTBIC number and searched the sheets.

Bingo.

That *was* interesting.

So much so he phoned a colleague of his who was a financial analyst. She worked a couple of floors down from him.

'I'll come up,' his colleague said.

Ten minutes later and they were getting somewhere.

'Look here, Matt.' The finance wizard was pointing at some numbers. Matthew had no idea what they meant.

His colleague continued.

'These six rows are all financial interactions with the Wang-Chang Credit Bank.'

'Not the Donchan Bank?' Matthew asked.

'No. Look ...' she was now pointing to a second screen which was open on a monitor to their left. It was showing more rows and columns of mind-numbing numbers, '... Wang-Chan's operational. Its BIC code is live. Donchan has a different code ... here.' She was pointing again, deftly juggling between the two monitors. His eyes were struggling to focus.

'OK. Thanks. What does it mean?' Matthew hoped they were getting somewhere. Just now he had no idea if they were.

'Well, your Swiss bank, PGB, is using an IBAN number ...'

'IBAN?' Matthew interrupted.

'International bank account number ... of CH67954. Here. And it's dealing with Wang-Chang's account, here ...' still pointing, '... which is NK62834532.

There is a hefty exchange, which took place ...' his colleague was following a cell on the spreadsheet up the page, '... three days ago.'

'What's the exchange?'

'It's not strictly an exchange, dollars say, for *won*, the North Korean currency. It's a futures buy. PGB are shorting the currency. They're not buying it, but betting on it falling.'

'Yeah, I think I get that. How much are we talking about?'

'An eye-watering amount,' his colleague responded.

'I'm an adult. You can tell me.'

'Eight hundred million Swiss Francs.'

Matthew breathed out. He'd spent an expensive holiday walking in the Swiss mountains last Easter. Then the Swiss Franc was worth about 80 pence. That made PGB's investment close to £650 million.

But, as his brain chewed over what he now knew, it didn't immediately add up to anything he understood.

The *won* was volatile; North Korean's inflation rampant. Surely any bet on the currency would be too risky to make, certainly one close to a billion pounds? He pressed his colleague.

'But the North Korean currency is mad. This would be like betting on a murmuration of starlings?'

'You would have thought. Unless the currency is going to crash – badly. It's interesting. Look back here.'

The finance wizard used a finger to send the sheet to the right. She stopped it after a couple of swipes, fiddled with it and then enlarged a single cell. In it the figure was too large to be displayed. His colleague hovered the cursor over the cell. A dialogue box appeared. It contained a single number in green type: *CHF 5,200,000,000.*

That's a lot of francs.

'Why is the figure in green, not black?' Matthew asked.

'It's a prediction.'

'Of what?'

'The post-short sum. The prize.' His colleague's eyes were wide open, her lips curling into a smile.

'What? That's ...' he took out his phone and opened up the calculator app. '... That's a six times return. That's crazy?'

'It is. And look back at the *won* versus the US dollar exchange.'

Matthew followed the woman's hand back to his second screen. In one corner his colleague had thrown up a graph. Time along the bottom, the value of the *won*, vertical. Rather than a constantly changing graph over time like a mountain range, the diagram showed a currency that lost and gained in chunks – big vertical chunks, but with plenty of short-ish periods of horizontal stability.

'Why does the graph look like that? Squares and rectangles?'

'Because the DPRK manipulate their currency and, ordinarily, they do not exchange it on the open market. Any change is affected by the government.'

'So how come PGB have managed to make this transaction?' Matthew pressed.

'I don't know. Maybe they have someone on the inside who has enabled it?'

'Someone who might know that the currency is going to crash in … how many days?'

'Ten.'

Matthew closed his eyes. He tried to put this in the context of Sir Clive Morton … and what he knew of 5toa. What was the connection?

Was there a connection?

He had no idea. And thinking about it made his ears tighten.

He thanked his colleague very much and popped across to the kitchen to make himself a cup of coffee. As he stirred his sweetener into the drink a thought occurred to him.

The Chief of SIS knows a major event is going to happen on the Korean peninsula.

An event that will undermine the DPRK's economy so much so the government has to revalue the *won*. And he uses a Brit contact to make a killing using that intelligence. What had the SMS said? *Meeting successful. There is benefit on both sides.*

But was this really about money? Sir Clive Morton was known to be a wealthy man. OK, people who got wealthy stayed wealthy. What was the maxim? How do you make a million? You start with a million.

It made sense.

Does it?

What other options were there?

He rested his backside on the worktop and sipped his drink.

He could think of two. Both of them were lame in comparison to making more money than the GDP of a small country. And both of them relied on the Chief of SIS running his own personal op, a notion which Matthew's pal in Sir Clive's organisation had laughed out of the stadium.

But he was paid to consider every possibility.

So.

Here goes.

First, Sir Clive was testing Anne Bertram, her brother, Tilsdent and PGB. In short, doing what MI5 had been doing but, in his case, aggressively rather than passively. Was the Chief of SIS running a financial honey trap? And, if so, why do it on his own? Indeed. Why do it at all?

He didn't like that option.

Second, he was shorting the *won* for a reason. It was a conspiracy within a conspiracy. By betting against the North Korean currency, was he somehow warning the North Koreans they were facing an existential threat? Somebody would spot a transaction of that size and put the North Korean government on guard?

But if he wanted to warn them, why not just warn them?

They wouldn't believe him.

How did that fit into the 5toa intelligence?

Did it?

Does it, in any way?

Matthew made his way back to his desk. He had some decisions to make. And more intelligence to gather. Probably not in that order.

No Bai International Airport, Hanoi, Vietnam

Sam was in the customs hall. It all looked remarkably efficient. It was clean and very modern. And well lit. Which was helpful, as it was as pitch-black outside.

The aircraft had, surprisingly, been the same: clean, organised and modern. She'd caught the low cost, national carrier which scored one-and-a-half stars on *airlinequality.com*. Expecting the worst, including unannounced flight delays and rude staff, she had boarded the smart Airbus 320 on time and been treated with utmost respect. It just proved the myth: only idiots with chips on their shoulders pen really bad reviews.

The flight was a couple of hours; she'd ordered an orange juice and some pretzels and tried to sleep. But it wouldn't come.

So she mused instead.

There had been no time to think through the bigger picture over the last couple of days. Driving the small minibus along, allegedly, Cambodian A-roads was akin to an off-roading course she'd attended in the army. The heavy afternoon rain hadn't helped the, more often than not, badly compacted mud surface. Nor had the other drivers, who Sam assumed thought the road had been laid just for them. The L100 had been a star, though, and she felt a pang of regret when she abandoned it a kilometre short of the Vietnamese border.

She'd lost a couple of kilogrammes of sweat by the time she'd reached the frontier and with the red dust of the road clinging to every wet patch, she looked more Dakar Rally motorcycle competitor than international traveller. Two litres of water and ten bribing dollars lighter, she was in Vietnam. And then into a taxi, which dropped her at the port.

Her subsequent conversation with Frank – and whoever Riley was – was both helpful and disappointing. Between the three of them they had nothing. Not really. Certainly nothing which might help them locate Jane. What they needed was to find the Toyota. Or for the man with Jafarov's phone to recharge it and turn it on so they had a 'ping'.

At that point her decision to head north had been spontaneous and probably pointless. But that was her way.

In a previous existence, say three or four years ago, she had been – even if she said so herself – a pretty decent analyst. She had an almost savant eye for detail and her wiring, which she reckoned put her somewhere on the autistic spectrum, meant she was undeterred by outside influence. She learnt quickly and she stuck at things. No amount of paperwork was too big. No pile of photographs too daunting.

She got results.

Since her case-officer training and her now many field operations, she was uncomfortable with sitting still. Her ten-month recovery at Frank's broke that mould, but as soon as her cognisant functions were back in working order, her leg would bounce incessantly and her eyes struggle to stay fixed on one point in the distance. It was as though there was a coiled spring inside her, which someone had wound too tight. And the only way to resolve the problem was to place her on parquet flooring, flick a switch and watch her frantically clockwork off into the distance.

She needed to be doing something.

Hence, abandoning the port and heading north.

There was no indication that Jane was in, or close to, Hanoi. Less still the mountain village of Lào Cai, a location plucked from a selfie of Jafarov with a Mr Wang from an email thread.

But it was a destination. A pin in a map. Somewhere other than where she had been.

If they could find the house in the photo, if nothing else Sam could poke around. Make a nuisance of herself. Let someone's tyres down.

If they were lucky the place might point to where they were keeping Jane.

Unless something else came up between now and then.

Which was possible.

As the plane made its descent Sam considered the wider picture.

A senior member of SIS had been kidnapped, possibly killed. Three reasonably high-profile Pacific Rim businessmen had been brutally murdered; all of them linked to the said SIS officer. The smart money was on Jane being broken in captivity, and handing out their names. One of the men had been about to offer intelligence which pointed to a Level One threat in the region. At the same time Beijing Station was calling a major operation – that was wobbling like a jelly on a dashboard. They couldn't get a hold of it.

That was pretty much as big and as messy as it got.

The Chief knew that. And was that why he had restricted knowledge to the smallest number staff?

If that were the case, why had he chosen the staff he had?

The team running the operation was two strong, maybe three, if you included Riley. And one of those three was an erstwhile case-officer who had been dumped by MI6 three years ago for being a maverick. Frank was a very decent analyst, but hardly a driver. And Riley was clearly subordinate to him.

A Level One threat, originally under the scrutiny of one of SIS's rising stars was now the responsibility of the three *amigos*.

It didn't make any sense.

As the lights in the cabin dimmed and Sam's ears popped, she couldn't get her head round that.

And now it was her turn at the smart glass and metal border desk.

She handed over her passport.

The woman with the military-style blue hat with a light blue central band nodded curtly as she took her document. Sam stared at the cap.

Big gold badge.

In fact, the woman's jacket was adorned with so many official badges it must have been a bugger to clean.

Undoing all those pins.

Then putting all the badges back in the same place. Did she have a photograph to refer to? Or was there a whole day's lesson of badge-pinning at the Vietnamese customs and excise college?

Pass or fail ...

She hated border checkpoints, even internal ones. She had been undone by them a couple of times. She had to keep herself occupied.

As the woman with the blue hat and multiple badges handed back her passport after just a casual glance at her photo, she realised this wasn't going to be one of them.

Phew.

Sam had no baggage, other than her carry-on rucksack and, without further direction from Frank, all she had was an outline itinerary: airport to central Hanoi, and then Hanoi to Lào Cai. Google had told her there were three ways to get to Lào Cai. First was by train, but they only travelled overnight and she'd have liked to cover the two hundred odd miles today.

Second was by coach or taxi. Third was to hire a car.

Which was a problem.

She had been in South East Asia for six days. She'd used her credit and debit cards fifteen times, which was fourteen times too many if she wanted to remain incognito. And she had crossed an international border – twice. For anyone looking to track a player, border crossings was the biggie, certainly if you were in government.

As someone trying to be furtive, she wasn't making a very good fist of it.

Hiring a car gave her flexibility. But it required handing over her driving licence and, again, for anyone interested it would be a big marker. A bus or taxi was a cash transaction, but it was also a one-journey pony. At the end she'd need to take another coach. Or hire another taxi.

Whatever she chose, it would be a compromise. And that needed some thought, which her brain was currently unwilling to process.

Get to central Hanoi. Sleep in the taxi.

She would make a decision when she got to the city.

The main airport atrium was not busy. Most of the desks were closed, as were the shops and cafés. A small number of passengers had adopted the sleeping position, lying on three chairs with their feet poking out into the gangways.

The signs pointing to the taxi-rank were pictorial and Sam had to engage only the tiniest segment of her brain to find the first cab, a white Hyundai i30, sporting a wide, lime green flash.

'Hanoi railway station, please,' she asked, as she flopped into the passenger seat. She hadn't yet chosen to travel to Lào Cai by train. The station was the first central destination which popped into her tiring mind.

A weary smile from the taxi driver was followed by, '*Vâng.*'

The man, a youngish local, tapped away at his smartphone which was on a plastic stand attached to his dashboard. Once Google Maps showed the way, he set off.

With her backpack on her lap, Sam was asleep in seconds.

She woke to the stop/start of East Asian city traffic. She wiped the sleep from her eyes, arched her back and stretched. The clock on the dash read 3.37 am and yet the traffic was as mad as rush hour in any British city. There were three times as many scooters as cars and trucks, and whilst most of the street vendors had closed down, their goods were simply lying about the pavement covered in tarpaulins and plastic sheeting. In amongst the covered goods, one or two kerbside cafés appeared to be offering food of various descriptions.

I could do with some of that.

'*Đây,*' the young driver said as they pulled into a disorganised car park. They'd stopped in front of a train-station-looking, Russianesque, two-storey yellow building with a central, low clock tower displaying the words: *Ga Hà Nội.*

Sam had ten dollars in her hand – which she thought would probably be enough – when movement in the taxi's wing mirror grabbed her attention.

Man. Just got out of a car behind us. Purposefully heading this way.

What?

No ... not again.

Not now.

Sam didn't wait to answer her own question. She threw the ten-dollar bill at the driver and was out of the car a second later, turning from the advancing man.

She ran – away from the building. Across the car park, dodging static cars, to the busy main road.

She was quick, even on an empty stomach.

She glanced behind.

The man was there, half in shadow, maybe 30 metres away. Mid-build. And moving fast. In her direction.

Fuck it.

The road was one way as she looked at it, left to right. It was a miasma of cars and scooters and trucks. Crossing the road was going to be dangerous – even if she took her time. The alternative was left along the pavement, which was more a repository for street vendors' gear than it was for pedestrians. And what bits of pavement there were, were littered with bins, plastic chairs and broken slabs.

Move.

She darted across the three, might be five, lanes of traffic ... which was moving erratically, go – don't go. The scooters, which were travelling quicker than a running man, were doing a better job than the cars.

She stopped briefly, mid-street, to avoid two scooters and a battered Honda Accord and checked behind her. The man had made it to the pavement edge. He was breathing hard. He clearly wasn't expecting a race.

Good.

She glanced to her right.

Shit!

A second man. In the traffic. Maybe 20 metres from her. He wasn't out for a casual stroll either.

Run!

Sam made it past the front of a scooter by the material of her shorts, but got knocked over by a second, which was undertaking the first. She was lifted off the ground, spun and landed awkwardly on her back, the wind pushed from her.

Fuck.

Her breathing was shallow and something hurt somewhere, but she couldn't get her mind to focus on it.

She had to get away.

From whom?

That was too big a question for now. She ignored it.

In any case, it was too late. Against the dark of the night sky, peppered with neon flashes from nearby shops and stools, the man was on her.

But ...

It wasn't the man. Not yet. It was a scooter helmet; small, grey-white with no chin protection. Like Wallace, out of *Wallace and Gromit.* Except it wasn't Wallace ...

... it was an Asian Audrey Hepburn.

What the ...?

'Are you OK?' Perfect English with a soft American accent, silkily lacing through the noise of the traffic.

303

Sam didn't have time to answer. She was scrambling to her feet whilst looking for her assailants.

Shit, my back hurts.

The traffic was causing as much a problem for the two men as it had for her. They had paused; looking confused. Maybe they had lost her in her fall? The original man was halfway across the road, looking beyond and to the left. The second man had made the far pavement, one she was now very close to. He was looking in Sam's direction – but she was shielded by the scooter-beauty.

'Take me away from here. On your scooter. Now … please. I am being followed … by someone who wants to do me harm?' She ignored the words that had come out of her mouth. She looked for hope in the beautiful woman's face and tried very hard to appear as desperate as possible.

Initially there was confusion. Then acceptance.

How does that work?

'Come,' the beauty said.

Her bike was a few metres ahead of them, on its kickstand – the motor still running. Sam waited for the girl to knock the scooter off its stand and perch (oh so elegantly) on the front of the saddle. Behind her, Sam threw her a leg over the bike, grabbed her rescuer by the waist – and then they were off, snaking through the traffic with ease.

She couldn't tell if either of the two men had spotted her. She'd lost the man in the traffic, and the

304

second, on the pavement, moved past them at a jog in the opposite direction.

But she did have a chance to glance over her right shoulder back towards the station car park.

For sure, there wasn't a whole lot of ambient light. And there might have been fifty cars in the car park. But she was confident she spotted a grey or silver Toyota down from where the taxi had dropped her off.

And the men?

Were they as described by the Frenchman at the campsite in Kampot?

Possibly.

How ... ?

Chapter 11

It was 5.45 am. Sam wasn't picking up either phone, which always made Frank nervous. She had been due to land in Hanoi in the early morning. She should be contactable by now.

They'd had some good news. Jafarov's phone was *pinging* which meant someone had turned it on. GCHQ was following it and they were sharing with him the same map application they used in Cambodia before it died at the border. The phone had made it a long way. Currently the *ping* was travelling north on the CT01, about 200 kilometres south of Hanoi. At the current rate it would be in the city in three or four hours.

Riley had pulled together all the intelligence they had on the house in Jafarov and Wang's selfie – and she had a fix. In Lào Cai. Cynthia's database had given a reasonable overhead of the property: detached with a large, park-like garden surrounded by a thick blanket of trees. There were no side shots other than the one from the selfie. He'd ordered some new overheads from Langley – the CIA's satellite database was always more up to date than SIS's. The images would be with him in the next couple of hours.

He'd also woken up the SIS duty officers in Hanoi and Beijing Stations. He had pressed them for anything they had with any connections to Lào Cai, or its environs. Frank sensed initial frustration at being hoofed out of bed at some ungodly hour. But their tune had changed once he'd handed over the op code which finished with an 'x'; the code that gave Frank wide-reaching and pretty immediate powers.

Beijing had returned something within half an hour. And he was looking at that now. It was a month-old paper titled, 'A New Gang Of Four?' He'd scanned its seven pages and then read it in detail. It was interesting stuff and, unbeknown to the writers, seemed likely to have some bearing on Op Mandolin and Abraham. It was sound, if speculative work. And, in one aspect, he was ahead of them.

The Gang of Four were countries not people: China, Vietnam, Cuba and North Korea – the very same Jane was investigating regarding the US mil-spec arms shipment from Cuba to, probably, the DPRK. That was where he was ahead of Beijing.

However, they had more.

Two Beijing case-officers were investigating a series of meetings, backed up by dark web conversations, between senior individuals in the four countries. So far the meetings had all been between two of the parties – never four at the same time. The case-officers had identified a senior DPRK politician, a Cuban minister, a Vietnamese politburo member, and an as yet named member of the Chinese Politburo Standing Committee.

Frank thought the Chinese Standing Committee member might well be called Wang, but it was too early to come to that conclusion.

In isolation the meetings between the four senior politicians were, according to the report, innocuous: trade bilaterals; the sharing of ideological maxims. An email between the two Cuban and Vietnamese politicians was titled: Achieving high level sporting success using the Marxist/Leninist model.

Ordinarily this would not have warranted SIS interest.

However, what was of interest was the conversations had been hidden on the dark web. And the liaisons had been going on for almost a decade, seemingly taking place without entourages and held in unlikely, out of the way, locations ...

... one of which was, and this was the best the report could do for now, Lào Cai. Four separate meetings had been staged there in the past three years. Three were between the Chinese and Vietnamese officials. The fourth, surprisingly as neither were Vietnamese, between China and the DPRK.

Frank was also pretty sure he knew exactly where these meetings had taken place: a detached house, set in parkland surrounded by lots of trees.

Which left his small team with a problem.

Sam was heading in that direction.

Soon?

Now?

He didn't know which.

Once there she might be able to get eyes on. But, as the house was likely a location for high level diplomats to conduct clandestine discussions under the banner of some pretty banal headings, the place would be heavily guarded. And, contrary to the movies, SIS case-officers weren't trained in breaking and entering, disarming multiple guards and potentially rescuing kidnapped British subjects.

The latter thought had only just formed in his mind.

Was it possible?

No.

The chances were incredibly unlikely. Jane had been snatched on the southern Cambodian/Vietnamese border. You could lose an army in the fields in either country as the Americans knew only too well; hide a company forever in the suburbs of one or two of the sprawling and chaotic cities; conceal a squad in the watery jungles of the Mekong.

Jane could be anywhere.

Anywhere.

And even if she were in Lào Cai, they'd need a highly trained force to extradite her.

The UK had one of those: the SAS. Not that he'd ever heard of the Special Air Service operating on the

Pacific Rim. Or, frankly, anywhere east of Afghanistan. But what did he know?

He had to tell the Chief. And he had to speak to Sam.

Which first?

Phone the Chief.

He was eight hours ahead of them. That made it close to 2 pm.

Text him.

He did that:

Sir, I have some new and potentially important info. Timing could be key. Could we speak ASAP? Frank.

He then dialled Sam satphone. It rang twice.

This time ...

'Hi, Frank.'

'Sam. Where are you?'

He wanted to say, 'Where the bloody hell have you been?', but thought better of it.

'Hanoi. I'm in a house. I met someone. It's a long story. And not a pretty one.'

That confused Frank. He mentally stuttered.

'Eh ... I've got something for you. Do you want to go first?' he asked.

'No. Send.'

He took a deep breath and then explained about the Beijing report, the *pinging* phone and the location and description of the house. He finished with, 'I'm trying to get in touch with the boss. To ask what to do next.'

There was silence for a while.

'It's communism,' Sam said.

'What?'

'It's communism. That's the link here. We missed it all along. The ship, with its Cuban, Vietnamese, Chinese and North Korean links. Those are the four remaining communist countries.'

Frank sat back. That made sense – in words. But what did it mean?

And what about Laos?

'What about Laos? They're the fifth "practising" communist country. Doesn't that break your mould?' he suggested.

Sam was quiet.

Riley, who had been sleeping on a small sofa in the station's kitchen, had joined Frank. She presented him with a cup of tea. Frank nodded and pressed the 'speaker' button on his phone.

'Well, Sam?'

'Laos is a red herring. It's not really communist and small fry in comparison to the other four. Wait ... let me think,' she replied.

Frank reached for his tea, raised it to Riley and mouthed, 'Thanks'.

'It's just odd.' Sam had started again. 'That there is a below the radar grouping whose only unifying connection is their political ideology. Maybe they're trying to keep the old guard alive? Keep everyone on the straight and narrow, as Mao and Lenin would want. Goodness knows there's plenty of pressure in all four countries to drop a Marxist approach to life. Hong Kong, for example. And here, the Vietnamese kids are desperate for more freedom. I should know, I've just spent three hours with a couple of them.'

Frank couldn't undo Sam's line of thought.

'If you are right, are these meetings taking place with the sanction of the political leaders? Or is it more subversive? And what about the arms shipment? Is that connected?'

There was more quiet.

'Beats me,' Sam eventually replied.

Silence again. Frank took another sip of his tea.

'Anyway,' Sam continued. 'That's all far too high powered for now. I'm off to Lào Cai. I've got a ride. So I should be there by about lunchtime.'

Frank was quick to interject. 'Hang on, Sam. I'm waiting for a call from the Chief. If Jane is in the building, which I know is a long shot, there's no way you can get her out on your own.'

There was another pause. Frank looked at Riley. Who stared at him back.

'Maybe not. But I can get eyes on. Speak to the boss. If I spot Jane, then I'm going to need back-up.'

The phone went dead before Frank had the chance to say, 'I'm not sure Special Forces work on this side of the world.'

Farm Street, Mayfair, London

Matthew was parked illegally on a single yellow line down from the London residence of Sir Clive Morton. He checked his watch. It was 9.47 pm.

This is madness.

He tapped away on the steering wheel. And then dipped his head so he had full view of the two-storey, yellow-brick façade of No 23a Farm Street. It didn't look much. Like the rest of the houses in the street, the frontage was butt up against the pavement, which was butt up against the narrow road. Apart from a church and an ornate, out of place, half-timbered house, this could be any old-town, city street, with the houses all different but all leant against each other. Sir Clive's house was mock-Georgian terrace, with a gloss black front door and eight, white-surround sash windows, three above two, below three. It was inelegant, but functional.

But this wasn't any old city street.

This was Mayfair, where real estate prices were among the most expensive in the world. And properties, even inelegant ones, were owned by the richest people, or the oldest families ... and Matthew reckoned the interior of Sir Clive's inelegant house would be beautifully, if soberly decorated.

After some thorough research, he thought he now knew a little more about the Chief of SIS. Public school educated, from a distantly rich family and with a degree from Edinburgh thirty years ago, after a short spell in the navy, he joined Secret Intelligence Service. His career with SIS took him to all of the hotspots, including Iraq and Afghanistan. Before becoming the 'Chief', or 'C' as he was colloquially known, he was head of SIS's counterintelligence. His decorations included the MBE, CBE, CB and then a knighthood. To add to an unblemished record, he was still married to the same woman he'd met at university and they had two children; one was an army officer, the second a vet.

It had taken Matthew most of the afternoon to piece together a picture of Sir Clive Morton. He'd had to be careful not to look too hard, but he reckoned he'd got the balance right. Sadly, but not surprisingly, there was nothing in his investigations which threw up a flag. Sir Clive was the perfect candidate to lead the country's overseas intelligence agency. And, by all accounts, he was incredibly good at it.

Matthew had read nearly all of his previous speeches, most of the relevant newspaper articles and a good number of his papers. There was nothing, no ideological anomalies, no political infringements, nothing that pointed to the fact he might be running an illicit operation with a Swiss bank to short the North Korean *won* to the tune of £650 million.

He was the perfect patriot. An exemplary civil servant.

And ... it was very likely he'd just pulled up outside his house.

With cars parked on both sides of the street, the heavy black Jag had stopped in the middle of the road. Out of the kerbside back door a male figure – bespectacled, just short of six foot and with grey hair which was thinning on top – got out.

In poor light it was difficult to be absolutely sure it was him.

I'll take that chance ...

... especially as the figure would be in his house in seconds.

Matthew threw open the door of his car and moved quickly down the pavement towards the Chief.

'Sir Clive!' Matthew was 15 metres away from the man who was placing a key into his front door. The pavement between them was empty. His voice would reach.

The figure stopped what he was doing, stood up straight and turned to face Matthew.

Smack!

Matthew was on the floor, his legs taken from him by a rugby-style tackle. His elbow hit the concrete slab first and pain shot up his arm to his shoulder.

Bugger, that hurt.

Then his left arm was behind him, his wrist pushed towards the nape of his neck, so much so he thought it was going to dislocate. It was a classic arrest technique. He shouldn't have expected anything less.

Stupidly, he hadn't expected anything at all.

But he was a strong forty-year-old. Boxing training fit. And he wasn't yet prepared to give up the fight.

'Sir Clive. I'm from The Box. I want to talk to you about Anne Bertram,' he shouted. His face was squashed flat on the floor and he was unable to move because he now had a knee in his back.

And the man had started to open his door again.

Fuck it.

'I want to talk about 5toa!' he shouted.

Everything was happening quickly. He was being pulled to his knees and his hands cuffed behind his back. Another bodyguard, and the driver of the Jag, was out of the car and heading his way.

The man had his door open and had taken a step in.

'The fifth tunnel of aggression!' Matthew screamed. His final effort.

Immediately time stood still.

Yes, he was still being expertly manhandled by the two men. His tackler was behind him and he heard him call for a back-up car to 'pick up an arrest from his location'. Matthew hadn't seen any police-style radios, so he assumed this was all earpiece and lapel microphone

316

stuff. Worryingly, the driver who was now a couple of metres from him had drawn a pistol, the short barrel of which was pointing directly at Matthew's chest.

But the Chief, it was definitely him, was no longer entering the house. He had stopped, mid-threshold. And his face was outside, rather than inside the house.

Time was still struggling to reset itself.

The Chief was looking directly at him. Matthew didn't waver, even as he was being manhandled to the car.

Then; 'Let him go.'

There was momentary confusion from the two bodyguards.

'Let him go. Check his credentials and get him in here. Quickly,' the Chief ordered.

Thirty seconds later, still sore and with grazes to his face, he was inside 23a Farm Street, Mayfair. London.

'Drink?' The Chief held up a square decanter, three-quarters full of a tea-coloured liquid.

Matthew had been asked to sit on one of two cream and red sofas in the front room of the house. He guessed Sir Clive would call it a 'sitting room', or maybe even 'the drawing room'. It wasn't a huge space, but easily big enough for two mid-sized sofas, a couple of ornate, wooden chairs, a delicate coffee table, a drinks table, some bookcases and a display cabinet full of silver and enamel objects. The decor was a combination of light creams, dark reds and walnut furniture. There was a small glass chandelier and other tasteful table lights. It was elegant and not overdone.

'No, thanks. Unless you have some water?' Matthew replied.

'Yes. Of course. I'll just pop to the kitchen.'

It seemed as though the Chief lived on his own in London. No maid. He was fetching the water himself.

And the bodyguards hadn't come into the house. They'd un-cuffed him, checked his ID and then, with only a grunt, escorted him to the front door where Sir Clive had courteously showed him in.

Sir Clive was out of the room for less than a minute. Matthew stayed where he was and took in more of his surroundings. The walls displayed four paintings. All of them landscapes: rugged mountains – snatches of desert. A camel in the distance. Some tribesmen and a tented camp.

'Helmand.' The Chief was back in the front room. 'A local artist did them. They're not fabulous works of art, but they provide immovable memories. I'm very fond of them.' He passed Matthew a cut-glass crystal tumbler of water. It had ice and a slice of lemon.

'Thanks.'

The Chief sat on the second sofa. He looked at ease. They were now perpendicular to each other. The Chief had crossed his legs and was sipping a drink out of a cognac balloon glass.

'So, Matthew. You're the Service officer who made the enquiry concerning 5toa? Which, as I understand it, you got from a CIA source in Zagreb?' The Chief's tone was relaxed. Comforting.

Matthew nodded. And took a sip of his water. He was sitting forward in his seat, his elbows on his knees.

He wouldn't say he was nervous; more like tense.

But he was here now. He had crossed the Rubicon.

As a result, he had no choice.

Everything has to come out.

'You're the man who got that thug to threaten me with a dead rabbit?' Matthew was eye to eye with the Chief.

Sir Clive didn't reply straight away. Matthew couldn't see any emotion behind the glasses. No hint of surprise. Or anger.

'Is that what they did?' Sir Clive tutted. 'Sorry about that.'

'So it was you? That's hardly the way to treat a fellow intelligence officer?'

The Chief took another sip of his drink. And didn't answer his question.

'It may be difficult for you to believe, but we are on the same side,' the Chief said. 'Tell me about 5toa. And Anne Bertram. Please.'

Matthew had decided to meet Sir Clive Morton because he couldn't think of any other way of taking what he had discovered forward. He would either have to leave well alone – as instructed by the man with the dead rabbit – or confront the whole thing head on.

He'd chosen the latter.

And he had already got much further than he had expected.

Which was why he was pleased he had covered his back.

Before leaving Thames House he'd documented everything and printed it out. He'd then put the papers in a double envelope and sent it first class to his brother. It was a hugely dramatic act but, in the time he had, he couldn't think of a better way to protect himself. The top envelope was plain – just his brother's address. The inside envelope bore the words: *Only open if you don't hear from me in the next 36 hours.*

His brother was a police sergeant in Bristol. He knew what Matthew did for a living and would know what to do if he hadn't heard from him by close of play tomorrow.

So, after another sip of water to moisten his dry mouth, he told Sir Clive almost everything. Including his disdain for his current operations manager and his general concern for where the senior echelons of his organisation were heading.

But he didn't mention the shorting of the *won*. He felt that was just a little too close for comfort.

The Chief didn't interrupt him. He just sat there, slowly getting through a medium-sized balloon of brandy.

When Matthew had finished, he felt as though a weight had been lifted. He sat back in the sofa.

And waited.

Eventually, 'Why do you think the request concerning the abbreviation "5toa" came from a CIA analyst? Not, say, director level to one of the deputies in my organisation?'

Matthew still wasn't sure.

'I don't know. Unless he felt unable to ask the question of his own chain of command?' Matthew answered.

'Mmm.' The Chief put down his drink and brought his hands together. He then continued. 'Do you know that Zagreb Mission Centre was recently bombed?'

'Of course.' Matthew tried not to look affronted. 'I'd heard about the IED and that there may be a US connection. The reports I've seen from our embassy were vague but, certainly amongst the desk officers in The Box, we suspected an in-house job. There just wasn't a credible threat before the attack.'

'They killed an agent … case-officer,' the Chief added, unnecessarily noting the two different national titles for the same job. 'Didn't get him in the blast, so they finished him off in the hospital.'

Wow.

Matthew hadn't heard that.

'And you think this is connected? This is to do with the North Korean's fifth tunnel of aggression?' Matthew asked.

'Possibly.' The Chief sat up. 'OK. We need to get you properly security cleared. And then I want you to call in sick. Can you do that?'

That caught Matthew completely off guard.

What?

What is going on?

'Why?' It was the best he could do.

'Because what you have unearthed is just part of a top-level SIS investigation that is on the closest of holds. I currently have a crack team in South East Asia working an operation which might be moving too quickly, even for them. I'd like you to join them. Please. How soon can you get to an airport?'

Off guard certainly wasn't a strong enough description.

South East Asia?

Away from the lunatic operations manager currently running the asylum?

Where do I sign?

22°26'50.0"N, 103°59'27.0"E, Outskirts of Lào Cai, Vietnam

Sam wasn't a nervous passenger. Not really.

That's what she told herself.

Unless she was asleep, she was a fiddler. Pushing buttons, touching surfaces – anything that dissipated the energy that overtook her when she didn't have hold of the steering wheel.

Hau Trần – Sam's new best friend and scooter-borne rescuer – was, thankfully, a careful driver. The road from Hanoi to Lào Cai could best be described as adequate. The road users, less so. Sam had experienced road and driving conditions in many non-first world countries, so the lack of consistent tarmac and the continuous ambition for two lanes to become three, or sometimes four, didn't surprise her. But it couldn't stop her involuntarily breathing in on more than one occasion. Hau had done well.

It had taken some time for them to get out of Hanoi but once they were free of the city traffic and the road started to climb into the mountains, Sam's anxiety had become less persistent. It spiked occasionally on mountain corners where a coach or lorry would assume it was safe to take most of the road. Inevitably, though, Sam wouldn't be completely relaxed until she was out of the car – a Mark 1 Nissan Micra, brush-overpainted in bright red, with hand-sketched yellow flowers on its bonnet.

Which put Hau in a box. She was, like the few Vietnamese youngsters Sam had encountered over the past couple of days, very keen to be free of the shackles of Vietnam's past. To move beyond the one-party state

323

which was still struggling to look forward, rather than back to the horrors of the civil war. Unlike her parents she was educated and starting off on a university degree. She had ambitions to become a graphic designer. She had entrepreneurial bones – and her colourful car was a statement of that intent. Sure, she had little money. But she had talent and class. And vision. Hau, like the friends she had introduced Sam to in her tiny flat, were the new Vietnamese. They had their parents' stoicism and work ethic. Yet they also had young people's eyes, and a purpose shaped by a future they glimpsed from social media.

Unfortunately it was clear to Sam that Hau and her friends were shackled by the system. Not completely. Not so much there was rioting in the streets. But enough to clip wings.

And it didn't look like improving anytime soon.

Which was a worry. Especially if what she and Frank had spoken about early this morning had even an element of truth. A communist – or Marxist/Leninist – pact between maverick elements of the four remaining communist countries, working collectively to prevent the breakdown of the old order.

Hau and her friends versus the system.

The system would win.

Social media was non-existent in the DPRK. It was tightly state-regulated in China. Both Cuba and Vietnam restricted access to some sites, such as WhatsApp and Facebook. And it wouldn't take much to close internet access in those countries, if that's what the governments wanted to do.

Sam hadn't said as much to Hau. She didn't want to dent her and her friends' enthusiasm. She had just enjoyed the company of four wonderfully ebullient and positive young women; girls almost. They had fed and watered her. Encouraged her to shower (in a sensitive way) and, when she'd been in the same room, hadn't stopped talking to her even though it was only just beyond dawn and all Sam wanted to do was sleep.

And Hau had insisted she drove Sam to Lào Cai. Sam had concocted a story that she worked for the British Council in Saigon. She was in Hanoi meeting friends when she became separated from them after a night out. The man who was chasing her (Sam cut the chasing party to one) was a taxi driver whom she hadn't paid in full because he'd massively overcharged. She'd run away from the man and, in fear of her life, had dashed across the road.

Bang! Sam had clapped at that point, and Hau and her friends had jumped – so entranced were they with her fairy-tale. Next thing Sam was on the road with a helmeted Hau looking over her. And then they were racing through traffic.

Escape was theirs!

The four young women had all cheered at that point.

Which made Sam uncomfortable, because most of it was untrue.

325

She hated lying. And she particularly hated lying to such innocence.

But it was a case of needs must. And she did take some solace from the fact the actual story would have elicited wider eyes and a much bigger 'hurrah!'

And now, here she was. Hau driving meticulously, and Sam still grimacing with every near miss.

I am hopeless.

In so many ways.

The scenery was fabulous. And it was cooler in the hills. If it wasn't for the temperature and the stepped and cascading tea plantations, they could have been making their way through the foothills of the Austrian Alps. The distant mountains were rugged and tall, but not snow-peaked, although Hau told Sam they would attract some snow in February and March.

And they hadn't been tailed. She was sure of it.

Which was some relief.

Sam tried every possible permutation, but couldn't work out how they, whoever they were, had found her. Only two people knew of her itinerary: Frank and, she guessed, Riley.

Maybe three? Frank had said something earlier about briefing the Chief.

She was an easy target. Her name was on her plane ticket, if that's how she had been discovered. Her passport had been examined at both airports, a prerequisite even for internal flights in Vietnam, so she could had been tagged then?

But where did it start? When did someone say, 'Find Sam Green'?

And was it the same people who had taken Jane?

The silver Toyota.

She had seen it. Hadn't she? At the train station.

She couldn't be sure; it had been fleeting.

And were these people connected to the 'Gang of Four' in the Beijing Station report?

Were she and Frank up against the totality of a communist pact?

More important ... by travelling to Lào Cai, was she walking into a trap of her own making?

She should be careful.

I will.

Sam checked the map on her phone. They were within a kilometre of the villa.

'Pull over, Hau, please.' They hadn't been speaking for a while. The traffic had picked up and Sam didn't want to break her new friend's concentration.

'Here?'

'Yes, please. That's fine. Thanks. I'll walk from here. I need the exercise.' Sam nodded and smiled.

Actually what Sam needed was to get Hau out of harm's way. The last time she had been rescued by a beautiful woman had been in Miami, two years ago. On a gorgeous monster trike.

Ginny.

Sam had abused that friendship. She had overstayed her welcome and exposed Ginny to the forces chasing her. As a result Ginny had been ritually murdered, and a message daubed in red lipstick on Ginny's bedroom mirror.

This is your fault.

It had been.

And it wasn't going to happen again.

Not to Hau.

The Micra came to a stop. Sam who, as always, had her backpack on her lap, reached across and, rather uncomfortably – as it wasn't her natural way – gave Hau a hug. As she did she dropped a twenty-dollar bill behind Hau's back.

'Thank you so much.'

'You're welcome. I'm so glad I could help.' Hau smiled so brightly it lit up an already very bright day.

Sam paused. But not for long.

Come on.

She got out of the car, waved shyly and, as she headed off down the street, immediately tried very hard to forget about her new friend.

It took her ten minutes to find the house or, that is, the grounds of the house. Sam approached from a side street and stopped short of the road which, according to Google Maps, circled most of the grounds. The perimeter looked to be surrounded by a brick wall, 2 metres tall, topped with barbed wire. Behind the wall was a jungle of pines and scrubby-topped evergreen trees. She couldn't see beyond the green mass. The house was hidden.

She walked to the junction and was met by a stream of scooters, taxis and cars heading in both directions. She stopped. And looked across the road for surveillance devices: cameras; stalks; antennae.

Nothing

Left, about 30 metres away, was a double gate, set back from the wall. It was guarded, interestingly, not by soldiers. Or policemen. That told her something: this was not an overtly-government facility.

Town-side of the gate were two men. Mid-sized, suit trousers and open-necked shirts. They both carried walkie-talkies. Sam couldn't be sure from this distance, but it looked like one of the men wore a holster in the nap of his back.

She turned right and, staying on the non-walled side of the road, followed the pavement as it bore left. There were cars parked haphazardly on her side of the road, but none on the other. There were no signs to say 'no parking' – not that anyone took any notice of signs in this country. But someone had put the word out.

No cars on the road by the house.

The locals knew who was in charge.

As Sam reconnoitred she had to venture onto broken tarmac to navigate a street café and later a line of tatty scooters which looked to be for sale from what might well be a workshop-cum-garage. Poor quality houses of varying descriptions accompanied her

329

journey, as did all shapes and sizes and ages of locals. At one point she was offered some fruit from a tray by a toothless woman wearing a paddy field hat. Sam dismissed the seller with a flat hand and a polite, 'No, thank you.'

And then the wall stopped abruptly, turned left and headed into scrubby, plastic strewn wasteland – which looked at worst impenetrable; at best, very scratchy. Sam stayed on the wrong side of the road and followed the scrubland for a little while.

There.

A gap. Certainly one she could disappear into. She stood on tiptoes. And couldn't see beyond the tall scrub. She looked around. To her rear right was a large hole in a poorly rendered wall, masquerading as a café. Small, primary school tables and chairs were scattered around.

No one in the café?

She stood on one of the chairs – and craned her neck.

Gotcha.

She could see the wall in the distance. And she could pick out a route to it.

Sam jumped off the chair.

If there weren't so many people kicking around …

She could wait until it was dark. Wrong. She *should* wait until it was dark.

That was the textbook solution.

Which she didn't take.

'Do you speak English?' She had stopped a young lad, maybe fourteen years old. He was Sam's size but as skinny as a fistful of bamboo.

'Yes. A little.'

'Do you want ten dollars?' She had pulled the lad to one side, checking that he wasn't with anyone.

Sam took a ten-dollar bill from her waist bag. His eyes lit up. He reached for the money.

'Wait.' She stopped him, pulling the bill away. 'I want you to do something for me ...'

Sam waited until the diversion was in full swing before she darted across the road and slipped into the bushes. She left behind a small version of chaos. The lad had taken a stick and a metal bin and was walking up and down the pavement making a helluva racket. Every so often, he took his drum onto the road and stopped the traffic. There were hoots and shouts and, by the time Sam disappeared from view, a small crowd had gathered to watch the boy beat the bin with all his might.

She was skirting the wall, maybe 5 metres from it. In less than a minute she was out of view of the street, although she could still hear the melee. The boy was earning his ten dollars. A couple of minutes later the wall turned left again, at an angle. She been expecting this – Google Maps had given a reasonably clear view of the wall and the extent of the scrub. In another 30 metres she would hit a second road and her cover would be lost.

Sam stopped ... and looked up at the wall. It was still 2 metres high and still topped with barbed wire, although one or two of the trees' branches poked over the wall like an uncontrollable fringe.

But it was out of sight of the road and the houses.

And it would have to do.

She checked her watch. It was 3.17 pm.

Shift changes across the world happened at breakfast, lunch, tea and supper. She wanted any guards inside the grounds to be nearing the end of their shift and not be at a changeover, where the guard size would double. Half past three in the afternoon was as good as it got in daylight.

In three strides and after a fight with a bush she was at the wall, under one of the branches.

She fingered the red bricks, running her thumb along the mortar, some of which was dislodged by her touch. She glanced up. 2 metres. 7 feet. Maybe six and a half. And then a roll of concertina wire.

Sam was five six in her socks.

I need help.

She looked around.

Nothing.

She followed the wall right for 5 metres, her bare skin scratched by thorny bushes.

Nothing.

Then ...

... a log, sticking out from the bottom of a bush. About the size of an upright vacuum cleaner.

It would have to do.

She pulled and pulled. It gave a little. *Pull.* And then it gave a lot. She fell on her backside and bumped her head on the wall.

Shit!

Idiot.

Nothing dented, other than her pride.

She placed the log against the wall, fat end set on the ground, thin end a metre up the wall. She looked up. There was a branch a little to her left. *Nope, not quite.* She slid the log so she was closer to the branch.

And then ...

... she stopped. Took her own phone out of her bag and SMSed Frank:

I'm at the house. Going over the wall.

She pressed, 'Send'.

And then, with her rucksack as protection against the wire, her feet on the log and her arm – the one which didn't pop out of its socket when she least expected it – grabbing the top of the wall, she was up ... and wavering ... and – *shit, that's a spike of wire in my knee* – she reached and wobbled comically. And ... *just get the damn thing* ... she now had both hands on the branch on the far side of the wall.

She launched herself. Twisted.

Swung.

And dangled.

Her feet a good metre from the ground. Her backpack caught on the wire.

Her upper body strength was good. Almost a year of concentrated yoga, press ups, pull ups ... she could hang on for a good while.

But she needed her backpack. It had both the phones. And a pistol.

She slid one hand along the branch towards the wire. And the second.

Did the same again.

This is going to be a one-shot weapon.

She grabbed the backpack with the closest hand and, knowing that she couldn't hold on with one arm for more than a few seconds, looked down ... and let go.

Rip, thud!

...

She was down. Safely. As was most of her backpack. It was pretty much intact. A couple of tears.

Sam crouched. And listened.

She couldn't see beyond the trees, the undergrowth was thick bushes. But she sensed she was no more than 10 metres from the edge of the wood.

She listened some more.

...

No dogs.

Nothing unusual.

Good.

She got onto her hands and knees and, pulling her rucksack along with her, she gently crawled her way through the bushes.

Cobwebs brushed against her face. A rustle from her left. Too quiet to be human.

She had to double-back once and alter her course twice. And then a clearing, no bigger than a bedroom, with a passageway at the end leading, she thought, to the house.

In the middle of the clearing was freshly dug earth, a few centimetres higher than the surrounding woodland detritus of rotting leaves and bark.

A wide line of freshly dug earth.

Maybe a couple of metres long. And a metre wide.

Freshly dug earth.

She touched it. Felt it.

And then, with reason slipping away, she scooped some from the top of the pile.

Slowly at first.

She scooped some more.

Both hands now.

Quicker.

This is madness.

And more. A steady rhythm.

Sam moved to the centre of the mound, both hands cupping and pulling, the mud flicking towards her, over her thighs. Onto her chest.

Her rhythm picked up. It matched the tempo of the spinning thoughts in her head. Her hands were dirty. Bits of damp mud was cementing on her thin cotton trousers and blouse, turning them from pale colours to dark brown.

Her pace didn't slow. In fact it got quicker. Bordering on frantic.

She continued to dig. Her nails weren't long, but they started to break. One by one. Mud splattered in her eyes. Sweat poured from her face ... the picture now of an unhinged woman, scratching at the ground, digging as if she were unearthing a hoard. Or saving something that had been buried ... alive.

Come on.

She had moved again, half a metre maybe, away from the wall. Towards the house. Now working the far end of the freshly dug earth. Her rucksack had been inadvertently covered, hidden from view. It didn't matter.

Nothing mattered.

Still she dug.

Tears now. And snot.

Snot and tears. And sweat. Scoops of mud.

Nothing mattered. Just the earth. The freshly dug earth.

She was a mud monster.

Now manic. Depraved.

Scared.

Shit!

That hurt. A finger had caught something that didn't want to move. There was no give. It wasn't hand on flesh, which was maybe what she was expecting. It was something more solid ... more *plastic*.

She pushed now, with a flat hand. Making way for the object she had hit. Clearing the earth. Pushing and scraping.

Brown gave way to black.

Organic to inorganic.

Oh fuck.

She knew straight away.

She knew all her fears were coming together at a crossroads. That they were smashing at each other like a gigantic car crash. The worst of the worst.

She had come this far.

Today. Since she'd left Frank's. Since the army had medically discharged her.

She had come *this* far.

And now it ended.

A black, heavy plastic body bag. Her finger had caught a seam. A seam that ran alongside a zip. A zip which finally shut the light from a human being.

Sam knew Jane was in the bag. It was the only answer.

And she hated it. Despised it. The question on its own was horrendous. The answer, unspeakable. They had broken Jane. Tortured her, like they had Jafarov and Zhao. And then murdered her.

Stuck her in a bag in a shallow grave.

Sam's rate slowed, but she didn't stop. There was no reason for her to go on, although she had to be sure. Didn't she? But it was futile, wasn't it? What would she do when she saw Jane's face? Would she zip up the bag and rebury her friend's body?

She didn't know.

But she kept scooping and pushing, following the zip, clearing in the direction she thought was headwards.

Scoop. Scoop. Push.

She had slowed. Become more methodical. Her tears had stopped. That was over. She was devastated. Smashed. But, somehow, not broken. There were many times in her past where she had been so overwhelmed, she couldn't have cared what might happen to her. She had longed for death. For the trigger to be pulled. For the fire to consume her.

Now, after Switzerland, that along with her dreams had gone.

Moments ago she thought she would break completely. Collapse into the mud. Join her friend with the maggots in the ground, side by side.

Finish it now. What else was there?

But that thought, that image, had been fleeting.

Fear and pain and wretchedness had gone.

Now she felt rage and drive and complete commitment.

And it had coalesced.

Her teeth were grinding, her joints straining. Her hands and arms working relentlessly, but not in panic. She *was* a mud monster. That was now an apt description. But monster was the stronger of the two nouns.

She was crazed. Determined.

But in control.

Jane might be dead. She wasn't.

And that was the way it was going to stay.

There.

The zip bridge and puller.

She brushed the final pieces of earth to one side.

And stopped.

She crawled across the mud pile she'd created and dug out her rucksack. She brushed her hands as clean as she could, and then took out her phone. She found the camera app.

She had to do this. And she would be quick about it. She needed a photo to prove it was Jane. And she didn't want to expose herself to her friend's body any longer than was needed.

Still on her knees and with one hand on the puller and one ready to take the shot, she exposed the head of the corpse.

Fuck.

Her heart was beating in her head and her mind spun so quickly she felt light-headed.

She shut her eyes and pulled the zipper closed.

Fuck, fuck, fuck.

It wasn't Jane.

Fuck!

It was a man. That's all she could tell – his face had been cut hundreds of times with a sharp blade.

It was a man?

She had to be sure.

She pulled the zip down again, this time to the corpse's chest.

It was definitely a man.

She took some photos, and then closed the body bag.

Fuck.

She had been diverted. Wasted too much time, and far too much energy.

Move.

Fuck.

Sam placed her now muddy phone back in her backpack and crawled down the path until she had a view of the house.

Fuck.

She was filthy. And sweaty. And tired.

And resolute. And determined.

She was a different Sam Green to Switzerland. And Italy, and Venezuela.

Something had bypassed something else; some synapses weren't working.

Her treatment of Frank. Her acceptance of Jane's death. They were bumps in the road.

Just bumps. The road ahead now clear.

There.

It was 25 metres away. A turn of the last century, colonial villa. Two-storey, dramatic roof – all in all about the size of a couple of tennis courts. It had bay windows, a side door – she guessed there was a grander entrance round to one side – a balcony … and a set of six first floor windows.

Which were all barred.

She ducked down, and slid back into the bushes.

And a roving guard.

Who had a rifle. With an optic sight.

She watched, wide-eyed.

Taking it all in. Every little thing.

And then a fleeting image. First floor, second window from the right.

A woman. *Must be?* The silhouette making it clear.

A Westerner – as tall as Jane. Too big for a local.

She looked very frail with rounded shoulders, which wasn't like her friend. The female frame stopped briefly at the window, her face half-obscured by the bars.

And then her head moved to one side, the lowering sun catching her features. And then she turned and was gone.

Chapter 12

Triệu Quang Phục, Lào Cai, Vietnam

Jane was tired. Close to exhausted. It had been a long day. Certainly long for her. This morning she had managed a strip wash with the help of Jingfei, her female guard. There was a basin in her new room and, since the event with the mirror, she had discarded all dignity. She was more than happy to let Jingfei undress her and then mop her down with a flannel and some carbolic soap. Her guard avoided the dressing which, if routine was adhered to, would be changed tonight by a man who Jane thought was probably a doctor. Like Jingfei, he didn't speak English, and Jane little Mandarin, so she would never know. In any case, words were beyond her at the moment. Nods and smiles, and the odd grimace, were her current methods of communication.

Jingfei also fed her. Jane could have managed, but she preferred the attention. And it wasn't that she was being force fed – she wasn't trying not to eat, she just wasn't hungry. She had made an attempt on her own her life once and that had been enough. It wouldn't happen again. Starvation wasn't on her mind.

She really couldn't go through that again.

She thought she had lost consciousness within a minute of the cutting. The next thing she knew it was days later. She still couldn't be absolutely sure. She'd woken in what she had named the cosseted room, lying comfortably on a single bed, one wrist bandaged and as sore as hell – the other attached to a drip. It was, she thought – having glanced out of the window – morning.

It had taken her a couple of hours to come to fully, by which time Jingfei had visited twice, checking her vitals and smiling incessantly. Once fully with it, Jane had taken in the room. It was as she had coined: cosseted. Or, more accurately, the suicide prevention room. There was a bed on which was a mattress – no cover or sheet. A sink, no towel. A wooden chair. And a bucket, for emergencies – as when she needed to go she knocked on the door and Jingfei accompanied her to the loo, which was now mirrorless and unlockable.

She was wearing cotton pyjamas; no cord. There was nothing on the wood-panelled and plaster walls, other than wood and plaster. And there was a single window, which was locked and barred.

Nothing else. Nothing which she might be able to use as a weapon against herself.

Waking from that dreadful sleep was two days ago. Since then she had been fed three times a day and washed in the morning. There had been no visitation by the stockbroker and no one had asked anything of her, other than Jingfei, who had used words Jane didn't understand, but actions she did.

And, having now had time to reflect, she had no idea how she felt.

Why were they keeping her alive?

She had all her faculties back, so why wasn't there a full-on interrogation? Why hadn't the stockbroker come back with the Nirex folder of devastating photos?

Which led to the question which she had banned herself from thinking.

Jane refused to ask herself about her mum. And her brother and his wife. And Sophie.

So she didn't.

Instead she had slept and, when awake, had tottered around the room dragging her drip stand with her. Every so often she paused to glance out of the window to the hills beyond.

It was late afternoon now. She had just stopped to look out across over the trees. The mountains were beautiful. She'd heard that northern Vietnam, which is where she guessed she was, was a 'must-see' on the tourist trail. That the stepped paddy fields were outrageously photogenic. She couldn't tell much from where she found herself, but she sensed that was the case. The greens she saw were vibrant, and the sky a brilliant, metallic blue, cluttered in one corner by gathering clouds. Rain would come soon, but for the moment there was peace.

She felt that too. Something close to peace.

Since the cutting.

It was as though she had been squeezed through a mangle and, like a cartoon character, had re-formed.

344

The same model, but updated. She was calmer, but not completely serene – especially when the door unlocked and she had to second guess who might be entering. Her nerves always jangled then.

But it was nearly always Jingfei. Happy Jingfei, who must have been about Jane's age, but acted older. She came in wearing a mother's smile, carrying a plateful of tasteless food and mucky coffee. Jane found herself beginning to smile back. To share some of her guard's warmth.

It was turning into an acceptable routine.

Eating and sleeping. Washing and dressing.

It was unremarkable, but something close to tranquillity.

The room didn't have air-conditioning, but it was never overly warm. In the middle of the night, when she woke from a bad dream with sweat on her shoulders and moisture plaiting her hair, she was never cold. It was a steady, workable temperature, like baby bear's porridge.

It had only been a couple of days of an unremarkable existence, but she sensed a rhythm. No highs, no lows. Just pleasantness accompanied by an aching wrist.

Was she depressed? Was that what it was? She had reason to be, surely?

Once, when they had been doing yoga together, her friend Sam Green had described her own depression. What had she said?

It's like drowning, when everyone else is breathing.

No, she didn't feel like that. It wasn't that dramatic.

What was it like then?

Jane remembered her maths from school. Those waves – sine waves which oscillated up and down like a skipping rope. Highs and lows.

That was normal life. Life back in London. Ups and downs.

But it wasn't her. Not now.

She felt more as if someone had taken hold of the dial and turned it down, so the graph was still making waves, but they weren't as big as normal. Like a ripple.

She didn't feel much. If anything. The beauty of the vista seen from the window was a watercolour wash. It was pretty, but there was no depth.

That was her. That's how she felt.

No depth. No ups and downs.

And she was happy with it.

She liked not having to feel. She relished the calm. The horizontal. The uncomplicated.

And she really hoped she could cling on to that for as long as possible.

She certainly wasn't ready for someone to play with the dial.

Frank's phone rang. He was in the embassy canteen. It was Sam.

'Sam?'

He stood, picked up his tray and headed to the kitchen hatch. He needed to take this call in the station's office.

'I've found her.'

What? Shit.

'Hang on, Sam. I need to move back to my desk. I'll be a minute.' He dropped off the tray and then headed for the corridor which led to a set of stairs, down to the station. 'And don't hang up. I have something for you.'

She's found Jane.

Shit!

He was jogging; a novel concept.

'I'm almost there ...' He pushed the door open, entered and closed the door behind him. He skirted around the desk which he had been given by the admin staff, and sat down.

'OK.' He took a shallow breath. 'I'm ready.'

There was nothing. An empty earpiece.

'Sam!'

'Shhh.' A whispered response, delayed slightly whilst the security algorithms did their thing.

Frank waited.

He had a pen in hand and a notebook open. He doodled. His favourite was a flower: a circle, petals, a stem and a pot. He finished one, drew in some shade and started on a second.

'Frank. 'You still there?' A hiss.

'Yes.'

'I've seen her in a window, which is barred. The villa is medium-sized, two floors. There's a single, roving armed guard. Nothing else on the outside as far as I can see.' She was cantering. 'I've done a full circle of the building. There's at least one other person inside ...'

Sam continued whispering her expert briefing whilst Frank scribbled. With her help he could've sketched a pretty accurate picture of the building including strengths and weaknesses, entry points and escape routes. He wrote down the make and registration of the car that was parked in front of the house, and he drew a sketch of the wall which Sam had scaled. He had everything he needed ... if they had been planning a release operation.

Which they weren't.

The Chief had been very clear after Frank had briefed him of Sam's latest location, and that she was going 'over the wall'.

'You must stop her!' His order had been sharp. 'Now!'

Frank had tried, but Sam had not picked up either of her phones. And now, an hour later, she was over the wall and had staked out the house.

'So, Frank. We need to get Jane out of the villa. I can't do this on my own.' Still whispers from Sam.

He took a breath.

'We can't do it, Sam.' He grimaced as he uttered the words. He knew to expect a fusillade in response.

Instead there was nothing.

'Look ...' he continued, 'In the last hour I've had fifteen minutes with the Chief. He agrees with the Gang of Four line. It was what he was expecting and, on its own, it's dynamite, albeit uncorroborated intelligence.' He stopped and listened. 'Are you there, Sam?'

Nothing. Then a grunt, which he accepted as 'understood'.

'And, apparently, bravo to us, and Jane, and Beijing.' He took the handset away from his ear and looked at it, hoping for some response. There was nothing. He put it back and continued. 'The thing is, the Chief is into that there's a major event going down. Possibly orchestrated by the Four; possibly from the building you're looking at. He reckons we're getting close to working out what that is. And an operation by us to release Jane will scare the horses and burn any leads we have.' He paused and listened. Nothing.

Sod it.

He continued.

'The best plan would be to target the villa passively, using GCHQ. Maybe establish some form of long-term electronic surveillance. Perhaps target a guard. Get an agent inside.' Again he paused, hoping for a response. Nothing.

Now irritated – on a Frank level – he continued.

'In any case, he was clear that the PM wouldn't sanction the use of SF in this part of the world.'

Frank thought he got the Chief's line. That, should a foreign intelligence agency expose the Gang of Four, they would go further to ground. And, if there was something big going down, they would close ranks and the chance of uncovering more useful intelligence would be lost. Although it was an appalling thought, he could see that Op Mandolin and Abraham were bigger than Jane Baker.

Which hurt. But not so much that he couldn't encourage Sam to do what the Chief had ordered.

'Sam?'

Nothing. A breath.

And then more nothing.

'He reckons he may need us. He doesn't want you getting in harm's way. He says we're ahead of the curve. And he's sending out another guy. To help. He's an MI5 intelligence officer. He's flying into Hanoi. Tomorrow morning.'

Still nothing.

Shit.

He knew what was going on in northern Vietnam. He could picture Sam's face. He'd seen it before. Last year, when Jane had tried to call them back from Switzerland to Rome: twice. Both times Sam had resisted. She had been set on a plan which she thought was more important than the one Jane was pursuing. And she had done what she thought was right.

And sod the consequences.

'Sam. You have to listen to me. I'm with the Chief here. We can't fly SF to Vietnam and, even if we could, it would take a couple of days, maybe more. And they'd need eyes on – you know – to confirm the target is still in the building. And you can't stay there indefinitely waiting for them to dispatch a recce team. When you sleep, or go and get some food, Jane could be whipped away from under your nose. And then the operation would close. Or, worse still, fail.'

He knew he was whining. But he got the Chief's line.

I get it …

… even if it meant that whoever was in the building might be torturing Jane. Or that she might die.

And Sam was already in harm's way. If she stayed where she was the odds of her being exposed rose by the hour. She couldn't stake out the house by herself. Not for any length of time.

The Chief could order a couple of case-officers from Hanoi to help her. But that wasn't their primary role and they weren't trained for long term surveillance.

Using them in that way was only ever sanctioned for exceptional circumstances. Which, if he thought about it, Jane's incarceration might apply. But to what end? The UK only had one answer to a land-borne hostage situation. And that was the SAS. And the Chief had ruled them out.

'Sam?'

Still nothing.

Come on, Sam.

'I need you to acknowledge that you've heard me. That you understand the Chief's orders,' Frank added.

Nothing.

Then, 'I don't work for the Chief.'

And the phone went dead.

Triệu Quang Phục, Lào Cai, Vietnam

It was dark now. Not quite dark enough to lose herself completely in the shadows of the trees, but that would come within the next half an hour. Sam knew about the dark. She understood its secrets. Not the dark that brought on dreams and demons, although she understood that too. No, the dark for hiding. For disappearing. If you stay perfectly still and smell like the dark, then you are lost.

352

She certainly smelt like the dark. Having showered this morning at Hau's place she'd started off whiffing of cleanliness. That had been lost in the afternoon heat and replaced by the distinctive smell of human sweat, which was nearly as easy to recognise. The good news was her pathetic grave-digging exercise had enhanced her disguise. She had smelt herself; her hands and under her arms. She smelt like dirt, which was good. And since then she had smothered her face and hands with mud, like the soldier she had been. She was, now in the dark, at one with the wood. If she stayed perfectly still, only a decent search dog would find her.

But she wasn't going to stay still.

She was going to extricate Jane.

The mound of freshly dug earth had been the catalyst. It had set her on a path of no return. She had sensed Jane's death. And then her resurrection – Jane's highlighted profile in the late afternoon sun. And Sam had come through that absolutely determined.

She had found Jane. And now she was going to rescue her.

No matter what Sir Clive Morton's instructions were.

Sam had turned off both phones. She needed to save batteries and, ten minutes after she cut Frank off, a new call had come through. First to the muted satphone, and then her phone. It was a London number and she recognised the dialling code. It was Vauxhall; very likely

Babylon. The Chief, or the Chief's PA, was trying to get in touch. And Sam wasn't having any of it.

She heard his logic. That kicking over this applecart might dislodge any future opportunities. And she understood why a longer-term electronic tag on everything in and around the villa would be the textbook thing to do. Indeed, it might well be the intelligence coup of the decade.

But it didn't remove Jane from danger.

And Sam wasn't having that.

There was another thing.

The Chief, or certainly Frank's version of the Chief's intent, wasn't the whole story. There was something missing. If this was as big as it seemed, she and Frank and Riley, and maybe this new MI5 bloke, weren't the answer. This was the perfect tiger team operation: SIS, Special Forces, the six Far Eastern SIS stations, from Seoul to Singapore, MI5, a CIA liaison officer, and not forgetting GCHQ. What a job! And, sure, the boss might be concerned about leakage, but there were many ways to reduce that risk. She'd heard of multi-agency teams working for ten months from a single room, with no outside-contamination. It was possible.

No. Something wasn't right.

And she sure as hell wasn't going to abandon Jane when she hadn't been given the whole story.

Now all she needed was a plan.

Which she thought she had.

Plan A. Which would morph into Plan B. Because no plan survives first contact with the enemy.

She had waited long enough. Now was the time.

She made her way through the trees to the main gate. As expected the two guards were still there, both on the roadside of the gate. One was armed – a pistol, in a holster. That would take a practised shooter a second and a half to prepare. The handgun would need to be extracted, then cocked ... and then aimed. A second and a half. The other man was unarmed. They both had walkie-talkies. The gate was ornate metal, sturdy and looked like it opened electronically. And it was not visible from the house.

Just down from the gate was the first part of Plan A.

A stand alone, electrical distribution box of some sort, the size of two bedside cabinets. It was set back from the drive and in partial shadow, but still in view of the guards.

It would take her two minutes to break into the box and tug at some wires. Hopefully that would disable power to the house, drop any surveillance and alarm devices, cause a little bit of mayhem and give her an opportunity to get into the building unseen.

There was, of course, the subsidiary issue of a generator. If this had been Africa she would have bet on a back-up power source. But, Vietnam didn't seem to have power outages and so a generator was unlikely.

And on her five circumnavigations of the villa, she hadn't spotted anything which looked like it might house one.

She looked to the gate. One of the guards had moved out of sight. The men were talking to each other, although she couldn't hear much above the noise of the traffic.

Good.

Sam checked her watch. It was 7.46 pm. If there were to be a handover it would be on the hour. She had ten minutes.

Go.

She slid round the front of the distribution box; her penknife between her teeth and her own pistol, which was cocked and safe, stuck down the back of her trousers. She'd left her backpack in the trees.

She paused, crouching in front of the box, her eyes on the gate.

One guard in view. Facing away from her.

Small, slow movement was key. The eye alerts the brain to sudden motion in its peripheral vision. An auto-response.

Slowly.

The front of the box had one of those annoying plastic triangle within-a-metal-circle locks that requires a special key. It was tricky, but not impossible.

Sam opened her penknife.

Movement. To her right. By the gate.

She stopped. Dead still. Not a breath. Both guards were in sight now. Neither looking her way. They were laughing at something.

She looked back at the job. She forced the blade of her knife into the recess between the plastic and the metal – and took a breath.

Twist

No movement. The lock was stuck.

She tried again.

Nothing.

One more time.

Nope.

Movement, again. From the front gate.

Still.

Perfectly ... still. She held her breath, looking away from the gate; her camouflaged face would be muddy-white against the dark of her surroundings. A good effort, but probably not good enough. The sergeant major wouldn't be happy.

More laughter. She was in the clear.

And there was still power being delivered to the house.

Think.

Still crouching, she moved slowly back behind the box. Darkness within a shadow, so much so she couldn't make anything out.

She felt.

No door. A flat, metal surface. No ... *hang on.* At the base of the box was a thick cable.

357

Feel.

It came out of the bottom of the box and sank into the ground. She managed to get her thumb and index finger around a wide sheath holding a group of wires. It was as thick as her wrist.

There was only one thing to do.

Sam always kept her stuff in good order. Everything she owned was fit for purpose. If it wasn't, she fixed it, or got it fixed. Or she recycled it.

Her penknife was one of her things. It was only two-bladed, but those blades were as sharp as a cutthroat razor. It was always like that. She made sure of it.

The blades were metal, which was a perfect conductor of electricity. For this purpose, a double-edged sword, as the body of the penknife was also metal.

Not so good.

She retrieved her rucksack from a few feet away and felt for a pair of pants. She wrapped them around the handle of the knife. Tightly.

...

She took a deep breath ...

... and started cutting. The first cut went through the sheath of the wire with ease. The second found some resistance.

The third blew her backwards a metre, the accompanying spark lit up the dark like a firework, and the noise of too much electricity going to places it shouldn't, sounded like a car backfiring.

Her right arm felt bruised and on fire, as though an acupuncturist had set their novice class to practise on any spare piece of flesh they could find. Her heart was racing, except it was missing beats, and her head throbbed where she had banged it against a tree.

But she had her pants-covered knife in her fist, which was locked tight ... and her rucksack was a foot away.

Without a second glance at the gate, she grabbed her backpack and crawled into the trees.

Noise from the gate. Loud voices. Then rattling of the gate, metal on metal.

It's electric. She'd forgotten about that. A win-win.

A torch!

Still fizzing, she pushed herself further into the undergrowth. She couldn't release her grip on the knife so had to doggy-crawl with one hand clenched. But she moved quickly and was 10 metres into the bush by the time the men had forced open the gate wide enough for them to get through.

A torch beam flashed around the distribution box. There was a hint of smoke in the air and the smell of burnt rubber.

More talking. High pitched and at a rattle. The walkie-talkies were in operation now. A metallic response from someone, probably in the house.

Sam lay down so she and the ground were an entity. And watched.

Three men now, the third scuttling down the track from the house; no rifle. *The roving guard had stayed put?* That would be the SOP. None of the three were round the back of the box. All of them staring and poking at the front. One was crouching. Sam couldn't see, but he was probably trying to open the door that Sam hadn't managed.

More talking from the two standing men. A smartphone was out now. She didn't get a word.

Move.

With her grip on the knife loosening and her arm now more of a tingle than on fire, she set off on elbows and knees. And then in a crouch. And then upright. She knew the route, she'd rehearsed it – and she knew she would be out of sight.

Left here.

Stop. By the edge of the trees.

She crouched again.

The house was black. No lights. The back door of the house was 25 metres away. The roving guard, who appeared more vigilant than usual, was in view, walking left to right along the gravel path which followed the boundary of the villa. She couldn't make out the path, but she could hear it. *Crunch, crunch.* In ten seconds he would be round the corner of the building. Out of sight. For about two minutes – one hundred and twenty seconds. And then he would appear from the left. That's how long it took to walk the perimeter. She'd counted his circumnavigation eight times.

One hundred and twenty ... one hundred and nineteen ... one hundred and eighteen.

She stood. Her rucksack stowed on her back, her knife away and the MP-443 in her hand.

Sprint.

She was across the patchy lawn in three seconds.

One hundred and thirteen ... one hundred and twelve.

She continued to count as she tried the door.

One hundred and nine.

Shit. It was locked.

There was a further set of patio doors on the next wall, round the corner. In the direction the guard had walked.

One hundred and six.

She walked quickly and silently to the corner and stuck her head round ... and pulled it straight back. The guard was standing still. His rifle's butt was on the floor, its muzzle brake leant against his groin. He was smoking a cigarette.

She stopped counting. Plan B was now in operation.

Sam dropped to her knees. And looked again.

Shit.

She immediately pulled back.

The guard was looking her way!

Had he seen her - she had purposely dropped her eye-line so it wouldn't be the same as his?

She stood up swiftly and pulled back 3 metres. Her pistol steady in her right hand, her left creating a platform underneath the grip. She held the weapon out front at head height, her elbows slightly bent so her arms weren't strained and any recoil would be absorbed. Both eyes open, looking along the short barrel.

If the guard came round the corner. She would …

Would she?

Could she?

She gripped the pistol more tightly. And held her breath. She couldn't miss from where she was.

…

Nothing.

She breathed. And dropped the barrel of the pistol a fraction. And shuffled forward. And crouched.

Her head and pistol turned the corner at the same time.

The man was gone.

Move.

She was at the patio doors a second later; they were locked.

Shit!

She bent down and peered inside. It was dark; her fault for fusing the electrics. But she could pick out a key in the lock.

Sam didn't need to process her next action. She took the barrel of the pistol in her left hand and tapped the pain of glass next to the lock with the butt of the pistol. There was a tinkle of glass on wooden floor tiles. She put her right hand in through the hole she'd created, turned the key and was inside a second later, kneeling – her focus on the room ... her pistol again at eye line. Her head made short, sharp turning moments. Her shoulders, her arms and the pistol followed.

Lounge. Not much furniture. No pictures

No LEDs in the corners of the room. No security.

She listened.

Nothing.

She stood, pushed the patio door to, locked it and took out the key. She placed it on the floor to the right of the door, more than an arm's length from the broken pane.

And now Jane.

Sam had no idea who was in the building. She had seen one man wandering around, and that man might be outside with the guards trying to work out why their electrics were a mess. Jane should be upstairs, and Sam would be able to find that room with ease. But were there others in the building?

If there were, that would be Plan C.

She'd take it a room at a time.

Door, ahead.

She moved silently to it, turned the doorknob and pulled it slightly ajar.

And listened.

The roving guard would be coming round to her side of the building about now. She had maybe ten seconds? Would he notice the break-in? She had to move more quickly.

Nothing.

She pushed the door open with her foot, wide enough to slip her body through. And then knelt.

Nothing.

She stuck her head round the edge of the door, below keyhole height.

A large, high and dark hallway, with double entrance doors at the far end – wooden and strong. One was ajar. Where the third man had exited through?

A staircase to her immediate right. Up to halfway on one wall, and then ninety degrees to the top. Leading to a single doorframe – no door. No balcony.

Good.

She sprinted, taking the stairs two at a time. The risk was piling through the doorway at the top without knowing what was beyond it. Should she wait, or take a chance?

The heavy wooden front door made that choice for her. It creaked open just as she reached the doorframe at the top of the stairs. She shot through ...

... and immediately dropped to her knees, presenting a smaller target. Her feet just in the upper hall, out of sight of whoever had entered downstairs – her back arching and turning, her pistol following her gaze.

Looking. Searching.

Darkness, apart from a small amount of ambient light from behind her, and a little from the grey skies in a far window at the end of the hall.

Nothing.

She waited. And watched.

There was someone downstairs. Heavy footsteps. A man. He was likely unarmed, but he might have access to a weapon. The roving guard with the rifle would be at the patio doors now.

Listen.

Nothing.

She had another two minutes before the guard reached the patio doors again.

Sam stood, pistol still at the aim, the barrel still along her sight line.

Left, to the corner. Then the next door on the right.

She stopped at the corner. Waited. And listened.

Talking?

She dropped to one knee. And peered round.

The noise was coming from what she assumed was Jane's room.

A lyrical female voice. Possibly.

Not Jane?

She crept along the wall and found Jane's door. There was a key in it.

More talking. One voice. Vietnamese. Or Chinese. Definitely a woman.

Not Jane's.

Is the door open?

She tried the round, brass handle. It turned ... and stopped when it reached its limit. The door was ready.

Now!

The next ten seconds was a blur. Sam's brain worked as quickly as it could to take in what she found in the room, and what she had to do about it.

Jane, at least she thought it was Jane, was lying in bed, attached to a drip. She looked dreadful. White, pallid, a nose too big for her face and a frame that looked as if it would snap in a breeze. Next to her was a local woman. Originally she had a tray in her hand which carried a bowl of food and a glass, but that dropped to the floor as Sam burst in. As did the spoon she was using to serve Jane.

And then she screamed. Louder than the most petulant of children who have had their ice cream taken from them. Her eyes were wide and her mouth a gaping hole. Both hands were close to her face, but they were doing nothing to stop the noise that was bellowing forth.

Initially Sam raised her pistol to take aim, but that just made matters worse.

What the fuck?

And Jane wasn't helping. She was mouthing something that might have been, 'Sam?', but it wasn't clear. But she didn't move. She was lifeless.

Sam did the next thing that sprung to mind, other than shoot the screaming woman.

She took a step forward and smacked the woman on the forehead with her pistol. It wasn't a huge hit; not with all her might. But the *crack* sounded tough, and the woman's head dropped downwards – blood following the trajectory.

The screaming stopped. Immediately. Then, still with her chin on her chest, the bleating started. Pitiful sobs, her shoulders shaking and her head nodding with each whimper.

Sam looked at Jane. Who was still staring at her, her mouth slightly ajar. Sam noticed she was missing a front tooth.

'Jane?'

'Sam?' A croak.

'We have to go.' A quiet order followed by half a smile.

Jane dithered and then, 'I can't.'

The bleating woman was competing with her conversation with Jane.

'Ssshh.' Sam spat the order at the sobbing woman. She half-obeyed, the noise lessened.

'Why not?'

We haven't got time for this.

'It's ... just ...'

If Sam had thought about it, she might have expected Jane's reaction: being broken and then surviving. It was one notch down from the Stockholm syndrome. Jane might not yet have taken up arms with her captors, but she had lost all will of her own. Sam had

367

not been there, but she had been to similar places. She understood.

'You're coming with me. And we're going now.'

Sam didn't wait for any acceptance. She reached across, closed the drip's butterfly clip and pulled out the main tubing, leaving the cannula in place.

She then offered Jane her hand. There was a momentary standoff ... and then she took it.

Jane's mind was all over the place. The shock of this zombie-like creature smashing into the room, Jingfei's scream and then the recognition it was Sam Green, was too much for her synapses to keep up with. Sam's assault on the woman – the woman who had cared for her over the past three days – was horrifying. And the realisation that her old friend had come to rip her away from the security of her current life added to the distress, and sent her brain into a meltdown.

But, compliance was her current natural state. And someone new had arrived. And that person had taken control.

Sam pushed open the door, slipped out into the corridor, and pulled Jane with her. Sam then skirted round her and turned the key in the door. She handed the key to Jane.

'Take this,' Sam said. 'Drop it somewhere away from here.'

She took the key.

Thud, thud, thud ...

The sound was feet on a set of stairs. And immediately Sam was pulling her away from the noise, down the corridor, round a corner ... already tired she tripped over her own feet but, somehow, Sam held her up. They were at a door, leading off from the corridor. Sam opened it ... carefully, pistol at the ready. She entered and pulled Jane in with her

It was a dark room. A bedroom. Single window – no bars. Sam had let go of her hand and was at the window, pushing aside the lock on the meeting rail between the lower and upper panes. She tried to lift the bottom window, but it wouldn't budge.

'Fuck it!' A quiet expletive.

Noises from down the hall. They were coming for them. They would find Jingfei, and Jane would be punished. They would capture Sam and do the same to her. *They will hurt my family.*

Sam was trying the top window.

Jane was scared now. It was all too much. There was too much noise ... too much angst. She needed to rest. She pulled away, towards the door ...

... and, as the top window budged, her hand was on the knob.

She turned it.

Sam looked back. Anger immediately scratched across her face.

'No you don't.' Sam lunged at Jane and grabbed her hand roughly; she reeled. 'You're coming home, Jane. With me.'

Sam tugged her toward the window as shouting now echoed from the corridor. Knocking and banging.

'Out!' Sam was firm, her finger pointing to the open window.

Jane looked at the task. There was no way she was going to make it through the gap. It was too high. And what would she do on the other side?

But failure wasn't an option. That was clear from Sam's face.

Jane didn't have time to think about how she might even begin to lift her body. Sam grabbed her around the stomach and dropped her onto her shoulder – so Jane's face met Sam's backside. And then, with a strength Jane couldn't imagine in a man, let alone a mid-sized woman, her feet were out of the window, her stomach caught on the latch.

'Ow!' She couldn't stop herself.

And then with Sam's hands around her waist and then her chest, she pushed her, inch by inch until her chin was resting on the meeting rail, Jane's forearms now in Sam's hands.

'Ready?' Sam asked, this time with some tenderness.

Jane nodded, sheepishly.

'This may hurt. Try not to cry out.'

Jane didn't have a chance to reply before Sam launched her out of the window. She fell maybe 4 metres, her feet and bottom hitting the gravel at the same time, her torso collapsing so that she lay on the

370

floor like a discarded glove puppet. A few seconds later, Sam landed softly beside her.

Again, before any communication was possible, she was on Sam's shoulders – with everything hurting. She thought she might have broken something. Maybe an ankle, or a leg. But the exhilaration, something she feared just six hours ago, had begun to flow through her. Some sense of her old self prickled and fizzed inside.

Sam Green is here to rescue me.

I am going to get out.

Jane's face was side on to Sam's bum, bouncing with every stride. She couldn't see much, most was a blur, but she spotted movement by the house.

And then a man's shout.

'Sam!' Jane hissed. 'There's a ...'

The end of the sentence was lost to the *crack* of a high velocity round which sailed far too close for comfort, the *thud* from the explosion at the rifle's end, following instantly.

Sam's fast walk became a run, now in a weaving pattern across the lawn.

Crack-thud!

One dreadful noise. Another shot.

Still Sam ran.

More shouting. Then *crack-chung-thud!*

That was close.

And then they were in the trees.

Branches and bushes scratched at Jane's exposed forearms and calves. Sam drove into the woods, but then immediately turned left and appeared to be moving through the trees along a badly designed track which ran parallel to the house.

Shouting. From behind them. Possibly in the trees, maybe not yet?

Still Sam pushed on. They must have made it halfway round the house by now.

The noise from the men was getting quieter, Sam's route putting distance between them and the men. And Sam was slowing. And then she paused, turned to her right and headed further into the woods. A few seconds later she stopped completely, took a breath and dropped Jane. Her legs almost gave way, her right ankle throbbing, but her arm – which had found some brickwork? – stopped her from falling.

Jane couldn't see Sam. It was too dark. But she could hear her: panting.

'The wall ... next,' she said.

The bricks were black as soot; Jane could only feel their texture. The top of the wall was highlighted by the dark orange and blue hue of a night sky mixed with the ambient light of what she imagined was the local town. Jane's brain couldn't currently manage calculations, but she knew the wall was tall. And on top of it, there was ... she couldn't make it out, but it could be barbed wire.

'I've made a makeshift ladder.' Sam's instructions were short, quiet; mixed in with gravelly breath. 'There's barbed wire on top, but I have flattened it with some plastic bags I found in the grounds. There will be spikes.' Sam again. Jane's eyes had adjusted to the dark. She could just make her rescuer out. She had her hands on her knees, her head level with Jane's chest.

'Can you do this?' An almost noiseless question.

Jane still couldn't see Sam's face, but she sensed pain in her voice.

'Yes,' Jane replied. She could. *I will.*

Sam took Jane's hand and placed it on what felt like some bark. Sam traced Jane's hand along the outline of a branch. It seemed to be leant up against the wall.

'There are two branches side by side. I'm going to stand between them with my knees bent and my hands cupped by my waist.' She paused. Her whispered words were getting weaker. 'Stand on anything you find. Including my head and my shoulders. Go!'

At first she was unsure. She dithered. It was too much. Too soon.

'Jane. You have to do this. You have to do this now.' Exhausted sympathy from Sam. It inspired something deep inside.

Jane fumbled. And slipped. Sam guided one bare foot onto one of her knees and then she helped Jane's other foot find her shoulder. As her legs bent and stretched, Jane used the logs as handrails and soon she had both feet on Sam's shoulders ... at which point she was sure she heard Sam let out a muffled cry.

Jane's stomach was on the barbed wire, her head and shoulders at freedom's gates. In front of her she made out the lights of the town.

'Move!' A rasp from below.

As Jane pivoted on the plastic bags, and as the barbed wire cut into her flesh, she heard the sound of men shouting on the house side of the wall. They were moving this way.

She pushed off with her arms, her pyjamas ripping – and let go. She fell as a sack, this time landing in a bush which, whilst it pierced and scratched, did no permanent damage and her ankle survived the fall. It took her a few seconds to right herself and get clear of the bush.

Come on, Sam!

Jane looked up at the wall. She could hear the men's voices. They appeared louder – closer – but their tone was lost with the sound of the street beyond the bushes.

And still no Sam.

Come on, Sam!

More shouting.

The men were definitely close to the wall now. Just the other side.

What do I do?

She started to crouch – to hide – in case the men appeared at the top of the wall.

Indecision flooded through her.

And then she made the only choice she could. If Sam had been taken, then she had no choice. She had to find help.

Jane stood, wobbled, steadied herself ... and then, one tentative step at a time, pushed through the bushes towards what she thought was probably a road.

It seemed to take an age. She was slow and tired and kept falling. Her ankle was hell and dragged behind her, but freedom was eventually just a few feet away. Ahead of her in the neon dark of a Far Eastern town, she could make out a steady stream of traffic. Beyond that, buildings and shops.

Be careful.

This would be the most dangerous time. The men might have sent someone onto the road. They'd be waiting for them ... her.

Shit!

Jane tensed as someone grabbed her shoulder from behind. She turned to face her attacker knowing that what resistance she had would be futile. As she rotated a body fell towards her, collapsing in her arms. Jane's reaction was to fall back, her bad ankle instinctively stepping towards the road. Her legs started to give way and she tensed, expecting the body and her own to tumble onto the road as one.

But she didn't. From somewhere she found strength. She locked her knees and tensed her stomach muscles. Her ankle screamed as she pushed against it.

She wobbled and settled. And she held the figure tight, like a mother holding a distressed child.

Because the body was Sam's.

And she was hurt, her head was on Jane's shoulder; she was close to unconscious and there was blood everywhere. Jane's hands and arms felt a backpack. And, round her waist, a money belt.

Find a taxi.

Move.

She took a single step backwards to the edge of the shrubland, her neck craned in the direction of the oncoming traffic. Cars and scooters shot past.

A taxi!

Jane lifted a hand, releasing Sam – she hung like a very heavy ragdoll in one arm.

'Taxi!'

It shot past.

Sod it.

Another. Coming quickly. She put up a hand again. But it was too much. Her own weakness; the weight of Sam's lifeless body. The pain in her ankle. Sam slipped from her grip and fell in a heap on the floor, smashing against her ankle – the pain profuse.

Bugger!

Tears rose. The futility of it all smacked her like a falling mattress.

She couldn't help herself. Her own legs buckled and she fell …

… but didn't hit the floor.

She had been caught. By a man's hand. And then an arm. Two arms, around her waist. She cried out, but the cry was lost in hooting traffic. The man was quick and efficient. A car door. She was in, headfirst, her bum pushed across the seat by the man's hand. And then Sam's head, the blood very real in the headlights of cars coming from the opposite direction. Then she was in. Both of them in the back seat.

A door shut behind Sam. A short delay. Then the one in the front.

And they were off.

'Get your head down!' English from the passenger seat. Sam's head was already in her lap. Jane, who was back in submission mode, dropped hers, so that her lips were next to Sam's ear.

As she whispered, 'Thank you,' she felt for Sam's carotid artery. There was a pulse. But it was weak.

'She's been shot. She needs to see a doctor.' Jane directed weakly to the front.

The man in the passenger seat turned his head. He grimaced.

'We know. We're on it.'

At that moment, Jane thought she felt safe, safe enough to continue to ask questions.

'Who are you?'

The man turned again. And smiled.

'Frank sent us.'

Chapter 13

British Embassy, 31 Hai Ba Trung, Hanoi, Vietnam

Matthew stood his suitcase upright. He'd made it to the rear of the embassy via a number of passages and one very secure air-lock. Here he was separated from everything other than his clothes, before passing through a full body scanner – whilst something similar did the same to his gear. On the other side of the lock he was met by a young woman named Gene who presented him with a visitor's pass. She accompanied him through an open-plan area with numerous desks and maybe ten staff, to a door that led into a smaller conference room.

And there he came face to face with a scene from an ER.

There were six people in the room, two of whom appeared to be patients. One was a thirty-something woman. She was topless and flat out on her front on the conference table, lying on top of multiple sheets of A1 flipboard paper. Originally the paper had been a light beige, and that was still true below the woman's waist. Anywhere north of that was mostly blood red. In one area the liquid was dripping off the table onto the carpet. Aside from the wound and the blood, the woman looked like she had literally been dragged through a ditch. She was filthy, the side of her face he could see was daubed brown as if she'd been paintballing.

And the floor was covered with disused, blood-red dressings.

She was being attended to by a proficient looking, fifty-something man who might well be a doctor. There was a drip – of sorts – probably from an emergency kit. It was being held aloft by a second middle-aged man, who didn't look very comfortable with what he was being asked to do. The maybe-doctor man was holding one end of a long metal instrument, like an elongated pair of scissors, the other was currently imbedded in the woman's shoulder.

Beside him was a fifty-something woman who was mopping the wound. Neither of them spoke. And neither of them were wearing surgical gowns, just office clothes suitable for a warm climate. Bandages tied at the back of their heads provided makeshift facemasks. Their gloves looked to have been taken straight from the kitchen cupboard.

'Over here, Matthew.' His thoughts on the horror were interrupted by Gene who took his elbow and walked him to the far end of the conference room where there were a number of upright chairs. 'Sit here and I'll make you some tea.'

How English.

Matthew didn't sit and only managed a nod. He couldn't take his eyes off the operation that was continuing in front of him.

He assumed the prostrate woman might be the one Chief had mentioned in his briefing: Sam Green. Whoever she was had a nasty hole in her shoulder and she had clearly lost a lot of blood.

But she was awake. And not at all comfortable with having a piece of metal stuck in her shoulder.

'For fuck's sake!' The comment, which was spat out through gritted teeth, didn't seem to be aimed at anyone in particular. And, considering the circumstances, he was amazed the woman was able to remain still. But she did.

'I've got it. Hang on, Sam. Hang on.' The words distorted through the bandage-cum-mask.

And then the maybe-doctor pulled a slug out through the hole in Sam's shoulder. He studied it, turning it left and right.

'Got it.' He looked very pleased with himself.

Matthew looked back at the patient, who he now knew was Sam. She had closed her eyes and seemed to be drifting into unconsciousness.

'Over to you, Hetty,' the maybe-doctor muffled to the woman who was acting as his assistant. He moved to one side whilst the woman took his place. With a square, fat dressing in one hand, with her free hand she set to the wound with a gel which Matthew didn't recognise.

The maybe-doctor hadn't finished his round. He quickly moved to the second patient whilst pulling off his red and goo gloves, one finger at a time.

It was another woman. She wasn't lying down, although she looked as though she ought to be. She was sitting on a swivel office chair. She was also attached to a drip which was hung from a latch belonging to an opaque window by her side. She looked dreadful. Her face was wan, her eyes sunken and her nose looked as if it had been recently broken. She had one leg raised – it had been placed on a cushion on a table. It was purple and black and swollen. Oddly, she was wearing pyjamas. She looked as if she'd been on the tiles for a week, slept in the bushes and twisted her ankle in the process.

'How are you doing, Jane?' the maybe-doctor asked.

Jane? Jane Baker?

Someone had found her. And rescued her?

Bloody hell.

Was that what this was all about?

'I'm fine, thanks, Timothy.' She didn't sound it. And she certainly didn't look it. 'Do you think the ankle is broken?'

Timothy, the maybe-doctor, placed his hand gently against the swelling.

'Does it feel numb, or tingle?' he asked.

'No. It's bloody sore,' Jane replied meekly.

'It doesn't look out of line to me, nor the lower leg. And pain rather than numbness is normally a sign of ripped ligaments rather than a break. But it could be both. We will need to get you to an X-ray machine.'

Matthew got a nudge. It was Gene. She had some tea. So entranced was he with the drama he took the mug without acknowledgement.

'And Sam?' Jane continued

'As far as I can tell, she has been very lucky. The bullet was small calibre and lodged in her scapula. It cut through tissue and muscle, missed the subclavian artery, but nicked the vein. Hence the blood, but not a deadly amount of it. It didn't smash the bone, so I think the bullet may have taken a deflection. With pressure on the wound and a couple of stitches, in time it might fix itself. But, like you, we need to get her to a friendly hospital. I also need a bucket load of antibiotics for both of you; I've only got a limited number. I'll get the ambassador onto that.'

He smiled at Jane. She smiled weakly back.

'We need to get both of you out of the country as soon as we can. Again, that's the ambassador's problem.'

'I'm not going anywhere.' The slurry of words didn't come from Jane's mouth, but from Sam's. 'Not until I speak with Frank.' She was clearly conscious, although barely so.

The doctor, who had been kneeling next to Jane, stood.

'Put a top on me, get me sat up, and then patch him through on a video link. Do it now. And then clear the room.' Sam seemed to be trying to push herself up, but it was a futile attempt. The pain overtook her before she made any progress.

'For fuck's sake!' She spat the expletive out.

The doctor moved to her side.

'OK, Sam. Whilst I don't recommend it, we'll sort that in the next half an hour.'

It was clear to Matthew who was in charge. As Timothy gave directions to the team looking after Sam and Jane, Matthew turned to Gene.

'How much do you know about all this?' He waved his hand vaguely in the direction of the operating theatre.

'Not a great deal, I'm afraid. Frank ... do you know who that is?' she asked.

'Yes. I've never met him. But I know of him. He's in Singapore? Still?'

'I think so. We've been helping him for almost a week. Low level stuff. And then we get a frantic call early yesterday evening. He wants a support team in Lào Cai. Immediately. So H1, the boss, dispatches David and Roger, these two guys ...' she pointed to the end of the room, '... who are helping Timothy and Hetty. They pick up Sam and Jane and we get another distressed call asking for medical support. Timothy's the embassy's MO. Hetty, his wife. She's an ex-nurse.'

Matthew got all that. But did anyone know anything about what the Chief had briefed him on?

'Thanks. But do any of you know about the operation? About Jane's incarceration? And Sam's attempt to find her?' He needed to know how far any details of Op Mandolin and Abraham had spread.

'No. Nothing. Unless H1 knows something, no. We're all a bit clueless. Sorry.'

Good.

'Well, all I can do is reaffirm Sam's request. We need to speak to Frank. And we need to do it alone.'

Sam was feeling distinctly groggy. Her shoulder ached like someone had just pulled a tooth, and a combination of a heavy dose of painkillers and 200 milligrams of morphine had replaced her brain with heavy fog. But she was awake. And she was determined to take this video call with Frank. They had a lot to discuss.

Jane was beside her – they were both on swivel chairs, with Jane's foot raised and rested on a third seat. She was still in her jimjams and Sam in her filthy cotton slacks, although someone had lent her a t-shirt. Thankfully Hetty had given her face and hands a wash. The fourth chair, a row of three and one for Jane's foot, was the domain of Matthew. After a brief discussion with him she had just got her head around Matthew's role. Which didn't make sense. The Chief had sent him out to help. But he didn't know any more than her. And, knowing Frank had been on the phone to Vauxhall at least twice in the time it had taken the MI5 man to fly to Hanoi, Frank would be better briefed than the man from The Box.

So why send him here? They had staff they could call on. Two of the team here had more than enough time last night to leg it up to Lào Cai and pull her and

Jane from the jaws of some real unpleasantness. And Sam had worked in one of the busiest SIS stations, Moscow. Having been waddled to the loo earlier by Hetty, from what she saw here, Hanoi had more than enough capacity to help.

So why send him?

She wasn't sure, other than maybe the Chief thought having an MI5 officer who had some knowledge of Op Mandolin and Abraham knocking around the intelligence services in London wasn't the securest of options.

When it came to the Chief, there was lots she wasn't sure about.

Jane coughed, which made Sam glance at her. In a moment of serendipity, Jane looked at Sam. Their eyes met and Jane, who was still looking dreadful, reached for Sam's hand and squeezed it. It was a touching moment, especially as they hadn't spoken to each other since Jane had dropped on the other side of the villa wall. Sam had been unconscious for the whole journey in the back of the car. And since then it had been a whirl of makeshift stretcher, a trip through the side entrance of the embassy followed by a bullet extraction and a clean-up.

'Thank you,' Jane said quietly, tears welling up in her eyes.

Sam was immediately uncomfortable and looked away.

'You're welcome,' she whispered.

Jane squeezed her hand again and then let it go. Sam then bent forward and collected a mug of tea which Gene had delivered five minutes ago. She was sipping it a second later.

The TV screen, which had been set up on the conference table in front of them, threw up a blue Skype-like telephone icon. It was accompanied by an annoying ringing tone.

Matthew, who was easily the least incapacitated of the three of them, reached forward and tapped 'Enter' on the keyboard.

Two seconds later Frank appeared. Immediately after that, the three of them materialised in a smaller box, bottom right.

Sam wanted to laugh. The whole episode seemed unreal. Three convicts sitting side by side in a prison bus. The main warden, a two-dimensional Frank, sitting opposite.

I'm not quite right.

It must be the shock. And the lack of sleep. *And the hunger.* She'd get Gene to fetch some chocolate later.

There was a pause. Frank's face turned from nondescript ... to one of pain ... and then, quickly, disbelief.

'Oh my God!' he blurted. 'It *is* you, Jane. They told me an hour ago that you were out. But ...' Frank closed his eyes, dropped his chin and squeezed a finger and thumb on the bridge of his nose. There was no disguising it. He was crying.

He carried on, regardless.

'Sorry. I'm so sorry ... it's so good to see you.' He looked up. 'Are you OK?'

Jane smiled, a pathetic smile. She was a sketch of her former self.

What has she been through?

It was more than a battered nose and smashed ankle. Sam had been awake the whole time in the conference room, even if her eyes told a different story. Not once had Jane mentioned what they'd done to her.

'I'm fine, Frank. I'm a bit battered and bruised, and I need a good sleep, but I'm fine. Thanks to Sam.' She pointed to her left.

Sam followed Frank's eyes. He was definitely looking at her now. His eyes were damp, and there was a trace of a tear down one cheek. But he couldn't hide his affection for her.

'Thanks, Sam. From all of us. I don't know how you did it. But, thanks. And ... my God! What's the dressing for?'

Sam didn't want to talk about it. She knew Frank would be overcome at seeing Jane. She guessed, if she paused for just a second, she might feel the same. Although she would never show it. But they had things to talk about. Like, why had the Chief sent over a boy from The Box? And, what the hell were they going to do next?

She certainly didn't want to discuss the hole in her shoulder.

388

'It's nothing. Really. I got shot, but it was small calibre,' she added quickly. 'Probably an HK 4.6 mil, fired from an MP7 – I didn't get a good look at the rifle. But, even so, it must have taken a deflection, otherwise I wouldn't be awake now.' She was gabbling. Getting it over with. 'Anyway, you see we've got Matthew.' She flicked her head to her left. 'He's here, although I'm not sure why. Care to enlighten us?'

Matthew shuffled in his chair.

Frank took a deep breath.

'Where do I start?'

Answer my question.

'Tell us about Matthew. I'm intrigued.' Sam hadn't let him take a second sentence.

There was so much emotion and tension filling the room, and that was being reflected in the screen. Frank literally bit his lip.

'No. First, let's redraw some boundaries.' He had put on his stern face, one Sam knew he would be uncomfortable with. He'd obviously spoken to the Chief and there were new orders. Orders Sam knew she wouldn't be happy with.

She looked across at the MI5 man. He tried to ignore her and stared straight at the screen.

Who the bloody hell are you?

Frank started.

'I've spoken with the Chief. First, Sam, he's full of admiration for you having rescued Jane ...'

'Could have fooled me,' she said under her breath. Jane heard and shot her a quizzical glance.

Frank pushed on.

'Whilst you and I, Sam, know rescuing Jane wasn't his preferred option … Jane, hear me out … the Chief was hoping to secure the digital-rights to the building in Lào Cai and gather, over time, a detailed intelligence picture from that location. Rescuing you would put that at risk. But, it is what it is. And the Chief is delighted.' Sam wasn't sure if Frank had just made the last bit up. 'The good news is whilst Sam was doing what it normally takes a troop of Special Forces to pull off, GCHQ have picked up five phones from the building. Four are still there. The fifth has taken flight and is already over the border into China. And, just after midnight, Jafarov's phone arrived in the grounds – which is all good linkage. We have yet to get any usable intelligence from any call transcripts, but it's only a matter of time. The question we have is, who was in the building, other than a guy driving a silver Toyota?'

He paused at that point, clearly hoping someone would answer.

Sam described the guards she had encountered and noted that, because of the light conditions, she wouldn't be able to Photofit them.

'The silver Toyota makes sense,' Sam added. 'I was hounded in Hanoi – before I left for Lào Cai. I was tailed from the airport and chased, just for a bit, by a guy travelling in a silver or grey Toyota. Clearly with your int, Frank, *the* silver Toyota, the one from Krakor. I have a good image of him and a glancing image of a co-pilot. I could do at least one Photofit there. It's not much ...'

Jane then described Jinfrei, the doctor and the Chinese stockbroker, making the point that the latter was, as far as she was concerned, the kingpin.

This was news to both Frank and Sam.

'It could be Wang,' Sam interrupted her.

'Who?' Jane replied.

'Mr Wang Huwinh, He's "Secretary for the Central Commission for Discipline Inspection", a member of the Chinese politburo. Hang on ...' Sam reached for her now very tatty rucksack and picked out her phone. She turned it on. Everyone waited. Jane leant her way.

'Here.' Sam showed the photo Riley had found of Wang and Jafarov outside of the villa.

It took Jane a couple of seconds.

'That's him. On the left. And that's Jafarov!'

'Correct,' Sam concluded. 'Frank. I've only got so much energy. Back brief Jane.'

Frank did as he was asked. He explained how they'd got into Jafarov's emails, found the photo – how Riley had matched it to a senior hood in the Chinese government, and how that might be linked to a North Korean bank, the Wang-Chang Credit Bank.

When Frank got to the bank link, Sam sensed that Matthew had become tense.

Which is odd.

'Wow,' Jane added at the end of Frank's briefing.

'Indeed,' Sam added. 'We may be getting somewhere, Frank.'

Having been animated, Frank now wore his stern face again.

'The Chief wants you both home. Jane and Sam.'

That's not going to happen.

Frank, sensing even more tension, continued. 'But I think he was unaware both of you might require hospital treatment. I appreciate using a local hospital is probably out. So we might need to send an RAF casevac team. Which will be tricky ...' He was thinking out loud. 'The ambassador will need to look at suitable extraction plans.'

'I can't fly. Not straight away,' Jane interjected.

Sam looked at her. 'Why?'

'If my foot goes into plaster, it has to settle before I fly. The doc told me. It's a pressure thing.'

Sam, who was definitely not going home, looked back at the screen.

'OK.' Frank was in uncharted territory. 'Leave this with me. Sam, can you travel?'

'Yes.' She didn't have the energy for an argument. Not now. So she answered the question truthfully. She could travel. She just wasn't going to.

'Good. I think, with both of you convalescing, Matt and I will take this forward. He's got the full briefing from the Chief, so has now joined the inner circle, if you will.' Frank fidgeted his shoulders.

Something was coming. 'The Chief has suggested on the basis that this is Top Secret, UK Eyes-A – and with Jane heading home – I only talk to him now. Unless there is something ...'

That was more than enough for Sam. She lost it.

'You can tell the Chief to stick his security classification up his backside.' She was trying her best to sound reasonable. And was failing. 'It seems likely we have enough intelligence to confirm the existence of the Gang of Four, and possibly the most important player: Wang. But we still have the threat of a major incident going down. Somewhere in this part of the world. This is not the time to be reducing those in the circle. Especially as both Jane and I have first-hand experience of these thugs.'

She glanced at Jane, who looked more weary than she had five minutes ago.

She needs some food and some rest. That's all.

'Well ...' Frank started, but Sam broke in.

'The guy in the silver Toyota might well be the Vietnamese lead? Or at least point us in that direction. All we then need is a North Korean and a Cuban and we have a full pack.' She knew she sounded exasperated.

'Well, yes ...' Frank started.

'And, for fuck's sake, how did they know who I was, or where I was? The only three people other than me who knew I was in Vietnam were you, your woman Riley, and the Chief. Think about that for a second!'

393

Frank was about to add something more, when he was interrupted by the door of the conference room opening. It was Gene.

'Out, Gene.' Sam didn't shout, but her intent was clear.

'Sorry, Sam. No. We have a situation.' She was standing in the doorway. She glanced at the TV and then back at the three of them.

'The station's had a "Critical" threat warning, via a grade one agent. The attack is imminent. The agent reckoned a concerted assault. Possibly a combination of a bomb and handheld weapons. H1 is recommending the ambassador call Operation Dovercourt, which is maximum evacuation ...'

Gene didn't have time to finish her brief. The blast from the van-bomb that had pulled up outside the front of the embassy blew her into the room and across the conference table, which upturned and followed her trajectory.

It took Matthew a couple of seconds to get his bearings. He was on the floor, no longer attached to his chair. His ears were ringing but above that he could hear the sound of distant gunfire.

What the hell is going on?

The room was filled with dust and, as his eyes adjusted, he made out the upturned conference table, scattered chairs and a blown-in half of the partition wall which had separated their room from the larger, main office. The other half was still standing.

Sam was on her feet. She was bent over Jane who was still in her chair, but lying sideward, the tube of her drip at maximum stretch. Gene was on her knees, coughing and spluttering. Her face was a mixture of beige dust – and there was blood on her forehead

Shit.

He didn't think about himself although, as he stood, no part of his anatomy screamed at him. *Which is good news.* He was at Gene's side in a couple of seconds.

The gunfire continued. It was sporadic, but intense. He flinched, but didn't cower. The shots were accompanied by multiple voices. He thought he heard some screaming.

'Are you OK?' He knew he was shouting.

Gene looked up at him. The blood was coming from her hairline, a candle drip had made it to an eyebrow where it accumulated. Any minute now it would rappel to the floor. She was initially confused. And then gave a tight smile.

'Fine.' She put out a hand. He took it; she stood.

Nearby, a spray of bullets sank into something that sounded like concrete.

More shouting. Definitely screaming. This time closer.

'Hey, what's happening?' It was a metallic squawk.

Matthew looked around. The noise confused him … until he realised it was probably still Frank. The monitor was on the floor, facing down, wires spewing out of its back and accumulating at a small metal hatch in the carpet.

'I've got to go.' Gene had grabbed his forearm. 'You stay here with Jane and Sam. Make sure they're OK. I'll go and find out what's happening.'

Another stream of shots. Distant this time. Gene was steadfast – which impressed him.

'But you've been hurt!' He was pointing at her head.

She looked confused again, and felt for a wound. She winced as she touched her head,

'It's fine. I've got to go.'

Matthew's eyes followed Gene's route as she scrambled over the table and through where there was once a door. The main office was a mess. Two men were at a heavy metal cupboard, its doors open. It was a small armoury. One of the men had started handing out what looked like big pistols. Gene was there now. And now there were two others: an older man and a woman – both dusty as hell. He recognised them from his short walk through the room earlier. None of them appeared badly hurt.

It was clear.

SIS Hanoi were getting tooled up.

I bet they weren't expecting their sunshine tour to end up like this.

Then the man by the armoury seemed to be giving some instructions. Seconds later he was out of the door which led to the main embassy building, the others following.

He had closed the metal cabinet. But one door was slightly ajar.

And still the gun battle raged from beyond the far wall.

'Matthew!' It was Sam. She had Jane back in her chair. Neither of them looked any worse off than before the start of the assault, other than a powdery coating. Sam had a plastic cannula in her arm, but had lost the drip. Jane's was still attached, and now she was upright it looked less prone to snapping.

Before he had a chance to reply, a volley of gunfire from the far wall sounded too close for comfort. They all involuntarily ducked.

Half crouching, he shouted, 'Yes!'

She beckoned him over with her hands and, with a pause in the gunfire, he stepped across to her. Their faces were inches apart. Her expression was more intense than he'd seen before. She looked wired – tightly sprung.

'That's the armoury.' She was pointing at the metal cabinet in the main office. 'Go and find whatever weapons you can. And grab any ammunition. I'm preparing Jane to move.'

Move?

397

A really loud burst of gunfire came from just beyond the door the staff had just disappeared through. Then some single shots. And shouts.

A scream.

It was something from a war movie. This was a whole new world to him. Security Service intelligence officers were taught how to fire a pistol in training. In the same way they were taught how to splint a broken leg. But they never expected to use their skills.

His nerves were jangling, but he felt on the right side of control. That is, until Sam had mentioned they might be going somewhere.

'Move? Where are we going?' He tried to lose the unease from his voice.

'Away from here. Now, get the weapons. You and I need at least one. And find something to carry the ammunition in. Go!' The immediacy in Sam's voice was penetrating.

He paused ... torn between arguing with the woman with the hole in her shoulder, and getting hold of something to defend himself with. *Who do I think I'm kidding?* The intensity of Sam's stare broke through any indecision. He was at the cabinet a few seconds later.

And still the gun battle raged.

Twang! Twang! Twang!

Muted orders from a distant room.

Another burst of gunfire.

He pulled open both doors of the cabinet. There was a top shelf which looked like it held ancillaries.

Underneath was a custom-made rack. There were slots for various weapons. There were two left. Both were handguns. He had no idea what type.

Thwack! Thwack! Thwack!

He couldn't stop himself. He threw himself to the floor. Whatever that was, and it sounded like the wrong end of a bullet, had landed very close – maybe on the other side of the wall to where he was now.

Shouting.

More bullet sounds. This time they seemed to be outgoing, rather than incoming.

'Matthew! Get a move on!' It was Sam. Her voice cut through the mayhem. There was no way he could disobey her. She had a power. He'd rather take a bullet to the back than not follow her instructions.

And he had no idea why.

He just knew what she was going to suggest would be better for all of them. Somehow.

More gunfire. The smell of cordite was now stronger than the settling dust.

He grabbed the two pistols, reached down to the bottom of the cabinet and picked up three boxes of bullets. The colour of the packaging wasn't consistent, but what did he know?

Just then the door leading to the embassy was thrown open. Gene rushed in and slammed the door behind her. She was carrying something bigger than a pistol, but not as big as a rifle; different from the ones he was holding. If he got out of here alive, he would sign up for one of the MI5 voluntary range days and get to grips with all this.

'I need the ammunition.' She sounded desperate, but still in control.

He held out what he had. She took the two green boxes and left the blue one with the white diagonal stripes. And then she dived into the cabinet and picked out some more of the same colour.

'Are you all OK?' Matthew blurted.

She stopped. Closed her eyes. And quickly opened them. She looked every part a soldier.

'Fine. We're now moving forward room by room. We've no idea how many casualties there are – on both sides. But our people are all accounted for.'

There was more gunfire.

'I hope,' she concluded.

As she opened the door to the chaos of war, she shouted, 'Keep them safe!' And was gone.

'Matthew!' It was her ladyship.

Blue and white boxes. The only ammunition left.

He picked up the remaining three from the bottom of the cabinet.

On his way back to the conference room he found a bag, emptied its contents onto the floor and put the ammunition in it. But he kept the pistols in one hand. And then he was with Sam.

She had Jane on her feet – she was now dripless. She looked dreadful, as if she might collapse at any moment. The upturned TV caught his eye. The back of it was now wireless. Somebody didn't want to talk to Frank.

Sam looked set. She had her rucksack on her back getting ready to go – somewhere.

She looked at his handful.

'Give me the Browning.'

Which ...?

With undisguised impatience she took one of the handguns, expertly released the magazine and checked its contents. Matthew recognised the brass and copper of a bullet resting on the top of the magazine. Sam pressed it down. The bullet didn't move.

'Good,' she said to herself. 'Full magazine.' She reassembled the weapon and cocked it. 'OK ...' she turned to her friend. '... are you up for this, Jane?'

Jane nodded, reluctantly. She didn't look ready for anything.

Sam turned to him.

'Matthew. We're getting out. The attack is meant for us. They want me. And Jane. They're prepared to attack a British embassy to get to us. We need to get away from here ... and I need you to come with me. I can't manage Jane on my own.'

'But ...' He started to interrupt.

'No buts.' There was grit in her voice. 'The team here are capable of looking after themselves.' To add to Sam's confidence, the sound of gunfire echoed from a distance that was further than the far wall of the main office. 'We are not safe here. They know where we are.

The Chief knows where we are. We need to distance ourselves from authority ... for now. Then we can regroup.'

It was madness.

'That's madness. Are you saying the Chief is involved with this?' He almost forgot he had a pistol in his hand as he remonstrated.

Sam blew out through her nose.

'I hope not. I really do. But let's put air between us and everyone else. So only we know where we are. And then we can engage. I've not risked everything to get Jane free from these thugs, only to lose her.'

He really wasn't sure. And going out ... there – now. It was a crazy idea.

'But it's like a bloody gangster movie out there. We'll be cut to ribbons!' His voice was slightly higher pitched than he hoped.

'No. Not where we're going.' She smiled, but her face quickly assumed one of dramatic determination.

He didn't get it. And she didn't give him time to have an argument with himself.

'Put the pistol in the bag and give it to me. And then put Jane over your shoulder; fireman's carry. And follow me.'

He ...

'Now,' she rasped.

Five seconds later, with Jane on his shoulder, he was just behind Sam as she scarpered through a door he hadn't noticed before and then through two more and out onto a street devoid of conflict. And, even though his carry was as light as a summer duvet, soon he was struggling to keep up with the madwoman with a hole in her shoulder.

Vanmiou 2 Hotol, 159 Khâm Thiên, Thổ Quan, Dống Du,

Hà Nội 116765, Vietnam

It was an odd hotel. It was big, and she wanted big. But it was more backpack central than Hiltonesque. They'd eventually got there after their fourth taxi hop. Sam had followed the training she'd practised at Fort Monkton, one she'd used many times before: if you're confused by your route choice, then any tail would be too. She'd issued a series of lefts and rights to the first taxi driver, without any sense of where they might end up. After ten minutes, they'd changed vehicles and done the same, with Sam always cognisant that they needed to remain in the depths of the city where there was more chance of being lost amongst the thousands of tourists. This time she'd stopped the taxi outside a street vendor which was selling fake or seconds of high-end trekking clothes – they were two-a-penny in the city. There, on the street, amongst scooters and people and heat and noise, she and Jane had pretty much disrobed and then dressed in lightweight, fashionable stuff which sort of suited who they were. At that point at least Jane was out of her jimjams – although she was asleep on her feet. Sam had to get her bedded down – and soon.

Whilst they shopped, Matthew – who Sam was beginning to warm to, a little – had kept watch.

The third taxi was a means to a furtive end. By the fourth Sam had made up her mind where they were going to spend the night; they had passed the hotel on a previous taxi drive-by. Fifteen minutes later they were at the Vanmieu 2 Hotel, which looked like something that might have been made in miniature by *Blue Peter* with sticky back plastic – all boxy in bright whites and yellows. They'd paid for two rooms with cash and used Matthew's passport as ID. Fifteen minutes later, with the light fading from their fifth floor window, Jane was flat out on one side of the double she and Sam would share. Matthew was sorting himself out in the next room.

Just as Sam was administering oral antibiotics to Jane from the pack the doc had given them at the embassy immediately before the dogs of war had been slipped, Matthew had knocked on the door.

Five times.

It was a simple and effective code.

'Come in.'

The room wasn't large and between them, the double bed, a dressing table and one of those slatted contraptions for resting suitcases, they nearly filled it.

Matthew was stocky, Sam reckoned early forties, with a face full of a skewed nose and a lived-in forehead. But he had warm eyes and a lovely smile which suited his demeanour. As they'd broken clean from the embassy through the emergency back door, he had constantly checked on Jane as she dangled across his broad shoulders. Sam had run at speed, directly away from the noise of the gun battle which had then seemed to be dying down – and he was always at her heel. Two blocks later she had hailed a taxi and, with Jane and Matthew taking the back seat, she had slipped in the front. As she barked orders at the driver, the MI5 man had continued to engage with Jane as if she were an injured child.

And, as she looked at him over in the calm of the hotel room, she could report he was in good shape. Which was a bonus.

'How are you, Jane?' he asked across Sam.

Jane didn't respond. Sam had the back of her head in one hand and had just pulled a plastic beaker of water from Jane's mouth. Her eyes were already shut.

'I think she'll be fine. But I can't be sure.' Sam put the cup on the bedside table and moved to the window. Hanoi looked as busy up there as it was down at street level. There was no space, just concrete and brick and plaster and tiles and satellite dishes. Lots of satellite dishes. 'As a gentleman, you won't have been looking when I dressed her in her new clothes on the pavement. So you wouldn't have seen the red marks on her stomach. And you may not have noticed the burn marks on her un-bandaged wrist?'

Sam turned away from the window. She stared at Matthew and gauged a reaction. Her assessment of Jane's condition hadn't been totally honest. She hadn't mentioned the now healing slash marks on Jane's left forearm, which was covered by tubigrip.

Sam had cleaned and redressed those wounds ten minutes ago whilst Jane had purposely kept her eyes shut. Sam knew what they were. She knew what, at some point, Jane had tried to do. And that had dragged her own heart downwards and formed tears in her eyes.

Sam had tried to take her own life just over a year ago. She hadn't cut herself – that level of courage was beyond her. She had taken the easy route: a company's worth of paracetamol and a bottle of vodka. Her mum had stopped her; technically, a vision of her mum who had appeared through the mist of Sam's drunken haze, had stopped her.

But death by an overdose wasn't the same thing. It wasn't the same as slashing at your wrists.

Nowhere near it.

As Sam gently washed each red-raw line with some soap and toilet tissue, she tried to imagine what must have happened.

Jane had been broken. For sure. She had given away things she should not have. She had put other people's lives in danger. Likely leading to their death. Maybe they had taken photos of Dusit Rattanatari, before and after, and shown them to her?

Then she had been pressed some more? Possibly photos of the dead dog. Maybe a close up of Mum in the shops.

Jane had been forced to make a decision. And she'd gone for redemption.

What a choice.

What bravery.

No wonder she was lifeless. That level of trauma must wreck a person.

Sam sniffed away another tear and smiled across at Matthew.

He shook his head, confused. His face contracted; empathy was the outcome. Sam noticed the crow's feet around his eyes for the first time.

'How did all that happen?' he asked.

Sam looked back at Jane. She was flat out, her mouth now slightly ajar. Sleeping. She reckoned Jane had been hung by her wrists and then abused with electric probes, maybe a cattle prod – or similar. Maybe first doused with water. Jane was a tough girl and it would have taken a lot for her to give up her three Asian agents. Sam mind wandered to her time in a warehouse in Munich, but gave it up. They had things to do.

'Hung by the wrists, I reckon. And then poked with a cow prod.'

Matthew took a short step backwards.

'What? Are you serious? Do people do things like that nowadays?'

Yes.

She knew.

She smiled again. It was forced, but she held it.

'I think we need to have a chat? You know, form a plan. And, I don't know about you, but I'm famished. And I need sleep. My shoulder's a touch sore and ... we should go downstairs. Is your phone still off?' Lots of sentences with tiny gaps. She was in a hurry.

Sam had told Matthew to turn his phone off in the first taxi. She had to know they were safe and his phone wasn't already a target.

'Sure. What about food for Jane?'

'We'll bring some up.' Sam already had her backpack in her hand, her face grimacing as she threw it over her shoulder. She studied Matthew briefly. The bag he had taken from the embassy was hanging from his right hand. It looked heavy enough to be carrying a pistol and ammunition.

She squeezed past him.

'Let's go.'

An hour later Matthew was full. He'd had a burger and chips from the hotel's less than charming bistro and, even though his new boss, Sam Green, had frowned, he was two bottles of Tiger to the better.

Sam had munched her way through a plate of chicken and rice, using chopsticks like a local. No alcohol, though.

'How's your shoulder?' Up until now they'd not said a great deal to each other. He had a million questions, but Sam had pulled up a drawbridge – so much for forming a plan. It had been yes and no answers to the few questions he'd asked. After fifteen minutes he'd given up and instead concentrated on his burger and beer.

Her reply surprised him with something more than a couple of syllables.

'Sore as hell. I can't lift my arm easily. But the dressing's holding.' She paused. 'I might need your help to replace it, if you don't mind, after I've showered.'

A spark.

It was not nothing – but it was something. There was no way Sam could have meant it to be anything other than a practical statement. She needed help with her dressing. It would be impossible to reapply on her own. But as soon as she finished her sentence, she glanced away, embarrassed by a silly connotation.

At that point he thought he'd found a vulnerability. She was no longer the woman who had singlehandedly rescued a senior SIS operative from the clutches of a four-nation conspiracy. Side on, her face was nowhere near as intense as it was full frontal.

Matthew found her attractive, there was no doubting that. She was slight and pretty – but not gorgeous. She had an open, round face, with high cheekbones and some freckles. Her lips were thin, her nose Cleopatran and her complexion clear. But she was no beauty. She was a supporting actress to a lead star. More Jodie Foster ... than Angelina Jolie.

409

More Jodie than Jolie.

'What?' She was looking at him now. 'Don't get any ideas. You're not my type.' It was a sulky response, as if she'd been caught out.

Attractive? He smiled to himself. *Maybe not.* She had a way of putting distance between herself and the rest of humanity.

To prove it, she scowled.

'What are we going to do, boss?' He had no problem mocking her a little.

She looked away again towards the double-aspect window which, with a glass door, was the entrance to the hotel.

She didn't reply.

OK. We're back there again now.

But they weren't. Sam turned to him, smiling thinly now, and nodding curtly at the same time. The embarrassment was over. They were back to work.

'I need to speak to Frank. But not here. I have an embassy satphone which is secure, but also pings a location. I have my own phone, which someone will be monitoring ...'

'Why?' he interrupted. 'It's what doesn't make sense to me. Your line about the Chief. It's as though we're – or you and Jane – are getting between him and something he wants?'

Sam took a sip from a can of coke.

She didn't reply to his question, which infuriated him.

410

'Tell me how you ended up here, Matthew. Everything.'

Chapter 14

ICM Coffee Lounge and Pub, 2R9P+5P Hanoi, Hoàn Kiếm,
Hanoi, Vietnam

The – *what would you call it?* – café, which mostly sold alcohol, was a good 200 metres from the hotel, and a couple of blocks away diagonally. Inside the decor was light wood and multicolour plastic, with 70s-style furniture. A local on an upright was playing well, singing recognisable classics in tune but with an accent which could only be South East Asian. It was packed with aspiring young, who were managing to drink, converse and manipulate their phones all at the same time.

It was noisy. And she was lost in a crowd. Which is what Sam wanted.

Over supper Matthew had given her the complete paperback on why he might have dispatched him to Hanoi. As such she was better informed, but none the wiser. It seemed incredulous that the head of SIS had set up his own private operation with a senior Member of Parliament in order to influence her brother, a businessman, who had his mucky fingers in pies which spread as far east as North Korea.

Matthew's further investigation seemed to indicate someone, it might be the Chief, was trying to short the North Korean *won* for a reason which no one could be clear on.

And then there was the issue of the tunnel between the DPRK and South Korea.

'It started with a strange email from a CIA analyst named Ron, who I met on a course last year,' Matthew had said. 'He's based in Zagreb, Croatia.'

'I know where Zagreb is,' Sam had replied curtly.

Matthew had snorted and taken a swig of his third beer.

'Well. That's how this kicked off. He wanted to know if anyone at The Box could decipher the term, "5toa".'

'Tango-oscar-alpha?' Sam had asked.

'Yes.'

Her brain was doing the thing it does, when it searches all of her mind's deepest recesses at the speed of a supercomputer – and then, as if by magic, it picks something out.

'Was the context Korea?' she'd asked, trying to narrow down her search engine list.

'Yes. How did you ...?'

'T-O-A. It's an acronym for "tunnel of aggression". It's a South Korean term to describe tunnels dug by the DPRK under the DMZ into South Korea ...'

She stopped, mid-sentence. It was Sam's turn to be interrupted. Matthew hadn't said anything. But she could tell by the way his mouth was hanging open that she'd surprised him.

'What?' she'd said.

'I put a charlie-charlie out on that to a wide address list. The only person who had any idea was a guy in Babylon who has a PhD in Korean history. Do you?'

No.

'Must've read it somewhere. Luck?' Which was probably the truth of it.

That's what they had. A fifth, as yet unpublicised, tunnel. And the Chief possibly messing with the North Korean currency. On that basis Matthew had turned up in the station's conference room earlier that day. Sam still thought it was because the boss wanted him out of the way. And, according to the LED-screen version of Frank, before he was upturned and blown to the floor, neither she nor Jane were welcome any longer in Vietnam. They had been ordered home.

One to replace two.

It was all far too murky for her.

Something isn't right.

Anyhow, after Matthew had finished his third beer she had dispatched him up to her room to feed Jane with a high-protein meal of beef burger and fried chicken they had ordered from the menu. He'd added a can of *Tiger*, which he'd picked up from the bar. She, and her now very achy shoulder – *more morphine required* – had walked the 200 or so metres to any bar she could find that would not easily lead a tail back to their hotel. She hoped she'd found it where she was.

She took out her own phone from her backpack; a backpack that still held a fully loaded Browning 9mm.

She turned it on. And phoned Frank …

… who picked it up after one ring.

'Bloody hell, Sam. Where are you? What are you playing at?'

She took the phone away from her ear and stared at it for a second. One part of her wanted to hang up and carry on drinking.

The more sensible part, however …

'I guess GCHQ are monitoring this phone?' she asked absently.

There was quiet.

'Yes. Of course. We're worried sick. I'm worried sick.' Frank's voice was irritatingly high-pitched. Her shoulder ached far too much for this. 'Do you know how many we lost at the embassy?'

Sam didn't. She had purposely not looked at a TV since they'd arrived at the hotel, or since she'd gone walkabout. Interestingly there was a TV on in the café, over her left shoulder. She glanced at it; it was showing the news. The pictures of the embassy looked horrendous. It was unrecognisable. There was fire and smoke. And bent metal and charred concrete.

'No,' she replied flatly.

'Four LECs (*locally employed civilians*) and one British member of staff. Four others were injured.' Frank was still sounding frantic.

'Any of ours?' she asked, thinking of Gene.

'No. The news we have on our wires is they saved the day. Frankly, I was surprised not to see your name on the casualty list ... knowing how you never shirk that sort of duty.'

It was a good point and one which Sam had considered as soon as Gene had been blown across the conference room table. But she had Jane to look after. And, for some reason, she and Jane were a precious resource. Sam felt the need to protect that.

'I had to get Jane to safety. They want her. That's what this is about.'

'Do you think?' Frank was still sounding sharp. Normally by now he would have calmed down. He was clearly worried. Or maybe he was under pressure? He had, after all, failed to keep his asset on a leash. And, even now, she was wandering around Hanoi doing her own thing.

The Chief wouldn't be impressed.

'Yes. I do. And I don't get it. The villa in Lào Cai is compromised, they must assume Jane would have talked as soon as we got her out. So why chase? Why attack a British embassy with all of the ramifications which fall from that?' It bugged her. That and the fact they were onto their location so quickly.

There was silence for a minute.

'To save yours and the Doughnut's effort ...' she continued, '... I'm still in Hanoi. Trying to work out what to do next. Jane's not well. Mentally more than physically. She needs professional help. Soon.'

A young man came to Sam's two-person table and asked, in international sign language, if he might take the empty chair opposite her. Sam nodded and, as she did, glanced back up at the TV screen. They had moved on from the attack. They were now showing an animation of the raising of two flags: the Stars and Stripes and the red and blue, horizontally striped and white star-adorned ensign of the Democratic People's Republic of Korea.

Fuck.

'What are we going to do about that?' Frank asked. His tone had dropped a notch.

'Wait.' Sam was thinking. 'When was the last time you checked the news?'

'Dunno. It's all embassy attack stuff, even here in Singapore. It's CNN's main lead as well. I guess it will be that way for the next couple of days.' Frank sounded confused.

'OK.' She was still staring at the TV. 'I think I know where this is going. But first, answer some direct questions for me.'

Sam waited. Frank was struggling with an answer. Then ...

'OK.'

Good. Frank couldn't lie. He'd had that gene surgically removed at birth.

'Why does the Chief want me and Jane back with him?'

'Specifically?' Answering a question with a question irked her.

'Specifically.'

'Apparently, he says you're compromised. You're a danger to yourselves and others in the field.'

Which others? And compromised to whom?

'Compromised to whom?' she asked.

'He wasn't clear, although I reckon it's the Gang of Four.'

That's obvious.

Or?

She thought some more.

'OK. Next. Where's *La Teja* at the moment?'

'The boat?'

Of course the bloody boat.

'Yes.'

'Wait.' He was checking something. 'Last known LOCSTAT is ... somewhere in the Taiwan Strait.'

'Between Taiwan and China,' she confirmed.

'Correct.'

Sam did some maths.

'That would make it about two days sail from Pyongyang?' she added.

Frank didn't reply straight away. He was obviously doing the same calculation which had taken her less than a second.

'Yes. If it sails directly to the DPRK. Why?'

The news article had moved on. The screen was now showing a TV ad. It was a beer commercial with

418

middle-aged men getting thirsty by cutting down a forest with chainsaws.

'Matthew was sent here because he outed the boss,' Sam mentioned casually. She was on an open line and had so far not mentioned full names. She hadn't wanted to use the secure satphone as it was bulky and it might draw attention to her. It would also mean she would need to talk out on the pavement. And she didn't feel safe standing still out there.

'What?' Frank replied.

Without naming names she told him Matthew's story about the Chief and Anne Bertram ... and then the additional intelligence about 'a Swiss bank' shortening the *won* to the tune of hundreds of millions of pounds. She didn't mention the fifth tunnel. That intelligence was far too sensitive for an open line.

'What? You don't think ...'

She still didn't know what to think.

'No. I don't. We've both known the boss for a good length of time. I've got to believe he's working with us. But I just can't see how?'

There was more quiet. Sam had a quick check around the room. It seemed busy, but safe.

For now.

It was time to move on.

'I've got to go, Frank. I'll call you again later. Next time on the satphone, but only when I feel it's safe to do so. In the meantime do me a favour ...'

Another pause.

'Sure.'

He sounded much more like her old Frank now. He was back on side.

I hope.

'Get anything you can on the just announced summit in Seoul. It's in four days' time. We need to know everything.' The images from the news clip had painted a canvas in her mind in which she was in a small figure in the bottom corner; next to the frame. Sam was convinced what was happening in the picture was where this all was heading.

She didn't wait for him to question her.

'We need to get Jane somewhere safe, which will definitely mean offshore. See what we have off the coast. Merchant or Royal Navy.' Sam had stood and gathered her bag. She had spent too long on the phone. If GCHQ was triangulating her number, everyone else would be.

'Protect us, Frank. And keep the boss at arm's length. For now. Tell him you're doing what you can.'

Sam pushed through between two crowds in the bar. As she did a man turned and her shoulder thumped into his back. The pain which erupted made her brain spin and she almost fell. She was a metre away from the front door and managed to reach for it. She held it tight as the surge from her shoulder heightened ... and then died down.

If Frank had replied whilst she was recovering, she hadn't heard him – the pain had been too overwhelming.

He hadn't. He'd been thinking.

'OK, Sam. I'll do what I can.'

'And ...' she added, managing to stand upright and take a step out onto the pavement.

'Yes?'

'Get on a plane to Seoul. We're going to need you in the thick of it.'

Heading East along the OL14 short of Ha Long Bay,
Vietnam

Sam reckoned they had three days, maybe four if they were lucky. The summit was planned to start on Saturday, spilling over into Sunday if things went well. Between now and then they, that is her and Matthew, had to get Jane out of harm's way before making their own way to Seoul – all without bumping into anything unpleasant.

So far, so good. It was hardly a red letter day, but at least they had almost made it to the Vietnamese coast.

Which would be leg one of a journey, a journey which currently lacked rigour. But she wasn't one for sitting still.

In her book, the only way to get Jane safely out of Vietnam was by boat. She knew that the SAS had an STOL (*short take-off and landing*) Hercules flight which could land in a hastily prepared field. But that aircraft was probably a couple of days away and likely being used for much more critical tasks. The UK Special Forces also had a number of helicopters, but again, they were days' flights away and would need a series of airports to frog leap into Vietnam.

Overland was very complicated, long-winded and prone to cock-up. The whole of the north of Vietnam bordered China. That was out. They could head south or west, into Laos and/or Cambodia – the way she had come in. But that was a long and uncomfortable road journey and she wasn't sure Jane was up for it; the last thing her friend needed was any more angst.

And Sam wasn't sure she was up for it either.

That left linking up with a friendly ship. Or, better still, the Royal Navy.

Frank was working on that.

And, apparently, it wasn't easy – she'd spoken with him first thing this morning by satphone.

The MCA had reviewed the ships in the region. Having ignored all Vietnamese and Chinese flagged vessels off the northeast Vietnamese coast, there were three within 100 miles which looked big enough to warrant having a doctor on board. One was a Malay tanker, the second a German freighter and the third was a South African container ship. The closest Royal Navy vessel was HMS Gosport, a Duke-class Type 23 Frigate. It was in the South China Sea, sailing south for Australia, via Singapore. The good news was it was carrying a Merlin helicopter. Sam had read that the Merlin had a range of almost 1,000 kilometres, if fitted with extra tanks. But even with the helicopter, HMS Gosport was well out of range.

It was a start. But there were a lot of ducks to get in line, and Frank had some pretty big favours to pull.

First, they had to get to a port on the coast; safely.

Before she'd got back to the hotel and after her conversation with Frank, Sam had popped into a phone kiosk and bought herself a MobiFone pay-as-you-go SIM. With it installed in her phone, she had called Hau – who had been delighted to hear from her. Sam had asked a number of casual questions, just checking that her Hanoi friend hadn't been compromised – that there wasn't some thug taking up far too much room in her tiny flat, coercing her to let him know should Sam make contact. Thankfully it didn't take long for Sam to feel comfortable that wasn't the case.

So she changed tack.

'I have a proposition for you, Hau,' Sam had said.

'Ooh. How exciting, Sam. Does it involve me driving to somewhere exotic, like last time? Do I need to pick you up from Lào Cai?'

Sam smiled to herself at Hau's girlish enthusiasm.

'No. I'm back in Hanoi. How does Ha Long Bay sound?'

'Sure, why not,' Hau had replied to Sam. 'Shall we take one of the cruises around the islands?'

Sam could imagine it. Her with the beautiful Hau, sitting on the poop deck of a Vietnamese pseudo-junk, sipping pink gins as the sun set behind rainforest-clad, limestone stacks.

Yes, that would be wonderful.

'Ehh, no. Probably not. No. Just as a taxi there. I'll pay you.' She grimaced at her last sentence.

'Sure. And don't worry about paying,' Hau had flashed back.

'OK.'

I will.

'When are we going? Soon, I hope,' Hau continued, undaunted.

'How about tomorrow? The thing is, I have some friends now. We're heading to Ha Long for a break. We may take a cruise later. We can let you know.'

Sam grimaced again as she introduced her cargo. She was asking a lot.

'How many of you are there?' Hau sounded less certain now.

'Just three?' Sam replied quickly.

There was the slightest of pauses.

'OK. Fab. What time? I'll need to let my professors know I'll be missing their lectures.'

Sam closed her eyes and breathed out. She didn't like what she was doing. At all.

Needs must.

'Thanks, Hau. I reckon on, say, 9 am? I'll SMS you a pickup point first thing tomorrow. It'll be pretty central.'

'Great. Looking forward to seeing you again, Sam.'

That was last night. And here they were now. In Hau's hand-painted, red and flowered Micra, just short of Ha Long. In the back was Matthew and Jane; she looked marginally better than last night, but had still slept the whole two-hour journey. Sam, who hated casual conversation, was doing her best to entertain the driver, although Matthew was helping. Sam thought he probably couldn't stop himself. Hau was very pretty and Sam reckoned only the coldest heart could have ignored her.

And Sam got that. She absolutely did. There was something enchanting about her Hanoi friend. She was like an unknowing siren, sitting on a rock, drawing all to her, unaware of the shipwrecks she might be creating.

Sam was also beginning to get Matthew. When she'd eventually got back to her room last night, she'd found him sitting on Jane's bedside helping her sip from a bottle of Tiger, an empty plate parked neatly on the dressing table. He was nursing her with real sensitivity.

'Hi,' Sam had said.

Jane had looked across at the door, but seemed unfocused as though she couldn't make out who Sam was. Matthew, on the other hand, beamed a smile and said, 'The patient's doing well. We've even made it to the loo.'

Sam had silently choked at that point.

One of her dearest friends – who had been through hell – needed help to eat and ablute. And the newcomer, a professional, male intelligence operator who had the face of a front-row forward, had the kindness to make that happen. And he wasn't embarrassed by it.

'Good,' she had replied. 'You can help me with my dressing later.' She had pouted a smile, which Matthew acknowledged back with a nod. They'd built that bridge.

Before she showered, and as Jane slept, she and Matthew had stepped out onto her room's small balcony. He'd taken another beer from the minibar and she a diet coke. As they stared out across a city she was beginning to really warm to, she outlined her plan to Matthew. If he thought it was a stupid idea with too many variables and a Rumsfeld number of unknowns, he didn't show it.

Instead he took a swig from his bottle and said, without any malice, 'You're one crazy woman, you know that?'

She hadn't replied. She was intent on watching the neon lights change and flicker on the building opposite.

Crazy?

Now, as they headed to Ha Long Bay to check out the local sailing fleet, she was inclined to agree with him.

426

Café Sao Biển, 33 Đặng Bá Hát, Hồng Gai, Thành phố Hạ Long, Quảng Ninh, Vietnam

Sam was at the point of giving up. She and Jane were propping up a table on the veranda of the Café Sao Biển. Jane was staring unstintingly across the glorious sound and out to Ha Long Bay which was a magical view in daylight and just as attractive at night. She was still uncommunicative, no matter the topic of conversation. And whilst she looked more perky than she had in the past thirty-six hours, Sam could see that something wasn't right. Her face was bleak ... and earnest, as though she was being pursued by her recent past and was doing all she could to break out into a better future. Sam knew post-trauma better than most. She knew the only thing that worked for her was time, with no surprises. Sam had no control of the former. For Jane, she was trying her damndest to take control of the latter.

After they had said cheerio to Hau and in the heat of the day, Sam had left Matthew with Jane at the café, found a quiet corner and phoned Frank on her Vietnamese SIM. He had pulled a blinder with the BND (*German Federal Intelligence Service*). *Fraulein Mila*, a German-flagged freighter about 80 miles off the coast and sailing for Qinzhou in southern China, had agreed to take on three Brits in need of medical attention – provided they could meet at a suitable rendezvous.

And, with the Chief's intervention, HMS Gosport had turned through 180 degrees and was a day and a half's sail from Qinzhou.

She'd then spent a frantic three hours scurrying around the quayside, popping onto boats and generally making a nuisance of herself. But she'd had no luck. Either the language barrier was too great an obstacle, or there were really no boats for hire that could take the three of them the good distance out to sea they needed to meet up with the German freighter. She'd thought one fisherman had said he was heading out in that direction tomorrow, but wouldn't be leaving until after breakfast. That was too late for them. The freighter would be at the location at midnight tonight and was prepared to rest at anchor until 9 am tomorrow – no longer.

They were running out of time.

And Sam was running out of everything.

Her shoulder was weeping badly and she knew she had a temperature. Her legs and arms ached, her head throbbed like it had been beaten with a plank and she felt as if she were always on the point of throwing up. Both she and Jane were taking antibiotics, so it didn't make sense that she'd got a fever from the wound. She'd been bitten a couple of times whilst she had been crawling about in the woods outside the villa, so maybe she'd picked up something there?

Or she was just shattered.

Over the past week she hadn't slept well, or for long. She had been continually on edge; what with looking after Jane, as well as trying to keep ahead of whatever it was that was chasing them. And, she had to remind herself, someone had javelined a slug into her shoulder which had nicked a bone. Thankfully, Matthew was proving to be a perfectly capable partner – currently he was back out among the trawlers and cruisers trying to get a ride.

'He's coming.' Jane's soft voice broke through Sam's consciousness.

Shit. I must have been asleep.

Matthew was jogging towards them, up the street. The multi-coloured lights from the varying shops and restaurants flickered across his face. It was a smiling Matthew. It looked as if he had good news.

Thank Christ for that.

He was at their table a few seconds later.

'Ready?' He was looking very pleased with himself.

Sam was struggling to be bothered. Jane had returned to staring absently out to sea.

'Are you OK?' he asked.

'I'm fine. What have we got?' She had no energy for pleasantries.

'There's a guy at the fisherman's quay. He's just unloading a catch. He'll take us to the RV as soon as we're ready. Are we? You don't look up for much, Sam.'

As she stared at him she felt a rush of emotion. Just now he was a colossus. A knight in very sparkly armour. The way she felt she wasn't sure if she were capable of finding her wallet to pay the bill that had been left on the table. With Matthew, they might just make it to the German freighter.

'Yes. Just a bit bushed. What's the boat like?' She didn't really care.

'A small trawler. Looks sturdy, not that I know a great deal about boats.'

'How much?' If it was over $200 they would need to get to a cashpoint. And that meant unnecessary walking. Which meant more effort. Which wasn't going to happen.

'Five hundred dollars ...'

'Five hundred dollars!' That had broken through the haze.

'Don't worry.' He held up his hands defensively. 'I've been to the hole-in-the-wall and I've got the cash. Any case, it's that or swim.'

He smiled.

She smiled pathetically back.

'Let's go.' It was more a mumble from Sam than an order.

20°04'19.0"N, 108°12'24.9"E, Ha Long Bay, 93 Nautical Miles from Ha Long

Jane couldn't sleep. Something wouldn't let her. Maybe it was the slapping of the waves on the hull of the boat? Maybe she didn't want to – maybe she feared sleep? Or, just maybe, she was persecuting herself after the events of the past few weeks?

Yes, she had managed to close her eyes last night, after Matthew had spoon fed her burger and chicken mixed in with some beer. Then she hadn't been able to keep her eyes open. But she wished she'd had ... as last night had haunted her day. All of it. The drive to Ha Long with the pretty Vietnamese girl. The intolerable wait whilst Sam and then Matthew had found a boat. A wait where her brain had had a chance to relive the nightmares of the previous night.

The slashing, not by her, but by some demon – dark and spiky, panting – with a blade as menacing as the devil's scythe. Her arm repeatedly attacked, with her body left lying in an expanse of blood on her mother's kitchen floor.

And they were next. Her family. One by one. Taken down by the black fiend. Mum. Then her brother. The whole family. And Misty, the dog. Its limbs hacked from its body and then strung up on the washing line, pegged next to white linen which in turn had slowly coloured red. The nightmare had been recurring. And she was forced to relive the horror. The second and third time the terror was the same, but with each repetition she had become more ambivalent to the process. In the fourth, her family and Misty had died – at her hands. The looks on their faces were unspeakable.

She knew they were just dreams.

That the haunting was just that.

But then, as they were due to leave the café and trudge to the fishing boat, it occurred to Jane that she had no idea whether or not her mum was alive. Her mind whirled and sparks filled her vision. Had her actions put them in danger? Sam had rescued her ... had that set in train a series of vengeful messages from the Chinese stockbroker?

Your daughter has escaped. You will not.

Why hadn't that been the first question she'd asked when they were in the car driving back from Lào Cai to Hanoi? Surely her actions had consequences?

How careless had she been?

What sort of daughter – and sister – am I?

'We must get a message to my mum!' It was almost a shriek.

The three of them had been walking slowly down the quayside. Sam looked unsteady on her feet and had hold of Matthew's arm. Jane felt strong enough to walk with the aid of a stick they had fashioned from some wood they had found on the side of the road. Her mind might have been a mess, but her body was recovering.

'What?' Sam's response had been an over-the-shoulder slur. Matthew had kept moving.

'My mum and my brother's family. How do we know they're not in danger?' Jane was two paces behind them; she had stopped, both hands on the stick. A moment of weak defiance.

Matthew paused, sensing something wasn't right. He turned to face her. Sam had no alternative. She stopped, but didn't turn to face Jane. That riled her.

'We must keep going, Jane. I mentioned it to Frank. I'm sure he's thought this all through.' Sam's voice was weak – quivering.

What does she know? She doesn't care!

'I don't under …' Mathew started. Jane interrupted.

'They killed my brother's dog. They … they … who know what they're doing. Right now, as we saunter along this frigging Vietnamese quayside!' Jane knew she sounded indignant. Screechy. She couldn't stop herself.

Matthew stared, lost for words. Sam turned now. She looked dreadful, Jane thought. As though she was about to collapse.

I don't care.

'Well?!' There was panic in Jane's voice. She needed to know. To be reassured.

Sam took off her rucksack. It slipped to the floor, dropping with a metallic sound.

'Use my satphone.' She sounded drunk. 'Turn it on. Be ET – phone home. But be quick. Who knows who's listening.' Sam then gave Jane the passcode number.

433

Jane scrambled forward, handed her stick to Matthew and took out the phone. As she turned it on and dialled her mum's number, Matthew collected Sam's rucksack and threw it over his shoulder. As soon as Jane had dialled, he passed her stick back and they walked on as she talked. Matthew now with an arm under one of Sam's armpits and Jane a few steps behind.

It was one of those once in a lifetime conversations that you have with the people you love. She hadn't stopped crying throughout; nor had her mother. Jane's instructions had been clear: phone the police and get protection. And do it now.

Jane had been talking so much she hadn't paid any attention to where they were or where they were going. Eventually she'd been interrupted by Matthew. They'd arrived at the trawler. Sam was sitting on the floor and Matthew had come to ask Jane to get off the phone.

'Sam says we need to be careful we're not compromised.' He'd put his hand out to take the phone. Jane then whispered an, 'I have to go now, mum. Phone the police. Please. I love you,' and hung up.

But that hadn't made her feel any better. She knew what these people were capable of. There was nowhere her family could hide where they wouldn't find them.

It would have been better if I'd stayed as a prisoner.

So sleep wouldn't come. The demon and the dread.

Not that she wanted it.

What she wanted was to get home. To hold her mum in her arms. To build the tallest wall around all of them and put a machine gun at each corner.

That's what she wanted to do.

But first they had to get on the freighter which was rearing up in front of them in the gloom.

It was getting light. The sun was lifting the dark grey sky to Matthew's right, turning it an umber-pink. The sea was darker still and overpainted with a deep blue, blacker if he looked to his left away from the dawn. The water could not be calmer. Standing on the freighter's bridge he reckoned he was 30 metres above the surface of the water, which had just been broken by a pod of dolphins chasing along the length of the ship. It was a beautiful place to watch the sunrise.

He felt calm, certainly calmer than at any time since he'd arrived at the embassy in Hanoi. He'd just checked on Jane – and then Sam. Jane was in the captain's cabin. She was flat out and much more with it since she'd spoken again to her mum, and then to Frank using the ship's INMARSAT connection. At first the captain had been reluctant, mostly, Matthew thought, because of the cost. Voice-over-satellite was expensive. He was happier when Frank had agreed to pay any cost and had provided an email address where the captain was to send the bill. Matthew didn't listen to the conversation between Jane and her mum, but she explained afterwards the local police had been ordered to provide over-watch on both her parents' and her brother's properties. That had calmed her down considerably.

Sam was in the very small – a bed's length and a cabinet's width – infirmary. The doctor, who was also the second mate, had been waiting for them. First, though, they had to get the two invalids on board. The fishing trawler had pulled alongside and was met by a fifteen-metre rope ladder which hung from the main deck. Thankfully the sea was calm – although it wasn't flat. Jane, who was still edgy, showed no signs of weakness, nerves, or that her ankle was still too sore to bear her weight. She hopped up the ladder using her arms to hold herself steady whilst her good leg took a rung at a time. It was impressive stuff.

Sam, on the other hand, wasn't anywhere near as able. She could hardly stand up unassisted. Matthew was pretty sure they'd have a stretcher on board, but as Sam was awake – and willing – he went for the next best and much quicker thing.

'I'm going to carry you up there.' He'd pointed at the ladder: two ropes and some sturdy plastic rungs.

Sam, who was sitting on the raised side of the trawler, took in the size of the task.

'Good luck with that.' Her tone was flat and lifeless.

Matthew looked around the deck. It was dark, especially in the lee of a pretty big freighter, but he spotted a coiled rope.

'I need you to get onto my back. And then I'm going to get the fisherman to tie you to me. Hang round my neck as tight as you can. Do you understand?'

Her eyes were shut then and her head was bowed. But she managed a, 'Whatever.'

'Come on then.'

The fisherman had been holding the boat tight against the side of the freighter with a rope and mooring cleat. It didn't take him long to work out what was going on, and what was required of him.

It took Matthew a couple of attempts to get Sam on his back and she only squealed once when the fisherman tied the rope too tight around her shoulder. But his work held good and, with Sam weighing under fifty kilos, he was up the ladder in no time.

Since then he'd checked on her twice.

Initially the doctor wasn't sure what the problem was, even though Matthew had pointed out the wound. On the second visit Sam was stretched out on the narrow infirmary bed, her wound redressed and a drip feeding clear liquid into her arm. She was gone to the world – snoring like a wheezy child. But, she looked settled.

After that he'd found the doctor who was in the galley nursing a brandy.

'Is she OK?' Matthew'd asked.

'Miss Green?' the doctor had replied.

'Yes.'

'Yes, she's fine.' The doctor took a sip of his drink, found a glass from the shelf behind him and, without asking, poured Matthew one. 'She was badly dehydrated. I think that would account for many of her symptoms. The wound is fine. There's no infection, it just hadn't been properly closed in the first place. But I have done that now.'

You should have seen the operating theatre.

Matthew had gladly accepted the doctor's drink and they had chatted for fifteen minutes about life at sea before the man had retired.

That was a couple of hours ago.

It was now 6.35 am. Off to his right the sun was now hiding behind some very low cloud, above which she was painting a picture in bright oranges and yellows. The sea, which was still as flat as laminate flooring, reflected that glory.

He'd been joined by the captain, a German national, who had relieved the first mate at six. The plan was still to stay at anchor until 9 am. By then Matthew hoped the Merlin would be in range and could pick them up before returning to HMS Gosport. The captain had been adamant as soon as they had got on board: at 9 am his ship would weigh anchor and continue their journey to Qinzhou; they had sixty-eight containers to offload and seventy-five new ones to collect. Time was money, etc, etc, no matter what favours the company might be doing for the German government.

Matthew had spoken with Frank after Jane had finished earlier. HMS Gosport was making best speed and would be within 400 miles of *Fraulein Mila* at 1.30 am. That gave the Merlin four and a half hours to RV with the German freighter.

'It's not uncomplicated.' Frank sounded as though he needed to get his head down.

'Go on,' Matthew had pressed.

Frank breathed out audibly. 'I've been liaising with the Defence Attaché (*DA*) here in Singapore. He tells me that the Chinese island of Hainan channels ships from the South China Sea between it and Vietnam. Unsurprisingly, China is particularly sensitive to any non-Chinese naval vessels, more so helicopters, in the South China Sea – and particularly as they approach Hainan. Whilst Gosport will remain in international waters, China may see her projected route as a hostile act. And a Merlin flying close to Hainan, more so.'

'But legally there is nothing they can do?' Matthew had asked.

'Perhaps. Perhaps not. Normally territorial waters, over which a country has complete land and air control, is anywhere between three and twelve nautical miles, depending who or where you are. China, however, exerts control over much of the South China Sea and has been expanding reefs and building islands to which it then lays claim. It's a murky and dangerous area. The DA thinks Gosport will get away with it, and the British ambassador in Beijing has been given a line to cover Gosport's tracks. But it might be touch and go.'

'Wow.' It was all Matthew could think of to say.

'Indeed. Apparently Gosport's captain is going to sail on the Vietnamese side of an imaginary line drawn by China. So it may be we only piss off the Vietnamese.'

That hadn't helped.

But there was some good news: he'd checked with the captain, who spoke adequate English. The *Fraulein Mila* could take a medium sized helicopter on one of their forward containers. It had been tried before and they had managed it … just.

What could possibly go wrong?

'Hi, Matthew.'

It was Sam's voice.

She's up?

He spun around.

There she was. Standing, without grabbing on to anything, at the entrance to the bridge framed by one of those oval-topped metal doors. She was still wearing the North Face walking trousers and t-shirt they'd bought in Hanoi, and the same pair of flip-flops, the cannula for the drip still stuck in her forearm. And she was carrying her tatty backpack. It was hanging down beside her, the weight of the pistol evident.

'Hi, Sam. How are you doing?'

440

He glanced across to the captain who was sitting at a small navigation table. He was looking at a paper map and sipping a mug of coffee. He showed no interest in Sam's arrival.

'Fine.' Her lips couldn't disguise a scowl. 'Better, actually. Thanks.' She moved into the bridge next to him, her hand grasping one of the stainless steel, steady rails that ran at waist height around the misshaped, metal room. Matthew turned so that they were both looking out across the sea.

Neither of them said anything. The view was as expansive as it came. Corner-to-corner two-tone blue, split by a gently curving horizon.

'What's that?' Sam was pointing at a tiny chunk of land in the far distance off to their left.

'Bạch Long Vĩ island.' The captain's voice, which was gutturally German, answered her question. 'It's populated, but *nicht Tourist. Dreißig* kilometres. It has *Fischereiflotte*. And a *Leuchtturm* ... lighthouse. *Das ist alles*. The mainland is *ein weiterer* seventy kilometres *des Weiteren*.'

Sam nodded a reply.

'So. It's now ...' she checked her watch, '... 7.05 am. Do we know where Gosport is?'

It's always business with her.

'No,' Matthew replied. 'Frank said he would call us when they had the Merlin in the air. I was waiting for him.'

441

Sam continued to stare out across the sea.

'A Merlin can make 300 klicks an hour. But that's empty and there's a range and potential cargo issue here.'

How does she know all these things?

She turned to the captain. 'Do you have AVTUR on board?'

'No. *Nein*,' he answered.

She nodded again and looked back out to sea.

'Rough estimate, I reckon the Merlin will only lift when Gosport is 400 klicks out. That's an hour and a half's flight time to here – and the same back. That means, to meet the 9 am deadline Gosport needs to be pretty close to launch now.' Sam had done the calculations.

Matthew replied, 'I'm sure there's some wiggle room in this. Captain?'

They'd both turned to face the navigation desk. But the captain was no longer sitting with his coffee. He was up at the rail on the far side of the bridge, binos in hand.

'*Das ist nicht unser Problem.*' The Captain's voice was strained.

Matthew looked at Sam, but she was ahead of him. She was already halfway across the bridge as the synthetic ring of the ship's phone echoed around the metalled room.

The captain passed the binos to Sam as he picked up the phone.

'*Hallo, die Fraulein Mila.*'

'Shit. Matthew, look at this.'

Matthew had started to move to Sam when he was met by the captain's outstretched arm, at the end of which was the phone's handset.

'*Es is Frank.*'

Matthew was betwixt and between.

'Wait, Sam.'

He took the handset, which was old fashioned enough to be attached to the cradle with a curly wire.

'Hi, Frank.' He put his hand on the mouthpiece. 'What is it, Sam?'

'Matthew?' Frank was a squawk.

Sam had turned. She made a fist and then pointed out to sea.

A fist? What does that mean?

'Hi, Frank. I think we might have a situation here.' Matthew moved as close to Sam as he could, the wiggly wire now outstretched. He peered over her shoulder, but couldn't see anything.

The captain was clearly not happy. He was now perched on the navigation table, his head in both hands.

'*Scheisse! Scheisse!*' The German's frustration and anger was boiling over.

And Matthew was struggling to understand what the hell was going on.

'What situation?' Frank squawked some more.

'I don't know. Sam? What's happening?'

She was still peering out to sea, the binos plastered to her face. She answered with a question.

'Is the Merlin in the air?'

'Frank. Did you get that?' Matthew was searching the horizon over Sam's shoulder, his eyes straining. But he still couldn't make anything out.

'Yes.' Another squawk. 'ETA, 8.25 am.'

That's ... 85 minutes' flight time. What the hell has Sam spotted?

'Give me the phone.' Sam turned sharply so that she faced Matthew. They were half a metre apart. She held out an open hand to take the phone; her other, which held the binos, was also outstretched. 'Take these. And keep an eye on what's happening out there.' She nodded over her shoulder.

'*Wir müssen* ... sail now. *Sofort!*' The captain was on his feet. He had both hands in the air.

Sam and Matthew ignored him. He'd have to wait. They exchanged phone for binos.

'Frank. We have an incoming ship. It's difficult to tell, but it looks military. It's heading from the north-north-east. Likely Chinese.' Sam turned to the captain and barked, 'How far away is the ship?'

'We must ... sail ... *jetzt*. This is *nicht gut*.' Panic and spittle at the same time. The captain took a couple of steps towards Sam.

The captain was a big man, in all dimensions. And his belly was very soon in Sam's personal space. Matthew, who had found the grey ship but couldn't make it out, dropped the binos from his eyes and was now watching the scene unfold.

'How – far – away – is – the -ship? *Wie weit weg, Kapitän?*'

The captain, whose face was beginning to burn, shot a glance over his shoulder and then blurted out, *'Fünfzig Kilometer'*

Sam held eye contact with the German. 'Frank. Let's assume we have a Chinese patrol boat heading our way. At 30 knots it'll arrive here at the same time as the Merlin, give or take. We might have a situation.'

The captain, whose complexion was now more beetroot than rouge – with thin blue veins now defining his nose – had given up with Sam. He moved to the central console and started pressing buttons and pulling levers.

'Wir gehen jetzt,' he murmured through clenched teeth.

What happened next surprised the bejeezus out of Matthew.

In what can only be described as an instant, Sam had dropped the phone – which twanged plastic on metal against the bridge's instrument panel – opened the top of her rucksack, pulled out her pistol, cocked it and took aim at the captain's head.

Foresight, first finger knuckle, elbow and left eye – all in perfect alignment.

The world stopped at that point, save for a squawking Frank ... 'Sam? Sam?'

445

'*Lass – die – Instrumente – in – Ruhe.*' Sam's order was given a word at a time. Matthew only spoke *Biergarten* German, but he absolutely understood what Sam had told the captain to do.

The captain stopped, mid-switch. He lifted his face and looked directly at Sam, and then, over her shoulder, to Matthew.

The look on his face told Matthew where this was going. And it was not going to end well.

For someone.

'*Nein.*'

Still looking their way, he pressed another button. In the distance Matthew heard a new sound: the low throb of engines turning over.

Sam took a pace forward. She was now no more than a metre from the captain.

'Turn off the engines, captain.' As cool as a cucumber.

Matthew didn't know what to do. He didn't know if Sam was capable of pulling the trigger. Of killing an innocent man. She had surprised him at every turn. Even her recovery overnight had been gobsmacking.

The captain hesitated. Even in the air-conditioned comfort of the bridge, sweat was beading on his forehead.

But he didn't flinch. His right hand moved slowly across the range of buttons and switches to a black, plastic dial which was larger than most.

He turned it. Slowly.

Deliberately.

At the opposite end of the ship to where they were Matthew just about made out a new, metallic clunking sound.

Anchors.

'Sam? What's happening?' Frank hadn't left them.

Then ...

Bang! Ping!

The noise of the gunshot and its ricochet was deafening. The scream that followed filled any void left in the bridge.

The captain collapsed to the floor, his hands reaching for his calf, the noises emanating from his mouth a combination of German profanities and a girl's scream.

'What the hell are you doing?!' Matthew stepped forward and immediately dropped to his knees so that he was next to the captain. A small pool of blood had already started to form on the metal floor, dripping from between the man's tubby fingers.

'You better wake the doctor.' Sam was ignoring what was happening at ankle level and was at the control panel. She was playing with the buttons and the dials.

'What? Are you out of your mind?' Matthew couldn't grasp what had just happened.

Sam froze.

Matthew stared up at her.

A mixed soundtrack of German yelps and Frank's tinny questions was the backdrop to his and Sam's first standoff.

Neither of them said anything.

Then, still with a composure that was bewildering, she replied.

'Possibly ... actually, probably. I don't know about you, but I don't want to spend the next twelve months in a Chinese prison just because one man couldn't hold his nerve.'

'But you bloody well shot him!' He sounded more incredulous than he wanted to.

'Check the wound. He'll be fine. It'll be less painful than my shoulder.' She turned back to the dials. Then, with her back to both him and the captain, said, 'Put a dressing on it. There's a yellow first aid box in the corner. Get him to apply pressure with his hand, and then wake the doctor. Oh, and get Jane up whilst you're at it. We need to be on the HLS in under an hour.'

Matthew took a quick glance around the bridge. He spotted the first aid box.

Here goes.

Chapter 15

20°04'19.0"N, 108°12'24.9"E, Ha Long Bay, 93 Nautical Miles from Ha Long

Sam could make out Jane and Matthew. They were on top of a grey Maersk shipping container which was close to the bow of the freighter. They had designated the one next to it as the HLS. That was bright blue with Cosco plastered on its side. She wasn't sure how the pilot was going to put the wheels down on a single container; maybe they'd need both of them? That meant that both Jane and Matthew would be too close to the downdraught as the helicopter came into land. Sam had relayed her concerns to Frank, but had yet to receive a response.

She'd also told him about the captain, who was in the infirmary with the second mate getting his leg patched up.

'What?! You did what?!' Frank's exasperation echoed all the way from Singapore.

'He's fine.' She really couldn't be bothered with this. The patrol boat, which was definitely Chinese – they could now make out its ensign – was ten klicks out, and motoring. And there was no sign of the helicopter.

She continued.

'Where's the Merlin? We'll have company within half an hour. And we've only armed with two pistols, and not a great deal of ammunition.' She was, of course, joking. Resistance would be futile. It was one thing shooting an unarmed German. Taking on the second largest navy in the world – North Korea had the biggest – was quite another.

Her attempt at humour was lost on Frank.

'You ...!'

'Don't worry, Frank. Just kidding. Find out where the Merlin is and call me back.' She'd hung up the phone.

The patrol boat was almost on them. She didn't need binos to make out the red, navy and muddy blue of the Chinese ensign. The ship would need to slow down soon, or at least turn sharply, otherwise there'd be an unnecessary collision.

Sam didn't do Chinese naval vessels, but she reckoned the boat was the same sort of size as a British Hunt class minesweeper: 60 metres long with a 30-millimetre cannon on the front, easily capable of bringing down a hovering helicopter. Now she could see the patrol boat clearly, it didn't look in great nick, but there were plenty of sailors on board running up and down the decks. She counted six long-barrelled weapons among them, probably a QBZ-95 – a very capable small arm. She knew a little more about the Chinese military's firearms.

As the patrol vessel loomed large, there were two key questions.

Would the Chinese Navy resort to violence?

And where was the Merlin?

The patrol boat had started to slow, and to turn, just as *Fraulein Mila's* first mate came onto the bridge. Sam had not met him before, but she recognised the shoulder tabs. He was short and wiry, possibly Eastern European. Romanian? And, by the look of it, he'd just woken from a deep sleep.

She still had her Browning in her hand. Without taking her eye off the incoming Chinese Navy, she raised it so the man could be sure who was in charge.

'Do you speak English?' Sam hadn't been with it when they'd boarded last night. She had no idea if he knew of them or, indeed, if he'd visited the captain in the infirmary.

He paused, not replying. He took a quick glance left and right. His eyes widened.

'Don't do anything heroic,' Sam continued. 'We've not taken over the ship. We're just waiting for a helicopter ride off here.' She hoped he spoke English. She really didn't want to shoot anyone else.

'Where's the captain?' Definitely Eastern European.

'He's had an accident.'

The patrol boat was 100 metres out and now side on. The cannon in the bulbous turret on the front of the boat was aimed at the centre of their ship.

The first mate moved into the middle of the bridge. He was looking at the patrol boat and shaking his head.

'What are they doing …'

The VHF radio interrupted the first officer's question. The only words Sam understood were *Fraulein Milu*. The rest was incomprehensible.

'Do you speak Chinese?' she asked.

The first mate shook his head. 'No. But their next call will be in English.' He turned to look at Sam. 'Why are they here? And, why have you got a pistol?'

Both good questions.

She needed him on side. She didn't want him fiddling with dials as the captain had done. And she certainly didn't want him thinking himself a hero.

Something close to honesty might help.

'Me and my friends …' she pointed to the bow, the first mate squinting as he looked in their direction, '… are British Secret Service. We're escaping from the Chinese authorities. There's a British naval helicopter inbound. It should be here any moment now.

'Hello *Fraulein Mila*.' English now from the radio. 'This is the PLA Navy. We need to speak with your captain.' The accent was clearly Chinese. The intent so far seemed benign.

'Are you going to answer it?' Sam pointed at the radio's handset.

The first mate looked unsure.

452

And then, music to Sam's ears, the faint *wocker-wocker* of a single rotor helicopter. She picked up the captain's binos and, looking in the opposite direction to the patrol boat, she scanned the horizon.

There.

'I need to go,' she said, matter-of-factly. She was already throwing on her backpack. She ignored the gnawing pain from her shoulder.

'What do I say to our Chinese friends?' The first mate had stepped forward to the radio. He had hold of the handset.

She stopped, halfway to the door. She smiled at him.

'The truth. Except the bit about me and my colleagues. Tell them that the captain is incapacitated and you've only just come on duty.' She made a further step to the door.

'Will they shoot at you?'

Sam paused.

'I think all I can say for certain is, they won't shoot at you.'

And then she was gone.

By the time Sam had run down the side of the deck and made it to the final two containers, avoiding all manner of health and safety trip hazards, the Merlin was almost on them. She couldn't see Jane and Matthew, they were two container heights above her. Nor could she see the patrol vessel. It was still on the far side of the *Fraulein Mila* and hidden by large metal boxes.

The two containers towered above her. Running down one side was a metal ladder.

6 metres of climb.

She shoved her pistol in her backpack.

I'm not sure my shoulder is up for this.

The grey Merlin – *God, I'd forgotten how bloody big they are* – was now hovering and turning, putting its back in the direction of the Chinese ship. Sam had no idea whether it was landing into the wind, or the pilot was getting some metal between it and the Chinese navy. It was 20 metres off the second container and descending gently.

The downdraught was terrific … but she had to climb.

Let's do this.

'British helicopter. This is the PLA Navy. Do not land.' Sam just about picked out the squeal of a tannoy above the percussion of the downdraught.

Sam was three rungs up and was already feeling wobbly. She looked up. The Merlin was still dropping – slowly.

'British helicopter. This is the PLA Navy. Do not land. If you try, we will fire.'

Shit.

The downdraught intensified. She wasn't looking up, but that meant the Merlin was still with them.

How many rungs were left?

Climb.

She managed two more rungs. Her arm, which was next to useless, was screaming at her. She really hadn't thought this through.

Thud! Thud!

That broke through the noise from the swirling blades.

Sam had been on the ground in Helmand when a Warrior infantry fighting vehicle had let off some 30-millimetre rounds at a Taliban bunker. It was like a rifle shot, but ten times louder. The Chinese patrol boat had just done the same.

The Merlin would be a goner.

She clung on, waiting for additional metallic crashing sounds, her shoulder delighted with the respite.

But there was nothing. Just the relentless drone of the downdraught.

Warning shots?

Likely? Possible.

Climb.

Three more rungs. She was past the top of the first container, her face now centimetres from the second. She looked up. The Merlin looked enormous. If the sun had been higher the helicopter would have delivered welcome shade. Instead it provided an unwelcome and almost debilitating storm.

And her shoulder and arm screeched at her.

She clung on to the ladder, her cheek pressed against a circular metal tube.

Climb.

She did as she asked.

Two more rungs ... *shit, that hurts!*

Sam glanced upwards. She was three rungs from the top.

Thud! Thud!

'Fuck!' She couldn't stop herself from thinking out loud. *That was close!* She pulled her herself tightly to the container, waiting for sparks and tearing metal as the Merlin spiralled and fell.

Nothing.

Just the bloody downdraught.

'British helicopter. This is the PLA Navy. Next time we will hit you. You have been warned.'

Climb.

One rung. *Nooo!* Two rungs.

Her foot slipped out from under her. Her body spun, pivoting from her good arm which clung on to a higher rung. Without warning her second foot popped out of the step it was resting on and she ...

... didn't fall.

Someone had grabbed her flailing, useless arm at the wrist.

It was a man's grip.

Strong.

And safe ... when, all around her, the world was being forced downwards, to the bottom of the sea.

She glanced up. Matthew's face was scrunched up in effort, his hair being blown everywhere by the helicopter's relentless, spinning rotors.

'Hold on!' he shouted.

She didn't fancy the alternatives.

A couple of seconds later she was being dragged onto the container, Matthew crouched on all fours, shuffling backwards – pulling her with him. Beyond him was the huge fuselage of a British Navy Merlin, three wheel pods just touching down, the side door pulled back with the green-helmeted and sunglasses-adorned loadmaster waving his hands frantically. Jane was already on her feet, hair blowing crazily as she stooped her way into his arms.

'Come on, Sam!' Matthew was pulling her. He was kneeling now, she was trying to do the same, but her balance wasn't yet right. And then they were both up, backs bent, hand in hand, running the short gap to the side door.

Thud! Thud!

The double-tap of the cannon was terrifyingly loud. Sam was convinced that the Merlin had taken incoming and her complicated life would soon be finished. She was to die in a mesh of bent, galvanised metal. Or her body split apart by a scything, composite rotor blade.

But none of that happened. She was in the helicopter's fuselage, her stomach pressed against the metal floorpan.

No sooner had the loadmaster launched her into the belly of the helicopter, than the Merlin pulled up its tail, twisted its chassis and started to accelerate away from the freighter ...

... and then it fell – no, *plummeted* like a toppling wine glass from a kitchen table. Maybe 20 metres? Her stomach stayed at freighter level, the rest of her braced for the crash.

At least the sea will be warm.

She closed her eyes.

But they didn't smack into the water. Their fall was beautifully arrested, a sharp but gracious curve dragging them along the top of the water. And the acceleration continued. The sea, which she could have touched if she had leant out of the cargo door, sped past them at ever increasing speeds.

They were getting away.

And we're using the freighter for cover.

The remained nap with the sea for what seemed like an age. She was entranced by the dolphin-eyed view. As was Matthew. She'd just noticed him beside her. He turned, looked and stuck up a thumb.

She nodded ... contently.

And then the Merlin climbed.

Hope?

Chapter 16

British Embassy, 24 Sejong-daero 19-gil, Jeong-dong, Jung-gu, Seoul, South Korea

The door opened. And there she was. Sam Green. The woman he loved.

This is not the moment.

The woman he knew didn't ... no, *couldn't* love him back. She'd told him that. And, over the past three weeks, her actions had made that abundantly clear. She was, as she always had been, mission orientated. Nothing else mattered. That didn't make her unkind, although sometimes it felt that way. It just made her focused.

Disregardful.

And it hurt more now than it had ever done before.

She smiled, a weak smile, and raised her hand.

'Hi, Frank.'

SIS's Seoul Station had labelled the room they were in 'The Small Conference Room'. It was no bigger than a medium sized office. It was filled with a six-person table, six chairs and an LED screen on the wall. Soundproof – no windows. Frank, the Station Deputy – Jim Dyer – and two male, Seoul case-officers, were already sitting round the table. Making up the six were Sam and the man from MI5, Matthew Stringer, who he hadn't yet met.

Frank stood, his chair hitting the wall behind him. He wanted to dance around the furniture and give Sam a hug. To let her know that nothing had changed as far as he was concerned. That he was *so* in awe of her rescuing Jane and then getting them out of Vietnam.

That he was still there for her. That he always would be.

But he didn't.

It wasn't appropriate. It wasn't the right place, or time. And, looking at her now, having flown from HMS Gosport into Osan US Airforce base and then driven straight to the embassy without passing 'Go', she didn't look in the mood for small talk. She looked tired, her left shoulder hung lower than her right, he guessed carrying the wound. Her clothes were unkempt and her hair a mess. Knowing her, she wouldn't have eaten much on the ship and probably slept even less. But Frank still sensed fire behind her eyes. And it didn't take her too long to throw her backpack on the table and sit on one of the free chairs.

She then moved the pack so it was perpendicular to the edge of the table.

Matthew, who stuck up a hand in acknowledgment of meeting a whole new bunch of people, took the empty chair next to Sam.

Frank had spoken with a friend of his in London. He'd wanted some more on Matthew Stringer. The news was unremarkable. Matthew had served three years in the Met and had then moved to The Service. He was in his early 40s and his career had flat-lined. He was an intelligence officer with a sound but not earth-shattering reputation – and he seemed to prefer it that way.

Frank wondered whether he was enjoying mixing it in the high-octane world of Sam Green.

Frank stared at him. The man looked comfortable in clothes which seemed to match what Sam was wearing – as though they had shopped together. He was unshaven, but didn't look rough. And he exuded calmness – which was a bit annoying.

Their eyes met and Frank looked away.

And then there was a moment.

Frank spotted it.

Sam and Matthew glanced at each other and there was a spark of something. A knowing. As though they had been through an ordeal. And that ordeal had brought them closer together.

And that hurt ... and it wasn't fair.

And he hated himself.

'Who have we got here?' Sam, her voice lacking any enthusiasm, broke through the temporary silence.

Frank led.

He introduced himself to Matthew, and then presented Jim, the station chief's deputy, and the two case officers.

'I thought this was on close hold?' Sam, straightforward as always.

'That's correct. But bringing in the deputy and some additional station horsepower ...' Frank showed a hand to the two case-officers, '... was the Chief's suggestion. His view is we now have a more bounded operation to focus on; that is, the integrity of the Korean summit. And we need all the help we can get.'

Frank watched Sam push herself back in her chair. She had control. The room was waiting for her to speak. Which was, in so many ways, odd to him. That this hugely significant operation was being controlled by an erstwhile, middle-grade SIS officer. A woman who was *persona non grata* in some intelligence circles. A civilian who, in order to rescue a friend, had disobeyed a direct instruction from the Chief of Secret Intelligence Service. And, as a result, had potentially blown apart a surveillance operation which could have reaped untold reward for years to come.

And her actions had likely caused the attack on the Hanoi Embassy.

Sam Green – the maverick.

If it were odd to him it must have been anathema to the three other SIS officers in the room. Frank had had to get the Chief to drop the deputy at the station an email, ordering him to let Sam Green take the lead.

'What? What the hell? This is our patch. And your friend Green has no experience here. She's not even a serving officer in the organisation for Chrissake!'

The deputy had stormed out of his own office.

Frank shot a glance at him now, an hour later. Like the rest of them he was waiting for Sam to say something. He appeared to have calmed down. Maybe he'd accessed Sam's file and seen what she'd been up to over the past five years.

But there was still an atmosphere of unease. A tension … a masculine tension that you get when you put men and a crisis in the same, small space. When men have invasion forced upon them. *My space; not yours.*

'No offence, but are you are all cleared for Op Mandolin and Abraham, because we must look at this against the wider context,' Sam continued.

Frank breathed in noisily through his nose. *That hasn't helped.*

But he knew this was coming. It was the obvious question. It was going to be difficult for them to make sensible decisions without everyone having full knowledge of all the facts, such as the location and intent of *La Teja*; of any decent intelligence coming from the phone taps from the Lào Cai villa, via GCHQ; of the output from the Chinese bot farm. He'd spoken to the Chief before he'd got on the plane to Seoul. The boss needed to know that Frank, using authority he didn't really have, had authorised the captain of the Gosport to continue to sail north with the aim of getting Sam and Matthew within Merlin distance of Osan. The Chief could have overridden his decision but he'd agreed – Frank thought reluctantly – Seoul was probably the best place for them.

'Get a team together. Small as possible. The deputy there knows the area like the back of his hand. Make sure he's in on it,' the Chief had said.

'How wide do I spread the intelligence?'

'As wide as you need to within the team, but be selective. And I want the names of those who are on the team. Clear?'

Frank had thought that order of detail was unnecessary for someone who operated at four-star level, but the Chief's approach had surprised him all the way.

Sam had questioned the main man's behaviour; fought against it.

And there was the issue of his relationship with Anne Bertram.

None of it was satisfactory.

But he had to trust him.

Surely?

'We share what we need to,' Frank replied. 'Although the two operational titles remain codeworded. So let's not associate any particular piece of intelligence with any one title.'

Sam closed her eyes at that point. Frank was sure he saw her mouth, 'For fuck's sake,' under her breath.

'Can we move this on?' The deputy was showing his impatience.

Sam opened her eyes and leant forward. She smiled wearily at the deputy.

Frank had a remote in his hand. He pressed a button and the screen burst into life. He then handed the control to one of the case-officers, who began the briefing.

'The summit starts tomorrow. It is being held over one and a half days. There are four main participants: POTUS (*President of the United States*); the President of the People's Republic of China; the President of South Korea; and the Supreme Leader of North Korea.' The case-officer was throwing up new slides every time he came onto a new point. The first four were photos of the leaders.

'POTUS is flying into Osan US Airforce Base in the early hours of tomorrow. The Chinese President is due to fly in at about the same time, but into Wonju International. Wonju is a lesser airport than Incheon International, South Korea's hub, so there should be less disruption. Apparently the government is restricting all flights into and out of Wonju until the summit is over.

'The South Korean President is clearly in situ and, by way of massive symbolism, the North Korean leader is taking the train from Pyongyang to Seoul. That journey isn't going to be without complication and requires at least one change of engine. But, it is possible. And it will be a first.' The case-officer now had a map on the screen and he was pointing with a laser. 'Freight trains used to run from South Korea to Kaesong Park, a joint industrial area just north of the DMZ, but no further. But those trains stopped rolling in 2016 when relations between the two countries deteriorated from an already low base. North Korea's track, like all of its infrastructure, is in a very poor state of repair and there is a real concern the leader might not make it. But he is, apparently, going to arrive by train – even if a flight would take one-tenth of the time. For the final and shortest section of the journey, between Dorasan – the brand new, South Korean border station – and Seoul, the North Korean leader will be accompanied by the President of South Korea. It will be a huge event and, if it goes without a hitch, would set the summit up for likely success.'

The case-officer paused. He looked around the room as if waiting for questions.

There were none.

Another slide, this time an itinerary.

'Tomorrow afternoon is ceremonial, with displays and banquets. POTUS is due to stay at the Park Hyatt; the other leaders, elsewhere in the city. Day two will start with a formal breakfast before a morning of bilaterals leading to a round-table meeting of all four leaders in the afternoon. The assumption is the summit would deliver some wording on the denuclearisation of the Korean peninsula including – vitally – a UN-led inspection programme of the North Korean nuclear facilities. The *quid pro quo* is a partial US troop withdrawal and the lifting of a number of sanctions which had been in place against the North Koreans since the 50s.'

The slides kept coming.

'The plan then is for all four leaders to move to the UN facility in the DMZ to share a symbolic 'cup of tea'. POTUS will fly via Marine One, the President's personal helicopter which has already been cargoed into Osan by USAF Galaxy. The Chinese leader is going to copy the move with his own aircraft. And both of the Koran leaders were due to travel to the DMZ by train.

'Once tea has been shared, POTUS and his Chinese equivalent will leave by respective helicopters and both of the Korean leaders are then set to travel on to Pyongyang ...' The case-officer paused for effect, '... by train. Which is one helluva gesture by the South Korean leader.'

467

The case-officer paused again, letting the latest slide sink in.

With no questions, he continued.

'Once in the North's capital, next on the agenda is, according to the brief we have from NIS ...'

'NIS?' Matthew interrupted.

'The South Korean's National Intelligence Service,' the case-officer clarified. 'Anyway, next is two days of discussions concerning further integration, sharing of resources and even the possibility of relaxing some of the border restrictions.'

The case-officer paused for the final time. He placed the remote on the table.

'It's fraught with opportunity,' the deputy added gravely. 'Although there is currently no intelligence, certainly nothing south of the DMZ, that indicates it will be anything other than successful. The NIS and the NPA ...'

'NPA?' Mathew interrupted again. Sam shot him a glance.

'The National Police Agency, South Korean's FBI.' The deputy answered the question curtly and continued.

'The NIS and NPA are stretched. Not in terms of boots on the ground, but making sure all of the four nations' close protection and police support are given the requisite amount of space and the right level of intelligence. We, which I guess means us and all other non-participating nations, have been told to stay indoors until this is over. Which does beg the question, why has the Chief sent you two here?' There was partially hidden venom in the deputy's last sentence.

He clearly hasn't calmed down.

The question was barked across the table to Sam and Matthew. She stared directly at the deputy. The tension was palpable.

Then Sam stood up

'Can I make myself some tea? I'm a bit parched.' She didn't wait for an answer and walked to the door. Matthew's head turned and everyone else's eyes followed her. With the door open, she lifted both hands. 'I'm happy to get a round in, if you like?'

Typical.

The only woman among them had offered to make a round of tea. It was an elegant put down.

'I'll come with you, Sam.' Frank was on his feet. The remainder of the room sat in silence. 'Where's the kitchen?' he asked.

One of the case-officers gave him instructions.

He squeezed past a couple of chairs and then jogged to catch up with her.

'Who the hell is he?' Sam spat out the question when she realised Frank was at her side.

'He's OK, Sam. You have to see it from his perspective. This is his AO. And none of us are Korean experts. It does seem presumptuous of the Chief to chuck us in a bit unannounced.'

Frank guided Sam to a small kitchen. She put the kettle on and took out six mugs from a wall cupboard.

'You're making tea for everyone?'

She paused, teabag in hand. She closed her eyes again, pursed her lips and then, with her eyes open, started making the tea.

'I'm going to assume everyone takes milk. Can you bring the sugar?' she asked.

Frank shifted his weight from foot to foot. This everything – was so much bigger than six cups of tea. The Gang of Four. Jane's rescue. The attack on the Hanoi Embassy. The imminent threat to the summit. Her and him. She and Matthew. A toxic conference room.

But ... that was what Sam had decided to do. Make six cups of tea.

Sam didn't know what she was doing. She wasn't one for mind games. She hadn't stormed out of the meeting, nor had she tried to play the deputy by acting as a brew bitch in a room that was overflowing with rabid masculinity. She just knew she had to leave. Find some space.

And, do you know what? She was thirsty. Her shoulder pulsed like a revolving door and she hadn't slept in any sense of the word since the hotel in Hanoi. At every turn she had met resistance. Jane wasn't talking to her – although Sam would have been surprised if she had the capacity to talk to anyone. The officers on the Gosport, even the female ones, had treated her like a passenger. It had taken a monumental effort, with Frank and her pressing and pressing, to get the ship's captain

470

to sail north for six hours, then fill up the Merlin and fly her and Matthew to Osan. And now another government official, one who should frankly know better, was pissed off because she and Matthew were warming his chairs.

Fucking people.

As she squeezed around the conference table carrying cups of steaming tea, she had been tempted to spill a bit. On a lap.

But that would then make her just like them. And, to be fair, Frank and Matthew were some of the good guys.

So she thought better of it.

'Thanks,' the deputy growled as Sam gently placed the mug in front of him.

'Frank's got the sugar,' she replied as she sat.

'OK.' She brought the meeting back to heel. 'Where's *La Teja*?'

Frank had just taken a sip of his tea. He signalled to the case-officer for the remote. He pressed it a couple of times and a map of Nampo, Pyongyang's container port, appeared on the screen.

'The latest MCA data has *La Teja* docked at Nampo, berth 11A.' He clicked again and the scale increased and the new slide displayed a satellite overlay. 'This is the latest overhead.' He used the laser pointer. 'Here she is.' Frank drew a continuous red circle around the plan view of a medium-sized freighter.

'How long has she been there?' Matthew asked.

471

'The DTG (*date-time-group*) of the overhead is three hours ago. A previous shot, which is four hours prior to that, has this berth empty.'

'That image repetition is impressive,' Sam chirped.

'CIA. It's not what you know ...' Frank said with an open smile. He'd been on edge since she'd arrived. He looked happier now they were back onto business.

'And can you remind everyone here of her cargo, that is, the cargo we're interested in,' Sam added.

Frank flicked through some slides until he had one that listed the cargo which had been discovered in Singapore. No one said anything as they read the bullet points.

Then one of the case-officers made the point Sam had thought all along.

'That's a huge amount of night fighting capability. I don't mean to be nerdy, but those thermal sights are the best in the world.'

'Correct,' Sam interjected. 'The Armasight Zeus rifle sight uses forward-looking infrared, comes in at about $10,000 a shot and has a restricted trade licence. It is banned from being exported outside of the US.' She stood, which immediately seemed to unnerve everyone. She dodged Matthew's chair and positioned herself by the screen. She pointed with her index finger as she spoke. 'Three top-end sniper rifles. State-of-the-art remote detonating equipment which can be used with any nature of explosive. These, the M141s rocket

472

launchers, are old technology but still in use by the US Army. They are, no pun intended, bomb proof and are colloquially known as bunker-busters. And all this ...' she ran her finger down the bottom of the list, '... is sighting equipment and other small arms. This is close to a company's worth, sorry about 100 men's worth, of warfighting equipment. At the top end. And, as you point out, it's been designed to be used very effectively at night.'

She stood still for a second. The case-officer who hadn't spoken throughout the meeting had his mouth open. The deputy was rocking back in his chair.

'So, it's tomorrow night then? What and where?' the deputy said, a touch of sarcasm laced in his words. 'How can they possibly hope to get that lot across the border?'

'The fifth tunnel of aggression,' Matthew added quickly.

'What?! What do you mean? There are only four tunnels!' The deputy was losing it.

Matthew looked at her. She looked at Frank.

They obviously don't know.

Sam nodded at Matthew. He started.

'The CIA in Croatia, of all places, came to me and asked if there was anyone in the British intelligence services who recognised the acronym 5-tango-oscar-alpha. I put out a charlie-charlie and came back with the answer: the fifth tunnel of aggression. I think it's agreed that one request led to the attack on the Zagreb Mission

Centre and the death of the CIA agent from where the request originated. We later discovered the agent was running a North Korean defector in Dubrovnik from where, the three of us believe, the information came.'

'All of that because of an acronym?' the deputy asked. 'And why don't we know about this, for God's sake?'

'Yes, because of an acronym. And you know about it now. Sorry.' Sam didn't mean it. Not the 'sorry'. They hadn't got time to collect the deputy's teddy bears and put them back in his cot. So she continued. 'We don't know any more about the tunnel, except that it is now common parlance in a small circle of Western agents and its knowledge probably led to an unhealthy situation in Croatia. It seems that whilst there used to be four tunnels, one of which is a tourist attraction and three others are cemented up, there appears to be – in a timely fashion – a fifth. We don't know where it is. Or indeed, who else knows about it.'

Nobody said anything. Then the vocal case-officer spoke up.

'The timings don't make sense. The third and first tunnels are within striking distance of Seoul and the summit. The second and fourth – and however many others there are, and nobody knows the answer to that question, now possibly five – are anywhere between four to eight hours' drive from here. And that's if you use the main roads – on both sides of the border. To get the gear from the port, through the tunnel and then here to

Seoul by tomorrow night is a particularly tall order. Certainly without raising suspicion.'

'He's right. And there's history, here.' The deputy's voice had settled a bit. He seemed more focused; less irate. 'The third tunnel was very close to completion when it was found. The view is it would have been able to move up to 3,000 men an hour, including light weapons. They were all being built for mass movement; an invasion. Not so a small band of determined men could infiltrate into the south. They don't necessarily need a tunnel for that. I know it's deep history, but in 1971 a 31-man detachment crossed the DMZ and made it as far as the President's official residence ...'

'The Blue House incident.' Sam hadn't needed to interject, but she couldn't stop herself.

The deputy looked across at her, his lips turning into something that looked like a smile.

He's impressed.

'Indeed,' he continued. 'Thirty-one DPRK soldiers infiltrated across the border, changed uniforms and eventually, even with a division of South Koreans searching for them, marched on the presidential palace. There was a firefight and sixty-odd Koreans from both sides were killed. So a cross-border raid would not be unprecedented. But, that was before the DMZ was reinforced. And, we should remember, the Blue House attack was sanctioned by the North Korean regime. With what's at stake, I can't see the Supreme Leader wanting

475

anything out of the next couple of days other than a successful summit.'

Frank spoke. 'I agree. And I know this is not my patch, but even the best trained North Koreans – soon to be equipped with state of the art weaponry – aren't capable of putting together something which would disrupt the summit. Not with the US and Chinese security apparatus all over it. Surely?'

Frank was right. They all were. None of the main players wanted anything out of this bar success; otherwise why would they be pursuing it?

But she was convinced it wasn't about the main players, or certainly the leaders of the participating nations. Their intent was clear.

But what of the Gang of Four?

Sam assumed the Deputy and his two boys weren't up to speed on that piece of intelligence. As a result, among the six of them she appeared to be the only one looking wide enough. Or deep enough.

She was still standing by the screen.

'Put up the railway map, Frank.'

It took him a couple of seconds to do as asked.

She stared at it for a second.

'What are you thinking, Miss Green?' the deputy asked, now with a touch of reverence.

That's better.

She turned to the group.

This is a long shot.

'In the past two weeks, and led heroically by Jane Baker who many of you will know, we think we have established a "Gang of Four" – a set of very senior officials from China, Vietnam, North Korea and Cuba – the remaining quasi-communist states. These men meet and communicate regularly and have been doing so for years. Whilst this is not clear, it seems possible that their meetings and their associated dark-web discussions are *not* sanctioned by their own leaders. Not wishing to be overly poetic, I believe their aim is to keep the earth in their countries red; blood red if necessary.' She let it hang. There was no response, so she continued. 'The ship, *La Teja*, is Cuban registered and has sailed from Havana. Via Singapore it stopped briefly at Cat Lai, in Vietnam. And is now berthed in Nampo. Cuba – Vietnam – North Korea.' She waited again. Still nothing.

Am I getting through?

If she could have paced around the room as she thought out loud, she would have. Instead she rested her hands on the back of Frank's chair.

'If the summit is successful the DPRK will pull away from communism. The four will become three. We know China is struggling in Hong Kong, but that's a blister on the side of an elephant. An elephant which is a tightly controlled state. But losing North Korea from the club could precipitate regime change in Vietnam. And then, maybe, Cuba?'

She waited again. The deputy was gently shaking his head. The two case-officers were nodding slowly.

477

'If we assume The Gang of Four's mission is to retain the virtues of communism, and indeed re-spread that message, they have to prevent the summit from being a success. There has to be an attack, of some sort. But it can't be the usual cake and arse affair the DPRK have pulled off in the past.' Apart from Frank, who she was standing behind, Sam looked at each of the men in the room as she briefed. 'We know they have the firepower; it's probably being unloaded as we speak. But we also know they can't make it to the South for the summit ...'

She lifted her hands from the chair as if to say, 'Can someone please complete my sentence?'

'They're going to attack the train. In the north.' Matthew did it for her.

Genius.

'When?' The deputy had his elbows on the table now, his face staring intently at the screen.

The vocal case-officer replied.

'The schedule for the Supreme Leader's train is for it to leave in the early hours of tomorrow morning. It is due at Dorasan, just north of the DMZ, at 10.15 am. They could ambush the train as it left Pyongyang?'

Sam waited for anyone to add something else to the mix. There was nothing.

'No. Wrong answer,' she said, flatly. The case-officer looked deflated. 'Sure, that would have an impact, but it would only stall the process. North Korean bandits kill North Korean leader. Sure, it's headline news.

478

However that would precipitate the election of a new leader with sympathetic support from China and the West. I can't see how that would make the regime more hard-line. If anything it's likely to reinforce the need for change. No. The Gang of Four need to be more ambitious than that.'

Sam waited.

The deputy had it.

'They're going to attack the train after the summit, as it moves from Dorasan to Pyongyang. There they get *both* leaders. The world would have a fit, the South Koreans would dismiss any chance of reconciliation and the DPRK would remain rooted in communism?'

We're getting somewhere.

'Yes.' Sam raised her finger to the side of her nose and then pointed it playfully at the deputy. 'Murdering the Supreme Leader is not enough. Taking out the whole summit is logistically impossible for the Gang of Four and, in any case, the DPRK would be toast if that happened ... either China or the US would make their life unbearable. Killing both Korean leaders would hit the right balance. It'll make the North Koreans look wholly unreliable and throw the peace process in the shredder.' She looked back at the map. 'Remind me, what are the timings for the return journey?'

The noisy case-officer replied.

'The details have not been formally announced. But if they move from the DMZ after tea, say 6 pm the

479

day after tomorrow, it would take them around 12 hours to make it to the capital. That's pretty much overnight. All of it in darkness. It's a turkey shoot.'

'If you have decent night sights,' Matthew added.

Sam stepped back so her head rested against the wall. Her shoulder was crying out for painkillers. And she was hungry. And she needed a pee; the tea had gone straight through her. And she needed a shower.

And some sleep.

But they didn't have a great deal of time for those things, no matter how essential.

The fact was there was no way this small cabal of middle and low grade staff had enough clout or intelligence to dent the ambitions of the summit; to change its itinerary. The Chief could speak to his opposite number at Langley, and maybe the team here could warn their opposite numbers in the Korean government. People could be put on their guard.

But there was no certainty.

No corroboration.

All they had was a theory. It was nowhere near enough.

And spreading their scant intelligence wider worried her.

Zagreb worried her.

The attack on the Hanoi Embassy worried her.

The Chief worried her.

The most heavily armed peninsula on the planet worried her. The South Korean Army was the largest standing force in the world, some three and a half million. The US military on the peninsula was 28,000 strong and tooled up to win World War Three. Over the border the Korean People's Army was more paramilitary than organised force, but it was a massive six million – one in four of the population.

Ten million men and women absolutely prepared to fight to save what they believed in.

The summit would bring peace. Or at least the start of it.

Peace.

Not everyone thought that word a good thing. In military terms peace was always associated with the word 'dividend'.

Soldiers would be sent home. Bases closed. Mission centres reduced in size. Ships and aircraft mothballed. Defence industries from around the world would lose huge orders; some would go bankrupt.

There would be a good number of people, just like the communists, who didn't want this thing to end. It was the longest running war in the past two centuries.

And it's a helluva gravy train.

The Gang of Four weren't the only people who wanted the summit to fail. She was sure of that. And, if it did fail, the fifth tunnel of aggression was a prize worth keeping secret. You never knew when you might need to invade another country.

'Matthew.' She looked across at him.

'Yes?'

'Get hold of someone in Zagreb. Quickly. Let's get whatever they have that came with the fifth tunnel of aggression intelligence. There must be more than just an acronym. It must have come from a larger document.'

'Sure, ehh, why?' he stuttered.

'Because you and I need to find out where it is.'

'What are you thinking of?' The Deputy looked perplexed.

Sam stared at the ceiling. She didn't know the answer to that question. She really didn't. All she knew was on this side of the border there were far too many self-interested parties who might go out of their way *not* to prevent an attack on two world leaders on a train.

So – if they weren't going to, it would be left up to the six of them.

And … *shit.*

She saw it then. It came rushing in from her blindside: what the Chief was up to. Why he had engaged Anne Bertram. He *was* on their side.

Definitely.

She looked across at the deputy and then to Frank.

'Matthew and I are going to cross the border. We need a vehicle, a weapon each and any night viewing aids you have. Frank …'

'What?!' the deputy and Frank blurted out in unison. 'That's impossible!' the deputy continued.

Sam didn't answer.

'Frank.' She was quieter.

482

'Yes.'

'The Chief is in the clear. I know what he's up to. I'll explain later. Get hold of him ASAP. Tell him everything we've discussed. My view is he won't want to share the intelligence. And we'll be on our own. There are too many people who don't want the summit to succeed. He knows that. That's why he was keeping this close ...'

Sam was cut off by the deputy.

'That's preposterous. We should get onto the Americans now. Straight away.' A little bit of venom had returned.

'No it isn't. Think about it.' Sam's tone was direct. Her sentences short. 'There are too many bases. Too many soldiers. This war is an industry. Which means money. Now ...'

The deputy half-raised a hand to interject, but Sam wouldn't let him. She continued to address him directly.

'... I want every army member of staff in the embassy, or anyone with a military background, in this room in half an hour.' She paused and waited for an acknowledgement. He nodded. 'Whilst we do an IPB of the northern rail route, you and your two officers can put a benign call out for anyone and anyone's wives. Find whatever intelligence you can. You're asking, you're not telling. Is there any information regarding a rogue grouping north of the border? Anything on a potential fifth tunnel? Anything. We need to know where they're going to hit the train. And Matthew ...' She turned to him.

'Yes?'

'We should be out of here within two hours. Get another satphone and a tablet. You can continue your conversations with Zagreb as we make our way along the border.'

'OK. Sure.' And then, 'What's an IPB? And are we taking a whole load of embassy staff with us?'

She smiled at him.

'Intelligence Preparation of the Battlefield. Me, and any army pals I can get my hands on, are going to plan an attack on a train. And no, we're going on our own.'

'OK.' His second response lacked the conviction Sam was hoping for.

Oh well.

Matthew's people skills had come to the fore – yet again. Jolene, a CIA woman in Zagreb had taken some convincing. In the end she'd sent over a file and three photos which, she reckoned, was all they had from the Korean defector which might be relevant to the fifth tunnel of aggression. She sounded completely convinced.

'I've looked over all of the documentation from the pen drive Jackson found in the Korean's apartment – three times. And I know what I'm on. The Word document and the three photos are linked in time and space. Everything else is dated much earlier. And that's all irrelevant stuff like bank statements and some unnecessary porno.' She had a lovely lyrical, mid-American accent.

'Thank you so much, Jolene. This is really helpful,' Matthew had replied.

'I'm about to send you the work I did for Jackson.' She paused. Matthew thought he heard her sniff back a tear. 'It's a clever cypher. They've used Morse code. Korean characters to English. The document explains how it works. I wrote it all down for Jackson. And, do you know what?'

No?

'No. Go on, Jolene.'

'I shouldn't have it. The Director has been sent very clear instructions to destroy anything on the defector. In fact, I shouldn't be talking to you about it now.'

'Then why ...'

'Because I smell a rat.' She was whispering now, but not making a very job of it. 'Jackson's murder was pushed under a rug. And I ain't worked for the Agency for nigh-on thirty years only to be part of a cover up, is all.'

Matthew now had the original document – in Korean. And three more folios explaining how Jolene, who was clearly a better cryptographer than whisperer, had ended up with: *We have found 5toa. It's operational. Could be used by both sides.*

485

And Matthew had the three photos on his screen. Without detailed interrogation they looked like they might show an entrance to the tunnel although, if you didn't know it existed you'd have struggled to make that leap. He counted a maximum of seventeen people between all three photos; there were some of the same folk in more than one image.

It was hardly helpful. As was the message.

Could be used by both sides.

What did that imply?

The people in the images – none of them looked official – were young and old alike. One or two were carrying objects: satchels and a rucksack. A couple, who Matthew couldn't make out, were hugging each other. Their embraces were close – meaningful. Stepping back, it was like the Korean equivalent of a village reunion.

Could be used by both sides?

Was the tunnel a casual find? Were these village folk? Celebrating a DMZ reunion? And who had taken the photos? And why then share it with a North Korean defector?

'Matthew.'

Sam was at his shoulder.

'How are you getting on?'

He pushed back his chair and showed her the photos.

'What's this?'

'I think it's the entrance to the tunnel.' He then pointed to a scrap of paper lying on his desk. He had scribbled down: *We have found 5toa. It's operational. Could be used by both sides.*

Sam didn't say anything. Instead, she glanced around and found a chair. She pulled up beside him. Their knees touched. It was a strangely intimate moment from a woman who had little idea what the word meant. When he had bandaged her shoulder in the hotel in Hanoi, he'd been gentle. He couldn't not touch her skin, although he did try to be as functional as possible. She had kept her eyes closed throughout, as though she didn't want to admit that some other human was being kind to her.

What have you been through?

'Is this everything?' she barked ... softly.

'Yes. And, according to "Jolene", I shouldn't have this stuff. It was meant to be destroyed.'

Sam didn't say anything. The intensity of her focus gave off its own glow. She was completely absorbed. In her element.

'Mmm,' she said, clearly not expecting an answer. She was professionally swiping, enlarging and reducing the three images.

She sat back; chewed on a finger.

And then leaned forward again, dabbing and swishing.

'Here.' The images were momentarily stationary. One was centre stage, the other two in the background. Sam had a finger on the screen.

Matthew leaned forward. Their faces were centimetres apart. He could smell her. A female smell. No perfume – maybe a touch of perspiration, but it wasn't unpleasant. Her breath was scented toothpaste. He glanced at the side of her face. He could make out the fine, wispy blonde hairs on her cheek. Her delicate, pointed nose and a thin, aerodynamic nostril. A wide, excited pupil almost overwhelmed a blue-green iris which itself was framed by a sliver of jet-black leading to unmarked, snow-white sclera.

Close up she was *very* pretty. There was no doubting that. Which was the wrong way round. Because as a package she was a car crash. As attractive as a porcupine.

She was unreachable – unless the connection was work.

'Look.' At this level concentration, even her voice was entrancing.

With a finger and thumb, she'd enlarged a section of a man's breast pocket from the central frame. As she did, the image pixelated – and then the SIS mainframe second-guessed the original photo and clarity was returned.

He moved even closer to the screen. Their shoulders touched. Flesh and thin cotton. Heat and a glistening of his sweat. She didn't seem to notice.

He couldn't not.

But her concentration – her potency – pulled him to the enlarged photo.

It was a Korean monogram.

How did she spot that?

'Any idea?' he asked.

'No. But ...' She didn't take her eyes off the screen, her slim fingers manipulating the three images so quickly that Matthew couldn't keep up. They ended up with the same enlarged photo. 'No. That's it.'

Sam stood and turned. The mid-sized office was open plan. She shouted across it.

'I need a translator here, now!'

There was some recognition ... and then a kerfuffle. A middle-aged woman stood and headed their way. Matthew moved so he and Sam created an avenue to the screen.

When the woman was close enough to the monitor Sam, with a finger on the image, said, 'What's that say? Please.' Her tone was direct, but not officious.

'My name's Bridget. Nice to meet you.'

Touché.

Sam didn't respond. She held her finger next to the characters on the man's shirt.

The woman leant forward.

'It says "Junsu's Garage".' A little attitude.

Bridget straightened her back and smiled at Sam.

'Can you google it for us. Please ... Bridget.' Sam forced a return smile.

'I'll do it on my machine.'

Bridget turned and strode back to her workstation.

489

'That's brilliant,' Matthew said. 'If we can find the garage, we might just be in the right place.'

He was talking to Sam's back. She was on Bridget's tail.

'Assuming that Junsu isn't the Korean equivalent of Smith,' she replied, over her shoulder.

They were both at Bridget's desk a few seconds later. And they were joined by Frank ...

... who asked, 'What are we up to?'

'Wait.' Sam put up a hand. Bridget was typing furiously. The three of them paused.

'There.' It was Bridget's turn to point at the screen. 'Junsu's Garage. And there's the address.'

'Google the address, please, Bridget.' Matthew beat Sam to it.

Bridget did as she was asked. A map and a red pin appeared. She pushed back in her chair so that the three of them could see the monitor.

Blow me down.

There it was. A red pin in a small bit of grey on Google Maps. Matthew couldn't do the perspective without finding the scale, but it looked awfully close to the DMZ.

'Bridget.' Sam had gone to touch the woman's shoulder, hesitated and then stopped herself. She pulled her hand back. 'You're fluent in Korean?'

'Of course. Most of us here are. But I'm one of two qualified interpreters.'

Sam took a breath.

'Can we borrow you? Just for a day?'

What?

Bridget stuttered. Frank looked quizzically at Sam. But Matthew now knew exactly where this was going.

'Eh. Sure. I'd need to talk with Jim. Why?'

'We're going to find the garage. Now. And then we will need someone who can charm like crazy ... in Korean. I think you might be that woman.'

Chapter 17

38°15'50.6"N 128°07'08.6"E, heading northeast on the 453

Sam was irritated. She was irritated by Bridget who was snoring in the back of the Hyundai i30, the best car the embassy could offer at short notice. Its plastic dashboard wasn't quite Volkswagen standard and the switches lacked the precision and weight of her old T5. That irritated her.

Matthew was irritating her. He was too perfect for his own good. They'd had words early on but, since the incident on the bridge of *Fraulein Mila*, he'd accepted everything she'd thrown at him. With some sweet-talking he'd possibly found the entrance to the tunnel and hadn't raised an eyebrow when she'd concocted a plan which relied on more luck than anyone deserved and would very likely mean they'd spend a good portion of the next decade in a North Korean jail.

Or worse.

And they had chemistry. Which irritated. Her emotional radar was irrevocably broken, but she'd felt it. He'd saved her from plummeting from the edge of the container. A masculine hand stalling her fall to more broken bones. He'd dressed her wound with maternal tenderness. And now she felt he was travelling with her, against the longest of odds, not just because it was work – no one in authority could possibly ask them to do what she was suggesting – but because he felt the need to protect her.

And they had touched – recently. By the computer screen at the station. It was brief, but it happened. She'd sensed it. A flutter of emotion; a fidget of hormones.

She had, of course, ignored it. She had no capacity. Frank had tested her love and found the cupboard bare. She hadn't been to bed with anyone since Austria, three years ago. That had been the briefest of affairs; the gender a different calling.

Sex couldn't be further from her mind.

Which is why the man from The Box – Thames House, MI5, The Service – was getting her goat. She didn't need distractions. Neither of them did. Split-second decision making required no distractions. Emotions, feelings – they were distractions. Unnecessary distractions.

He'd been a burden at the beginning. A brief passenger. Then he was at her side, stride for stride. And now they were partners: she leading; he – chief administrator and back-getter.

Which wasn't her. She worked better alone. It was as simple as that ... wasn't it?

But she'd encouraged him.

493

And now, here he was. Driving the plastic Hyundai through the dark, cold night with the confidence of ten men.

Which irritated her,

With the support of two army guys from the embassy, she'd uncovered three likely attack locations on the railway north from Dorasan. Concurrently he'd pulled together an H&K MP5 machine pistol and a second Browning 9mm, an additional satphone, a 7-inch tablet and two handheld thermal imaging binoculars. All with the scantiest of direction.

He was good.

And *that* irritated her.

A snort and a cough from the back seat.

Matthew looked across at her, his face lit up by an oncoming car.

He smiled.

Irritating.

She looked away to the dark shapes of the trees and the lighter gaps between them, flashing by.

What were they up to?

What chance was there they would find the tunnel? And, if they did, that it wasn't already compromised? Why wouldn't it be guarded? If not, why should someone lead them through?

And what about on the northern side? The DPRK's infrastructure was rubbish. There were few cars and the roads were dreadful. They had no maps, limited firepower and not enough time.

It was hopeless.

And dangerous.

Frank had spoken to the Chief. He had sanctioned her crazy idea, but there would be no support, no acknowledgment ... and no rescue. In the same call the Chief had confirmed what Sam had deduced. He'd used Anne Bertram. He'd paid for a massive shorting of the Korean *won*. It was a long shot but he was hoping that such a large deal – and its timing – wouldn't go unnoticed in Pyongyang. That the finance ministry would latch on to such a move and recognise their currency was under attack – so close to the summit. As a result they would investigate further and maybe root out their own member of the Gang of Four.

That might still be happening. But it was a longshot.

A longshot?

No more than her and Matthew's attempt to prevent a heavily armed attack on a train. An attack which might well be a figment of her imagination. And could take place anywhere on a 243 kilometre stretch of line. Sure, she and her army pals had undertaken a review of the route. They had pored over maps and satellite imagery. Reviewed distances and terrain from Nampo to likely ambush points on the railway. They had taken into consideration the strengths of the attacking force and those that might be on the train. They had looked at the environmental conditions – the next two days were calm, but overcast. There would be no moonlight.

And they had investigated escape routes for the attackers.

It had boiled down to three options.

In the military there were always three options. If you could only find two you invented a third. Sam had felt like she was retaking her sergeant's course. But this time the enemy wasn't fictitious. And the weapons very real.

She had yet to make a choice as to which one, if any, was the right option. She'd have to do that between now and ... whenever.

Odds of three to one.

Get real.

The odds were more like 10,000 to one.

But what else could they do?

Matthew had negotiated a left turn and they were now climbing into the hills. The village was twenty klicks up the road, the garage the third building on the left, set back behind a forecourt. There were forty-two separate dwellings in the village, the road dissecting the place: one-third on the west side of the road; two-thirds on the east. The lanes and tracks in and around the village were imprinted on her mind. She could have drawn a scaled plan. And she could navigate around the place in the dark. She'd seen the map. She remembered it.

They'd used the mapping tool to look wider. To see if they could find an open area of ground which they might recognise from the photos. But there were too many choices and they'd given up.

With what time they had, they needed to find the man from the garage in the photo. And then they had to persuade him to take them to the tunnel.

So many imponderables. Too many ducks and too long a row.

The vegetation was flashing past, the road twisting and turning – Matthew focusing hard on his driving. Bridget was no longer snoring, which was a relief.

And Sam was bored.

Do something useful.

'Bridget?' She'd turned her head and directed her question to the back seat.

'Mmm?' A snoozy response.

'The holdall next to you. The one with the weapons in. Can you fish out the pistol and the bigger gun?'

She and Matthew had only made a cursory check of the additional 9mm Browning and the Beretta machine pistol; time hadn't been on their side and they needed to get moving. He'd found a military-style holdall and put all of the equipment they'd taken from the station in the bag, which Sam had thrown on the back seat of the Hyundai.

They needed a proper look-see.

She'd check the weapons first. The sights second.

They'd have to be sensible with the thermal binos, which worked on rechargeable batteries via a USB charging port – like a smartphone. That was good news – if you could find an appropriate power source, which was unlikely. They'd have to use them parsimoniously.

Grunting came from the back. And then a handful of pistol emerged from between the two chairs, followed by the longer barrel of the MP5.

Sam put the Browning in her lap and the MP5, stock down, between her knees.

'Are you expecting trouble?' Matthew quipped.

'No. But you have been irritating me for a while. Clearly my wit's not working, so I've called for back-up.' She had the Browning in one hand and a handkerchief in the other.

She dismantled the pistol into her hanky: release the magazine; cock the weapon by pulling back the top slide; push the holding lever up; push out the safety catch lever; gently release the mechanism; careful not to lose the spring.

She couldn't see much, so used her fingers to feel for oil and dirt. The weapon was clean and had been put away dry. That wasn't the army way. A light oil would have been better, especially in the cold. But it would be OK. Pistols worked. They just did.

Sam used her handkerchief to wipe down the parts and then reassembled the weapon without the magazine. She cocked it twice, and fired off the action.

She then pressed down on the top round in the magazine. It hardly moved: a full load, thirteen rounds, unlucky for some. *Good.* She reloaded the magazine into the bottom of the pistol grip, tapped it closed and placed it under her leg.

Next, the MP5.

'Have you ever fired an MP5?' she asked Matthew.

'Sure. I've got a couple in a locked cabinet in my garage.'

She didn't acknowledge the sarcasm outwardly, but smiled to herself.

Damn. Why are you such good company?

The MP5 was new to her. It wasn't a standard issue weapon in the British military. She had seen one in SIS's armoury in Moscow – but had never fired it. Like any handheld weapon the mechanism would be straightforward, but she wasn't prepared to try and dismantle it in the front seat of a car, in the dark. But she needed to know where the cocking mechanism and the safety were, and where the magazine release was.

Magazine release first.

She felt for it.

Click.

The curved magazine dropped from the body of the elongated pistol. She stuck it between her knees.

Cocking handle.

With the hanky still on her lap, she felt for the ejection slot and turned the weapon so the opening was facing her crotch. She pulled the cocking handle back – no round dropped out. The MP5 had been loaded, but not made ready. She released the handle.

Clunk.

Now find the safety.

She fiddled in the dark.

There.

Exactly where it should be. By the thumb of her right hand. She pushed it down ... and then up: *click; click*. It should now be safe.

She found the electric window button on the car door and pressed 'down'. The more the glass dropped, the more they were joined by a cool fifty-mile-an-hour wind.

She turned her shoulders and stuck the machine pistol's short barrel out of the window. She looked across the weapon's iron sights into the green and black mass of passing trees.

'Sam?' Matthew, above the noise of the rushing wind.

She ignored him.

She fired off the action ... but the trigger wouldn't budge.

Safety works.

'Sam?!' Louder this time, with a touch of alarm.

She released the safety catch, fired off the action and then closed the safety.

Clunk. Click.

She pulled the barrel inside the car, closed the window, engaged the magazine and placed the weapon back between her knees.

'What?' she replied nonchalantly.

'Nothing,' Matthew said wearily, without looking at her.

A set of headlights appeared on the horizon They got bigger and bigger, and then flashed past them. It was the first car she'd seen since they'd pulled off the main road.

Sam checked the clock on the dash: *20.17*. At least they wouldn't be dragging people from their beds.

Ten minutes later the surrounding blackness lightened toward the horizon. A streetlight came into view, its mellow orange a welcome beacon against the previously oppressive darkness.

'I think we're almost here.' Matthew broke her train of thought.

Ahead of them was the start of a linear village. A road with houses on either side. The map had shown the details. The garage was on the left. Three buildings down. They were on it almost before they realised. Matthew pressed hard on the brakes and pulled the Hyundai off the road to the right. Sam had to bend forward and left to look through his window. They were close again, almost touching. She forced the thought from her mind.

'What now?' he asked.

'Let's go and wake someone up,' she replied.

Bridget took longer than the pair of them to get herself sorted. Whilst she straightened her clothes and pushed her hair behind her ears, Sam and Matthew peered in through the garage's office door, beside which was a large and closed roll-over mechanism which Sam assumed led to a workshop.

There were no lights in the office. But there was a lamp lit in a window above, on the second floor.

No doorbell.

'Bridget?' Sam asked.

She was with them now.

'Yes?'

'Can you phone this?' The torch on Sam's phone was illuminating a number on an advertorial stuck to the inside of the office door.

They had purposely not attempted to engage with the garage before now. She was worried ranks would close and horses would bolt. Both she and Matthew had agreed that any contact would be best done face to face.

Bridget had her phone to her ear.

'What do you want me to say?'

'Tell them you've just managed to limp your car to the garage's forecourt. They can look out of the window and see it, if they wish. You need help. Do the best damsel in distress act you can.'

The phone was ringing.

A splurge of Korean.

Then she hung up.

'Well?' Sam asked a little too tersely.

'He's on his way down. Now.'

Blimey.

A light went on in the office and a short, late-middle-aged man shuffled to the door. He undid some bolts and a lock; the door opened.

It wasn't the man in the photo.

Bugger.

He bowed. They all bowed back.

'어떻게 도와 드릴까요?'

Bridget turned to Sam.

'What do you want me to say?'

Sam had worked with interpreters before in Afghanistan. The key to developing a relationship with a person whose language you cannot speak is to talk to them directly. Engage them. Eye to eye. Let the interpreter do their work to the side, but make it about you and your new companion.

Ignore Bridget.

'Hello. My name is Sam Green.' Sam caught the attention of the Korean.

Bridget interpreted. The man, now a little confused as to who he should be speaking, replied in Korean.

'Hello. My name is Beom-soo.' Bridget interpreted. 'Would you like to come in? It is cold outside.'

Sam bowed, a semi-bow.

'Thank you.'

Bridget did her thing.

The man led the way. They all took a seat on soft chairs which were placed around a Formica-topped coffee table on which was strewn a set of dog-eared motoring magazines.

There was a momentary silence which allowed Sam to get her thoughts together.

'We need your help,' she said.

Bridget translated. The man nodded.

'My uncle served in the Korean War.' Sam paused, just briefly. She didn't know how good Bridget was and she wanted her message to get across, including its tone. 'He was a gunner in 14 Field Regiment. Artillery. He was here in 1951. His name was Peter.'

The Korean offered a comment.

Bridget translated, nigh-on simultaneously.

'You are British?'

'Yes, sorry. I should have made that clear.'

More Korean.

'We are in your debt. You lost many soldiers to secure our future.' From Bridget.

'We lost over a thousand soldiers. My uncle Peter was injured in the arm.' Sam reached unnecessarily for her shoulder realising it was the same arm where she was currently nursing her own bullet wound. 'There were over one hundred thousand South Koreans lost in the war?' Sam finished with a question.

Whilst Bridget did her thing, Sam looked intently at the man opposite her. It was difficult to guess his age.

504

He was, like most of the East Asians she'd encountered, short, wiry and, as they got older, wrinkled. She reckoned he was maybe in his 60s. But his eyes were bright and knowing. His hands were those of a mechanic, etched with dark oil that had penetrated the grooves and lines of his skin. She wouldn't have been surprised to see him pop out from under a car with a spanner in his hands.

And a smile on his face.

The Korean spoke; Bridget translated.

'Here, we don't talk of losses to the South, or to the North. We are one Korea. And there are many numbers. Some say over a million of our family lost their lives in that war. We do not want another.' His face remained sombre as Bridget translated.

Sam shut her eyes briefly. The numbers were staggering. Without a successful summit, who knew whether or not they would be adding to the total sometime soon.

The man spoke again.

'What do you want, Miss Green? This is not about your car, is it?' Bridget was doing an excellent job. She was matching her voice with the sincerity of the man's face.

'No. We are from the British government.' Sam nudged Matthew and whispered, 'Get your ID out. You too, Bridget.'

505

The Korean heard the translation and waited to see the cards. He picked up Matthew's and turned it over in his hand.

'너는 어디 있니?'

'Where is yours?' Bridget interpreted. The man was staring at Sam impassively.

Sam didn't answer, because she couldn't. Instead she took out a folded sheet of A4 from her backpack. She opened it. And showed it to the Korean.

It was a cropped photo of the man with the garage's logo. She had cut it in a way which didn't show the background. That was for later.

'Do you know this man?' Sam asked.

The Korean, who up until this point had been sitting forward, leant back in his seat and folded his arms.

That's not a good look.

There was a moment. Then he spoke.

'I ask you again, Miss Green. What do you and your friends want?'

Sam sat back as well. She then smiled and nodded.

In for a penny.

'We know of the fifth tunnel, Beom-soo. And we know it's here, near this village.' Her first white lie. 'This man, who wears your garage's logo, knows where the tunnel is. And we need to speak with him. He is not in any trouble.' She forced a defensive smile.

As Bridget translated, the Korean kept Sam's gaze. And she couldn't, for the life of her, work out what was going on upstairs.

And then he stood. At first Sam thought there was a finality about the move, that the conversation was over. That he would ask them to leave. At which point Sam was ready to try an altogether different approach, which might include her MP5.

Instead, the Korean turned and walked away from the table ... and made it as far as the counter. He then picked up an old fashioned phone and dialled.

After a pause for a connection, a conversation ensued. Which Bridget translated.

'Hello, Jae-joon. It's your brother. You need to come to the garage. Now. I have some people who want to talk to you. I think it is over.' There was a pause, and then, 'Good. I will see you in five minutes.' He hung up the phone.

He then addressed the three of them, which Bridget translated.

'My brother is coming now. He will be here in five minutes. He will talk to you.' The man moved to a door at the back of the office. He opened it. Sam spotted steps leading upward. He shouted some Korean and then turned to them.

'I have ordered some tea. My wife will bring it presently.'

Half an hour and two cups of sweet tea later they were making progress. Beom-soo's brother, a civil servant, part time mechanic and the man who had unexpectedly discovered the fifth tunnel of aggression, spoke reasonable English. At first the conversation had been stilted. Sam had given a little of their story and how the British hoped to prevent a major incident north of the border. After that, and with an integrity that Sam warmed to, Jae-joon explained how he'd accidentally discovered the tunnel and how, over time, the village had used it to bring families together – as well as a conduit for provisions to support people on the other side of the DMZ.

'I knew, and the village elders know, it was only a matter of time before the authorities found out. One side or the other. We have tried to be as discreet as we might, but this is too large a secret to keep.'

Bridget was translating for the other brother as the conversation went on.

'Someone senior in the DPRK knows. The secret is wider than just among your families. That's how we found out,' Sam said.

Jae-joon didn't reply. He looked at his brother.

'끝났다,' he said.

'It is finished,' Bridget translated.

Beom-soo and his brother, who were sitting next to each other, joined hands and nodded. It was a poignant moment.

508

Sam let the gravity of where they found themselves sink in. And then, 'We need to use the tunnel.' Sam broke into the mood.

Jae-joon let go of his brother's hand and faced Sam.

'But if the North knows, it will be dangerous to use it now?' The Korean showed real concern.

Tell me about it.

'May I have some more tea, please?' Sam pointed at the pot. Beom-soo did the honours. Once he'd finished, she picked up the cup and took a sip. She then gently put the cup down and placed her hands on her knees.

She nodded slowly as she spoke.

'Matthew and I need to get into the north. Tonight. On the other side we require a driver and a car.' She waited, letting Bridget translate for Beom-soo. 'We believe someone is going to attack a train, possibly tomorrow night ...'

'The train carrying the two leaders?' Jae-joon interrupted.

Sam wanted to slow things down. She had to convince the two Koreans she was telling the truth and, whilst the gravity of the situation was huge, she needed to reinforce that what they were discussing must remain only between them.

'Yes,' Sam replied, nodding gravely.

'*예*,' Bridget added.

509

Jae-joon glanced at his brother. And then to Sam … and then Matthew.

'We have been sent by the Chief of the British Secret Intelligence Service.' Matthew hadn't spoken throughout. He clearly thought now was the time to add his piece. 'There are people in Seoul looking at taking action to prevent an attack. But, in case that doesn't work, we have been tasked to get on the train.'

Get on *the train?*

That wasn't in Sam's plan.

She didn't say anything.

'Are you armed?' Jae-joon asked.

Sam looked at Matthew. And then reached into her bag and pulled out her Browning. She offered it to Jae-joon. He took it.

'We have more weapons and ancillaries in the car,' she added.

Jae-joon handed the pistol back. He stood, placing his hand on the back of his head, stretching. He then walked to the centre of the room. He seemed to be staring at a calendar on the far wall. Nobody said anything for what seemed like an age.

He turned back to face them.

'What will happen to the tunnel?' he asked.

'I'm pretty sure your government – the government in the South – haven't heard about it. And we are the only people who know exactly where it is. I can't guess who in the DPRK knows, but we didn't find out from government sources – so your secret may be able to be kept safe. For a while at least,' Sam replied.

Jae-joon dropped his hand to his side, turned again and looked out of the window of the office to the road beyond. He appeared unsure. Contemplative.

'I know of someone in the northern village who has a van. He is my cousin. We can pay him.'

That easy?

'That's ... that's great.' Sam sounded as surprised as she felt.

'And I will drive you,' he added.

'But ...' Sam thought she might object. She had no idea why.

'If I am going to facilitate this, then I have to be sure you are who you say you are. And that you do what you say you are going to do. That is my duty as a Korean.' Jae-joon's face displayed a mixture of honesty and stoicism.

Matthew glanced at Sam. Bridget was translating. Her expression reflected her own astonishment.

Sam stood. She walked over to Jae-joon. They were half a metre apart.

'Can you use a pistol?' she asked him quietly. Bridget matched her softness.

'I was conscripted into the Marine Corps when I was eighteen. I served for two years. I can fire many weapons,' he replied.

She nodded. And handed him her Browning.

511

'Keep this. And let's hope you don't have to use it.'

38°19'48.7"N, 128°06'16.2"E, North of Ihyeon-Ri, DMZ, Korea

Matthew had to duck his head a couple of times. And for a 20-metre section he was bent right over. The tunnel wasn't made for Western men. Jae-joon was leading. He had a torch in one hand and Sam's Browning in the other. Sam followed on. Considering her shoulder injury she was faring well. She'd taken a pair of the thermal binos, the MP5 and some ammunition. The binos and ammunition were in her backpack, the MP5 was slung and she was also carrying a torch Jae-joon had lent her. She was a dynamo. There was no questioning that.

He had the remaining gear from the embassy in the holdall which he'd thrown over his shoulder. And the Browning was in one palm – a torch in the other.

'It's another 25 metres or so.' Jae-joon's voice from the front carried easily in the dank, lifeless conditions.

And then what?

Matthew had no idea what he was doing. That is, he knew what he was doing – or being asked to do, but he had no idea why he had agreed to it. His Security Service role had not been without excitement. Whilst most of the time he was stuck behind a desk searching

512

through financial evidence, written transcripts, call logs and CCTV clips, he did venture out. He'd kept count: in his fifteen years of service he'd run sixty-one informants. He currently had four on his books. Making those connections required face-to-face meetings, often with some very unsavoury characters: gangsters; would-be Islamic terrorists; hardened criminals; men and women on the edge. He'd had a knife pulled on him twice. And whilst, thankfully, he hadn't needed it, both times he'd been wearing a stab vest – just in case. But at no time in his career had he been armed.

He'd been a witness to three shootings. In all occasions he'd been in over-watch; out of harm's way. He'd seen one man die, killed by a police marksman. Two others, both men, had been shot, but not fatally. There had been blood. Lots of it.

But not at his hands.

Sam was clearly happy carrying and using a weapon. She was ex-army and probably had a lot of practice. And she'd shot the captain of *Fraulein Mila* in the calf, just to keep her eye in.

Bang.

And then she'd ignored the man on the ground as she righted the ship so the Merlin could land.

Yes, she seemed very comfortable using a weapon.

He'd not asked her whether she had killed someone, although there'd been plenty of quiet times when he could have posed it. It's not a question you asked. He knew that. But if he had asked, he knew it would be a question to which there would be no answer. There was something in her demeanour. A coldness; a distance ... no, *a cloak*, that enveloped her. That protected her. Shielding other people from the truth.

It was like he was dealing with a crystal tumbler which was protected with more bubble wrap and stuck with more Sellotape than any one person could remove. But a fine glass was no good unless you could see it. Drink out of it.

On the other hand, by exposing it you risked dropping it, shattering it into a thousand pieces.

That was her.

And Sam Green wasn't having any of it. She was protecting her past from her present. And doing a damn good job of it.

Was he in the tunnel because his professional conscience told him that's what he had to do? His country needed him? Or was he following Sam Green because, if he didn't she would dismiss him as half the man she thought he might be?

He had no idea. Although the former was nonsense. He'd been given no direct instructions from his leaders. Indeed, it had been made clear that they would abandon him and Sam if they got caught out in the north.

The latter was a crazier notion still. That, in less than a week, he'd fallen for a woman who showed almost no interest in him. A woman who might well be using him and, just as likely, abandon him as the authorities had said they would if things went awry.

But.

She couldn't do this on her own. Their escape from the embassy. The ship. The Merlin. If she'd been doing any of that solo, she'd have come unstuck. They wouldn't be where they were now if he hadn't stayed with her ... and more so now – under the DPRK's soil.

She needed him. Even if she didn't acknowledge it.

'We're here.' Jae-joon had reached a set of steps carved out of the stone. Moisture trickled down them into a milky puddle on the tunnel floor. The light of Sam's torch caught the Korean's face. He looked as serious now as when he'd accepted the challenge in the garage. And Matthew felt very comfortable that he was with them.

'Go.' Sam motioned with her torch.

'You're staying here whilst I wake my cousin?'

'No. We'll come to the surface with you. It will be dark for a while yet. We'll find somewhere to hide,' Sam directed.

Jae-joon didn't look sure. But then he nodded and started to climb the steps.

'Sam?' Matthew asked.

She turned and looked at him, her face lit by his torch. The irritation in her face answered the question.

'Nothing,' he said.

She turned and followed Jae-joon up the stairs.

Jae-joon was gone for half an hour. Sam had chosen to lay low in a small copse on the edge of the village. She could make out the silhouettes of one or two buildings, but without moonlight it was difficult to get a decent picture. And she wasn't prepared to use the precious thermal imaging equipment. Not yet.

'Psst,' she called, as Jae-joon approached the wrong set of trees.

He changed his tack and headed toward them.

When he was in whispering distance he said, 'I've got the keys.' He held them up between finger and thumb.

'Good.' She pulled him further into the trees. She then opened her backpack, pulled out the satphone and turned it on. A light green hue shone from the small LED screen. Sam put her back between it and the buildings.

She waited. It took the phone a minute to connect.

When the screen showed she had a signal she dialled Frank's number. It took him five rings to pick up. Matthew moved to her shoulder so he could listen to the conversation.

'Sam. Where are you? Why haven't you been in touch? I've got stuff for you.'

She didn't need a lecture.

'We're in the DPRK, via the tunnel …'

'What? Bloody hell!' Frank squealed in response.

'We're about to head northwest. Depending which of the three options we choose as the most likely attack point, it's going to take anywhere between five and eight hours to make that trip – assuming we don't encounter any delays. I'll need to make a final decision in about three hours' time. At which point I'll phone again, unless you have further int now?'

'How are you travelling?'

Is that important?

'Jae-joon?' She brought the LED screen to her chest. 'What vehicle have we got?'

'A Russian, UAZ-469,' he replied.

She brought the handset back to her face.

'A Russian 4x4. It's pretty reliable. Why do you ask?'

'Good. The road network is rubbish and, having made a detailed review of possible routes, there are very few places where the roads and railway intersect. We're working the surveillance hard here. We have your three army options and we're overlaying them with whatever we can get. Our best hope is to follow the weapons. It's a needle in a haystack, but we're doing our best.' Frank sounded less than positive.

'What chance do you have?' Sam needed everything and anything.

'Dunno. The problem is the operation here is closed. It's me, the deputy and the two other guys. We've been restricted to the conference room and have been instructed by the Chief to stay put. He's also stuck a restriction on who we can email and what sources we can push. I've managed to get the satellite feed via Singapore, who are abusing their local CIA mission centre contacts. We're getting an hourly refresh of the overheads and that's where we're hoping to spot a pattern – maybe a couple of trucks moving east from the coast. Nonetheless, not being able to pull all our contacts is tying one hand behind our backs.'

Why?

Sam closed her eyes, not that that changed what she could see. She didn't get the bigger picture. It had eluded her since the beginning. And just when she thought she knew what the Chief was up to, she lost it.

But … she couldn't be bothered with the politics. Not now. Anything other than the train was a distraction.

They needed to move on.

'OK. What visually have you got of the whole area?' Sam asked.

'As an overview we're working on pretty detailed paper maps. We stuck some together – it's on the table.'

An image of Churchill's map room in the War Office, replete with pretty WRAFs manoeuvring flights of Junkers across a table with push rods, was quickly dispelled.

Get. A. Grip.

'Good. Look one-third up from the DMZ in the west. Find Pyeongyang. Have you got it?' Sam asked.

'Hang on … yep. Is that where you're heading?'

'Yes. To start with. I'm pretty certain there's road and track from here to there … and the railway travels through the town. And there's a station. It's a central launch point for any of the three options. Or whatever you lot come up with.'

'OK, Sam. One other thing.'

'Go on.'

'The Chinese bot farm is back on the air.'

'And?'

'It's low-level stuff at the moment. But the message, which is China, South Korea and US-wide, is the summit is going to Westernise the DPRK. One bot Facebook site is named, "The North is the US's bitch". Another, "There must be oil in them there hills". And there are hundreds of others.' Frank sounded depressed.

'It's anti-summit. Pro status quo.' Matthew whispered loud enough for Frank to hear.

'Correct,' was Frank's response.

'OK, Frank. Let's wrap this up. We have to get going,' Sam interjected.

'Sam?'

She knew what was coming now.

'Yes, Frank.'

'Be as safe as you can.'

Whilst it was wholly expected, Sam was briefly overcome by Frank's concern, yet again, for her welfare.

She dismissed it.

'Find me where the weapons are heading.' And she hung up. 'Let's go,' she ordered to Matthew and Jae-joon.

38°37'21.9"N 127°59'13.9"E, Kangwon, North Korea

Matthew had never been off-roading. And now he knew why. He and Sam were sitting in the back of the Russian 4x4 – and it was hell. On inspection the mini-truck looked like a Land Rover Defender, but it was nothing like it. It was small and hurtful. The suspension was non-existent and they were sitting on facing bench seats, which had no cushions. It was flesh on angular metal.

And it was cold. The whole cab was open-backed with a canvas roof, and a metal half-tailgate above which was a cloth cover with a rectangular, opaque-plastic window – which wasn't sealed against the elements. As a result, cold air mixed with petrol fumes was a constant companion.

It was particularly unpleasant.

And he couldn't stretch his legs, which were beginning to seize.

'We're coming into a town,' Jae-joon called from the front. 'Get down.'

He and Sam dropped to the footwell so their heads couldn't be seen through the front window. Between them they pulled a canopy over themselves, a disappearing trick Sam had insisted they practised as they left the village.

It was cosy – and slightly warmer – under the tarpaulin. Their heads were at the same end of the footwell, inches apart. His chin above her forehead. He could smell her breath; with the constant clanging of the suspension it was his only sense he had working. His knees were touching, he guessed, her groin. Her elbows pushed against his chest and the barrel of an H&K MP5, which she clung to as if it were a sickly child, was resting against his forearm.

His own Browning was crammed between his legs.

They were armed – and potentially dangerous.

'Are you OK?' he whispered. He found it a comfortable question in uncomfortable surroundings. She was sure to have heard him.

There was no response.

'How's your shoulder?' he pressed. He wanted to know. He wasn't just passing the time of day.

Still no response.

Then, 'You didn't have to come,' she said.

She speaks.

'Who was going to carry your ammunition?' he quipped.

There was quiet again.

'Promise me something,' she continued.

'Mmm?'

'Look after *yourself*.' It was almost a mumble. An apology.

There was a pause, before she continued. 'I've been here a number of times. It's a blur to me. I don't have much to go back for. That makes me ...' She seemed to be struggling to find the right word.

'Reckless?' Matthew finished her sentence.

More quiet. A pothole shook the 4x4 and bits of body rubbed against other bits of other people's bodies.

'Yes. Reckless.' A further pause. 'You seem like a nice man ...'

'Nice man?' he interrupted her.

'Well, you know what I mean.' She sounded frustrated that he was interrupting her when she was trying so hard to communicate. He chastised himself for stopping her flow. 'I don't want you to get hurt ... unnecessarily.'

He smiled to himself.

There is some warmth in her.

'OK. I promise only to get hurt if it's necessary.'

She jabbed him in the chest with her elbow.

'Shut the fuck up,' she muttered.

The vehicle slowed. Matthew's concentration heightened.

'We've got company! A road block. Hang on.'

Matthew moved his arm so his hand was on the pistol grip of the Browning. And he felt the barrel of the MP5 move as Sam did the same.

Am I really going to shoot someone?

He had no idea.

Chapter 18

38°37'21.9"N 127°59'13.9"E, Kangwon, North Korea

It all happened so quickly. Matthew heard Jae-joon and another man have a quick-fire exchange in Korean, probably through the window of the driver's door. The 4x4's engine was then switched off. There was a pause, possibly for Jae-joon to get his documentation out (he had borrowed his cousin's ID and was dressed in his clothes) and hand them over.

Then more Korean. This time Matthew felt the inflexion in the second man's voice was more immediate, if that could be possible.

Shoes on gravel followed by a whisper from the driver's seat.

'A soldier is coming round the back.'

Sam shot straight back.

'How many are there?'

'Just him. There's another one with a gun ahead of us manning a ...'

Jae-joon didn't have time to finish his sentence.

Matthew heard the rear flap being undone, and then a *swoosh* of air and a soft *thump* as the canvas and plastic sheet folded over itself and landed on the roof.

He held his breath. A torch beam flickered in a dark corner under the canvas where the sheet had left a gap ...

... followed by the sound he was dreading. And the rushing of colder air.

The soldier had lifted the tarpaulin at their leg ond.

As he did, and in one smooth movement, Sam sat upright, the MP5 – held expertly in both hands – pointing straight at the soldier's stomach.

'Don't. Do anything. Stupid,' she said quietly and calmly.

The soldier, who had his weapon slung behind his back, fidgeted – his torch mimicking the motion, spraying the inside of the UAZ-469 with a shaft of light.

Sam pushed the barrel of the Heckler & Koch forward until it found the soldier's stomach.

He froze, the torch spotting a far corner of the back of the van. And then he started to raise his hands in submission, the torch beam following the trajectory.

'*Ani*,' she said; sharply, but calmly.

The soldier stopped, hands shoulder high, his mouth slightly ajar.

Quiet filled the void; the man's breathing was the loudest noise Matthew could hear.

Sam broke the impasse. With one hand remaining on the pistol grip of MP5, she reached into her waist belt and pulled out a piece of paper.

The North Korean soldier's eyes widened as they followed Sam's hand.

In it she held a $50 bill. More than a Korean soldier might earn in a year. Then, still with just one hand, she folded it expertly and placed the note between her teeth, side on.

The man watched every single move ... nervously.

Sam nodded. Slowly.

Her hand then moved slowly back to her waist belt and pulled out another note. Again she showed it to the soldier. A second $50 bill. She folded it like last time and it joined the first bill – between her teeth, her hand now holding the end of both bills.

She then took both notes and presented them to the soldier – so that the bills were a few centimetres from his face, side-by-side, but set apart like a V-sign. Matthew was sure the soldier went slightly cross-eyed.

'무슨 일이야?!' A shout in the middle distance from, Matthew assumed, the guard at the checkpoint.

Without taking his eyes off the notes, the soldier shouted back some indecipherable noise.

Sam nodded.

'Well. Done. Fella.' Very slowly she placed the bills in the soldier's breast pocket, patting it when she was done. And then, very deliberately and without removing the barrel from the soldier's stomach, she waved her free hand. Gently. Deliberately.

The soldier smiled, nodded quickly and reached up for the rear flap. He dropped it.

'*그것들을 놔 줘!*' he shouted.

Matthew had no idea what that meant, but Jaejoon did. He started the engine of the 4x4 and took off, with a touch of wheel spin.

Sam dropped the MP5 by her knees and secured the rear flap which was straggling behind them as the UAZ picked up speed. When she was finished she lay down, back in the foetal position they had rehearsed as they left the village a couple of hours earlier. He did the same.

Matthew thought he ought to say something, but he didn't know what. Throughout the ordeal with the soldier, his heart had been in his mouth, clattering away at a speed that he'd struggle to achieve in the gym. But, he'd had both hands on the Browning and, without really thinking, had very quietly cocked the pistol when the soldier had been entranced by Sam's extraordinary piece of theatre.

The vehicle hit a pothole. They bounced about. The barrel of the MP5 dug into his bicep, which hurt.

I'll survive.

He wanted to say something. Maybe 'thanks'. But that didn't seem right.

What do you say when someone has the perfect temperament and agility of mind to prevent a bloodbath, in which you might well have been a casualty?

She had, without a doubt, saved their lives; or, if nothing else, saved them from a long incarceration in a shitty North Korean cell.

He owed her. And he had to say something.

'Will he let on?' He'd eventually juggled some words together.

'Your guess is as good as mine. Maybe not initially. We'll just have to be on our guard.' A muffled reply from around his chest.

'Would you have shot him? If he'd called us out?'

'Would you?' Sam answered his question with a question.

He didn't reply straight away. He imagined what that might have looked like. The soldier, who was just a man who happened to have been born in a country different from his, screaming that he had found two Westerners hiding in the back of the truck. He'd have been frightened as anything.

Would Jae-joon have driven away? Would that have been followed by a volley of shots from both soldiers? Would he, Matthew, have taken aim with the Browning and fired off a round?

He didn't know. He really didn't.

'Probably not,' he replied.

They didn't speak for a while. Jae-joon was driving more quickly than he had previously and took a couple of sharp turns which Matthew assumed was to keep everyone guessing. He and Sam were thrown about like chickens in a cage. He thought he heard her cry out in pain.

Then he asked, 'How does Jae-joon know where he is going?'

Sam shuffled about. He thought she was hoping to get more comfortable. And, maybe like him, she was hoping soon to be given the all clear by their driver so they could sit up. Although, lying crunched up in the small footwell was no more or less comfortable than sitting on the angular metal seats.

'During conscription the South Korean soldiers have to learn everything about the potential enemy. Weapons, tactics ... North Korean topography. And, as I remember, there aren't a great number of roads in the DPRK. So it must be pretty easy to follow a route.'

'Oh,' he said, not very intelligently.

She was talking. He followed on.

'Do you have a job, other than as a mercenary for SIS?'

She didn't say anything for a second.

'I used to work in Asda.'

'Oh,' he said again. 'Fruit and veg. Or that rarely used aisle where you bribe North Korean soldiers at gunpoint?'

She let out a small laugh. Which was a good feeling.

'I'm ex-army, then SIS, first as an analyst and then a case-officer in Moscow. It all went a bit wrong there, and I ended up in Asda. Shit happens.'

'Oh. Well, if you don't mind me saying, I don't know anyone who could have made that happen with the soldier without someone pulling a trigger.'

She didn't say anything.

He continued. 'By the way, what does "*ani*" mean?'

The vehicle swerved and then slowed, and they were thrown about again like a blackjack ball coming to rest on the roulette wheel. They finished up closer together than when they started.

Another checkpoint?

God, not again.

Matthew held his breath, expecting something which might cost more than $100 and maybe involve a few rounds of 9mm. But the 4x4 steadied itself and kept on driving.

'It means "no",' Sam replied.

'Where did you pick that up from?' He was genuinely interested. The language was a mystery to him.

'I listen. And I remember,' she replied. 'Now shut up, because I need to get my head down. I suggest you do the same.'

'Oh,' he replied.

38°23'22.9"N 126°28'07.3"E, Ryesŏng River, East of Pyongsan

530

Sam woke with a start. It seemed her body had become accustomed to being thrown about by Jae-Joon swerving the UAZ from side to side to miss potholes, but a new experience of off-roading woke her from a fitful sleep. She was immediately alert and she closed her right hand around the pistol grip of the MP5.

It was getting light. She reckoned the UAZ, which Jae-Joon had now brought to a halt, was facing east. Through the front window and above the black silhouette of a distant tree line, she could make out the pinky-grey glow of dawn struggling against a blanket of cloud.

'What's happening?' she asked.

'We are a few kilometres short of Pyongsan. I've pulled off the road. I'm tired and we need to decide what to do next.' He sounded weary.

Matthew stirred beside her. He grunted and coughed. But didn't add to the conversation.

'OK,' Sam replied. She had started fishing in her rucksack for the satphone. 'Get your head down now. I need to speak to my man in Seoul. And then Matthew and I will discuss a plan. Happy?'

'Yes. I need to pop outside first, and we can break into the rations my cousin gave us. After last night I'm not happy about driving in daylight. You?' he asked.

'I don't know. Ideally not. But we'll see.' Sam was metaphorically crossing her legs; Jae-joon's implied mention of the toilet had sent her bladder into spasm. She poked Matthew gently in the chest. 'I need to pop to the loo. And then phone Frank. Are you happy to stay with the van?'

'Sure.'

Matthew's face was half in darkness, but she could see enough. He looked a little drawn, not helped by the fact he badly needed a shave. She didn't take to hairy men, so she hoped he kept his fledgling beard until this was all over.

She undid the rear flap and unhooked the tailgate. She left it drop slowly. Then, with the MP5 in one hand, the phone in the other and her backpack hanging from her good shoulder, she hopped out.

They were in the trees by a river, well away from a track which she could just make out under the lower branches. Jae-joon had trotted off to the left. She made her way down to the river.

Under almost any other circumstances, it was an idyllic position. The river, all dark green and cold, was wide and slow moving. Upstream it bent left and disappeared behind a shallow mound. Downstream it was pretty straight until, in the far distance, it turned towards her and went who knew where. Beyond the river was ... *what does it look like*? As she stared, her initial sense of serenity lost its glow. Across the river was agricultural land, but not as she recognised it. It wasn't helping that it was still not fully light, but the wheat-like crop was grey and patchy, as though the land had its own form of cancer and was losing its hair as a result.

Overgrown ditches broke the fields into segments, and shabby copses, like the one she was in, were dotted around like acne. In another, more distant field, the earth looked overgrown with weed – unkempt and ignored. And beyond that the ground rose up into a hill, the agriculture stopped and an untidy forest line was just catching the morning light from over her shoulder. The trees were irregular, and clearly not managed. The whole place had a sense of failure.

Of lost potential.

Apart from the gentle gurgle of the river, there was no sound. Nothing. No people. No cattle. Obviously no vehicles, as few people could afford them. But there was no noise from the indigenous nature. She'd visited the German concentration camp, Belsen, when she was serving over there. Once it had been a place of mass murder. Now it was a highly manicured site of remembrance.

And she'd noticed the same thing there.

No sound, apart from the wind cutting its way through the trees.

No birds.

She'd asked a guide if she were imaging things. The guide had replied that they weren't yet ready to come back. And it wasn't the death, the stench of human tragedy they didn't take to. It was that anything living in the grounds had been eaten by the inmates. And that memory lingered, even now.

That might well have been folklore, but Sam sensed the same thing here. The ground wasn't giving – certainly not enough to feed many hungry bellies. So the locals ate anything that moved ... or flew.

It was a peculiar comparison.

And it unnerved her.

She knew she had to phone Frank. And she knew she was close to wetting herself, but instead she listened.

Nothing.

Nothing at all.

It was very odd.

...

Come on.

Sam placed the MP5 on the floor and the satphone next to it. She dropped her far-too-thin-for-this-climate walking trousers – and her pants; she crouched and peed. As she did she kept her eye on the fields opposite. She had no idea what she was looking for, other than maybe some signs of life.

Nothing.

Not a thing. A strangely deserted non-desert.

South Korea was the twelfth largest economy in the world. It was self-sufficient in rice. Its people were hugely industrious and made electronics and cars that either dominated or would soon dominate world markets. And yet, ten miles north the same race of people with the same land and the same climate couldn't even manage to grow a field of barley without it shrivelling and dying.

And the Gang of Four wanted to keep it that way.

That made her very angry.

The summit *had* to be a success. She'd known all along. And her first glimpse of North Korea reaffirmed what she already knew to be so.

She wiped herself, pulled up her clothes, slung her MP5 and turned on the phone.

It took a minute to get itself organised.

She rang Frank. Who picked up on the third ring.

'Where are you?' He sounded tired.

'East of Pyongsan,' she replied.

There was a pause. Sam imagined Frank looking over the paper map on the conference table. He was no more than 100 miles from where she was. But he might as well have been in a different solar system.

'Good. I've got some stuff.'

She walked as she listened and talked, making a lazy-arc with the UAZ at the centre, keeping an eye out for anything which shouldn't be there.

'Hit me.'

Frank took a breath. 'We think we've managed to follow the arms shipment. We've got near-real time overheads, with a pass of every twenty minutes – better than we were expecting. Initially we were following four trucks from the quayside, which is easier than it sounds. In the end only two headed anywhere near the railway.'

That sounded hopeful.

535

'Go on,' Sam encouraged.

'Both trucks made it to a small hamlet 3 kilometres south of your Option B, the river plain north of Munmu Station.'

Sam could picture it from the historic overheads she had seen. An old provincial station serving a small industrial town. They'd had access to some of the embassy's files on the track and it was at Munmu that the train would need to stop as, for some inexplicable reason, the line terminated at the station and the carriages had to be shunted to a parallel track. Whatever, there would be a halt.

Sam and the army team reckoned that the station at Munmu would be heavily guarded. But, just north of the town towards Pyongyang, the railway crossed a river. At that point the track, river and a half-decent side road coalesced. The vegetation looked to be all paddy fields, so the fields-of-view would be excellent. And she'd done a calculation on the back of a fag packet. First, the distance from the station to the river/railway bridge was under 800 metres. A good distance from the town, but not enough for the train to pick up much speed. Second, at that point the gap from the road to the railway was under 150 metres. With decent night viewing equipment and no vegetation it would be a fairground shoot.

'Good.'

'I'm not finished,' Frank continued. 'The hamlet where the trucks eventually stopped was empty

536

yesterday – the satellite shots show that. However, the last snap has nine vehicles of varying descriptions gathering in the courtyards and side roads of the hamlet about three kilometre to the west of the railway. We've counted twenty-three individuals. And we've seen weapons.'

Shit.

Sam didn't need to do the maths.

They had two Brownings, a Heckler & Koch MP5 and 120 rounds of 9mm ammunition. All three were at best self-defence weapons with effective ranges out to tens of metres, no more. There was no way they could take out twenty-three men with more firepower than the Death Star.

'So,' she said. 'Good news and bad news? You've found the attack point. And there's no way we can stop it.'

'Maybe.' Frank sounded like he was trying to be positive. 'I do have something else. It might help.'

'Go.'

'We have a contact on the train. It's one of those bizarre coincidences; someone knows someone who knows someone...' Frank paused, perhaps waiting for Sam to say something. She didn't. He continued. 'She's a captain in the Korean Army. Presidential detachment. I had to clear it with the Chief first, as contacting the captain would cross a line the boss had drawn, but he said it was OK.'

What the hell's with the Chief?

Frank continued.

'We have the train details. Do you need to write this down?'

No.

'No,' she replied.

'Seven carriages, pulled by a single diesel locomotive. The first three carriages will be manned by North Korean guards. The fourth is the Supreme Leader's carriage. The fifth is purposely empty – an air gap. The sixth is the President of South Korea's carriage and the seventh will be stacked with the South Korean Army. Happy so far?'

'OK. How does this help?'

'The Chief thinks you should get on the train.'

What?

'What?'

'Yes. My thoughts. He suggests you and Matthew board the train. The captain is IC of the South Korean presidential detachment and will be in the last carriage. If you can find her, you might be able to get on board.'

'And do what, for fuck's sake? Add to the casualty list?' Sam wasn't happy with the plan.

Although … her brain was catching up with her mouth.

'I don't know. Warn the President?'

'Why can't the captain do that? Why can't the Chief do that? He could stop it now!' She was still walking round in circles, but now she had been joined by Matthew. *What are you … who's with the gear?*

538

She put the phone to her chest and whispered to him, 'Who's with the truck?'

'Jae-joon.' He looked hurt for being asked.

'Oh.' She nodded.

Frank continued.

'He said, he's trying. But he's only a few levers and is coming up against a lot of pushback.'

Sam pulled the phone from her ear. Matthew was standing in front of her, unattractive beard and everything.

'Option B,' she said. 'The weapons and a team of at least twenty-three fifth columnists are gathering as we speak, west of the target. The Chief reckons we should get on the train and warn them.' She tilted her head to one side and raised a hand as if to say that everyone else obviously thought they might be the stupid ones.

'Does he?' Matthew wasn't communicating much at the moment.

Nor was the phone. Frank was silent.

'We have a friendly on the train. This might just be possible,' she added to Matthew.

'What, clamber aboard a moving train? Who am I, Harrison Ford? Do we have any horses?'

Sometimes crisis brings out the best sarcasm in people.

They were both on the edge.

'No. Which is a shame ... that's the answer to the first question. As to the second, I know where the train

539

stops. We *can* get on. No saddle required.' She brought the phone back to her ear. 'Frank?'

'Yes,' he replied.

'We'll go with the Chief's plan. I need as much on the layout of the train carriages as you can get. And timings. And anything on Munmu station. And the captain's details. Tell her there'll be three of us. Matthew, me and an interpreter. OK?'

'Sure, and Sam?'

She hung up the phone. She didn't need to be told to be careful. Not this time. What the Chief was expecting them to do was akin to invading Normandy with a shotgun and a canoe. He was out of his mind.

And so were they.

38°26'14.4"N 126°04'03.3"E, short of Munmu Station

Jae-joon pulled the UAZ off the road. Sam could pick out where they were heading through the windscreen, the Russian 4x4 headlights giving adequate illumination. Ahead of them was a dilapidated wooden barn. The Korean parked the truck next to it, furthest from the road. He turned off the engine.

It had been an incident-free journey; a little over four hours. Sam had counted five other vehicles on the road. And no checkpoints. She had chosen to approach the station from the northeast, which was the direction they were coming in from in any case. The aim was to

540

stay on the other side of the track to where Frank reckoned the hamlet with the weapons and the bad guys were.

So far, so good.

Jae-joon breathed out noisily. If he were scared, he wasn't showing it. As they waited for night to fall by their initial river stop, Sam had outlined the plan. Once in sight of the train – and assuming it was shunting rather than driving straight through the station – she would phone Frank who, in turn, would contact the 'captain'. The captain should, hopefully, make herself known. The signal was a torch pointing to her feet. With Sam and Matthew providing cover – if extraction were needed – Jae-joon would approach the captain. He'd also have his torch pointed at his feet. A conversation would follow with the aim of Sam, Matthew and the Korean climbing aboard the last carriage.

Once in the carriage, the only thing they'd agreed was that Sam would lead, Matthew second and Jae-joon would be third in line. From then on in, they would wing it.

That was the plan. Not that it was much.

The three of them remained silent, lost in their own thoughts. The only discernible noise was the *tick* and *clunk* as the 4x4 cooled down after its 150 kilometre drive.

Sam tried to visualise the route from where they were parked to the station, but couldn't. It wasn't that her photographic memory was failing her. It was that she hadn't studied the satellite overheads much beyond the ambush point. That was a kilometre from here, northwest. In the embassy the train station had been a blur in her peripheral vision as they'd studied the attack point. It remained so now.

However, from what little she could recall, the road they had just left led perpendicularly to the railway and a crossing, with some dwellings either side. The station building, not much more than house-sized, was on the far side of a double track, with more buildings beyond that. She had no idea where the shunting carriages might do their thing. Nor did she have much idea of detailed distances. Thankfully Frank had painted a clearer picture when she'd last spoken to him. The track closest to them ran out of rails just beyond the station. There was a joining track and points to the far rail 80 metres southwest of the station.

Her best guess triangulation put them pretty much due north of that siding, with nothing but vegetation between them and the track. So, if they headed south ... maybe no more than ten minutes?

'What are you thinking?' Matthew broke the silence.

'Not much. Just getting my bearings,' she replied.

'Due south; maybe 100 metres?' he offered.

God, he's good.

'Yes. That's my view.'

She checked her watch. It was 2.17 am. Frank had said there was no exact itinerary. He'd done a better than cursory time and space review and reckoned the train would be at the station at 3.30 am, give or take an hour. That meant they could already be late … and their opportunity lost. But Jae-joon hadn't been prepared to drive from their stop by the river in daylight, and both Sam and Matthew had agreed he was probably right. So they had holed up during the day and set off after dusk.

'We should go.' She leant forward to the cab. 'Jae-joon? Turn the truck around and put the keys in the glovebox. Let us get out first. OK?'

She motioned Matthew to dismount and she followed him. They moved away from the truck, under the darkest lee of the barn. She had her thermal imaging binos out and her MP5 was slung. Matthew looked as if he might copy her.

'Don't.' She raised a near invisible hand.

'What?' He was confused.

'I'll scout with the binos. You and Jae-joon make your Brownings ready. I want one of you on my shoulder looking forward, and the other scouting behind.'

Matthew stopped what he was doing and re-slung the holdall. Jae-joon had now joined them, extinguished torch in one hand and Browning in the other.

'Jae-joon? Keep our backs,' Sam ordered.

'OK,' he replied.

The beauty of dealing with trained men, no matter what nationality.

Crouching, she moved away from the barn, up a low rise between some bushes – slowly; stopping every minute to listen. Both men did the same. As they reached the brow Sam knelt behind a bush and turned on the binos. She then closed one eye, brought an eyepiece to her good eye and scanned ahead of her.

Dark blue on top, dropping to shades of green where the vegetation had kept its heat from the day.

Nothing to report.

Without any announcement, she lowered the binos, half-stood and moved forward, a couple of paces at a time. Listening. Watching – the eye she had closed when she used the binos had kept its night vision.

A piece of barbed wire, ankle height.

She knelt. Matthew was just behind her, on her right shoulder. The short barrel of the Browning was 50 centimetres from her, pointing forward.

She lifted the binos to her face. Same action.

And dropped them immediately.

Fuck.

She reached over her shoulder and felt for Matthew's face. She touched his cheek. She then raised a fist and pointed off to their right.

She'd seen a warm body. Fuzzy reds and yellows amongst the blues and greens. A peculiarly shaped, truncated head; as if the shape was wearing a cold, steel helmet – Korean War vintage. The target was 20 metres away.

She lifted the binos and looked again – one eye.

544

Two men. Within a metre of each other.

And weapons. Which were slung. The cool dark blue of their long barrels pointing to the sky.

She listened.

Noise now. A crackle of a radio. Laughter. A joke. A response.

More laughter.

North Korean guards.

She guessed there might be. These weren't the fifth columnists. These soldiers were an extra ring of steel around the station. It made sound, tactical sense.

And if there were two, there would be more.

She pulled the MP5 round to her front and grabbed the pistol grip with her right hand, the binos hanging from her left.

Still crouching, she moved back off the ridge, Matthew sticking with her, Jae-joon allowing them to pass him, before following on.

Once she knew she was out of sight, she bore right ... and then right again, still pausing to listen. And then to look.

Finally, when she thought they were at least 50 metres from the soldiers, with plenty of scrubby wasteland between both parties, she led her team back to the railway.

Slowly.

She stopped frequently. And listened.

And then the noise which she was hoping to hear ...

The hum of the tracks.

Shit.

She widened her ears to full volume.

And there it was. The distant thunder of an engine and seven-carriage train. She had absolutely no idea how far away it was. All she could tell was it was coming.

They needed to get where they could see it.

Still crouching, but now moving a little faster, she summited a small knoll, knelt, looked through the binos, and spotted nothing within range.

She moved on, 10 metres, the ground falling away in front of her. She stopped.

Listened.

The noise from the train was getting louder. The tracks singing now, reverberating like an off-key tuning fork.

Binos.

There. The train. Plenty of heat in bright yellow. But tiny.

800 metres away?

She wanted to get closer.

Move now.

She took a couple of steps and then froze, putting a hand up.

And then, very slowly, she knelt down, tucking in behind a rock that was on her right. Matthew, still just off her shoulder, followed suit.

546

She had spotted the tell-tale sign of a burning cigarette.

Another soldier.

Do they always deploy in twos?

Matthew dug his elbow into her ribs. Their faces were close.

'Two men,' he whispered.

She nodded.

Thought so.

The North Koreans had the station surrounded. It was simple but good skills. The train needed to stop. It would be a target. Surround it with armed men, looking outwards.

She did a quick combat estimate in her head.

Enemy. Ground. Weather. Friendly forces. Mission. Timings. Options.

The factors ran through her mind at speed; the process took less than twenty seconds.

Timings: Frank reckoned the train would be at the station for no more than fifteen minutes.

It would be here in three.

Surprise was on their side, accentuated by the fact that everyone liked to gawp at a train.

The noise from the engine was getting louder.

They had a couple of minutes.

She raised the binos and looked in the direction of the soldier, who Matthew thought might be two.

Definitely two.

They were standing side by side, looking down the track to the arriving train.

Perfect.

She turned to Matthew ... who was gone?

What the ...?

'Cover us!' she barked under her breath to Jae-Joon.

She picked up Matthew amongst the scrub, a dark moving shape amid even darker static objects. He'd dropped back 5 metres and was now moving parallel to the railway in the direction of the soldiers. Sam moved quickly, less concerned about the noise as the train was filling the void. She was at Matthew's shoulder ten seconds later. She grabbed his arm and pulled him to a stop.

They both went down on one knee – they couldn't have been any more than 15 metres from the soldiers.

And still the train came.

'What are you doing?' Her head was at right angles and millimetres from his left ear. The inflection in her whisper very clear.

The noise of the train was covering everything. It must have no more than 50 metres from them ... and now, its engine noise was accompanied by the screech of brakes, metal on metal.

'We don't have time! They'll be looking at the train!' He was pointing in the direction of the soldiers –

her free-spirited lieutenant had been thinking along the same lines.

'What are going to do?' Sam could have shouted and the soldiers wouldn't have heard her, the noise from the train was overwhelming now.

In a stamping motion using the butt of his pistol he made it clear what his plan was.

'Go! Take the right. I'll take the left,' she half-shouted.

And he was off, she scurrying after him ...

... now in completely new territory.

Sam had defended herself before, but it had never been premeditated. The scissor stop, with your arms crossed in front of you, your palms away from the attacker who's coming at you with a knife. The cross catches, focuses and slows the assault to the point where your arms meet. And then, by twisting and grabbing a forearm – letting your attacker's momentum do the work – you pull them to the floor in a wrist lock, grab their thumb and force it back to their forearm. Finally a knee to their elbow, ready to break an arm, and your job is done.

She had proven to be good at it in training.
Self-defence classes. The clue was in the title.
Defence.
She wasn't defending herself now.
She was attacking. Arm-to-arm combat.
Accompanied by the soundtrack of a goods yard.
How poetic.

The soldiers had their backs to them, black silhouettes against a dark grey sky. 10 metres.

5.

The MP5 was already in her hands, butt first. She couldn't remember how that had happened.

Smack!

Matthew was all over the soldier on the right and it wasn't like the movies. It was neither silent, nor clean. The man fell to his knees, turning. His mouth open in a scream. Matthew collapsed with him ...

... but Sam lost sight of the affair on her right.

She had other things on her mind.

Her man was moving, lifting a weapon which hitherto had its butt on the floor. His body had gone from a large, static rectangular target, to a side-on, slimmer figure, turning and bending.

She launched the butt of the MP5 at the man's head with everything she had, her 45 kilogrammes of bone and flesh following on.

But he wasn't where she thought he had been.

The MP5 flew past the back of his head, but her body hit him, side-on, the wind taken from her. Two became one. They both fell. Two bodies, two weapons. She was dazed, fearful, her shoulder screaming blue murder. He was angry, and tough. And shouting.

He writhed. She reached for his mouth to stop the noise.

He threw a punch over his shoulder, that found the side of her head ... which sent up a spray of stars.

And that was enough.

Time for the red mist.

It was a weapon she couldn't completely control. It came when she most needed it, but its form was inexplicable ... and erratic. Untrustworthy.

The man was moving, struggling free. Sam had the MP5 in one hand and she was momentarily pinned down; her other arm under the man's body. But he was lifting and turning. Which allowed her to push back with her legs. Sliding across the damp ground. Creating space between the soldier and her. Finding room to aim her machine-pistol. A weapon she had never fired before.

Which she knew was not the right thing to do. Not now. Not yet.

Don't pull the trigger. It will be too noisy. Any element of surprise would be lost.

But she still made space for herself. Still she made herself ready. Still she watched the man rise in slow motion, a black, moving mass.

A target against the lighter sky.

Easy.

The man was steadying, he was bringing his own weapon to bear.

The barrel of her MP5 was rising.

She was going to beat him. She was quick. Quicker than him. She knew she was.

Don't pull the trigger. It was the wrong thing to do.

Milliseconds. That's what this was going to take. The MP5's barrel was almost in line. Her thumb had flicked the safety. Her finger was closing on the trigger. She was about to kill a man.

And then ... blur.

A second blob had joined the fray. An outstretched arm. A fist.

A connection.

The soldier's head jerked violently right. His legs buckled. And his weapon fell.

She closed her eyes, hoping beyond hope that she hadn't pulled the trigger. That she was too late.

The train rattled and snorted behind them. The noise was cacophonous.

Who would know?

Did I pull the trigger?

'Sam!' A half-shout.

Matthew pushed the short barrel of the MP5 away and reached for her arm. She stared at what she could see of him. Their arms made a connection. He pulled her into the sitting position. As he did, he bent down. His head came to within a few centimetres of hers.

And still the noise of the train deafened: screeching and howling.

'Good work! We got both of them,' he exclaimed excitedly.

You got both of them.

Jae-joon was with them now and, in the dark, he was already disarming the men, removing the slings of their rifles to tie their hands. And taking off their jackets, ripping off the arms as makeshift gags and using the remaining material to tie their legs.

'You OK?' Matthew asked.

I didn't fire. Did I?

She didn't. She couldn't have done. There would have been an additional noise. Recoil from the weapon. The man would be dead.

She would have known?

'Fine, thanks. We should get going.'

He lifted her off the ground and held her by the shoulders, looking into her face.

She forced a smile, not that he'd be able to see much.

'What about you?' She was having to raise her voice above the noise of the train.

'Fine. Thanks.'

Good.

She took a short breath, listened to her heart which was beating far too fast to be of any use and, without further comment, carefully headed off down the slope to the track.

Chapter 19

38°26'14.2"N 126°04'03.0"E, Munmu Station, North Korea

Matthew hadn't given Sam the whole story. His right hand was a mess. The first guy had been a cinch after he'd taken a blow to the back of the head with the base of the Browning. All Matthew had to do, once he'd got his bearings having fallen to the floor coupled to the soldier, was take him from a dazed state to one of unconsciousness. That had required a second 'tap' with the pistol to his forehead. And then he was out. But it wasn't over next door. As Matthew turned and rose, even in the dim light, he could see where Sam and her opposition were heading. Someone was going to shoot somebody else. It was inevitable.

Instinct and ten years training in a boxing club kicked in: a straight arm punch with his right hand – the one still carrying the Browning. It would have hurt less and possibly broken fewer fingers (he couldn't be sure, but he reckoned that was the problem), if he'd used the Browning like a hammer. But there was no time for that. A straight punch was the solution. And it had done the trick.

Whilst breaking a couple of fingers.

That's what it felt like.

I'll survive.

554

And, he reckoned, so would Sam. She was odd immediately after the fight. Massively pent up ... dazed, and angry. It was as though she had lost control and was hating herself for it. Which was madness. Without her taking on the second soldier, he would have been dead. Maybe they all would have. She had put him down and, Matthew reckoned, would have put a bullet through his chest before the man had had a chance to loose one off.

That was no mean feat.

She *was* one crazy woman.

And she was ahead of him now. Back in control. As she liked it.

Having come off the mound, they'd made it to the edge of the track. Sam knelt; he did the same beside her. Jae-joon was on his tail, but facing backwards. Matthew knew very little about the military, other than watching the odd war film, but he reckoned they were doing a good job.

The train was beyond them now. It was difficult to see any detail in the dark, although a single arc light by the station building – beyond the wagons – gave a clear view of its silhouette. The noise was down to a loud *hum* from the engine.

There was movement.

A man. Two.

More.

A small crowd appeared to be disgorging from the train. Medium sized bodies closest to them. Much smaller ones in the far distance.

South Koreans close to.

And North Koreans in the distance?

Sam whispered.

'We're going to move fifty metres along the track, from bush to bush. And then we'll wait for a signal. Acknowledge.'

'Got it,' Matthew responded.

'Me too.' Then Jae-joon.

He kept as close to her as he could, always looking left and right for danger. Unseen by him, she had put the binos in her backpack and held the MP5 expertly in two hands. They could see enough for now.

And you can't take out a North Korean guard with surveillance equipment.

They dropped down on one knee. Together. Three, in a tight line.

Looking.

Nothing had changed.

Up. Move.

Sam half-jogged in the crouch position. He followed suit – it wasn't long before his thighs were screaming at him.

Down.

10 metres that time.

The same again. A slightly shorter hop.

Down. Look.

Then again. Eight strides. *5 metres*. At the next break Matthew counted five soldiers at this end of the train. Maybe eight or ten at the other. Both parties were keeping their distance.

Up. Move.

On their right. A bigger bush which sprawled up the mound, back towards their truck.

Down.

Matthew got behind the bush. He couldn't see the train. Sam was at the edge of the shrub. Jae-joon was a few feet from him, still guarding their backs.

Sam pulled back, unslung her rucksack and dug out the satphone. She pressed a button, holding it down. As she waited for the phone to connect, he slipped past her and took pole position.

Definitely five men this end. They were alert, but not 'on guard'. Two of them were smoking cigarettes, the glow of the lit tips burning bright orange against the black of the train.

Shit! Two new men.

The far side of the train, out of nowhere, from the direction of the station. One was carrying what looked like ... a crowbar? And they were heading in their direction.

'Sam!' He nudged her.

The men were jogging towards them now, along the far track. They'd be opposite them in a few seconds.

'Wait ...' she replied.

'Enemy!' A bit too loud, but needs must.

She placed the phone on the ground, screen side down, and joined him.

The men were right there. Just ahead of them. 15 metres away. On the opposite side of the tracks. They had stopped, dark shadows of small stature men – made darker still by the shade of the trees on the opposite side of the track.

Matthew checked Sam. She had the MP5 in the shoulder, the weapon's barrel aiming at the pair.

It was really difficult to tell, but the two men appeared to be gathered at a pole that rose from the ground. There was a *grunt* and some words.

A *clang*.

Some more words. And more *grunts*.

A metallic *clunk*.

Matthew had it. The men were operating a points lever. The train had to back up, swapping tracks as it did. That would be the next move.

Where is the lever on this side?

Both sets of points would need to be changed. There would be a lever.

Had they passed it?

He couldn't recall seeing it. If it were behind them the men would have to walk straight by them, either to or from the lever.

They were moving across the line. Heading towards them. Maybe to their right?

Hop – *crunch*. Hop. *Crunch – crunch – crunch*. Hop. Hop. *Crunch*.

They were here. Matthew stopped breathing. His index finger tightened around the trigger.

There was literally a bush between the North Korean railway workers and the three of them. They were on one side, the three of them on the other. They said a few words to each other.

Then ...

A metallic, screeching noise. Dull but loud enough.

Shit.

From the satphone. A connection? He didn't know.

Sam silently and quickly picked it up and stuck it down her jacket.

He listened. Every muscle tensed. Every nerve ending exposed.

He was ready. The men weren't soldiers; and not armed as far as he had seen. They would be easier than the two they had taken out earlier.

Some Korean voices. From further away than he thought the men were. Was it the same pair? Had they been joined by others?

He still wasn't breathing.

More Korean. Same distance. Same tone. It was hard to tell if they were discussing the strange noise that had just come from behind the bush – or it was business as usual.

The engine was still chugging away in the background.

Clunk.

The points had moved.

An exclamation in Korean. It might have been their equivalent of 'hurrah'. Maybe the points were tough? Maybe if they couldn't get them to work they'd be off to the DPRK's version of the salt mines?

More Korean. And the *crunching* sound of feet on gravel.

Heading away from them.

Phew.

He breathed out.

Sam dug out the phone from her jacket. The green hue from the screen lit up her face. The air was still cold, but Matthew spotted sweat on her brow.

I know how you feel.

'Frank,' Sam whispered into the mouthpiece.

'Yes?'

'We're here. The train is at the station. Make your call. Acknowledge.'

'Will do.' He cut her off.

Good.

She took a deep breath, stared at the screen for a second, pressed down and held the 'off' button and a second later shoved the phone in her backpack.

It had been tough so far. They had almost been rumbled – twice. And this was meant to be the easy bit.

She grabbed Matthew's arm and guided herself back around the bush so she could see the train. It was as she'd left it.

Shit!

She hadn't been thinking. None of them had. They'd been too busy dealing with the distractions. The train would need to back up. The engine would have to reverse beyond the points. That meant they would be in full sight of anyone on or associated with the train.

'Jae-joon. Matthew.' Hushed tones. Sam used a hand to call them to her as she kept an eye on the dismounted Koreans closest to them. 'We need to get in better cover. The train must come this way ...' She paused; distracted. 'Wait!'

In the distance she picked out the shrill, polyphonic melody of a smartphone's ring-tone. *The boy band, BTS?* She squinted, trying to work out who might be picking up.

I do have binos.

Not enough time.

Two of the five men closest to them were moving about. There were still two cigarettes lit. She couldn't tell who was doing what ...

... and then.

A torch beam. The silhouette closest to the last carriage. Pointing downwards.

'That's it!' Matthew was at her shoulder. 'That's her!' he whispered.

She looked around. Jae-joon was two feet from her, doing his job. She reached out and grabbed his jacket, gently pulling him around her so he could see the woman with a torch.

Jae-joon seemed to steady himself. Sam could just make out his face. He was nodding.

The engine made a loud *crunching* noise. There was a squeal of metal against metal as the wheels found traction. More *clunks* and shunts. And the train started to reverse.

'You go higher on the hill. In the bushes Assuming she walks this way, I'll wait until the captain is beside me and then I'll make my move.' Jae-joon was taking control.

It made sense.

'Let's go!' she snapped at Matthew. Half-crouching, she moved up the rise, keeping as close to the bushes as she could.

She glanced behind. He was with her.

He was always with her.

How far?

There. A gap had emerged between the bushes to her left. She found space and squeezed in. Matthew did the same. She squatted. He sat on the floor. Both of them had their weapons ready.

'You OK?' she whispered.

'Yeah. Fine. Is this going to work?'

She couldn't make out much. Just an outline of the side of his face. She imagined his chin covered with too much hair.

'Who knows?'

She really had no idea.

'What happens if the connection with the captain doesn't work? If they arrest Jae-joon?'

The noise from the train was getting louder, the tracks protesting at the weight of their load.

'We let him go. A South Korean picked up by South Koreans. He'll be fine.'

'And us?'

She had thought that through; but only in outline. There were two options. Take out the driver of the train and stop the wagons in their literal tracks. That might create some delay and heighten the awareness of both sets of soldiers, but it wouldn't stop the fifth columnists from amending their plan and bringing the fight to the station.

The second option was two against twenty-three. Wait for the soldiers to load and for the train to head off. Then cut across the track and make for the road where the enemy were preparing their ambush. Create their own little piece of madness for them. And, hopefully, balance the odds a little.

Neither would work. Sam knew the weaponry they were up against and guessed at the fanaticism and training of the enemy. A couple of shoulder-launched munitions and the train would be off the bridge and into the river. And if they'd wired up the detonators to some quarry explosives, the train would be in the drink without a shot being fired.

End of.

The chances of success for her and Matthew in either scenario were zero.

They needed to get on the train. Either stop it before it hit the bridge. Or get the two leaders off the train. And maybe galvanise both of the protection parties and take the fight to the enemy.

That's what she was hoping to do.

And exactly what language should I inspire the troops in?

It was a shit plan. The whole thing was – from the beginning. They were peeing into a volcano.

She answered Matthew.

'I have a couple of options. Neither of them helpful. Both of them likely to fail.'

The word fail made something deep inside of her shiver. It was an uncomfortable feeling. One close to dread.

And it wasn't about her.

It was about him.

The thought she might well be leading Matthew to his death was unconscionable.

What am I doing?

It was her first feeling of self-doubt since she'd left the UK. Up until now she had been bulletproof. Nothing mattered. She would prevail. Everyone else was wrong. She was perfect.

What had changed that?

Hand to hand combat?

An overdose of adrenalin combined with little sleep and an empty stomach?

What was I thinking?

A wash of humility swept through her. Bizarrely she thought she shed a tear.

She reached up, fumbled for Matthew's face and finally found his bristly cheek. It was a strange feeling, one she didn't quite understand. She wanted to say, 'You stay here,' but she knew she couldn't. She wanted to protect him. To send him home. To enable him to live a full life. But she knew she wouldn't.

I won't.

Because the mission came first. It always had. It always would.

So she didn't say anything. Instead, she forced her mouth into a smile; a smile in the darkness he would never see.

Then something happened which made her insides shiver again.

He placed a hand on hers. And ...

There's no time for this.

She pulled her hand away. The moment was lost.

The back of the end carriage was now level with them, bending away, following the track that connected the two rails. A single soldier, weapon in both hands, was walking just ahead of the buffers.

Then a torch beam, pointing down belonging to a second soldier – *the captain*? And a third; no torch. Then a fourth. And a fifth.

Below them. From nowhere. A second beam, pointing to the floor. From by the bush. It was Jae-joon. He was on his feet.

A shout! In Korean, from the third soldier. His weapon raised. He shouted again.

The train kept moving – the first bogey had struck the far track. The noise of protesting wheels hurt Sam's ears.

Their Korean friend stopped halfway to the train. He stood still. He said something. A shout, but only for it to be heard above the noise of the train. The tone was calming. Measured.

The captain turned off her torch. It was too dark to pick out the details, but she walked over to Jae-joon. There was a conversation which Sam couldn't hear above the second bogey hitting the far track. A follow-on carriage, all blacked out windows – was with them now.

The North Koreans will be here soon.

The captain and Jae-joon turned smartly and, side by side, followed the sixth carriage as it twisted its way onto the rear track. It was slow progress, but soon they were 30 metres from her and Matthew.

Sam waited.

The fifth carriage.

Then the fourth, carrying the Supreme Leader, accompanied by three North Korean soldiers. Drilled. Sharp, almost dancing along the track keeping exactly in line with the carriage.

The third. Three more soldiers.

566

The second.

The first. Four more soldiers.

Ten this side. Ten the other? How many still mounted?

There were maybe thirty North Koreans. What were they carrying? She couldn't see, but likely the Type 58, Russian AK-47. Made in-country and as reliable as they come. A 30-round magazine of 7.62mm shorts. If one of those hit you in the arm it would rip it off.

Not a bad armoury.

If she could guarantee it was on her side.

The engine now. Diesel. Noisy and oily. It twisted and chugged across the intersecting track, which protested louder than ever. And then it screeched to a halt. It was right in front of them on the far track. Job done. There was a light on in the cab. Sam could make out the driver.

Clunk. She picked it out just above the noise of the engine.

The two railway men they'd spotted earlier must have reset the points.

A shout from one of the North Korean soldiers. Followed by lots of movement. The soldiers jogging to two separate carriage doors. Ten of them – she counted again. More shouting. And then, in seconds, they were on the train.

The engine gasped, its revs climbed, Sam imagined huge plumes of black smoke rising from its exhausts.

And then metal wheels spinning on a metal track.

A shudder. A *screech* – more like a whine.

A *snort*.

And the train started to move.

She looked back to the last carriage. It was 200 metres away. A dark snake in a black pit

What should they do?

Move. Down to the track. If they were spotted the train wouldn't stop. And, whilst the North Korean carriages had their doors pulled back and an armed soldier hanging out of each, getting off an accurate shot would be close to impossible.

She grabbed Matthew's forearm and led him down the hill, doing her best to stay close to the bushes as she could. A few seconds later they were by the track – wheel height. She'd forgotten how tall the bogeys were.

The third carriage was moving back the way it had come – maybe three miles an hour.

The fourth. A bit quicker. Nobody was giving them a second glance.

Fifth. The train was travelling faster now.

Sixth.

Eight miles an hour? Not quite sprinting speed, but getting close.

There!

A torch from the last carriage's door. Right at the back of the train. Heading towards them.

Timing was everything.

One ... two ...

The start of the last carriage had just passed them.

Matthew was on his feet. *What the ...?* He had her arm. She sprung up and sprinted like crazy. The middle of the last carriage was 10 metres ahead of them and was moving faster.

She glanced left. The torch at the end of the train bouncing, flashing, coming towards them. At speed. Someone shouting.

Now they were train-side. *God, it's bloody big.* Jae-joon was close now, motoring their way, hand outstretched.

This isn't going to work. She'd have her arm pulled from its socket.

Run! Same direction as the train. It was obvious.

She did. Immediately Matthew was on her tail.

But she was still quicker than him. A lot quicker.

The end of the train pulled alongside. Jae-joon was there. Just there. She could have reached out and touched his hand.

But she didn't.

She side-stepped away from the train, creating an air gap for Matthew, who was lagging behind.

'Get on the fucking train!' she screamed over her shoulder. Her hands were pumping. Her knees lifting, nobody would hear them. There was too much metal on metal, too many monumental *clunks* and shunts.

Matthew didn't wait to be asked. He knew she was quicker.

He was beside her, the train so close and so big; the seventh carriage's back end was still there. Jae-joon's arm providing a hand grab. The train was pushing on. She had something left in the tank. Matthew didn't. He reached. Floundered. Reached again. An extended arm. A stretch. *Contact!* Hands on wrists.

And he was on. One foot on a metal step ...

Fuck!

She fell.

Arse over tit. And rolled, someone thrust a knitting needle in her shoulder and a sharp piece of MP5 caught her in the stomach, which probably created a gash ... not that she knew.

Shit. Shit. Shit!

Get up.

She did. She'd lost a couple of seconds and the train was beyond her. It was leaving her. She had no idea at what speed.

She sprinted. Flat out. Like a school sports day. As if she were being chased by a monster. The rear of the train was 10 metres from her.

Then eight.

Four.

Matthew was on the footplate, his whole body extended as far as it could go. His hand was there ... reaching.

'Come on!' he screamed.

She ran. And ran.

Catching. Breathing. Getting closer. She had the MP5 in her right hand and her left was pushed out in front of her, centimetres from his. It stayed that way for an age. Her strength fading. Her hopes diminishing.

And then the train jumped and lurched, and slowed momentarily. And Matthew's hand was just there.

She leapt. Like a keeper saving the goal of her life.

Matthew had her. His hand around her wrist. And then a second, grabbing her shirt. He might be a rubbish sprinter, but he was strong. And safe. A second later she was on the plate with him, her face on his chest, his arm wrapped tightly around her shoulders.

They held it there for a second and then ...

'Thanks,' she mumbled loudly. The warmth and security she felt from his embrace dissipated. Embarrassment and a spike of anger took hold. She prised herself from his grasp and pushed past him into the carriage ...

... where they met Jae-joon and, looking at her rank slides and taking a guess, the captain.

She was wearing army fatigues, very similar to their US equivalent. Sam recognised a Daewoo K2, 5.56mm carbine which was slung over the captain's right shoulder. And she had a walkie-talkie on her belt. Her eyes were partially shadowed by a combat baseball cap which displayed a vertical set of three flattened, gold stars.

Sam held out a hand.

'Sam Green. Do you speak English?'

The woman half-bowed and took her hand.

'Captain Min-sung. This is highly irregular, Miss Green.'

The train *clanked* and rattled. Sam reached for an upright – with the hand that wasn't gripping the MP5 – to steady herself. It was a squeeze, the four of them in the small area between the two train doors and what looked like a janitor's cupboard. It was all she could do to stop herself from bumping into the Korean captain.

'We have maybe five minutes, at most. Are you prepared for an attack at that point? Maybe explosives on the line. Coming in from the west?' Sam was speaking at a gallop. She hoped the captain's English was up for it.

'We are always ready for an attack, Miss Green. That's our job,' was the reply.

I know, I know.

But, with rockets, and a bridge that's down?

'What about the North Koreans?' The train lurched. Sam had to step back to stop herself from falling. Her foot landed on Matthew's toe. Neither of them acknowledged it.

'They are ready, also. If your question is, "Do they know about a potential attack beyond the station, which I was briefed on by text from the British Embassy, after the train had left Dorasan?" the answer is, I haven't told them.'

Sam felt that she was hitting her head against a brick wall.

What is *the point?*

'Listen.' She wanted to grab the captain's lapels. 'My government has tracked weaponry, ammunition and ancillaries to an exact location about 1,000 metres away. There are over twenty men. The gear will shred this train and everyone in it. It will be carnage.'

She waited to gauge a reaction. The woman's mouth twitched. She must be getting something. Surely? The British government don't metaphorically parachute agents into North Korea and catapult them on board a presidential train for the gig. Her and Matthew's presence must mean something?

The captain set her face to 'stern' mode ... and was about to say something.

'You could be a hero, Captain Min-sung,' Jae-joon pleaded.

She turned her face to him. And winced. Sam could see the conflict writ large across the captain's face. Suddenly something snapped. She said, 'What do you suggest we do, Miss Green?'

Sam breathed in. The motion of the train was picking up. At any other time she would have started to feel a bit queasy.

Not now.

'How are you communicating with the DPRK contingent?' Sam asked.

'We're not. There's an empty carriage between us and them. I spoke to my opposite number at the beginning of the journey. We'll speak again at the end, that is all. We have no compatible comms.'

Great.

'Is your President's carriage guarded?'

'Of course.'

'OK. Brief your team. And take me to the President.' There was a pause. 'Now!' Sam barked. She then turned to Matthew. 'See if there is an emergency cord. Find it and pull it!'

He didn't wait for an answer; he was already looking up and around.

The captain turned. She was already snarling Korean into the walkie-talkie as she opened the carriage door. Sam was on her heels.

The carriage was a shell, just four windows – all painted black – and a smattering of chairs. Sam counted twelve soldiers – quite a few women. They all stood up and braced to attention as the captain entered, although against the rocking of the carriage one or two of them were struggling to look smart.

The captain strode through the centre of the carriage barking more orders. This resulted in a flurry of activity; two of the soldiers rushed through the door from where they had just come. Sam assumed they were going to overtly guard the rear doors – *why not all the time?*

Others were grabbing their weapons trying not to look bewildered.

Bring ... bring ... bring ...

The rattling ringtone from an ancient loudspeaker above the door broke through the melee.

Matthew's found the emergency stop.

She braced herself ... the captain kept striding.

Bring ... bring ... bring ...

One or two of the Korean soldiers stopped what they were doing and looked around.

Come on.

Nothing.

The noise rang and rang. The train continued to pick up its pace.

The driver was ignoring the distress call.

Fuck it.

Sam kicked off, following the captain who was now at the far door ... who pushed through into the airlock, and then the second door; she held them both open with her feet, her body swaying with the motion of the train. Sam was with her a second later, Jae-joon just behind.

And into the presidential carriage, which caught Sam.

It was a bizarre set-up. Another open carriage with no partitions – possibly an ex-goods train. Four windows, not painted black this time, but with shutters dropped. Poorly decorated in red and some strange flower wallpaper. There was bedroom furniture, including a double bed which was side on to the carriage, and two high-back chairs. One was directly in front of them, pointing their way – it was occupied by an armed soldier. The other was identical, but facing the far door on the other side of the bed, replete with guard. Over her left shoulder was a makeshift bathroom, with a plastic portable toilet, a sink and a couple of buckets. There was a suspended shower curtain which looked as if it might provide some privacy.

How the other half live?

The carriage was lit by three overhead bulbs. No shades.

The *bring ... bring ... bring* of the emergency stop siren was still blurting out.

And the train continued to *rattle* and roll.

The soldier closest to them was on his feet, the butt of his weapon on the floor, the front handstock gripped – another man at 'attention'. In the distance the second soldier was now also on his feet and was copying the posture, facing away from them.

On the bed a man-shaped counterpane moved. A head appeared.

Sam double-took.

The President.

She was on the left of the captain, Jae-joon now to the woman's right. And she sensed Matthew entering the carriage behind them.

'Mr President.' Sam raised her voice above the *bring-bring* of the alarm and the *clattering* of the train.

The man was now sitting up, his hands collarbone height, hanging on to the blanket.

'Yes?' It was an uncertain response. He was clearly petrified.

'We need to get off the train. Come with me now, sir.' Sam offered a hand, even though she was 5 metres away.

Matthew had stepped ahead of her.

'I'll head into the spare carriage and try to warn the North Koreans?' he interjected ... searching for an answer from her.

What?

The door in front of them led to ... serious injury. Or death.

No! Please, no ...

She dithered.

'I'll come with you. You'll need an interpreter,' Jae-joon answered, filling the void left by Sam's non-response.

She was flummoxed.

The mission.

Or the man.

What?

She was in uncharted territory.

She glanced at Matthew, who was poised. Ready. She looked back at the President, wasting a further precious second.

But that was all it took. She couldn't give Matthew a direct order. She couldn't send him through the door. She couldn't.

So she ignored him.

She took four steps forward so she was closer to the bed and unable to see Matthew's expression. The captain matched her, and then took another step; she was now at the bedstead.

'Mr President. This woman ...' the captain thumbed over her shoulder, '... is British secret service. Do whatever she says.'

Matthew moved to Sam's right, towards the far door, ahead of her now. It was a dance.

He looked across at her. And nodded.

He had made his own decision ...

... and was gone, without looking back.

Shit!

'Wait ...' It was a plea from Sam. But it was half-hearted and not as loud as the surrounding noise of the train and the damn ringing from the alarm.

Shit! Shit, shit, shit!

This wasn't what she wanted. No matter how right it was.

Shit, shit, shit.

Anger rose in her, but it didn't peak. It faltered. And then fell.

She still had a job to do.

Sam blocked everything but the President.

Eight steps forward and she was at his bedside. 'Come on, Mr President!' He looked bewildered – lost.

Scared.

Who wouldn't be?

'Come on!' Through gritted teeth.

They didn't have long.

Matthew and Jae-joon have even less time.

The man dithered, and then acted. He slid his feet out from under the covers – he was wearing a white t-shirt and a pair of tight-fitting blue boxers.

'Where are your shoes?' Sam felt as if she were dressing a child.

'Here.' He was pointing under the bed.

'Get them on!' She was struggling to contain her frustration.

She looked around. There was a wooden chair opposite the bed. Hung on it was a suit jacket.

That'll do.

She moved and grabbed it, and met the President coming back – she almost knocked him over.

'Captain! Get this on him.' Sam handed over the jacket. 'And follow me.'

The train stumbled. She half-fell. The soldier closest to the door toppled comically backwards and ended up sitting in the chair from where he had started. Sam turned to check on her quarry. The captain had her arm round his shoulders.

God help South Korea.

She kicked off again, towards the rear of the train.

The door.

She opened it. And the one on the other side of the airlock. She stood between the two, letting the captain and the President through.

Sam followed on … but, *wait?*

The train was slowing. She was sure of it. The driver had recognised the signal?

But no brakes. *No screeching*?

Had Matthew and Jae-joon passed on the message? Had they been quick enough?

The sound of a massive explosion answered the question.

Everything rocked. She fell on one knee. She wasn't sure how the train had stayed on its rails.

And then …

Bang! Whoosh … boom!

An explosion. And a rocket-propelled grenade? Behind them. Maybe one of the front carriages.

Then an almighty *clatter* and *screech* from the same area. Her brain couldn't reconcile the noises with likely actions.

And still the carriages moved forward.

Rat … tat … tat … tat … tat …

Crack … ping … ping … ping … crack …

Gunfire.

Fuck!

Lots of it. High velocity rounds. A very sharp and clean sound from a distance, the *cracks* as the bullets flew overhead; the *pings*, the rounds finding their target.

Whoosh ... boom!

An earthquake off the Richter scale. Somewhere up front again. Then more incoming fire, but not yet on them.

And still the carriages trundled forward, *but their momentum was slowing*?

The captain released the President, who cowered against the far wall. She started shouting orders in Korean. The soldiers reacted, running around. But there was nothing they could do. Not without a view – not without targets.

'Smash the windows!' Sam screamed, as she grabbed the President and pushed him forward ... a frightened deadweight, hunched and staggering as the world as he knew it headed towards its end.

The captain shouted out again. It seemed to resonate among the soldiers; bringing them to order. One was immediately hacking at the window closest to the enemy with the butt of his rifle. A second followed suit on another window.

The mayhem continued. A gun battle of epic proportions; a more violent exchange than anything she'd experienced in Helmand. Another incoming RPG – much closer now; she couldn't stop herself from flinching. *Matthew!?* She dismissed her concerns. There just wasn't space for him and the task.

581

And still the train moved, albeit now at a dirge, slowing all the time.

She and the President were now at the far door of the carriage. Sam pushed him through.

Whoosh ... bang!

The whole carriage pivoted left and both of them fell, their fall arrested by the wall of the janitor's cupboard.

Sam braced herself for the carriage to continue to topple, maybe off the tracks and into the river, if they'd got that far. But it didn't. Instead, it rocked back onto the track, and wriggled and shouted – and stopped ... dead still.

Gunfire. Incoming. It had their names on it.

Twang. She thought a round hit the metal wall just by her knee. A second made it through, the resulting slug bouncing around the small area between the three doors and janitor's room.

Go!

She grabbed the President by the arm, turned left and was met by an open door, a black void – no soldier. He must have gone.

Whoosh!

Sam didn't wait for the explosion. She wrenched the President from behind her with all her might. He shot past, teetering on the edge of the open chasm of unknown depth ... he wouldn't jump.

So she straight-armed him on the back ...

... and he was gone.

Boom!

Reds and yellows. Noise and smoke. Twisted metal and a cacophony of *pings* as bullets sprayed into the carriage.

She launched herself from the footplate.

The fall seemed to last forever. She was expecting to die. To land on rocks, or get spiked by a bush or a tree. Something horrible was definitely going to happen.

As she fell the sound of battle reverberated around her. She was pretty certain a round flew past her ear. Maybe one above her head.

Splash!

Water. Not a great deal of it, but enough to offer a safe landing. Her MP5 fell from her hand. She was arms and legs, like an upturned turtle. It was cold. And dark. Her feet now on the muddy floor, her shoulders above the water level. The current pulling at her.

And still the ambush raged.

Sloop ... sloop!

Bullets hitting the river close by.

The enemy had decent night sights. They'd be able to pick out targets, even small ones.

She was such a target. They were.

There must be some protection from the bridge?

Sloop ... sloop!

Obviously not.

Where's the President?

Where's my MP5?

Sod it. That's gone.

Sloop.

Another round. Just next to her. She was being shot at. She *had* to get going.

Sam worked her leg muscles hard against the current. Toward the bank.

Two steps. Three.

Where's the President?

A body.

Oh my God!

No. Not the President. It was a Korean soldier. On his back. Floating like a lilo. Panic rose. And then she calmed herself.

God, it's cold.

She felt for a pulse, which was a next to useless action in the water.

What was she thinking?

The water had turned orange, illuminated by fire from above. She turned to see the source of the light … and her stomach tensed.

The train was in two halves.

The front five carriages were in the centre of the bridge, the engine teetering at a gap where the track used to be. Other than the engine, all five carriages were ablaze. She could see men alight. One, a human torch, had just jumped into the water. Two or three were already there. Rifle shots *pinged* around them. Sparks flew off the carriages as the rounds found their target.

Her two carriages, which were 40 metres from the original five, were a different story ... one that needed telling quickly. They were just above her, 5 metres up. The presidential carriage was alight. There was very little left of it. The soldiers' carriage had its forward bogey on the track. The rear one was off. It was a train version of *The Italian Job*. It could fall at any moment. Especially as it was still being peppered with gunfire.

Come on!

But ...

... where's the President?

How was she going to find him in the darkness?

She looked away from the bridge, to her left where the President would have landed.

Nothing.

Sloop ... sloop.

The rounds were still close.

'Help!'

A pathetic cry from right of where she'd just been looking. In the reeds, 15 metres away. *The President.* She was sure. He was sitting on something, waving.

Sloop ... sloop.

Bullets were landing at his feet. He pulled his knees to his chest.

'Get out! Get away!' Sam screamed.

Sloop ... sloop ... sloop.

Fuck! Right by her back.

She ducked under the water. Like they do in the films.

Fuck, it's cold!

And swam. She closed her eyes – the water was so cold it stung.

And swam. And swam, her lungs bursting for air.

And swam.

I'm tired.

Her knee hit a rock.

I need to breathe.

She popped her head up. Reeds. Rocks. A bank.

Air filled her lungs between gasps.

The President was set further back now, in the reeds. He was still hugging his knees. Shaking like a leaf. The orange from the fire – on his face – exposing his fear.

She was kneeling, her shoulders were now above water; she couldn't swim any more.

She clambered out, slipping and sliding on rocks, all her effort expended.

Crack! Crack!

Two rounds overhead.

They were still after her.

She dragged herself. And cried out loud in frustration.

She was next to the President. He was shivering, staring into the distance, the reds and yellows of the engulfed train reflecting in his dilated pupils.

Sam grabbed him by the upper arm. And yanked him so he half stood. She moved past him into the reeds, pulling him with her.

Three steps.

Come on!

Four. Five. Six.

And then they were in cover.

Just.

She pulled the main man to her and grabbed his head, a hand either side, her face centimetres from his.

There was something ... she dismissed it.

'We need to get out of here!' She could shout; it didn't matter. The firefight was still raging.

Splodge ... splodge.

Two rounds into the bank, just behind them. They had to move.

Then a massive *creak* followed by the sound of tonnes of metal toppling and splashing into the river.

She looked over her shoulder.

Oh my God!

'Move!'

The slow motion wave was 2 metres high. And was heading their way. It could drown them.

She was on her feet; the President had no choice. She had jerked him up and twisted him away from the wall of water.

Pulling. Dragging.

She drove forward into the reeds, the ground thick with mud. She lost a shoe. But still she pushed … and pulled. And dragged.

The wave hit them a second later. It knocked her off her feet and released her grip from the President's arm. He fell as she tumbled.

And spun, her back hitting a log and stopping her dead.

Fuck!

What next?

Whatever next!?

She coughed and spat. And sat up. And coughed some more.

Crack … crack … crack.

Thud … thud … thud.

More incoming. But wayward, off to her left.

She stood. And fell. And stood again.

She spat out something unpleasant that had lodge itself in her mouth. And coughed some more.

Where's …?

He was there. Off to her left. He was sitting up, blood on his forehead streaking down onto a cheek. She scrambled over to him.

'You OK?' she demanded.

He nodded, his eyes still wide with disbelief. Staring. Completely out of it. The only positive was he'd stopped shivering.

'We should go. Come on.' Softer this time. Sam offered her hand.

He took it.

38°26'14.4"N 126°04'03.3"E, North of Munmu, short of
Munmu Station

Sam drummed her fingers on the steering wheel of the
UAZ. How long should she wait?

How long?

The only thing keeping her awake was adrenalin.
The President was sitting in the passenger seat; the
scantest of damp bed clothes and a drenched suit jacket.
A stranger sight you would not see. The first thing he'd
done when he got in the truck was to pull on a safety
belt. She could have laughed out loud.

It had taken her twenty minutes to cajole and
drag the President to the UAZ. They had to lie low whilst
a couple of North Korean soldiers, who were probably
part of the original cordon, jogged in the direction of the
firefight. Which was, by then, beginning to die down.
After that all they needed to do was to cross the road in
the village, and then make their way to the barn. She
knew exactly where it was. And she knew exactly how
best to get there without being compromised.

She was good at that. Even though her teeth
were chattering. And everything was aching.

And now they waited. She'd turned the truck
over to warm it up. Both she and the main man were
perishing. The heater was making an adequate fist of it.

589

To waste more time she had taken the jerry can which was tied down on the inside of the truck and filled up the tank. They now had more than enough diesel to make it to the tunnel in one go.

All they had to do now was decide how long to wait.

For what?

Was Matthew alive? And Jae-joon?

Her heart lurched at the thought.

Stop it.

Had the North Koreans done enough to see off the enemy? Were the fifth columnists out there now scouring the countryside for her and her quarry?

How long?

A clock ticked in her head.

Tick – tock.

It had been half an hour now since the attack. She'd heard a truck head towards the station on the main road just ahead of them; she guessed it might have been DPRK reinforcements.

She toyed with the choices.

Tunnel?

Or give themselves up?

She drummed her fingers some more.

Come on, Matthew.

She continued to wait, pushing her head forward, trying to see around the barn, something she knew was impossible.

590

So she sat back. Closed her eyes. Counted some seconds. Another minute.

One more minute.

She drummed. And counted.

Counted and drummed.

The beat of her fingers matched her numbers until, eventually ...

... five one thousand. Four one thousand. Three one thousand. Two one thousand ...

Sam slapped the thin Bakelite steering wheel with a force which hurt her hand.

'Fuck it!' she screamed.

The President flinched.

She panted through her nose. Then took a deep breath ...

... and released the handbrake. The reliable UAZ gently began to roll forward. She found the clutch, selected second and accelerated, turning onto the track heading down to the road. No lights.

She looked left or right.

Where's Matthew?

Nowhere.

She waited just off the main road, briefly.

Nothing.

Fuck it. This time to herself.

She grimaced. She let the 4x4 roll forward to the main road.

One last look up and down the street.

591

And then she turned the wheel, switched on the vehicle's lights and headed away from the station.

The UAZ rattled and lurched as she swung left and right to miss potholes. The man next to her, who had one hand on his seatbelt, said nothing.

They would either make the tunnel, or be stopped. Either were fine. Neither, she reckoned, would result in anything other than a heavy prison sentence for her. Maybe less if the Chief pulled some strings.

But something was bothering her. Something so deep it was almost hidden.

Something she couldn't access.

Which added to the pent-up anger, and prodded at her massive weariness.

The man in the passenger seat found the missing piece. He dug it up.

'I'm not the President.'

…

…

She ignored what she already knew deep in a recess to be the case. Instead she chewed on her lip.

She couldn't contemplate it. It was too much of a horror story.

Her. Matthew. Jae-joon. If she bit any harder she'd draw blood. So she ground her teeth instead, staring straight ahead.

Focus on the road.

She knew. She had known.

Her initial double-take when she had first set eyes on him. She'd seen plenty of photos of the real President. And she never, *ever* forgot a face.

And the man's cowering. His inability to dress himself. His lack of courage – in the reeds.

Nobody knew how they'd react under fire. But she expected the leaders of countries, if nothing else, to show some kind of grace when faced with adversity ... even if they couldn't manage bravery.

She ignored the man with his hand on his seatbelt.

He was just that: a man.

It wasn't his fault. He was doing a job.

So was she.

She drove on. In silence.

Let's hope we make it to the tunnel.

Epilogue

Three weeks later

Roseberry Gardens, Orpington, London, UK

Sam hugged her knees and stared out of the window. There wasn't a great deal to see; certainly nothing substantially different from the hundreds of previous times she'd studied this vista. A low, manicured hedge. A row of cars, the makes and registrations of which she could recite in an instant. A streetlamp, giving off a milky glow which turned everything a paler shade of its original colour. A second set of cars on the opposite side of the road, including a pearlescent blue Tesla 3 – all electric – which Frank's opposite neighbour-but-one cleaned to within an inch of its life every day after work. Beyond them a second set of late-Victorian terraced houses.

Above which a sky, the far reaches of which was as dark as freshly dug peat.

Which matched how she felt.

To be fair it was different from last time she'd sat where she was now. Then, post Switzerland, her brain had been mush. Like it had been sucked out of her ear with a turkey baster, liquidized and squashed back in again with a palette knife.

It wasn't like that now. She had all her faculties. Everything worked. She could talk and think and walk.

And cry.

She'd done a lot of the latter since she'd got back home. Since Frank had, bless his cotton socks, encouraged her to come back to his place. To use him as a base until she found her feet.

She didn't deserve him. His faithfulness. His kindness. She had never let him near. And, once launched into South East Asia, she had pushed him further and further away. In her head she blamed work. The mission – however trite that sounded. But she knew that wasn't it.

It was that he had got too close. She could have blamed Switzerland, coming back a mess and looking for any stump she could sit on. But it was her fault. She'd inadvertently let it happen. To allow Frank to believe there was a future.

And those bonds needed to be broken. For both their sakes. Chasing after Jane and then into Korea was the perfect scythe to cut away the ties. And she'd done that effectively and without feeling.

And yet there he was. At the embassy in Seoul. Tears rolling down his cheeks when she'd eventually made it into the station, his mouth slightly ajar. His shoulders shaking gently.

The image had been a fitting metaphor for the whole bloody mess.

And what a mess.

595

In the end the journey from Munmu to the North Korean end of the tunnel had been pretty uneventful. After the attack she had driven the truck through the last three hours of darkness and then thrown it into a small wood to wait out the day. Her passenger – she'd not asked his name; nor spoken to him other than necessities – had spent the whole journey staring straight ahead, one hand clutching his seatbelt at chest height. Once they'd stopped Sam had barked, 'We're staying here until it gets dark again.' She'd then popped out for a pee, climbed back into the UAZ and, with a stomach which had begun to chew on its own lining, slept fitfully for ten hours.

No dreams, though. Which was still a constant relief. Just empty sleep broken by stiff joints and a shoulder which throbbed away in the background ...

... and a heart that wept in a way it hadn't since Chris had been killed in Afghanistan. It was a deep, uncomfortable agony. Different from Chris, though. She and Matthew had never got anywhere close to having a relationship. But she already knew that she could have loved him, whatever that meant. She didn't know why, particularly. It was just ... that inexplicable something. That thing which sometimes happens between people. She didn't know if her fondness would have been reciprocated, but she sensed it might.

Whatever.

She'd never know.

And all of that gnawed away at her insides.

They'd driven through the second night and reached the tunnel in the early hours. In towns she'd expertly navigated off the main roads, down side-streets to avoid potential checkpoints. There had been little traffic and most of what they had seen had been heading in the opposite direction, towards the melee. She'd met up with the cousin who, and it wasn't a surprise, hadn't heard anything on the news about an attack on a train. Their discussion had been brief and a little tearful for both of them, the presidential body-double adding whatever gravitas was needed to make her story believable. And then they'd walked, shoulders hunched, the 400 metres underground until they'd popped up in the South.

At which point there had been more tears with the garage owner. The train story also hadn't made the news but, as Sam expected, there had been plenty of images of the two smiley leaders hobnobbing around Pyongyang, surrounded by throngs of dutiful, cheering and regimented locals. Sam had thought about making up some cock-and-bull story, but lost interest halfway through, mainly because the brother had broken down – in a reserved, South Korean way. Beom-soo knew as soon as she and the fake-president turned up the news was going to be bad. The pair of them looked a complete state. After a firefight, a dunking in freezing, filthy water, an awful vehicle journey, and 400 metres underground, her companion couldn't have looked any less presidential. The North Koreans were used to accepting what they were told. The southerners were clearly much more sceptical.

Not that it mattered. The context was irrelevant. All that was important to Beom-soo was he had lost a brother. And, in his grief, was looking for someone to blame.

Blame me.

For fuck's sake, blame her.

It was her fault. Heading across the border to rescue a non-existent president was the craziest idea she'd ever had. She should have known the system would never have let him and the North Korean leader take the train.

It was obvious.

Now.

It would have been madness to let the journey go ahead with only a handful of soldiers and two maverick British agents running around with their backsides on fire hoping to prevent it. The Chief wouldn't have let it happen. She knew that. Sure, maybe he'd have kept the Americans out of the loop because he couldn't fully trust them as no one knew who was in it for what. But he'd have spoken to someone, maybe his oppo in South Korea's NIS, and between them they'd have made the switch at the last moment.

Of course they had.

It must have been a closely guarded and masterfully choreographed pantomime. If the switch had got out beyond the tightest of holds the Gang of Four would have pulled the plug on the attack. Maybe redirected their efforts? After the switch Sam didn't know how they'd got the leaders to Pyongyang, she just knew they had. The follow-on summit had gone ahead as planned, in the full light of the world's media. What was just as clever, the attack on the train hadn't made any news cycle. Anywhere. The North had kept the whole thing wrapped, which was well within their grasp – although the loss of some South Korean soldiers would have needed to be tidied up. Someone in Seoul had ordered a news blackout on that.

It was a neat trick. Anywhere else on the globe, such an audacious operation would have been impossible.

North Korea? With support from their new friends?

Bring it on.

But why?

She could only guess.

In her mind, the Chief had allowed – *no, encouraged* – her, Matthew and Jae-joon to board the train. Everyone needed to think the leaders were on it. The attack *had* to happen. That way the Chief could be absolutely convinced the Gang of Four existed. That its ambition was to derail peace on the peninsula and then further the fortunes of the four remaining communist countries.

An attack equalled certainty. No attack, and the Chief would struggle to persuade anyone the Gang of

Four existed beyond his imagination supported by limited intelligence.

And the attack *had* happened.

She knew. In a way that caused her more pain than she wished to think about.

So why not broadcast the fact now that it was known? Why not expose the Gang of Four to the world?

Hypothesis - she'd pieced something together.

A double bluff as intricate as the filament of an incandescent light bulb.

The South Koreans were never at any point going to let their leader travel on the train. Ever. It was too dangerous. There was only one usable track and only one set of carriages. Any would-be terrorist could have a go.

So they set up a decoy.

Who wouldn't?

And, inadvertently, they'd enabled the perfect deception.

If and when the attack materialised, both North and South would need to keep a lid on it – until they worked out who was responsible. That would be standard operating procedure. It could have been any one of a number of terror cells; especially if you assume you don't know anything about the Gang of Four. So you enforce a media blackout. Cover your tracks ... and your face.

And whilst the machinations of the intelligence systems do their stuff, the Gang of Four could not be

600

sure their cover had been blown. Especially if, early on, SIS or NIS let slip a hint of some other parties they were interested in.

Then, maybe subtly or in a blaze of glory, the South Koreans supported by the UK take down any old lowly, Pacific Rim terror cell and pin it on them?

Result?

The world knows the leaders were safe having circumvented an attack on the presidential train – and the intelligence services have the culprits. Circled squared.

What should the Gang of Four do now?

They lie low for a while. And then, maybe in a couple of months, start to operate again. Unaware that a small group of determined and incredibly well equipped intelligence officials know who they are. And those intelligence services have at least one location in northern Vietnam and four phone numbers into the bag. Maybe more now.

It was the perfect play, enabled by a train journey that was never going to happen. It was genius, if she really thought about it.

Of course, the party would be over at some point. The Chief, or his successor, or his successor's successor, would eventually pull the plug on the Gang of Four.

But why not let it run for a bit longer? Widen the net. Recruit an agent. Find all the links.

And then ... haul them in.

That was Sam's hypothesis. That's what she would have done.

Her bum was going to sleep. She wiggled about on the window seat and checked her watch. It was 5.17 pm. Frank would be at least another two hours. She'd have something ready for him when he got in. There was, as always, plenty in the cupboard. Neatly stowed.

She put her chin on her chest.

Her hypothesis held water. But her musings hadn't really answered the moral question at the centre of this.

Why send two fellow countrymen all the way to their deaths? Were she and Matthew so wound up in the story that to warn the pair of them would alert the attackers? Who was following them? Had the Gang of Four tagged her? Had someone hacked the satphone's electronic hierarchy and managed to triangulate where they were? Was someone chasing them across the peninsula?

She didn't know.

And – and this was all adding to her dreadful feeling of hurt and misery – she *so* wanted to, but she couldn't blame the Chief.

She and Matthew had been on a suicide mission. But it should have fallen over long before they got to the train. And maybe that had been the point? Maybe the Chief had expected her to fail at some point. Get close to the target, yes, but then get arrested by the North Koreans. That way the Gang of Four, who were on her

602

tail, would know ... and *still* be confident the two leaders were in the carriages. The operation could still be given the green light?

But you didn't get stopped, did you, Sam Green? You made it onto the train against all the odds. I wasn't expecting that ...

So why not pull the operation when she and Matthew had got some distance into the north when it was too late to pull the attack? Or, how about when they'd got Frank to phone the captain? Wasn't that close enough?

No. Nothing that would enable the enemy to get suspicious.

Or, maybe, the Chief just wasn't paying enough attention?

Because, surely, they'd never make it that far. They'd end up in a North Korean jail eating rice and weevils for breakfast. Surely.

Let them run. And let them trip. Any interference would alert the attackers.

Sam lifted her head and looked back out at the scene which never changed.

She'd never know.

Well, she might. There was an open offer for her to pop into Vauxhall and meet with the Chief. A couple of days after they'd got back from the Far East Frank had brought back a security clearance paper which she'd been asked to sign before she was to be allowed in the building. It was an arcane document designed to give

Secret Intelligence Service as much leverage as possible over her should she decide to talk to anyone about her time in South East Asia, and particularly her trip into the DPRK.

She'd scanned it, sat at the kitchen table, realised immediately it was something she was never going to sign, and pushed it back across the polished pine top to Frank.

'You're not going to do it?' He'd asked.

'No. Sorry. Did you read the bit about, "SIS reserve the right to smear your name on every social media platform they can find if you break this NDA"? (*non-disclosure agreement*)' she said.

'It doesn't say that?' Frank replied incredulously.

She'd scoffed.

'Might as well."

But she'd needed to pick at the scab. She'd needed some answers.

And, to be fair to Frank, that evening around the kitchen table he had filled in some gaps – although he'd been tight with his intelligence. Clearly the Chief had stamped a moratorium on 'sharing' and Sam was now back in the long grass when it came to being important.

Having helped herself to glass of red wine and offered Frank an alcohol-free beer, she'd pressed.

'I guess there's no news on Matthew or Jae-joon?' She was looking at her wine slowly spinning in the Paris goblet. She'd purposely not looked him in the eye at that point.

Frank had stopped mid-swig and then tilted his head to one side.

'No. Sorry. Nothing.'

She took a sip.

'What about the Gang of Four?'

Infuriatingly he gave her a 'give me a break' shrug, his hands raised in submission.

She'd countered with a Paddington hard stare, but he was not forthcoming.

'What about the Chief shorting the *won*?' she pressed, her tone matching her rising infuriation.

He hesitated.

'Was I right?' Sam wasn't having any of it. He *would* tell her something. 'He was trying to alert the North Korean government by using the Bertrams and Tilsdent Holdings to pre-buy a shed-load of *won,* so big they'd have no choice other than to think something was up? Put them on their guard?'

They had made eye contact now. Frank's beer was midway between the table and his mouth.

He nodded in agreement.

'But in the end he needn't have bothered, because I found Jane at the villa in Lào Cai and, by then, we'd pieced together the Gang of Four intelligence and, with the *La Teja's* cargo he had enough to alert both governments on the peninsula?'

He nodded again. And then took a swig of his beer.

'And the attack in Hanoi? Did the Gang of Four orchestrate that? And the tag on the satphone? The silver Toyota?'

Frank stared at her. Not a flicker of recognition.

'For fuck's sake, Frank! I almost died out there. And two of my friends *did* die. Help me!'

He grimaced and his shoulders dropped.

'You could sign this ...' he tapped at the agreement which was still on the table, '... and I'm sure the boss would fill you in.'

She bit at her bottom lip, glanced at the NDA by any other name and then looked back at Frank.

'He may not. And you know that, Frank. He might just be asking me to come in to tell me that I'm to keep my mouth shut. I might be no better off than I am now.' All of a sudden she felt completely drained.

'Help me, Frank. Please.' It was almost a bleat.

He put his beer on the table and rested both hands in front of him.

'We're pretty certain it's all the Gang of Four. All of it. Everything. They have the reach and the intent. Probably with some help. We're working on that,' he said.

'And the bomb in Croatia. The CIA officer Matthew spoke of? The Gang of Four too?'

Frank's head wobbled from side to side and he grimaced an, 'I'm not sure'.

'So, there could have been some US involvement. Maybe in support of the Gang of Four, or just a group of

American crazies hoping to stop the summit being successful?'

Frank nodded.

They'd probably never know. The US intelligence services were very adept at washing that sort of dirty laundry out of sight of everyone else.

The Gang of Four supported by a CIA/military faction?

It wasn't a happy thought.

She'd asked some other questions that evening and got no more from Frank, other than a couple of grunts. The well had dried.

And, after that, they hadn't spoken about Southeast Asia again. The only other topic of conversation had been Jane. The latest was that she was still on leave and, according to Frank, might never return to work. Frank's view was that things in the office would never be the same again. Sam could see that.

Sitting in Frank's window seat she had filled enough of the gaps in the wall for it to hold. Another chapter of her life compartmentalised and hidden.

Let's hope it stays that way.

She continued to stare out of the bay window. Nothing had changed. Things were as they always were.

Ding-dong.

The front door bell.

Shit. She really didn't want to talk to anyone.

Ding-dong. Ding-dong.

Sam unravelled her legs and made her way to the hall. The front door was painted gloss white: solid wood with two opaque, side by side, glass panels above belly-button height.

There was somebody at the door. She could see an outline.

She had no idea. Taller than her. Unknown gender.

She was about to turn on the light and, all of a sudden, she felt on edge. Her heart rate picked up and her mouth dried. She looked round for a weapon.

There.

A letter opener on a narrow hall table where Frank kept his incoming and outgoing mail. Neatly. In a V-shaped wooden holder.

She picked it up, and held it behind her back.

She listened.

Nothing.

Ding-dong.

Multiple rings weren't the signature of a would-be intruder. She relaxed a little.

She took the handle of the front door. And turned it, pulling the door towards her.

...

...

Her hand with the letter opener dropped to her side. Her bottom jaw relaxed. Her tongue popped out. She tried to say something.

But nothing came out.

She tensed. She thought about taking a step forward, but her legs were lead.

'Hello, Sam,' Matthew said.

He lifted his opened hands a touch; a half-hug stance. She noticed his left elbow was in a cast and his right hand bandaged.

She didn't respond.

There was a pause.

He stepped forward.

One step.

Two steps.

And then she was with him. Still standing upright. Rigid. He closed his arms around her, his strength immediately washing through her.

'It's OK,' he said. 'It's OK.'

She hadn't realised but tears were already rolling down her cheeks. The weir gates had opened, but still she felt detached. Like a third umpire in a cricket match. Seeing everything, but experiencing nothing.

Her shoulders would have rocked if he hadn't been holding her. Her face was turned to one side; her wet cheek was dampening his jacket.

Her brain wasn't working. There was too much happening for her synapses to cope with. So many questions. It was really disconcerting.

They stayed together for a minute. Neither of them spoke. Her arms were still at her side; his were around her shoulders. His chin resting on her head.

So many questions.

So many.

Then, 'Jae-joon?' she whispered.

She felt his chin moving from side to side.

'Sorry,' was Matthew's response.

She scrunched her eyes together and a little flood of tears cascaded down her cheeks.

That was the big question – and the answer was rubbish. But it wasn't the only question.

'Why was the train split in two? Our carriages and those of the North Koreans?' she whispered, still behaving like a stick of celery in a bed of lettuce. Over the past three weeks it was the only question she'd not been able to force into a box.

'What?' His response was louder than a whisper.

'The train. We were decoupled from the leading carriages.' Her face was still pushed gently against his chest. The warmth from his torso was comforting, but that wasn't yet enough. 'As a result we got hit later than you. We were slowing down. Maybe they had to wait until we were in the killing zone before they opened up on us?' She scrunched up her face against his chest. She knew this was exactly the wrong reaction to seeing the man you had deep feelings for rise up from the dead. But …

He stepped back. Holding her by the shoulders. His head on one side. His face was one of consternation. *Why wouldn't it be?* Then, with a delicacy that only brought on more tears, he brushed away those which were already dripping down her cheeks.

But he didn't answer the question. So she asked it again.

'Why did you and Jae-joon decouple the train?'

He smiled. *Apologetically*?

'To give you a chance.'

Something spiked in her.

'But that would have slowed you down. Given you less opportunity to warn the North Koreans.'

He didn't respond. He just very slowly and almost imperceptibly shook his head.

Sam knew then. She knew what she didn't want to know. It now all made sense.

She stepped back, his arms dropping to his side. His elbow clearly hurt as he grimaced as it fell. She so wanted to ask him about that. *Were you shot? Are there any more injuries? How did you get out of the country?*

Are you OK?

The obvious, sensible, loving questions.

'You didn't try to get into the North Korean carriages, did you? You stayed with the President's carriage? You had no intention of doing so? Your plan, I don't know when you thought of it, was to save the South Koreans and let the North's soldiers and their premier take the brunt of the battle.' Her words were still a whisper. But they were deliberate; pointed.

He didn't respond immediately.

She waited.

Then. 'It's an awful regime, Sam. You know that.' Matthew's voice was raised. It was laced with a touch of

611

indignation. 'The leader is a mass murderer. He holds his people to ransom every day. You saw the fields. You had a glimpse of the towns. The North would be a so much better place without him. We were doing the world a favour.'

She didn't want to hear his words. Not from him. Not from the man she thought she could love, if she didn't already.

For her, what he had done had been unforgivable. He'd had the chance to save lives. Instead he had decided to expend them; offer a leader and his soldiers to the mercy of an ambush which would surely kill or maim them all.

He was as bad as the enemy.

And, just as important, he had shattered her dream.

My dream: that she had found someone like Chris. Someone who might replace him. Someone who was a giant in so many ways, but humble in so many others.

But he wasn't. He was neither of those things.

That was gone now. Shattered in a sentence.

'You don't get to play God, Matthew.'

'But ...' he stuttered.

'You don't.'

She was shaking. He took a step forward and put out his arms. She crossed hers in front of her chest.

'But, Sam ...'

'I think you should go now.' Her tears might have been unstoppable, but her commitment was unbreakable.

'What? But...?'

'Now.'

There was a long silence. They both held each other's stare, even though all Sam saw was a tear-filled view of something that looked like Matthew.

And then, without warning, he turned and left, leaving a gaping hole where there had very recently been a man she might have learned to love.

Sam Green books by Roland Ladley:

Unsuspecting Hero

Sam Green's life is in danger of imploding. Suffering from post-traumatic stress disorder after horrific injuries and personal tragedy in Afghanistan, she escapes to the Isle of Mull hoping to convalesce. A chance find on the island's shores interrupts her rehabilitation and launches her on a journey to West Africa and on a collision course with forces and adversaries she cannot begin to comprehend.

Meanwhile in London, SIS/MI6 is facing down a biological threat that could kill thousands and inflame an already smouldering religious war. Time is not on anyone's side and Sam's determination to face her past and control her future, regardless of the risks, looks likely to end in disaster. Fate conspires to bring Sam into the centre of an international conspiracy where she alone has the power to influence world-changing events. Blind to her new-found role, is her military training and complete disregard for her own safety enough to prevent the imminent devastation?

Fuelling the Fire

Why are so many passenger planes falling from the sky? Why are two ex-CIA agents training terrorists in the Yemeni desert? Why is a religious cult transferring millions of dollars to unattributable bank accounts around the world? Are these events connected? If they are, is this the mother of all conspiracies?

MI6 analyst, Sam Green, desperately wants to establish why her only surviving relative died in the latest plane crash. But can she put aside her grief and make sense of it all? Or is the clock ticking just too quickly, even for her?

The Innocence of Trust

Sam Green's been promoted. She's now working out of Moscow as an SIS 'case officer' and hates it. She loathes her boss, feels out of place among SIS's elite and loses her only Russian informant to a bomb that also had her name on it.

On the verge of jacking it all in, Sam promises a beautiful stranger that she will find her boyfriend's murderer. That promise propels her into a web of top-level industrial crime and savage international terrorism. With reliable friends and colleagues in very short supply, Sam starts something she cannot stop. And this time, she's going to need more than an expert analyst's eye and a complete disregard for her own safety to prevent the most lethal terror plot since 9/11.

For Good Men To Do Nothing

Someone's messing with the Global Positioning System and no one knows who, or why. The CIA has intelligence of a major terror attack planned for the Middle East, but they have no idea of when and where. And the ultra right-wing Christian sect, The Church of the White Cross, is back doing what it does best: laying down carnage and inflaming anti-Muslim hatred.

Sam Green's been fired from SIS/MI6 for being a maverick operator and is trying to get her life back together. Skiing on a shoestring in Austria, she spots a face in the crowd. And it's a face that doesn't want to be recognised. But it knows she knows - and that can't be allowed.

Then someone lets slip the dogs of war.

Sam's back; this time without SIS support. Pursued from Europe to Venezuela, via The Bahamas and Miami, her enemies are seemingly one step ahead. With a single act of terror the world could be plunged into a religious war that would last for decades. With only the help of her old German hacking pal, Wolfgang, together can they prevent Armageddon?

On The Back Foot To Hell

A new, undefined terror is spreading across the globe. Indiscriminate, low-level acts of violence have hit all five continents - and it's getting worse. The world's security services are at a loss. Who is behind the upsurge in violence? Where will the next attack take place? Will it ever stop?

Sam Green, now a lowly supermarket till girl in a small town in England, is oblivious to world events. She has her own inner demons to fight and they're consuming her every spare moment. All too soon those demons will take on human form. And then she will be faced with two choices: run or fight.

In Naples, Italy, a young Welsh student is innocently researching a link between The Mafia and the history of art. And two thousand miles away in Moscow, Russian intelligence services are struggling to contain a new terror cell that threatens nuclear catastrophe. Are all these things connected? If so, can someone force order from chaos? Sam has managed before. But now there are too many obstacles, the biggest of which are those plaguing her own mind.

This time the world might just have to rely on someone else.

+++++

Find Roland Ladley's books here:
https://www.amazon.co.uk/Roland-Ladley/e/B010MAOZOE

And keep in touch via his blog here:
https://thewanderlings2013.wordpress.com/

++++++

Printed in Great Britain
by Amazon